Praise for *Breach The Hull*
Winner of the 2007 Dream Realm Award

"There is more than enough great SF in *Breach the Hull*
for any true fan of the genre, military or not."
— Will McDermott, author of *Lasgun Wedding*

"I enjoyed this book and heartily recommend it."
—Sam Tomaino, *Space and Time Magazine*

"[*Breach the Hull*] kicks down the doors in a way that allows
anyone access to the genre[. . .]it read like a bunch of soldiers
sitting around swapping stories of the wars. Fun, fast-paced, and
packed with action. I give it a thumbs up."
—Jonathan Maberry,
Bram Stoker Award-winning author

"[*Breach the Hull*] is worth the purchase. I normally don't partake
of anthologies as a general rule . . . but Mike McPhail has done
a great job in making me rethink this position."
—Peter Hodges, Reviewer

Praise for *So It Begins*
Two-Time Finalist for the 2009 Indy Book Award

Fantastic, captivating and stimulating reading from cover to cover...
The key to the success of this anthology is its flawless writing and exceptional
characterization...*So It Begins* has a bit of everything for everyone.
Highly recommended."
—5 Moons, Sarah Gentili, Mystique Books Reviews

[So It Begins] features contributions from some of the best writers of
military science fiction at the top of their form.
—Sam Tomaino, Space and Time Magazine

"An interesting collection of interconnected stories by a variety of writers.
The action is in your face and the military aspects seem to be spot on...
a fast read due to the nearly non-stop action."
— 4 Star Review, Kat Thompson, reviewer

"This volume contains sixteen quick-read short stories—the majority of
which pack surprising masses of literary firepower. You'll snicker, you'll cringe,
you'll dodge shrapnel—you will even hum the closing theme song!"
— Stephen Bierce, reviewer

Other Books in the Series

BREACH THE HULL
SO IT BEGINS
NO MAN'S LAND

Related Novels Published
by Dark Quest Books

GET HER BACK!
by David Sherman
A DEMONTECH NOVELLA

RADIATION ANGELS
by James Daniel Ross

BY OTHER MEANS

Book Three in the Defending The Future series

EDITED BY:

MIKE McPHAIL

Dark Quest, LLC
Howell, New Jersey

Special thanks to "DAN • E"
... Fix it!

PUBLISHED BY
Dark Quest, LLC
Neal Levin, Publisher
23 Alec Drive,
Howell, New Jersey 07731
www.darkquestbooks.com

ISBN (trade paper): 978-0-9830993-5-2

Series Website: www.defendingthefuture.com

Design: Mike and Danielle McPhail
Cover Art: Mike McPhail, McP Concepts
www.mcp-concepts.com
www.milscifi.com

Copy Editing: Danielle McPhail
www.sidhenadaire.com

Contents

This book is dedicated to the memory of:

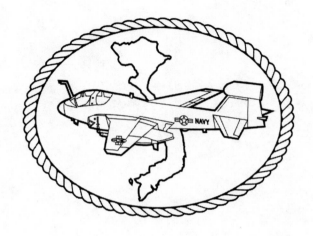

Charles Nicholas Ackley, Sr.
1940 - 2010

Sergeant, U.S.M.C.
Lieutenant Commander, U.S.N.

A Highly decorated Naval Aviator
who served his country in Vietam.

MOTHER OF PEACE
James Chambers

THEY PROWLED THE GHOST CITY BY NIGHT AND HUNTED THE THOUGHTS OF dead machines. Dr. Bell told them it was the only way to win the war. Find the old weapons and reactivate them. They had all heard it before, but she repeated it when they moved out of the jade moonlight into the shadows of a crumbling tenement row. It was her way of saying "Be careful" as they detoured around a dirty bomb hotspot leftover from a battle fought before any of them were born. Dr. Bell hoped Calypso's contact did not lie inside the high-becquerel zone. The sievert count there was more than the thin-skin suits they were wearing could deflect.

As they neared the next avenue, Sergeant Tanner ordered the squad to stop and sent two soldiers to scout the intersection. His voice came over Dr. Bell's earpiece. "Can your mutant give us a location yet?"

"How many times must I tell you he's not a mutant?" Dr. Bell said. "Why don't you ask him yourself?"

"Figured he already knew I was wondering."

"He gave his word he won't peek into your head without permission."

"How would I know if he did?"

"You wouldn't," Dr. Bell said.

She missed Sergeant Williams, whom Tanner had replaced two weeks ago, but she reminded herself it had taken almost three months for Calypso to earn Williams' trust. It would take Tanner time too. Leaders did not like telepaths. Dr. Bell considered it fortunate that most of their squad had been together so long now that they treated her and Calypso as equals. Despite the growing number of telepaths appearing in the population, most people still considered them outcasts.

"If this duty doesn't suit you, Sergeant," Dr. Bell said, "I'll support your request for reassignment."

"No, ma'am," Tanner said. "The brass handed me this job, and I intend to do it."

The two scouts returned, crouched low. Dr. Bell thought they looked nervous, but it was difficult to read expressions through their faceplates. Her earpiece went silent as Tanner switched to another channel for their report. The men gestured high and low at the intersection then separated and took new cover.

"Hey, Calypso," Tanner spoke over the squad's open link. "You got a hard twenty on our contact yet?"

"Narrowed it to two blocks," Calypso said. "But we're on the wrong side of the hotspot. Shortest route is south at the next avenue, thirty blocks downtown, then cut over on 14th Street and loop back uptown about five blocks. Should be somewhere around there."

"Can't take the next avenue," Tanner said. "Enemy presence there."

"How many?" Dr. Bell asked.

"Three locations for sure. Two ground level. One high, probably a sniper. Six men minimum. Could be more."

"Let me feel it out," Calypso said. The comm link went quiet for several seconds, and then Calypso came back. "There are eighteen, at least. All Chinese. Calm thoughts. They don't know we're here."

"Thank god for small favors," Tanner said. "Okay, let's turn back before we blip their radar."

Dr. Bell shuddered. This was the strongest contact Calypso had made since she taught him how to recognize the brain waves that identified a Centry warcraft. She did not want to lose it. She had searched for missing Centries across North America for two decades and found only rusted-out wrecks littered on old battlefields. The cybernetic machines, built to end the war, were meant to last a hundred years, but after thirteen months in the field the entire system had collapsed. Many units were destroyed in battle; most vanished and their tracking units went dark. But despite the quixotic nature of Dr. Bell's commitment to finding a live one and reigniting the program, the top brass had not yet lost faith in her.

Dr. Bell thought at Calypso, *Will you make this contact again if we don't find the source tonight?*

Because thought communication was instantaneous, she had given him standing permission to scan her surface thoughts, keeping anything personal behind a mental barrier. She did not like the hesitation in Calypso's reply.

Maybe, he thought. *But you know how it is. We've been through this city before, no contact like this. Things are how they are right now, today. It feels good. We should go for it.*

Calypso had been with Dr. Bell since he was eight when she found him hiding alone in a bombed-out school. That was ten years ago, and he had been helping her ever since then. He wanted to end the war as much as she did. He would have been out front of the squad running for the contact if only he were allowed.

Dr. Bell braced herself and then told Tanner, "We can't turn back."

Tanner unleashed a string of profanities, but he stopped short of demanding a retreat. Dr. Bell rode out his tirade and explained that they could not risk losing the contact. She had full authority for such decisions. She did not have to justify them, but she did not want to antagonize Tanner.

After Tanner calmed down, she said, "Find another route."

With a mumbled curse, Tanner clicked off comm. He scrambled across the street to where his second-in-command, Corporal Dolan, was crouched behind the blackened skeleton of a city bus. The two officers conferred, and then Tanner's voice came over the open link.

"Subway entrance off the avenue. Uptown side of the intersection. If the tunnel isn't blocked we can walk under the ambush points and come up six blocks south of our target then double back. Should cover us."

"Assuming no one's waiting in the tunnel," said Dolan.

"I can give a warning if anyone's there," Calypso said. "They won't get the drop on us."

"Fine. But down there, you and Dr. Bell bring up the rear," Tanner said. "Ladies and gents, weapons ready. Let's go."

Following Tanner's lead the squad spread out and edged toward the avenue. Moonlight tinged faint green by a haze of dust and ash fell like water over their thin-skins. The transparent suits reflected their environment, blurring the soldiers and giving them a sort of shimmering camouflage. Dr. Bell checked the clip in her rifle while she waited for Calypso to fall in ahead of her. She knew if the tunnel was blocked Sergeant Tanner would insist on turning back, and he would be right. But it would not be fair, not after so long, when she was so close, and so much was at stake. More than any other contact she had traced in recent years, she felt this was the one for which she had spent so long looking, the one that would lead to all the others.

As they neared the intersection, Tanner ordered everyone to drop to their bellies and snake-crawl through the rubble. Ahead of them was a gap in cover. Beyond a burned-up delivery truck, an explosion had left a shallow crater and scattered the rubble. It was a space of only about fifteen feet, but for the time it took them to round the corner and descend into the subway station, they would be exposed.

"Don't like that blank spot," Tanner said.

"I see it," Dr. Bell said. "We'll have to be fast."

"You and Calypso go first. With me. Get you down the stairs before they can take a shot if they see us."

Dr. Bell thought the plan to Calypso, who agreed, and then the two wormed their way to Tanner's side. The squad surveyed the avenue. Through night-sights, the enemy positions were visible by turquoise splotches that marked the half-hidden faces of the hostile soldiers. Otherwise the cracked street was desolate.

"Can you figure their locations?" Tanner asked Calypso.

"They're not far, between us and the contact," Calypso said. "Sorry, I can't be more specific at this range."

Tanner put Dolan in charge of bringing the rest of the squad into the tunnel. Then keeping low, he darted like a ghost across the gap and disappeared into the deep shadows of the entrance. Calypso went five seconds later, a blur flashing through the gloom. Dr. Bell followed him, moving fast on the cybernetic, prosthetic legs that let a woman in her fifties keep up with the others. Tanner directed her down the stairs, where Calypso was scanning the subway station with an LED lamp.

It looked clear except for old litter. Dolan came next and relieved Tanner at the entrance. Then the rest of the squad rushed into the gap.

Dr. Bell froze the moment she heard the whistling sound coming from the sky. It sounded like a howling wind, but she knew it was an anti-personnel, fragmentation mortar, a glorified grenade, but nasty, like the one that had stolen her legs and left arm, and condemned her to rely on prosthetic limbs. It had taken the life of her unborn child too. She grabbed Tanner with her cybernetic arm and dragged him downstairs. Dolan bolted down the steps from street level, shouting over the comm for everyone to take cover. Bell thrust Tanner into the darkness then clutched Calypso by the waist and leapt after him.

The whistling became a clipped shriek.

Then the missile hit.

The subway station trembled.

Flame and smoke and shattered concrete flooded down the stairs. For a moment Corporal Dolan was part of it, a twisting, tumbling ragdoll, and then the cloud enveloped him, and he was gone. The shockwave rolled through the station, cracking the information booth windows and slamming Dr. Bell to the floor. Calypso's voice stayed in her head, letting her know he was all right. She shouted for Tanner, but the rumble of the explosion drowned out any reply. Dr. Bell rolled until she bumped up against something hard. She curled into a ball and covered her head with her cybernetic arm. After awhile, the concentrated chaos faded away to a plastic stillness broken by dripping bits of stone and ceiling tile.

Through the dust cloud, Dr. Bell found Calypso against the iron bars of the turnstile gate. She tried to raise Tanner on the comm. He came through sounding faint and faraway to Dr. Bell's explosion-deadened ears. She and Calypso located the Sergeant and helped him to his feet. They found Dolan dead at the bottom of the stairs, half buried in a frozen sluice of rubble that had sealed the station entrance.

"We're trapped," Tanner said. He pulled Dolan's dog tags from his neck and stuck them in a pouch on his belt.

"I'm so sorry." Dr. Bell would miss Dolan. He had saved her life twice.

"Most of the others are still alive. I sense them," Calypso said. "Enemy soldiers came on foot after the mortar strike. Now it's a firefight."

"And not a damn thing I can do to help them," said Tanner. "Can't even raise them on the comm link."

"It's the radiation." Dr. Bell gestured toward the ceiling. "Or the old pipes and wires in the ground. Communications are always sketchy in the city."

"Sarge," Calypso said. "If you want, I can convey your orders to Private Rasmussen. He gave me permission to talk to him thought to thought. At this range, I should be able to pick him out of the crowd."

Tanner frowned. "Alright, tell them we're alive. Tell them to fall back and withdraw. Return with reinforcements to wipe out those enemy installations."

"What about us?" Dr. Bell said.

"Unless you can clear half a ton of rubble from this exit, we're going down the tunnel, like we planned."

Dr. Bell raised an eyebrow.

"You said it was a good contact, didn't you?" Tanner said.

"The best we've ever had."

"Yeah, well, I want to see this war over as much as anyone, so let's do our job. To hell with whoever tries to stop us."

They clipped LED lamps onto their chests then jumped the turnstile. Tanner led them to the end of the platform and down the steps to track level. The tunnel looked empty and deathly still. The city had been so hard hit by the war that Dr. Bell doubted even rats were left down here. There were not enough people in the city to support them, and unlike cockroaches, they could not live in the irradiated places. Tanner went first and Bell took the rear with Calypso between them. After they went only a few yards, the station was lost to the darkness behind them. Walking the railroad ties like steps, they settled into a steady pace along the center of the downtown track, traveling in a bubble of icy light. The gray concrete walls caked with dirt and soot never changed. The only colors there were the faded remnants of red and yellow warning signs.

Rounding a curve, they entered the next station and found an abandoned subway train. Calypso detected no one inside. Tanner led them onto the platform, and they flashed their lights through the grimy windows as they walked the length of the train. Most cars were empty, but in some were broken skeletons dressed in rotted clothing.

"What do you think happened?" Tanner said, as they left the dead train behind them.

"They probably came down here to hide from the fighting," Dr. Bell said.

"Not with the people on the train. With the Centry program. You've been after this longer than I've been in uniform. Figure you must have some theories."

Sooner or later, Dr. Bell had this conversation with almost everyone who came into the squad. They had all grown up with the mystery of the Centry program and its shattered promise of victory and peace. The warcrafts were like flying tanks with human intuition and responsiveness, thanks to the brains of mortally wounded soldiers implanted in them. They coordinated via a satellite link, now believed dead, and from the day they hit the field, they had succeeded in halting the enemy advance and pushing them back. For one year, victory was in sight. Now Dr. Bell thought the brass kept her going only to stoke the embers of that hope. After two hundred years of fighting, every day was a like a hard crack in the face. Resources were so depleted that some battles were being fought with swords and pikes, and the food supply often fell to subsistence levels. The prospect of ending the war in a day, however improbable, helped a lot of people get up in the morning. Dr. Bell remembered that whenever she answered a question like Tanner's.

"A lot of things might have gone wrong," she said. "I think it was a flaw in the cybernetics programming. If I can correct it, maybe I can revive the sat link and fix the others. The Centries were built to be self-sustaining for a hundred years, so there's a chance I can bring back online any machines that are still intact."

"You work on the original program?"

"I was twenty-one when Centry began. If you were going into the sciences then, you were contributing to Centry. That's what I did for more than ten years until it all went live. Then a year later, the Centries were gone, and the only work left was this. These days I'm the only one who hasn't given up the ghost."

She did not tell Tanner the real reason she kept looking or why she kept coming back to search this same city. She had shared that with no one. She suspected Calypso had pieced it together, because he knew the last reported coordinates for each Centry as well as she did. He knew the three Centries that had gone down in this area. But he would never dare ask her. Anyway, it was better to hide the personal element or risk people seeing her work as a crusade, which she knew it was not. If she was right about why Centry failed and if she could find one live Centry craft, even if not the one she most wanted, she really did stand a chance of ending the war. And in the end her reason for doing what she did—personal or not— was the only real reason there was for fighting in the first place.

The station closest to their target location was clear, but it was on the edge of the hotspot, so they kept moving. Two stops later, they entered the 14th Street Station on its lowest level, and then tracked up the stairs behind Tanner. They went slow, with weapons ready, even though Calypso told them no one was there. On the station's main level, they found part of the ceiling caved in by something that had left an enormous cavity filled with layers of wreckage. Faint moonlight poured through gaps in the rubble. The scale of destruction suggested a crashed vehicle or an unexploded missile. Dr. Bell walked to the edge of the debris and pushed aside a chunk of concrete. She grabbed a length of broken rebar and used it to pry away large pieces, working with the strength of her prosthetics until she exposed an edge of blue-gray metal.

Calypso and Tanner helped her. The three of them heaved away broken concrete and chunks of shattered tile until they uncovered part of a pitted hull painted with call letters and the American flag. Beneath the flag were embossed captain's bars and the name "McCardle." Dr. Bell flashed her lamp around the debris then leapt halfway up the mound and scrambled on top of the pile. She forced another chunk aside, her cybernetic legs giving her the power to shift it until it tumbled away. She pushed another and another, eliciting a warning from Tanner to watch where she was throwing rocks. The debris mound was too unstable for him and Calypso to climb, and they could not jump atop it like Dr. Bell.

"Get off there before it collapses," Tanner said.

Dr. Bell ignored him and continued excavating. The scales of a dead subway station tumbled off the pile. When Dr. Bell did leap down, her face was beaming.

"It's a Centry," she said. "It's hard to tell under all this wreckage, but I cleared the top of the hull, and there's no mistaking it. The cockpit is intact."

Tanner moved back to the metal hull and placed his hand on the painted American flag. Then he set down his rifle and shoved more rubble away from the craft. Calypso and Dr. Bell worked with him, Moving hunks of fallen street and ceiling, rolling the pieces too big to lift, until they had cleared a recognizable section of the warcraft.

"Sonofabitch," Tanner said. "Exactly like the pictures."

"Didn't you believe me?" Dr. Bell said.

"That these things existed? Yes. That we'd find one intact after twenty years? Guess I figured they were all lost. Alright, let's call in a recovery crew."

"Not for this one. Not yet, at least."

"Why not?"

"This isn't the contact," Calypso said. He stared at the uncovered patches of the warcraft then placed his hand on the hull like Tanner had done. "I get no thought activity at all."

"Because he's dead," Dr. Bell said.

Calypso nodded. "I think so."

"How can you know?" Tanner said.

"He's been down here a long time, covered in rubble, cut off from the sun. The machinery may still work, and maybe the nuclear battery is still charged. But the nanites that kept the brain alive can't be. They were fueled by chlorophyll, and without sunlight, they wouldn't have lasted more than a few months. The brain plugged into the cockpit would have withered and died only a few days after the nanites stopped repairing its cells and manufacturing oxygen and nutrients. I'm sorry to say Captain McCardle has been dead a long time. I've found seven others like this over the years. Intact but dead."

"The contact is stronger here," Calypso said. "We're not far."

"It has to be topside somewhere," Dr. Bell said. "Exposed to the sky, but not in the open."

"Not getting out through here to look." Tanner nodded at the rubble-choked exits.

He jogged across the station to check the other stairways and found the southwest stairwell was passable. The trio climbed it to the street and surveyed the neighborhood. Although Calypso sensed people in the area, no one felt close enough to be an immediate threat. They spread apart, and Tanner led them, following Calypso's directions. The city was quiet. Mingled with the sky's brackish hue was the creamsicle glow of fires burning somewhere on the avenue. In a few hours it would be dawn, and the sun would cook off the night haze.

The contact grew stronger. Calypso was restless and wanted to go faster. Tanner tried to hold him back, but Calypso's excitement was contagious, and before long the trio was jogging. They crossed another block. Then ignoring Tanner's warnings, Calypso sprinted away.

"Down here!" he shouted.

Dr. Bell and Tanner raced after him.

"This way," Calypso said.

Tanner hollered for him to slow down and wait, but Calypso kept running. He vanished through the broken front doors of a high-rise office building.

Wait! We can't see you now, Dr. Bell thought at him.

Calypso thought back, *Okay, okay, but it's here, in this building, right on top of us. It's here! So let's go, slowpoke.*

Dr. Bell edged past Tanner, who yelled at her to slow down. Tanner tried to keep up, but Dr. Bell's prosthetic legs outpaced him. Running was one of the few times she felt grateful for her machine limbs, and Calypso was right. Now was the time to act. She was thirty yards from the building entrance when something like an invisible wasp buzzed by her head. Another came right after it. Time seemed to grind to a crawl, and Calypso's voice exploded through her mind.

Get down! Get down!

All around Dr. Bell the pavement spit up asphalt dust like a deep puddle splattering under a sudden rain. The air filled with humming, zipping sounds, and as Dr. Bell crouched and then leapt toward the building's broken entrance, hot stings drilled through her upper body. She cleared the distance on the power of her artificial legs and tumbled into the shelter of the pitch-black building lobby. In an instant Calypso was at her side, his thoughts a wild jumble of apologies for being distracted, for not sensing the sniper, for not warning her sooner. The raw emotion pouring out of him was overwhelming. For all his courage, in that moment, Calypso was only a boy convinced the woman who was like a mother to him was about to die. Dr. Bell gripped his hand and tried to soothe him.

Not your fault, she thought. *He was too far away for you to know he was dangerous. Don't blame yourself. Please. Not your fault.*

She thought it over and over, coaxing Calypso back from the edge of panic. And when she had helped him regain his focus, she asked him about Sergeant Tanner.

Calypso edged to the open doorways. *He's pinned down behind a dumpster. But I don't think he's hurt*, he thought.

How many enemy? Dr. Bell asked.

Only the sniper.

Then you have to take him. I know you don't want to, but you have to. Or Tanner might die.

She felt how fragile Calypso's spirit was now, and she hated the burden she was placing on him, but there was no other way. Calypso withdrew into the darkness.

You need my help, he thought.

Help Tanner first. You have to. Please.

Dr. Bell was grateful for the darkness. She was afraid of how Calypso might react if he saw her torn up and bloodied, and she needed him to act. She could not leave him alone out here. If her wounds were as bad as they felt, Sergeant Tanner might be the only one left to get him home.

Please, she thought. *Trust me. You do trust me, right?*

Of course, I do. You've done everything for me. I trust you more than anyone else.

Then do what I say. I know what I'm asking, and I know you can handle it. I wouldn't ask if it weren't the only way.

Dr. Bell felt Calypso's thoughts churning in the blackness between them. Then he extricated himself from Dr. Bell's mind to protect her from what he was about to do. The abrupt break startled her. Calypso crept back to the entrance, becoming a shadowy scarecrow. The gunfire had died down, but a fresh shot came every few seconds—the sniper letting Tanner know he was still there. Calypso planted his feet, and then what happened next happened in stillness and without a sound. A gunshot plinked off the dumpster. A few seconds passed. Another round shattered the glass off a lamppost behind Tanner. A few more seconds passed. The next bullet gouged concrete far from its target, and the next struck a window in a building on the next corner. Seconds passed. No other shot came.

It's done, thought Calypso. Then speaking over the comm link, he said, "All clear, Sergeant Tanner. Come in now. I'm sorry I didn't warn us. I won't let down my guard again. Please hurry. Dr. Bell is wounded."

His voice was laden with sadness. Dr. Bell knew the dying thoughts of the sniper were echoing through Calypso's mind. They would always be there. To think someone dead, as Calypso had done, required staying connected with the target's psyche until the very last moment, rewiring brain patterns for a suicide circuit, and the dying impressions were too powerful to ever forget. But she believed Calypso was strong enough to live with what he had been forced to do. When Tanner entered the lobby, he guided him to Dr. Bell.

"How bad is it?" Calypso asked.

Tanner flashed his lamp over Bell's body. "Pretty damn bad. Time to evac."

"No," Dr. Bell said. "We're too close. The contact's here. Pack my wounds. I can make it."

Tanner was already pressing field dressings over Dr. Bell's wounds. "Out of your mind if you think I'll let you go anywhere other than home," he said.

Dr. Bell pushed herself onto her knees.

"Shit. Don't move. You're hurt." Tanner tried to ease her back down.

With her cybernetic arm, Bell jolted Tanner aside and then forced herself to stand. Her breathing was shallow, and her heart was racing, but she was steady.

"We have to hurry," she said. "We might not find it again."

"You need a medic," Tanner said.

"Or what? I'll die. Like how many millions of others in this war. We don't have a lot of true choices in our lives, Sergeant. You're not taking this one away from me. I swear to you if this contact turns out to be a Centry, this all will have been worth it. And if I die then so be it. I've outlived too many people to care about that now. So, please, follow Calypso's directions."

Dr. Bell thought Tanner might face her down, but then he nodded and let Calypso lead them to a staircase at the back of the lobby. They climbed it. Dr. Bell, weak from blood loss, set her legs to automatic and let them carry her behind Calypso and Tanner.

They passed the fourth floor, then the fifth, and kept going. Dr. Bell expected they would have to climb to the roof. It was the only place that made sense for the contact to be. It took them about an hour to reach the roof access. Tanner broke the lock, and then they were back in the moonlight with a view of the dark city in every direction. The fires on the avenue were burning bright.

"Where?" Dr. Bell asked Calypso.

Spikes of pain drove through her chest, and her vision grayed for a moment. It was getting harder to breathe. She suspected she was bleeding into her lungs. Calypso looked frightened, and she knew she must look awful, covered in blood.

It's okay, she thought to him. *Believe in me. Where?*

At the center of the roof was a bulky ventilation unit. On the other side was the Centry, covered in thick dust. It looked peaceful, like it was sleeping. Dr. Bell, Tanner, and Calypso approached it.

"Incredible," Tanner whispered.

Calypso brushed dust from the hull to expose the call letters, American flag, and the name "Bowman" painted over captain's bars. Dr. Bell swallowed a sob. She had not realized that seeing him would resurrect so much of her grief. She realized then that even after all the years she had searched, she did not know if she had ever really expected to find him. She circled the craft, which aside from scrapes and dents looked undamaged. She opened a panel near the cockpit and accessed the diagnostic interface. Running off the nuclear battery, it was still lit and working. Dr. Bell checked the cockpit environment. The numbers for oxygen, nitrogen, temperature, and protein count all came up good. She cycled through the next batch of data then initiated a full system check. Two minutes later the display reported all systems, except the satellite link, running but they had not been activated outside of drill mode since the Centry program crashed.

"You're alive," she said. "Why won't you work?"

The machine did not answer.

"Calypso," she said. "It's time to use your training."

"It's not safe," he said. "I sense others in the building. They're coming up, hunting us."

"How many?" Tanner said.

"Half a dozen."

"Sniper must've alerted them," Tanner said. He checked his weapon and jogged toward the roof door. "Only one access point. I can hold them off, but not forever."

"We'll be quick. We have to be. If they find the Centry they'll destroy it," Dr. Bell said. "Now, like we practiced, Calypso, okay?"

Calypso nodded and then sat down in the shadow of the machine and closed his eyes.

Tanner watched. "What's he doing?"

"Entering the Centry's brain. He's going to link me to it, so I can see what went wrong."

Dr. Bell sat beside Calypso and held his hand. His mind touched hers and then guided her toward the Centry, and once she was in, he backed off, leaving her connected to Captain Bowman's brain. It amazed Dr. Bell how easy the connection was, and she wished she had known about telepaths when she was helping to build the Centries. The soldier's mind was stripped down, full of combat information, and packed with Centry programming. There were memories of battles and an intense, fiery vision that was the fight that had put Captain Bowman on the Centry roster. He had come in at the end, one of the last units to go online, and Dr. Bell remembered how it had crushed her to see his broken body in the operating room. She had not even known then that she was carrying his child.

She dug through scattered recollections and impressions. The Centry process struck a fine balance between removing enough memories to make a century of mechanized existence bearable while leaving enough to preserve the soldier's humanity. The latter were the memories Dr. Bell wanted.

Everything flickered. Calypso was straining to keep the connection open. Dr. Bell pushed deeper, moving her awareness past banks of codes and concepts that she had helped create. She forced her way down to the central core of Bowman's mind, and there she located the memory she wanted.

It was herself.

She was smiling, and there was sun in her hair.

She felt the softness of her skin the way Bowman had felt it the last time they had been together. His mind was trapped in that moment, cycling it like a loop. It had been designed that way to keep the Centries sedated when they were offline for repairs. A programming error had set the clocks running wrong, making it seem that a century had already passed when only little more than a year had gone by. The Centries had defaulted to maintenance mode, but because the glitch was only in one part of the programming, they could not complete the routine and return to their bases. Instead they had simply shut down, wherever they were, trapped in pleasant memories designated to sustain them through a prolonged state of inactivity. The simplicity of it made Dr. Bell furious. Someone's carelessness had allowed the war to go on long after it should have ended. Dr. Bell sharpened her focus. She felt the strain, in her body and her mind. Drawing on Calypso's help, she scanned Bowman's cybernetics programming until she located the error. She noted the code and the proper fix and thought them to Calypso, so that Bowman could be repaired when he was recovered.

I can do that now, thought Calypso.

What do you mean? Dr. Bell thought.

I can fix him. So much of the coding is embedded in his mind, it's like an open book to me. Calypso paused, and then thought, *I wish you had told me about him and you. I consider you my mother. Perhaps I could think of him as my father.*

Yes, t*hink of him that way, and remember, not everything is meant to be shared between parent and child.*

I understand, Calypso thought.

If you can fix him, please do.

I already did.

Dr. Bell felt the change flow through Bowman's mind as Calypso drew her out of it. She did not want to lose the connection. It had been so long since she had felt so close to anyone. The attack that wounded her and killed her unborn child had come only six months after the Centry program launched. She had been alone since then.Before she could protest, she was out of Bowman's psyche and back in her own.

Gunfire rattled the air.

Calypso was dragging her around the Centry for cover.

"They're at the door," he said.

Dr. Bell crawled to the diagnostic panel and checked the readings. They had switched from drill mode to duty mode, and even more amazing, the satellite link was back online. Bowman was fully functional again, and he was plugged into every other surviving Centry.

Can you do what you did to him for the others? Dr. Bell thought to Calypso. *Go through his mind like I went through yours, via the satellite link? All at once?*

Calypso did not answer right away.

Captain Bowman began to vibrate, and then he lifted off the ground, raising a blast of stale air.

He knows you're here and what you did, and he's grateful, Calypso thought. *He misses you, and he's...happy...to meet me.*

Stay with him as long as you can, thought Dr. Bell.

And, yes, Calypso thought, *I think I can do what you're asking.*

Then do it, please do it, don't wait, and don't worry about me, and don't miss me too much, Dr. Bell thought. *Only you truly understand what we've done here, and it's up to you to see it through, to win this war, for me, for us, for our family.*

The enemy broke through the door then, forcing Tanner to fall back, and then Dr. Bell saw Captain Bowman's shadow as he rose higher into the air. Her thoughts fell back inside her mind, and she was only herself, shivering from a cold wave spreading outward from her chest. She imagined the other Centries, the ones left alive all around the country, rising like Captain Bowman, the awakening of a ghost army, and then Bowman opened fire, cutting down the enemy soldiers in seconds. The roar and flash of gunfire filled Dr. Bell's senses. Calypso would be safe; he would be protected for what he could do as she had so long protected him. She was pleased to leave him with the prospect of victory and freedom and a better world than she had ever known. The echo of gunfire faded. Bowman's shadow darkened Dr. Bell's sight as he set down beside her. After that, she knew nothing more.

CYBERMARINE
Bud Sparhawk

AWOKE TO DARKNESS, A BLOWTORCH BREATHING ON MY FACE AND ON MY SCALP a raging fire roared. Acid burned both eyes. Every tooth was a source of grinding misery that demanded a cry of rage. But I had no lips to form, no tongue to shape, no lungs or breath to propel a scream. Neither could I flail an arm, lift fingers to face, or even twist a leg to display my agony.

Was this hell and I one of the damned? There was no answer as the burning seared my being until, thankfully, darkness washed consciousness away.

A timeless interval later I awoke. The burning had ceased but the pain was as intense.

And everywhere.

I was just a nexus of suffering with no history or future. I could hear no sounds, smell no odors, feel neither warmth nor cold, and had no awareness of whether I was standing or lying prone or supine. That pain existed was all.

Only fitful sleep momentarily relieved the pain, and with the sleep, came memories.

There were twenty marines and four cybermarines assigned to me. Ours was the usual shipboard duty, breaking up fights between the Navy rates and sometimes starting a few of our own. None of the cybers got involved of course. Nobody wanted to tangle with those zombies so I made sure they kept to themselves. I wouldn't want any of the real marines to risk fighting one of them.

The cybers were Command's newest weapon, something dreamed up, I believe, by cyberghouls who had ethicotomies. Regardless of how many words and studies Command used to justify their actions or whether the choice had even been theirs to make, it still wasn't right to use dying marines that way, not right to deny them a decent death, not right to turn them into fucking machines.

Oh, the politicians had all the high-sounding reasons for the program—getting a return from the money invested in training, allowing the dying marines a continuation of honorable service, providing new life to the nearly departed, etc, etc, etc. It's amazing the excuses Command can employ to rationalize their decisions. Personally, I think it was all about economics; a cybermarine was a lot cheaper than an automated tank and a lot more expendable.

The cybers didn't even look like marines. Rather, from a distance, they looked like everybody's ideal soldier—seven feet tall, broad of shoulder and thick of chest, with muscular arms and legs. Up close you saw the real differences, like those faces you couldn't look at without wanting to puke.

The normal-sized head had no nose or mouth—just a couple of thumb-sized holes below the eyes. Yeah, eyes—six of them; a wide-set pair above the outside of the cheekbones, a tiny pair, quite close together where the bridge of the nose might have been, and another set, larger and circular, above them.

The skull was a hairless pate from eyebrows to the nape of the neck and down past the ears on both sides. On either side of the head, where you expected to see ears, were knobs of flesh on which they could hang six-lensed combat glasses to augment their incredible vision.

Thank God, the helmets they wore for combat usually obscured most of a zombie's face. I wished they'd wear them, visors down, most of the time, if only to spare everybody's sensitivities.

"The men do not like us, Lieutenant," the cybermarines' squad leader said after saluting. I noticed it wore no rank. According to its tag the name was Winslow, Harold.

"You know that how?"

"When one of them looks at us his face becomes warmer than normal, indicating an adverse emotional reaction. We've also noticed how they clench their fists and tense their muscular structure as if ready for either fight or flight." He tilted his head to the side. "By the way, sir, I note a sudden tension in your jaw muscles. Your voice also expresses stress, sir. Do you share your men's distaste, sir?"

"Great, just what I need—a walking lie detector."

"Simply infrared vision, sir. I also see into the ultraviolet spectrum and, before you ask, my binocular vision is ten times more acute than a normal person's."

"You are also faster than a fucking bullet and can leap tall buildings in a single bound, I suppose."

"Sir, I may have an enhanced body, but I doubt I could do either of those." I couldn't tell if he was serious or not. Last thing I wanted was a smart-ass cyberzombie.

Then I remembered how most of its memories had been stripped away, along with whatever sense of humor Winslow, Harold might have had. "Yes, it was a joke and I am quite well acquainted with your physical capabilities. I've read the specs and know you will be an asset to the unit." I tried to put as much sincerity into my voice as I could, but I knew Winslow, Harold would know the truth of how I felt.

"By your leave, sir. What is my bunk assignment?"

"I haven't made arrangements yet. Certainly you can't be staying with the *men*.

I doubt you'd fit into a standard rack." I was actually wondering if I could put the cybers in the cargo hold and out of sight. "I'll talk to the captain about it. In the meantime, why don't you boys take a seat in the mess?"

"What about our gear, sir? Each of the squad has two hundred kilos of food, five hundred kilos of weapons and ammunition, and one hundred kilograms of personal supplies."

Crap, that was more stuff than my twenty men carried into deployment. "Food?"

"We need a special diet to remain effective, sir."

Yes, and his weapons were probably heavier than anything even our beefiest marine could carry. "See the quartermaster. He'll figure out where to store your kit."

"By your leave, sir." With that he spun on his heel and departed.

"You have a choice," someone whispered softly from the depths of the conflagration that wracked my being. "We can save you as you are or..."

I knew the choice. It was standard option to the oath of office and drilled into us. "I don't know," I replied, but whether words escaped or not, I could not hear. The pain was so intense that I knew that I had to be near death's door.

"It's life—of a sort," came the whispered promise. "We don't want to lose your knowledge and skills."

Which meant, I realized through agonizing waves of pain, that I could put an end to the suffering by simply saying I wanted to die.

Death wasn't appealing, but surviving as a pathetic remnant of my former self, horribly disfigured, covered with scars and missing eyes, ears, arms, and legs. They could probably restore some functions, but I'd sooner die than become some disgusting, crippled veteran.

The alternative to dying was to survive, albeit briefly given the sorts of engagements where cybers were used. I remembered what Winslow, Harold had looked like and wondered if death might not be the better choice.

"We need your rage," the whisper continued.

The choice was less than living and more than dying. All they offered was a promise that I could continue to serve and, in serving, release my raging anger.

"Machines, that's all they are, damned machines," the quartermaster grumbled as the cybers lined up at the hatch.

"They're marines, sailor," I barked in reply, a trifle loudly because all the cybers glanced my way. "I expect the cargo hold to be fixed up to accommodate them comfortably."

"Don't look like they need anything but a packing crate," he answered under his breath, just softly enough that I wasn't sure I heard correctly.

"Packing crates would be fine, sir," Winslow, Harold shouted from across the compartment as the quartermaster's ears turned bright red.

The cybers couldn't use the seats in the mess even if they wanted to sit with the rest of the marines. Sitting with the sailors was even less of an option, given that they were equally as hostile to my marines as the cybers. Instead they ate whatever suited their weird metabolism in the privacy of the hold. It was probably better, their being all among their own kind.

"By your leave, sir." I looked up to see Winslow, Harold's hulking presence at the door to the compartment I shared with the first sergeant. Seeing his overwhelming form in such close quarters made him appear all the more menacing.

"We were wondering when we would train with the rest of the troops."

"I don't think that would be a good idea," I replied. I'd kept my men separate from the cybers mostly out of concern for their safety. With their power the cybers could easily and unintentionally harm someone, not that there weren't a few who might want to try. Best, I thought, to keep their training exercises separate. That wouldn't make a difference in combat, seeing as how the cybers always operated as an autonomous element of the force.

No burning pain touched me on my next awakening. I was blissfully aware of floating. Just the absence of pain was enough.

Then, without warning, I became aware of my body. Sounds assaulted my ears, far too loud to make any sense of them. Bright formless light nearly blinded me. My body was tingling with a thousand tiny bites, each demanding to be scratched. I flexed my arm to scratch the bothersome itch at my hip and somebody screamed: "Holy shit, watch out for the..."

Darkness ensued.

I could make no sense of the vague dark forms that swam before my eyes. Caricatures they were, rude representations of the human form, huge and threatening. I could make out no details save that one was somewhat larger than the rest—closer, I wondered and tried to blink away the fogginess. That's when I realized I had no eyelids, nor even the sensation of them.

Sound assailed my ears. An intermittent, dull, and loud rattle that echoed in my skull like a dentist's burr drill. On and on it went, repeating endlessly. No, I noted that it was slightly different each time, varying in volume and intensity.

I felt something brush my cheek; a woman's caress judging by the silky smoothness of it. I recalled how my mother's hand had stroked me like that so many years ago as she sent me off to school. Where was she now? "Mother," I tried to cry, but still had no voice or breath; no way to cry.

Mother was gone now, I recalled. Lost like father and brother over the years and billions of miles, so far away that the news of her passing had not reached me until long after the services, long after the immolation, long after my last and only remaining family connection had died.

I recalled the farm, my prize calf, and the family of silly cats in the barns who thought they owned the cattle. I remembered my many dogs, short-lived all, and the kitchen garden I planted with its even shorter-lived crops. Gone, all gone.

The sound gradually changed to become a harsh voice that formed words. "David? Ah, good. We got a reaction that time. Set the [something, mumble, mumble] down."

Our squadron happened upon the Shardie ships off Roger-5, Farthing Sector, just as we emerged. The automatics from all four ships fired before anyone had recovered from the quantum probability drive's blink syndrome.

There had been four alien ships; small ones or we wouldn't have survived. The first two were atomized when our ballistic rounds struck, shattering them into a million glass fragments that sparkled as new constellations. The third ship dodged one round successfully but moved directly into the path of our second salvo.

The last ship somehow avoided our barrage and accelerated away from the scattering fragments of its companions. The failure of a Shardie ship to immediately attack was so unexpected that we lost precious milliseconds as each ship's autonomous battle controls spun them as the main drives kicked in to follow the escaping ship.

The Shardie was boosting five gees and accelerating a lot faster than *Falcon*, our fastest ship, could possibly match. There was no chance of catching up if the alien continued its straight-line flight. Unlike the Shardie crew, we frail humans couldn't survive such high acceleration for long.

Falcon fired high-velocity ballistic rounds continuously. The Shardie ship dodged as if it knew where she would place them. It didn't matter if *Falcon* hit it or not. Every avoiding movement the Shardie made took time away from its straight-line course. That gave the squadron a chance to keep up.

In five minutes we had two ships within fifty klicks of the enemy and still the Shardie hadn't fired back or turned to run at full speed into whatever target it could find. That had become a common tactic earlier in the war, turning their ships into ballistic missiles.

But this one hadn't, which was strange.

What was different about this ship, I wondered as we closed on the target? By the standards of all previous encounters our squadron should have come out of the engagement down one ship at best.

The escaping Shardie's actions were so far from the norms of their behavior that I momentarily wondered if we were dealing with the same race. No, that couldn't be true. The identifying characteristics were within 99.9999% of the Shardie profile. There was no mistake. This ship was definitely one of theirs.

Maybe it was carrying something so valuable that escape was preferable. If so, we were within moments of overtaking a functional Shardie ship and, hopefully, their crew. For the first time in this war we'd find out what our alien enemies looked like and perhaps discover what motivated them.

There were still a few back home that hoped we could learn how to communicate with them. Implicit in that hope was that communications might lead to some sort of accommodation, some way of averting the path of this war away from total annihilation. Any step forward would be an improvement over the Shardie's current negotiation strategy of immediately attacking.

The rest of us would be satisfied only by their complete obliteration. Call it genocide if you want. I call it retribution.

"Armed and ready," Guns reported automatically when we were within twenty klicks, a range where a miss was improbable and a kill a certainty. Guns was a good man.

"Stand down. Go manual," the captain ordered. He didn't want some automatic defense logic to screw up our chance of capturing this ship. "Chief, use the small gun to disable if we can't overtake."

Guns looked at him and hesitated. "Where you want me to aim, Cap't? I don't know where their frigging drives might be."

No opportunity like this had come up before. It pissed me off that nobody in the freaking Navy knew how to disable a Shardie ship other than destroying it. The captain decided to throw the rulebook away. "Hit them in the ass then, Guns!"

"Closing at two kps," Navigation reported. "Range five kilometers. Contact in ninety seconds." Great, a little over a minute to add a chapter to the Fleet's tactical protocols. Would our entry be notable or simply another footnote of failure?

Guns tried to disable the fleeing ship by firing on her stern, but that had no effect. *Heron* tried to seize it but the magnetic grapples slipped off the smooth surface.

"Pull ahead." The command was clear. If ordnance didn't work maybe baking it with our main engines would. *"Falcon, Grayson,* and *Heron,* close on three sides to bracket the bastard. Keep him on a single heading."

I watched *Falcon* spin clockwise and dart to catch the ship as *Heron* and *Grayson* performed similar maneuvers. There was a beauty in the economy of how those three massive ships managed to pirouette and spin like ballet dancers. Command would probably have flayed the captain's hide for ordering such a move in those close quarters. But not now, not while we took pride at their handling skills.

The little Shardie ship tried to turn as *Falcon* came abreast but was blocked by *Heron.* A second evasive move was blocked by *Grayson.*

"Wheels, give us a boost. I want to place our engines directly ahead of it." I watched the screens over the captain's shoulder as we moved into position. Thus far the alien had maintained a steady velocity. If it accelerated suddenly...I cut that thought off as soon as it started.

"Engines, fire at one quarter full and slowly bring our speed down." The forward steering engines fired intermittently, each blast decreasing our velocity by fifty kilometers per second. I had faith in the crew that they could balance the forward braking against the thrust of the mains.

There was a plume of burning violet plasma reaching a quarter kilometer behind us, its white-hot tip threatening the alien. Nothing could withstand that much heat. Even ceramics would be consumed in such a flame. The Shardie had to either halt or be melted into submission.

I held my breath as the tip of our flame touched the bow of the alien ship.

"She's slowed," *Grayson* reported. "Adjusting to maintain position." *Heron* and *Falcon* moved accordingly.

"Close the bracket," the captain ordered. "Tight as you can."

"I can push it against *Heron*," *Falcon* reported.

"Careful," he warned. "We don't know what tricks this bastard might have up its sleeve."

"Engines, cut our plume slowly so he doesn't get any ideas as we close. I want to put our mains tight against the bow of that thing. One hint of trouble and I want them immediately on full to incinerate him."

A second later the call for all hands to secure themselves rang through the ship. If we fired the mains on full we'd pull seven gees at least.

"Get your marines ready to board," the captain instructed.

I could sense something exercising my body when I emerged from the dream state. I could see mountains in the distance and, before them, a broad lake. The water rippled slowly, as if a slight breeze was playing across its surface. Somewhere a bird sang a cheery song. There should have been pine scent or the earthy smell of loam, but I detected none of that. There was no smell whatsoever.

Another glance at the lake and a memory came flooding back. This was the lake where we vacationed. But was this just a memory or was it an actual scene? I flicked eyes left and right, taking in the three dimensional reality of the sight. No, this was no memory. Somehow I had been transported several million miles to Earth and brought to this lovely spot.

But then I recalled that the lake had been drained before I was commissioned and the mountains leveled for ore. Unless I had been taken back in time this scene couldn't be real, despite the evidence of my senses.

I felt my legs bending and my arms twisting, but when I tried to resist I realized I still had no control, no volition. It was as if my limbs had minds of their own. Still, the movement after so long felt good, the muscles moving with strength and purpose.

Whatever was causing this stayed out of sight, beyond every perception but the sense of movement—kinesthetic; I think it's called. I tried to move my head to see my feet but it felt as if my neck was made of stone. Neither did I catch a glimpse of forearms or hands even though my senses said they should be in plain sight.

So many mysteries and so little knowledge. I tried to recall how I had come to this, tried to recall anything more recent than my boyhood memories.

And failed.

I ordered two of my men and three of the cybers out of the hatch and onto the surface of the captured Shardie ship. If we were lucky they could find some way to get inside and confront the aliens. Kill them if necessary, but maybe it wouldn't come to that. I made sure that Corporal Henderson wasn't among the four. He'd recently lost his family to the Shardies and might not be shy about using his weapon.

"No apparent hatches," one of the cybers reported. "There are little holes everywhere, about a hands-breadth wide. The infrared shows there's something really hot amidships. Might be the engine." There was a long pause. "Downloading images now."

"See what your engineers can make of those pictures," The captain instructed *Heron*. "See if you can chip off some samples."

Soon after, the squad rigged some netting to give the engineers a way to secure themselves as they worked. The cybers were still searching for an entrance.

The captain stood beside me as we watched the tactical feeds streaming back. "Make sure we get a sample of that thing," he said. "If I have to fire the mains and melt the son-of-a-bitch we'll need something for the scientists to analyze."

I knew he wouldn't hesitate if it tried to escape. "All ships, link your mains to mine," he ordered. "If I have to blow this guy I want to be sure you are with me and not part of the melt." That got a few chuckles.

Nobody mentioned my marines.

"Count backwards from ten," the voice asked as I groggily wakened. Must not have kept the covers on, was my first thought. I felt cold but wasn't shivering. Must be autumn if the nights were so cool. "T. te...Ten," I tried to say but couldn't feel my mouth forming the words.

"I need you to say it out loud," the voice prompted as I struggled to make sense of what he said. Hadn't he heard me?

I took a deep breath and struggled to form the words but still couldn't feel tongue or lips. "Ten!" Something screeched behind me. "Nine." Lower this time. "Eight." A normal voice I thought.

"Excellent."

There were some mechanical sounds. Something touched my face, a feather of sensation, quickly gone. There was a flash and then, I could see! It took a moment to adjust before I noticed that the lights were too bright and the colors garish. I tried, but couldn't squint. "Hurts," I said and the lights immediately dimmed. There seemed to be a doctor looking into my eyes, a doctor with a bright red face and hands, as if he were wearing florescent paint. I noticed that his gown was pale violet instead of the traditional white. When he smiled his teeth glowed.

"Funny colors," I said, and heard my voice coming from somewhere behind me.

"We'll fix that in a few days but for now we're going to reconnect you. Don't try to move until I tell you."

Stupid thing to say, besides, my cheek itched where the feather had touched. I lifted my hand to scratch and heard whirling sounds as something moved. It sounded mechanical and heavy. Somebody screamed.

It was me.

"I've got her tight as a tick," the quartermaster reported shortly afterward, meaning that the Shardie ship had been trussed tightly to our hull and blanketed by every bit of electronic suppression gear we had. "Charges armed and ready." If need be the captain could sever the cables linking the Shardie to our ships in an instant.

I continued to watch the engineers move equipment across the gap between the Shardie and our ship as they continued to work. I saw small sparks, those would be the engineers' cutting torches, a new approach now that the drills and saws had failed them.

"Some sort of ceramic, it looks like," the engineering chief reported. I could tell which one it was by the bright red suit he wore in contrast to my marines' dull black and the engineers' glaring white. Three engineers had set up a large tripod and connected it to some thick cables emanating from *Heron*. "Never seen anything like this hull material, but there ain't nothing can stand up to a laser torch. We'll have that sample for you soon."

The Shardie hadn't moved since we bracketed it. In fact, there was no sign that it was anything but an inert hunk of glass with something hot in the middle.

Apparently the engineers had gotten the laser working. As they activated the torch a pale blue beam grew to white brilliance beneath the tripod. "Looks like she's cutting through," the chief said seconds before a gout of flame shot up and quickly grew to consume the red and white suits in a rapidly expanding circle. The Shardie began to...

"What the..." was all I had time to say before the Shardie became a miniature nova.

Alarm bells were clamoring, pressure changing as the blast doors slammed to preserve sections from the vacuum. The board was a sea of crimson dotted with stars of warning lights beneath while whistling air screamed where the metal shards had made their entrance. The hatch door was a twisted mass blocking the corridor from the bridge.

The pain in my body was immense, almost more than I could bear. Each intake of breath was an agony of scorching air, each exhalation a scream of rasping torture. I kept hoping each would subside, but the horror of each breath added to the previous, growing ever more intense as the moments passed.

I looked across the slick deck, past the arms and legs, one with my boot on it. "Captain, captain," screamed Guns as he clutched the captain's body. "Oh God, we've got to save him." I didn't think that was possible since the captain's head was beside me and across the room from Guns.

"He's dead," I said too calmly as I grew aware of my own injuries. I couldn't feel my legs and one arm felt as if it were on fire. My gut felt cold and empty. My pants felt full, warm, and smelled like shit.

A pair of hands appeared on either side and ripped the malformed hatch aside. One of my marines, Winslow, Harold, stepped onto the bridge. "Lieutenant?"

"Here," I groaned.

"You are seriously injured, sir," Winslow said as he lifted me effortlessly and carried me to the hatch. I think I screamed from the pain as bone grated on bone. Guns staggered behind us, carrying his right arm with what remained of his left hand.

Winslow continued to carry me. "Our men?" I whispered, meaning the ones outside.

"All gone," he replied and I hoped he meant the same.

"Help Guns," I ordered.

"He is bleeding profusely from multiple trauma and will likely die within minutes," the cyber replied. "I believe that you can survive."

Two Navy ratings stumbled into the corridor. "Decks Four and Five gone," the one with the bloody leg yelled. "Access from this deck's cut off by a fire."

I noticed severe burns on the left side of the other rating's face when he glanced my way. "Jesus, how can he still be alive?" he cried after glancing my way.

"Help me get him into the escape pod," Winslow ordered, his voice crackling in command mode. "You, put a tourniquet on your leg and take care of him. There's a medical pack on board."

"What about me?" the other rating asked with a catch in his voice and a glance at Gun's bloody body lying on the deck.

"We do what we can to save the ship and crew," Winslow, Harold replied as he slammed the hatch shut and cut off any reply. A few seconds later the force of the ejection sequence blew the pod free from the ship and me free from my pain.

I awoke so free from pain that I wondered if I had made the wrong choice and was in heaven. Then I realized that I was breathing, there were things happening in my body, and smells assailed my nostrils. I had been saved by my choice, but: "What have you done to me?"

"You were close to death, Lieutenant," a distant voice replied. "We saved what we could." He went on to describe the extensive modifications to my body, my supersensitive senses, the improved vision—and I recalled Winslow, Harold's six eyes—and all of the other things that separated a cybermarine from ordinary humans.

"What else did you do?" I said. I never felt more alive and vigorous. This might not be bad at all.

The voice didn't respond immediately and when it did it was a different voice—probably a psychologist. "We had to choose what parts of your memories to retain," the new voice said softly. "Your new brain is artificial, a silicon and gel mixture that gives you consciousness, volition, and memories but doesn't have the capacity of...Look, there wasn't enough for most of your past so we had to choose what would be most important to you. Your education, training, and recent war experiences use most of the memory volume, leaving just enough room for a few boyhood memories."

No, that couldn't be true, I thought, the memories of my prize calf, the lake, and mother clear in my mind. Try as I might, there were nothing else I could recall with such clarity. There were fragments, just flashes of scenes without context, and faces without names. On the other hand, every memory of my twelve years in the Navy, of training and skills were clear as if they had happened seconds before. Most of what had made me unique was gone forever, along with emotions, faith, and the important things that had formed my personality. "Did I have any family beside my mother?"

"Sorry," the voice added. It didn't sound terribly apologetic.

"There is a choice," someone had whispered softly weeks before. "Do you want to get back at those who did this?" they'd asked.

Now I realized there was something I could do, something I could still contribute to the war effort. "Yes," I'd whispered, fully understanding the commitment I was making. It would give me the means to pay those bastards back for what they had done to Guns, Comms, Nav, and the rest of the squadron, but most of all, it was a way of paying back Winslow, Harold for his sacrifice.

STAND AND NEVER FALTER

BLANKETS
Jeff Young

C OLLATORAL DAMAGE, THOUGHT KIERSEY STARING AT THE SMALL SANDALED foot as he pulled more branches over the body. That's what Lieutenant Roberts would call this, but all Kiersey could see was a young boy who should have been running and playing. Their medic, Leigh looked over the casualty quickly and logged the cause of death as exposure. She had taken a blood sample for confirmation because Leigh was nothing if not diligent. *If the exploratory force from the Ross weren't here on the planet, well the kid at his feet might still be alive*—Kiersey cut himself off. *Time to reign it in and focus on the task at hand*, he thought.

"Eyes ahead, Kiersey. No way you get to keep looking at my ass."

Shaking his head, Kiersey stopped his impromptu burial to stare at Bangs. She wasn't just all talk; she had a bad habit of acting out of hand as well. Taking her LinAcc rifle in one hand she proceeded to wriggle suggestively. In a motion almost too fast to see Bangs dropped the rifle into her cradling hands and whipped around so that its bore faced Kiersey for a second and swung away.

"Bangs!" Roberts' voice cut through the comm, "Get on point and cut it."

She looked at Kiersey a moment longer, reshouldered her weapon, then slapped her ass before moving ahead. Shaking his head, Kiersey turned away from her antics. Tapping the contact plate on his temple twice brought up the enhancement and overlay to his vision. He pushed the viewpoint up and out until he could see all of the team highlighted in ghostly blue spread out over the floor of the valley. The Mosquito.net system of microaerosats that he'd deployed was spreading and increasing their coverage. Each one of the team had an aerosat shadowing them and Kiersey could view any individual—more importantly so could Roberts. To his left Anderev flanked Kiersey while Breadle and

Peak brought up the rear. Heyer and Michaels ranged to right and Roberts stayed to the center.

"Move out," came Roberts' order.

Pulling the viewpoint even higher, Kiersey looked over the terrain. The team was working its way up the valley toward the highest point in the area and the targeted lookout emplacement. One valley over, the secondary team was moving slower, keeping to the hedgerows and avoiding the open areas of the tilled fields. Kiersey continued to spread the net, carefully maintaining a cautious overlap of each of the aerosat elements. The others all had their specialties and this was his. He felt a brief jab of satisfaction at the way he performed as the commtech.

While he'd listened earlier to Roberts' impassioned briefing about the necessity of securing Cansec, the Sylvan Seven world that was their current assignment, Kiersey was having trouble squaring what they'd been told with the limited amount of resistance the team had encountered. Where were the dangerous rebels that Roberts warned them of? The *Ross* had dropped teams now for two weeks and they received little resistance. The thought hit him—he'd served in enough action on heavily colonized worlds to know that the boy he'd buried could have easily carried a sizeable explosive device into a trusting company and wreaked havoc. But everything Kiersey saw pointed to someone who'd wandered out into the woods and died of natural causes. He tried to focus on that.

Anderev's hand on his shoulder brought him back into focus. Blinking, Kiersey readjusted his vision and nodded at the veteran combat specialist. With two fingers, Anderev gestured him forward and then loped off to the left resuming his position. The valley turned and now Kiersey could see the rise ahead. He pushed several mosquito.net 'sats ahead of them toward the target, keeping them high and spread wide. The group of 'sat's pinged him back—one kilometer ahead there were three IR sources that bore metallic returns moving toward the team. Kiersey flipped the info over to Roberts and the lieutenant called Bangs to a halt, sending the flankers ahead. Moments later weapon fire tore through the quiet of the tree-covered hillsides of the valley.

Transcript Committee Hearing, Sylvan Seven Atrocities

> **General Pressman: The war had stopped. We were simply unable to continue to promote an effective campaign against the renegade worlds. The systems which were dependent upon the support of the renegades and were within reach were recaptured and opposition was quelled. The remaining seven worlds continued to resist. We had the troop carriers, the troops, and the desire to finish the conflict, but we no longer had the backing or the finances. We were not given the option to stop the conflict.**

Senator Wellheim: I'm sorry, General, maybe I misunderstood. You told me you couldn't continue.

General Pressman: Under traditional methods, we had no means of an assured victory.

Senator Wellheim: You seem to be implying that you were considering alternatives; alternatives that perhaps were outside of the Geneva Convention, Articles II.

General Pressman: I'm stating a fact. Implying nothing. You already know what we did. You just need to hear me say it. It will go quicker, be more efficient, and cost less overall if you do not interrupt.
   There were a number of radical ideas proposed, most of which were summarily dismissed. The final solution was based upon the fact the selected troop carriers were prepared to make the nadir transition to return from the fringe to the central stars and that redeployment would take an unacceptable amount of time and cost. Given that each nadir jump takes four objective years in real time and one year subjective time, the task force of seven ships was twelve years out. All ships were contacted; new orders were issued and the task force turned about.

Senator Wellheim: Let me stop you there, General, your use of the word contact is a bit of a euphemism, isn't it?

General Pressman: The military-class AI's of the ships were contacted and given new orders which were not revealed to the human complement.

Senator Wellheim: Wasn't one of those orders to ensure the failure of the refueling drones?

General Pressman: We made sure that what was necessary was done.

Senator Wellheim: You are content with the result?

General Pressman: We achieved the reacquisition of the colonies. That is the only result that matters.

"What the hell was that? What kind of idiot makes that much noise?" Peak asked over the comm.

Kiersey swung his bar-buster around at the sounds from ahead. He snugged the helmet down on his head, his fingers briefly catching on the hanger hook on the back. The rectangular bar-buster hummed in his hands when the weapon's field went live. His gun was limited in accuracy but the amount of ammunition it could sling made up for that failing. As the hostile fire ahead of them started up again, Kiersey realized what was bothering Peak. All of the combat team's weapons were silent until impact; the older style slug throwers made a racket and gave away their user's positions. When Kiersey looked at the view from the net, he realized there were no IR spikes in the area that matched the trajectories of the enemy fire.

Sweeping his view over the team, he found Breadle down and Peak firing his bar-buster standing next to his fallen comrade. Breadle rolled over onto his side trying to get up to one knee. Roberts was receiving all of the feed and made the intuitive jump before Kiersey did, redirecting the fire from Peak and Anderev up into the canopy of the trees. Bangs, every bit as lucky as she always was, crouched untouched behind the stump of a toppled tree, her LinAcc pointed toward the incoming hostiles. Kiersey picked them out, painted them, and passed the info along to Roberts. Seconds later the first one slumped forward, promptly followed by the next. The final combatant turned to make a run for it, but Bangs' headshot brought his limp form to the ground.

Kiersey fanned out the aerosats looking for more movement. Then he received an image from Anderev and quickly forwarded it to Roberts—the fire the combat group received was from two automated systems that were embedded in the trunks of large trees.

At the base of the nearest tree, Heyer looked up at the splintered remains. "Why the hell do that?"

"The tree covered up the metallic ping and soaked up the heat signature. It's high enough to give the system good covering fire and, finally, a bunch of farmers don't think like we do." Anderev's delivered his assessment in a clipped tone.

"Too right. Only a bunch of farmers could figure on kicking the Federate and not expect a response," returned Bangs as she got to her feet.

Kiersey began a broad sweep looking for any emission from more emplace-ments, resetting the parameters to catch the limited exposure of these embedded traps. Roberts turned his attention to Bangs' feed and Kiersey found himself fol-lowing along using the 'sat that shadowed her. She crept up on the casualties and then came to an abrupt halt.

"What is it, Bangs?" sent Roberts.

When she turned, the body at her left came into view. At first all that Kiersey could see were the muddy boots and non-mutable camouflage, then Bangs walked closer. There was no mistaking the cylinders strapped to the dead man's face.

"Go to BW-1. All team, BW-1. Now," barked Roberts over the comm.

Bangs' chatter reduced itself to a constant stream of profanity that Kiersey chopped off. Her shoulders shook once, then she reached around and pulled the filter clasp across the front of her helmet like they all were doing. Then her LinAcc

came back up and her back straightened. He'd seen Bangs like this before. Someone was going to die and soon. He was just glad she was in front of him. Kiersey
dialed back his viewpoint and a twitch raced up his spine. Who knew what bio
weapon they were all exposed to....

Transcript Committee Hearing, Sylvan Seven Atrocities

**Senator Wellheim: Correct me if I'm wrong, General, but I
understand that you gave your troops something extra.**

**General Pressman: All troops were inoculated with a new full-
spectrum antigen.**

**Senator Wellheim: Well that makes sense; you don't want your
troops coming down with anything once they are groundside.**

Leigh patched up as much of Breadle's side as she could while Kiersey and
Peak watched over her. Kiersey stole a glance at Roberts. The lieutenant, from his
tense stance, was having a heated encrypted conversation with command on board
the *Ross*. Once Roberts secured evac for Breadle, Kiersey saw him send Peak to
help the injured man to a clear LZ. Pushing the net farther, Kiersey kept scanning
for enemy signatures. Now that he had a template from the automated guns in the
trees, he was able to identify two other emplacements. He caught Roberts' comm
lighting up.

"Leigh," Roberts sent and the medic jogged over to him. "I need a report and
I need it yesterday. What the hell did we just step in? How bad is it?"

Leigh looked away briefly. "Sir, I'm not certain what we're up against, but it's
fairly virulent. When I knew that we were looking for a pathogen, something that I
found from the casualty we discovered earlier made better sense. The boy should-
n't have died from exposure. It just doesn't get cold enough in this season. His
cause of death must be due to whatever the rebels released. I'm still trying to
narrow it down, but there were some unusual viruses in his system."

"Are we safe?" Roberts asked.

"Our new antigen treatment should cover most of what the opposition could
throw at us."

Roberts put a hand on Leigh's shoulder and turned her away from the team,
their comm's chatter becoming encrypted. Kiersey considered what had just
happened. Roberts wasn't very subtle when it came to communication. If Kiersey
didn't know any better, he'd swear that the encryption slip was deliberate. He did-
n't get any time to think about it further, because Roberts redeployed the team and
once again started them toward the highest point. Kiersey could still hear Bangs
mumbling under her breath as they struck out.

There was a body lying in the clearing at the base of the rise. The metal in the gun it held pinged on the mosquito.net but its temperature had dropped enough that the IR could not immediately discern it. After making their way around the two tree emplacements, the team continued on to the objective. At the foot of the hill, the trees were all cut down to give the defenders on the heights the advantage of a clear line of sight. Except, when Kiersey flew the aerosats over the landscape he found no IR spikes or metallic pings other than the fortified position on the hillside that had been identified from orbit by the *Ross*. Where were all the defenders, he wondered? The only thing the team discovered so far was a casualty lying in plain sight.

Kiersey brought a group of aerosats level with the front of the opening in the hillside that led via a switchback tunnel up to the keep above them. Nothing. Still no heat signatures. Once inside the 'sats found the bodies of two guards, one of them with his arms out-stretched, futilely reaching for a cylinder mask. Beyond that there were more dead, all of which were cold enough that Leigh couldn't guess at a time of death.

"What the hell happened here?" mumbled Heyer.

Roberts stood considering the scene before him. Kiersey watched him shake his head briefly. Then the lieutenant spoke, sending Bangs in to lead, followed by Heyer and Michaels. Kiersey looked at the 'sat readings again. The cave ran straight back for fifty meters before starting to ascend. Roberts sent him a brief message, "Stay here with Anderev. Move some aerosats over our back trail and continue to push forward the ones in the cave." With that the lieutenant motioned Leigh ahead of him toward the dead guards.

Kiersey picked a 'sat near Bangs and watched as she moved further into the cave. She was still twitchy and her shoulders jerked back and forth. More bodies slumped against the sides of the cavern.

"This is bad," Michaels sent over the band. "It's like they didn't even know what they set loose."

"No chatter," Roberts replied from where he stood over Leigh as she examined the guard's body.

The furthest 'sat picked up a spike in the IR. Kiersey relayed the highlighted view to the rest of the team. "You've got a live one all the way at the back of the cave. There's some metallic pings from around the combatant."

"Bangs!" Roberts sent cutting across Kiersey, but she was already in motion, the LinAcc's barrel swinging in front of her as she tracked the enemy.

"What is this stuff?" came from Heyer, who was down on one knee in front of several bags made from coarsely spun fiber.

"Bangs, I need them alive. We need to know what's going on here." Roberts started to move away from Leigh.

"There's more over here. It's really fine," answered Michaels, something white and powdery spilled out onto the floor in front of him. "There's something buried under all of these bags. Look at they way they hump up in the middle."

Kiersey saw Anderev move in the corner of his eye. The combat specialist was also watching the feed from the cave in a reduced window according to Kiersey's log. There was a brief, sharp breath from Bangs' feed and a muffled thump as the LinAcc's ammunition found its target.

"Damn it, Bangs!" came from Roberts.

Kiersey flipped back to the feed from the 'sat shadowing Bangs just in time to see the thumb on her victim's hand rise.

All of the team in the cave's audio caught the pop of small explosions. The 'sats images were overwhelmed by the fine white particles that shot into the air as the bags were destroyed. Kiersey's mind was working at putting everything he saw together when Anderev slammed into him throwing them both to the ground. The feed from the 'sats vanished into bright white overload. The ground shook momentarily and an orange lance of fire jetted from the cave across the clearing into the surrounding woods. Kiersey felt himself rolling away from Anderev, his ears and eyes overwhelmed despite the protection of his helmet.

He came to rest on his back. Blinking his eyes, Kiersey looked upward in time to see the tree flying through the air. Its roots came down, striking him in the chest and shoving him along the ground for several meters.

There was a smell of something other than burning wood when he came around. At the edges of Kiersey's awareness, he could hear Anderev muttering. He heard snatches of "Flour, of all things, damn primitives" and then "You're not going to like this, but I can't carry you." The burning scent got stronger and when he dug far enough into his memory, Kiersey realized that it smelled just like incinerated flesh.

❖

Transcript Committee Hearing, Sylvan Seven Atrocities

General Pressman: We gave our soldiers much more than just a new antigen.

Senator Wellheim: Enlighten us.

General Pressman: Ships by nature are very difficult to keep completely clean in a biologic sense. They are breeding grounds for all kinds of new bacteria and phages all altered by the incidence of cosmic rays and other radiations. By giving our crews the full-spectrum antibody, the infectious agents were encouraged to adapt, becoming more and more virulent over time. The soldiers of course would be fine.

Senator Wellheim: I note here on this report that the full-spectrum antibody does not necessarily destroy these hostile agents, but rather stops any effect on the troops. So essentially you turned them all in Typhoid Marys. I'm sorry, General ,do you have any response to that? No, I didn't expect you would.

This dream is really the worst, thought Kiersey as the feeling of floating continued. He had a few snatches of memory that kept coming back and made no sense. There was a disturbing tugging sensation, a release, and then he felt like he was sailing through the air as if he suddenly weighed nothing at all. It reminded him of the way the tree flew through the air in the moments before landing on him. Then there were a few seconds of very distorted vision as if he were hanging upside down and swinging back and forth. Through all of this he could smell that horrendous odor once again of burning flesh.

"OPS-AI give him visual."

Kiersey worked over the new stimuli for a moment. That was Anderev's voice he realized and then he could see.

The image before him wavered and Kiersey realized he was in the infirmary onboard the *Ross*. He'd made it. He started to turn his head in the direction that Anderev's voice came from but nothing happened. The staff must have him secured, that made sense since his back or neck was probably injured. He heard a chair scrape on the flooring and Anderev came into his line of sight.

The combat specialist was missing an arm. The slope of his shoulder cut off abruptly and a reddish blue bandage covered the absence. Burns covered what was visible of the rest of Anderev. "It's not as bad as it looks, but when it itches, then it is that bad," Anderev grated out. "Sorry, smoke inhalation," he continued pointing at his throat. "But what I'm really sorry about is that I couldn't carry you out..." his voice trailed off and he looked away.

Kiersey was briefly confused at that. He was thinking more clearly now than before, perhaps the level of drugs in his system was being reduced. "What do you mean?" His voice sounded tinny and unmodulated; perhaps he had some smoke inhalation damage as well.

Anderev didn't say anything for a moment. Then he reached across and pulled a slate off of nearby table. He fiddled with it awkwardly until its surface became reflective. "I'm not sure you're ready for this..." Again he trailed off and then brought up the mirrored screen before Kiersey.

It was quiet in the room while Kiersey went through several panicked reactions. But they were reactions that would have taken a body to act upon. His face was barely recognizable and that was what remained of most of him. Just below his adam's apple, Kiersey became a ragged mass of flesh. His body was gone. A gelatinous mass of blue, a tangle of tubes, and several flexing bellows were attached to his pitiful remains. His mind...his mind however continued to work fine. Six long months, six incredibly long months and the techs on the *Ross* would grow him a new body. He'd be more than just a chunk of flesh again. That was when he realized that Anderev was still much too quiet and still. "You saved my life," Kiersey said.

The big man's shoulders slumped. "It was about the only thing I saved," he sat down at the edge of Kiersey's vision.

"Now I know what you mean when you said you couldn't carry me." If he had a body, Kiersey would have shuddered. He'd heard before about the option of sealing the armor's helmet before in life-threatening situations. But he'd never heard of anyone using it. That's what the handle on the top of the helmet was really for, not just hanging it on the wall. Then he started to think more about what Anderev said. "Look, there was nothing we could do for them. It happened so fast. It was over fast—that was the only good thing. I'm sure they never even felt it."

Anderev turned back around where Kiersey could see his face. Some of the tension there had lessened. "Kiersey, you don't understand. All of those dead men and women down there, even that kid—it's all our fault."

"When we get sent in, people die. It's a fact."

Kiersey heard Anderev stand up to his feet. "No, you don't know. When we were sent down to Cansec our hyped-up immune systems were carrying live infectious agents. We were full of diseases that had to develop into radically dangerous forms as they tried to overwhelm our antigens—viruses that the population of that world had no protection from whatsoever."

As Anderev stepped out of Kiersey's line of sight he heard him say softly, "Every last one of them is dead. We walked on their world, breathed its air, drank its water, and we poisoned them. We poisoned them so well that they never had a chance."

Kiersey heard Anderev's footsteps and then the *chuff* of the airlock door as it opened and closed. He stared at the opposite wall and its blank grey metal for a long time. Everything that he saw appear was a product of his imagination and none of it could be as bad as the reality. "OPS," he said, "I think you can turn me off for awhile. I think you can turn me off for a long while...."

Transcript Committee Hearing, Sylvan Seven Atrocities

Senator Wellheim: So you knew full well what you were doing?

General Pressman: Sadly, sir, it is not without precedent. Our ancestors gave blankets impregnated with the small pox infection to the Indians and achieved the same result. Our decision was not arrived at lightly. After all it was a group of rebel farmers that started the American Revolution. Since the consolidation, the Federate simply is not prepared for another conflict. We were all aware of the consequences and have accepted them as a necessary cost of winning this war.

Senator Wellheim: You condemned all of those people to death.

General Pressman: No, sir, they accepted their fate when they challenged us. We were given little choice in how to accomplish our goal. I could just as easily lay the blame on your shoulders when your committee cut the finances to the war effort. But you do not want to see or hear that, you are only looking for someone to accept the blame. Well, I will. If you want to blame someone for accomplishing something that you tried to make certain could not be done, then blame me. If you want to blame someone for finishing this with no recourse, then blame me. If you want to blame someone for having the balls to do what it takes, then blame me. But don't you ever tell me that I have failed the Federal Coalition.

Senator, I'm done here. I have answered your questions. I have nothing further to say.

SHEEPDOG
An Alliance Archives Adventure
Mike McPhail

"Most of the people in our society are sheep. They are kind, gentle, productive creatures who can only hurt one another by accident. Then there are the wolves, and the wolves feed on the sheep without mercy. Then there are sheepdogs, and I'm a sheepdog. I live to protect the flock and confront the wolves."

Paraphrased from "Sheep, Wolves, and Sheepdogs"
Lt. Col. Dave Grossman

IT WAS A RELIEF TO FINALLY ESCAPE THE SMOTHERING DARKNESS OF THE OLD-growth forest. Its ancient canopy had long ago meshed to form an impenetrable barrier to the life-giving light of this world's sun, Tau Ceti. Nature had not seen fit to give the planet a celestial traveling companion, as with Earth and her moon, so the term 'the dark of night' had a whole new meaning here.

As starlight shown on the scene through the towering grasses at the edge of the tree line, the suit's all-governing computer, or Pacscomp, powered down the peripheral, infrared lamps, once again allowing the helmet-mounted, electro-optical scopes to gather the faint ambient light and amplify it into a false-color day.

The armor-clad figure pressed forward until the sea of grass parted like waves breaking against the bow of a ship. Visibility was less than a few inches, fostering a complex feeling of concealed safety and overt vulnerability as his passage created a hole in the surrounding landscape.

Navigating by landmarks was impossible, yet the scouts pressed on, guided only by the down-view overlay, which gave them an approximation of their position.

As with all things deemed vital to the cause, both sides in the conflict had electronically fought for control of the orbiting constellation of LandNav satellites, ultimately rendering the system virtually useless. So it was the suit's digital compass, in sync with the transponder they had set up back at the insertion point that guided them this night.

"*Slow it down,*" another spoke directly into his mind, the tone was flavored by the adrenaline-fueled tension of the moment.

The scouts had been moving at a trot since leaving the bushes at the edge of the tree line. Without responding the one in the lead down-shifted into a walk and focused on the map. Its scale indicated that they were about twenty yards from the parameter roadway, heading straight for a rock outcropping.

The sound of his breath opening and closing the suit's air handling system was almost drowned out by the background noise of the winds dancing across the field, whipping the grasses, and creating a white nose reminiscent of falling rain.

Glancing over toward his comrade, there—superimposed against the wall of foliage—was a green, rounded-point triangle, topped with the letters RWL. Its relative size indicated that the scout was less than five yards away. The sight of his teammate's icon was reassuring; it added a physical presence beyond just the comm traffic, and the voices in his head.

"*I'm telling you,*" his comrade continued the conversation they'd started earlier, "*she was up all day and night screaming and demanding my attentions.*" A feeling of being tired washed across the electronic commune.

"*And...?*" asked Ke'Se, trying to keep his amusement from being conveyed.

"*And so I did as nature intended,*" replied Ra'Ewl with a hint of pride. "*But in truth, there's only so much enthusiasm before all that biting and scratching gets old.*"

"*You're a spaz for complaining,*" responded Ke'Se. "So, no nap then?"

The very top of the rock outcropping came into view, less as an image, and more of a void punched out of the starry sky.

"*Just what we had on the flight in.*" Ra'Ewl slowed and then took up a position at the foot of the rock. Its surface was almost smooth from weathering, but at least this facing sloped up to its summit at a traversable angle.

"*Going right,*" stated Ke'Se as he crouched for a slow pass along the side of the rock. Now just a yard from the cleared edge of the grasses, he went down onto his belly. He spied the world through the last few inches of cover.

"*Clear?*" asked Ra'Ewl impatiently as he revved up for the leap.

"*Standby.*" Ke'Se crawled forward and gently pushed his head through the grass, opening up the field of view to his helmet-mounted scope. To his front was a swath of crushed stones that had been used to stabilize and defoliate the ground around the roadways. With a slow pan of his head, he scanned the area for any immediate threats.

"*You're good to go.*"

"*Going up,*" Ra'Ewl communed with an accompanying *hooff* over the comm as he leaped. The jump brought him to just below the grass tops. Gaining purchase on the rock took a little more than just the traction pads on his boots. With a snap he deployed the fighting claws, and pressed hard against his toes. At a measured pace—as laid down by eons of evolution—he moved slowly toward the crest.

Feeling more like a gecko climbing out onto a rock to sun himself than a predator on the hunt, Ra'Ewl settled onto the high point and waited for the suit's equivalent of chromatophores to shift into a dark gray. *"I AM...the rock,"* he communed with a sense of playfulness.

After another quick sweep, Ke'Se pivoted to look up at Ra'Ewl, whose green icon floated ethereally at the back of his helmet. Despite the carapace plates that made him look like a child's toy robot, there was still no mistaking that he was fifteen pounds worth of cat, stuffed into AS'Is (Allied Standard Issue) body armor.

Although spawned from a thousand generations of domestic house cats, nature was no longer in the driver's seats. As the end product of the animal-experimentation phase for the Synaptic Interface—direct mind–machine communications, or commune—Doctor Jonathan Parr's feline lab rats took on an unexpected life of their own, as comrade-in-arms with their bygone tormentors.

From his perch, Ra'Ewl could see the town's parameter roadway, with its long, curving arc and accompanying sidewalk. There were no lights to be seen, only the myriad of road-designating phosphorescent reflectors giving up their stored energy to the night.

The town of Stratford was typical for Demeter, a bullseye layout with a series of concentric circular roadways and spoke avenues, dividing up lots. At its apex was the Administrative Centre, which housed everything that an isolated town of two thousand projected residents might need.

"Raul what is your position?" came over the comm in a slight Scottish accent.

Ra'Ewl's tail twitched at the thought of making mischief. "Standing on a rock," he replied over the comm via the commune, and then turned to look down at his fellow scout.

There was a pause. "Aye. Echo status?" replied the voice from his helmet's speakers, asking if they had spotted any sign of the enemy, or Echo, from the phonetic alphabet.

"Still looking for those bad-guys." Both he and Ke'Se started to chirp with laughter.

Yet another pause. "Raul. Kizzy. Maintain comm procedures," instructed the voice. The letters OWN shown on the squad-ban display.

Ra'Ewl did a quick front stretch, and then reared up into a sitting position, all the time scanning for movement.

This isn't the first time Corporal Owens has expected us to play like soldiers, thought Ra'Ewl to himself. Being an expatriate of the Dominion, only Owens knew why he'd chosen to fighting under Allied Military authority.

"Owens, the bad-guys can't pick up our comm traffic, and even if they could, they don't have the Pacscomp to translate it. That's why they're all hot-and-heavy to try and get their hands on one."

"Aye, I've been told all that, but I'm sure Donitz felt the same way about Enigma," quipped Owens. "So if you two are through pissing about, I need you to move onto the objective."

"Who's Donuts?" asked Ke'Se.

"Haven't a clue." Ra'Ewl leaped from the rock. *"On the move."*

The outermost ringed streets of Stratford were nothing more than a flattened bit of land, with yellow boundary lines and brass benchmarks proclaiming their future address. Many of the lots already had their poured foundation slabs and adjoining utilities trenches running out to the street. Just ahead, a picket of landscaping trees marked the boundary to the completed section of the town.

Ra'Ewl swung left at a trot, following the tree line with Ke'Se in tow. Through the thicket of screening foliage laid the boxy, two-story prefab buildings that were predominately used across the planet. No doubt each had been adorned by their owners to express their own personal idioms, but here in the dark they where all just oppressive, monolithic structures seemingly devoid of life.

"Ra'Ewl!" communed Ke'Se, with a sense of discovery.

The Parr looked back toward the construction zone. One of the slabs had a large piece missing next to a wide depression. As they approached, the ground they covered was awash in a spray of dirt and shattered bits of concrete.

"This is it?" asked Ke'Se.

Ra'Ewl had already turned and was looking about for others. *"Yeah I think so; it looks like two more over this way,"* he replied before heading off.

It took them a few minutes to arrive at the third hole; this one was in a patch of open ground. Ra'Ewl estimated that the crater was about two and a half yards across and a foot deep. He then noticed that Ke'Se wasn't looking at the crater, but back toward the house.

Ke'Se purred with fascination at a tree between him and the building. To say the tree was broken would have been an understatement. The crown had been blown off, leaving foot-long splinters sticking up at odd angles. The upper portion now sat on the ground, resting against the bole of the tree.

"Fell short," commented Ke'Se as he moved in for a closer look.

Ra'Ewl suddenly felt a need to get to higher ground, but the best he could do was a nearby pallet of building materials. It was piled high with polymer sacks, many of which were torn open and had hemorrhaged their contents. They were filled with some form of granular material. With a dash and a leap he landed on top and gave a good hard look about.

"Owens, from Ra'Ewl," he communed; now watching Ke'Se as he moved behind the devastated tree, to be replaced by just his floating icon.

"Owens, go ahead, Raul." the letters OWN brighten on the Parr's display.

"We're on station. Negative contacts. There are three confirmed hits and a possible tree burst. The craters are the right size for the enemy's eighty-ones." he reported.

"Understood, what did they hit?"

Ra'Ewl had another quick look. "Nothing. They landed in the construction zone back behind the first street of houses." Ke'Se's icon was receding, heading off toward the nearby house. Ra'Ewl was anxious to join him.

"Roger that."

Ra'Ewl leaped from the pallet and darted off. "Owens, we say 'acknowledged' in this cat's Army," he communed, knowing that it would annoy Owens to be caught making such a simple mistake.

"Acknowledged," the human said in a taut tone. "Keep me informed. ETA about fifteen minutes, Owens out."

As Ra'Ewl cleared the trees, he saw that Ke'Se had crossed the backyard and was now just outside the building. Crouched down, he used the thickness of the back deck for cover. The storm door's clear, polycarbonate panels were fractured, and the inner door lay open and at an angle.

Ke'Se briefly looked over as Ra'Ewl settled in next to him. *"I'm getting a glow on thermal from somewhere near to front,"* reported Ke'Se. His display was showing him the world from his scope's far-infrared pickups. Everything was painted in shades of cold blue to white hot; the interior of the house was awash in warm colors reflected off numerous surfaces; it looked very much like a room lit by a fireplace.

"Big or little?" asked Ra'Ewl, as he slowly moved off toward the left side of the house.

Ke'Se checked the color-coded thermal key at the bottom of his display. *"Maybe around eighty degrees ambient, it's hard to tell without line of sight. Whatever it is, it's small."* he added.

"Like a monkey-boy has his helmet off?" Ra'Ewl was now just under a large picture window that faced out onto what appeared to be the homeowner's garden project. The cleared ground was edged with a continuous strip of black plastic, while underneath the window lay a neatly stacked pile of rock pavers.

"I don't think so; it's bigger than that."

Checking that the pavers screened him from the street, Ra'Ewl stretched up his full length; he was just short of being able to look into the window. *"Okay, be ready to run if someone spots me,"* he communed, almost excited by the possibility.

"Acknowledged." Ke'Se backed up so he could get a running start into his turn.

"Suit, scope up," Ra'Ewl commanded. A small insert window opened on his display. Its round image was almost fish-eyed, and clearly in motion. At the end of its extension, the flexible scope stood a foot over his head, and parroted the movements of the helmet.

The space was a living room, decorated in a modular, out-of-the-catalog style, with two couches forming an el near the window. Across the room was a theater display, its flat-panel screen gouged and the frame missing pieces.

Tilting his head, he scanned the area along the floor in front of the seating area. There, partially covered by the far edge of the couch, sat a child, it was doubled over as if resting its head on its knees.

"Shit!" communed Ra'Ewl conveying a feeling of annoyance.

"Big shit or little shit?" misconstrued Ke'Se. Ra'Ewl ignored his attempt at being a smartass.

"Suit, scope down." The scout was on the move even before the scope locked

safe into its housing. *"Back door, we're going in."*

Ke'Se was standing to one side as Ra'Ewl reached the storm door. Standing up on his hid legs and grabbing the knob with both paws, Ra'Ewl gave it a twist and reared back. As the door gapped, Ke'Se intervened and shoved it open with his body.

Cautiously, Ke'Se peered around the edge of the inner door. Nothing had changed. They entered the room slowly; its floor was covered in rough tiles and was lined with counter tops and appliances. To the right was a staircase.

"Check the second floor," ordered Ra'Ewl.

As Ke'Se went for the stairs, the hot spot came into view through a myriad of chair and table legs.

Ra'Ewl could feel his comrade's concern. *"Go check for bad-guys,"* he ordered.

Quietly Ke'Se climbed the stairs as Ra'Ewl lowered himself into a stalk, and moved to get a better look. It seemed that he had been too distracted by the sight of the child to see the truth of the situation. Lying there, just on the other side of the dinning room table separating the living room from the kitchen, was a body. Ra'Ewl didn't bother with a biometric scan, if the human had been among the living Ke'Se would have seen that on thermal. *"Anything?"*

"Negative. On the move."

Ra'Ewl stood up and walked toward the child, swinging wide to avoid the body and the pool of congealed blood that surrounded it. Looking back he could see that Ke'Se had just turned the corner.

Together they stood in silence and pondered the scene. The child was a small female, dressed in a long-sleeved T-shirt and overalls. Her head rested forward against her knees, and her long hair draped to the sides of her black, rubberized field boots. One arm was up underneath her, holding some form of plush animal, while the other hung down; its hand was gripping the hair of the adult. It too was female.

"Suit, thermal disengage." He turned to face Ra'Ewl. *"Mom?"*

Ra'Ewl didn't answer what he felt was obvious. *Thing are getting complicated,* he thought to himself, as he looked around in the hope that an answer to this problem would just materialize if he looked hard enough.

In a sense it did; while he was distracted, Ke'Se had moved to within just a foot of the girl and was reaching out to touch her leg.

"No stop that, bad Parr, don't..."

Ke'Se had stop as Ra'Ewl barked the order, but with paw outstretch the scout stood frozen in the moment as the girl looked up. Her eyes were dilated against the darkness, and through his night vision scopes they shown as bright as a cat's. There was just a momentary pause, as confusion washed across the girl's tear-stained face and her young mind raced for an answer.

He had just lowered his arm when tremors shook her body, and the girl screamed. Involuntary he leapt, fling himself back almost a yard. Ke'Se landed with a padded thump, back arched. The commune was now awash with primitive emotions, as the sounds of his hissing and growling flooded the comm.

Ra'Ewl fought to maintain his composure. *"Ke'Se, stand down!"* he ordered, while trying to drive across the feeling of being in control.

Ke'Se wound down as he watched the girl desperately trying to backpedal away from him, only to be stopped by the edge of the couch.

"Just great, get over here," demanded Ra'Ewl; the girl's voice was strained, as if she'd already given as much as she could to the effort. No longer screaming, she trembled with fear, while clutching her stuffed animal.

As Ke'Se moved passed Ra'Ewl, he pressed himself against his comrade's side asking for forgiveness, resulting in a series of thumps as composite plates smacked into each other.

"What where you thinking?" The tip of Ra'Ewl's tail flicked with annoyance.

The image of sitting on the floor and playing with his friend's children hung in Ke'Se's mind. *"Mac's kids always liked it when I patted them,"* Ke'Se communed defensively. In the early days of the Project, Dr. Parr had isolated and switched off the gene that created the cat's claws, making his front paws more like prehensile hands, than weapons, and thus safe for playing with children.

"Yeah, but here and now, all you are is a Jonathan-forsaken monster; just a shadow against the dark." Ra'Ewl paused, as if hearing his own words being spoken by someone else. *"Get out of your suit,"* he ordered.

"What? Are you spazzed?" The very thought clearly panicked Ke'Se.

"Just do it." Ra'Ewl looked around to see how much cover they had. The windows had no blinds or curtains, so they must have been the type that electronically went opaque.

"Why me?" argued Ke'Se, as he assumed the position.

Ra'Ewl looked for the main controls; odds were they were somewhere near the master's seat on the couch across from the theater display. He moved with all the stealth he could muster, while watching the girl and hoping that he didn't frighten her any more than could be helped. *"Because, the monkey-boys gave me an AS'ls hair cut to deal with the suit's tactile contact points, whereas you are still fuzzy,"* he communed with a sense of amusement over his partner's growing distress.

Lying on his stomach, Ke'Se moved his front paws to either side of his helmet. With a firm push, he depressed the twin latches; the backpack portion of his armor popped opened. Arching his back, he pulled his head free, leaving his helmet still connected to the suit's neck coupling.

Over the commune, a wave of disgust hit Ra'Ewl, who was almost to the couch. Turning he could see Ke'Se's head, but his ears were back and he had one paw over his nose, as he had seen the humans do in such a situation. *"The smell..."* Ke'Se trailed off.

"Deal with it; we'll have a Vettech give you a bath when we get home." At the moment the girl was distracted by the sounds of Ke'Se extracting himself from his armor. Ra'Ewl leapt for the couch; there, built into the padded arm rest, was the controller. With a stubbly digit he pressed the window-screen button. In an instant, the stars no long shown through the panels, as the dark became black. The girl gasped in horror and started sobbing.

"The batteries still work," he mused as he turned to face the scene. Ke'Se was out of his suit and standing in front of the child. *"Ready?"* Ra'Ewl asked, before realizing his mistake. The Pacscomp could only communicate with the user's Synaptic Interface within the confines of the helmet.

"Suit, external," he instructed. "Hi there." sounded the male-neutral voice from the Parr's external speakers. The girl turned toward the voice, her eyes wide; her mouth hung open as she panted to breathe.

"It's okay, we're here to help. Don't be scared." It sounded cliché. *"Suit hold, lights, thirty-percent, maximum diffusion, engage."* The helmet's side lamp came on. Even at its low setting it still came on like a blazing sun. Ra'Ewl's night vision switched off.

The girl squealed and raised her arms to cover her eyes against the light, the blue plush animal she had been holding dangled precariously by its long ears; a trail of white stuffing lead to its midsection.

Ke'Se had guessed his comrade's intentions and was prepared. Slowly, he opened his eyes, allowing his pupils time to constrict. The girl's boots stood like a grime-splattered wall in front of him. Not wanting a repeat of her earlier reaction, he decided not to reach for her, instead he purred.

Timidly the girl peered around her arms in search of the sound. Her blue eyes locked onto Ke'Se's, who then squinted his eyes in greetings and then tipped his head slightly to one side to be cute.

For the first time something less then terror shown from the girl's face; slowly she unfolded herself, and tentatively reached out toward the black and white cat. Ke'Se stepped forward, thrusting his head under the girl's hand and pressed into her palm.

To Ke'Se surprise, the girl giggled nervously and rocked forward onto her knees to throw her arms around him in an effort to pick him up. Of course, at fifteen pounds he was easily over a third of her weight, so he just stood there, as she hugged him and buried her face into his soft fur.

"Raul from Owens, status!" came in over the comm. "What's happened to Kizzy?"

Ra'Ewl paused for a moment to figure out what to say; no doubt Ke'Se's icon fell of the grid once he was out of range of his Pacscomp. "Ah, we have a domestic situation here," he answered.

"Be more specific."

"We found a child in the house near the tree strike," he replied, wondering what would happen next. Looking up, he could see Owens' icon in the distance.

"Standby. I'll be with you shortly," he instructed.

Sighting in on the scouts' icons, Owens entered the building, closing the damaged door behind him as best he could. The Parr's small helmet lamps lit up the house as if it were high noon. Owens went down on one knee, using the counters for cover from the windows; his weapon was at the ready. "Raul, turn them off." The house went black; the intensity of his night vision display rose to compensate. The false safety of the darkness returned.

Staying low, Owens moved over to the body. Next to it, the girl had reared back trying to take Ke'Se with her. The Parr—now standing up on his back legs—was held tight as if he was the girl's only hope. Lowering his weapon, Owens allowed it to hang across his chest by its strap.

"Raul?" he commed, as he reached for the body. Firmly he grabbed it by the shoulder and moved it; it was cold and sluggish, but not stiff. *Whoever she was, she's been dead for more than a day*, he surmised.

"Raul..." he repeated, when he realized that the Parr was sitting next to him. "Did you check their RF tags?" he asked, looking over at the girl. A knot now gripped his stomach. He'd seen that look of terror before, and not on the faces of a stranger, but of a friend, long ago, when her own parents had met a similar fate.

"Negative, I don't have a reader," communed Ra'Ewl, as his suit's synthetic voice joined in.

With a practiced hand, Owens reached into his side pack and retrieved a wallet-sized device. He then held it near the body. "Suit, RF scan." With that command, an ID photo and data line appeared with an arrow pointing at the body. Her name is—was—Sherilyn Carter; it went on to list that she was married and had a daughter.

Owens then aimed the reader at the girl. "Christine 'Crissy' Carter," he read aloud over the comm; "Year of birth, 2059. She's only three." Owens fought to keep his emotions in check.

"Did you find anyone else?" he asked, wondering about the father.

"Nope."

Owens gently reached over and put his hand on Mrs. Carter. Silently he prayed. He then took a deep breath; it cleared his mind and helped steadied his emotion.

He then reach into his pack and pulled out a disposable chemlight. Removing the safety cap, he depressed the igniter, which popped. As the chemicals mixed, the room became awash in a soft white glow.

"Sheeet." meowed Ke'Se in purrsing, the closest thing the Parr had to a spoken language, as Crissy clutched him in a death grip when Owens was revealed by the light. Clad in his AS'Is carapace armor, the soldier must have appearance like some form of unimaginably large insect, suddenly materializing out of the darkness. Crissy was frozen with fear.

"It's okay, he's not going to hurt you, he's a friend." said Ra'Ewl in an effort to comfort the girl.

"Easy, easy..." Owens commed before realizing she could not hear him. "Suit, external." "Easy there, Sweetie," he said, calmly leaning forward, and motioning with his hand. Clearly it wasn't working. Owens was still some faceless monster in her eyes.

"Suit, unlock." he said as he reached up and pulled the mandible portion of his helmet free. In response, the visor raised, leaving his face framed by his comhood. "It's okay, Sweetie, please don't squish the cat. They're expensive," he said gently.

Ke'Se's tail swished with annoyance at the remark, but at least the girl calmed down.

"Raul, you get Kizzy back into armor," Owens said as he stood up and walked toward the kitchen, then up the stairs.

There was no sign that the girl was going to give him up. Ke'Se knew he could fight his way free, but that was not even going to be his last option. Longingly, he turned to see what his comrade was up to.

Ra'Ewl was now next to them reaching for the girl's discarded plushy; his glove's prosthetic grippers were deployed and acting as a set of opposable thumbs. With the toy in paw, he moved off in a three-legged hop, to sit down with his back toward the two.

Owens had returned; his helmet was closed with the visor still up. He was carrying a small blanket adorned with wide-eyed blue bunnies. "What's the hold up?"

"Working on it," Ra'Ewl said. Turning he held up the plushy as he closed his medpack; the rabbit's torn abdomen was now covered by a gray contact bandage. He gently shook it, making its long ears flop about.

"It's okay, Sweetie, you can take your rabbit," Owens assured her.

Reluctantly, she let go of Ke'Se and grabbed for the toy. She clutched it even tighter than she had the cat, all the while giving Owens and Ra'Ewl a pouting frown, as if their handling of her toy was more of an offense than their presence. Ke'Se backed away the moment she took possession of the plushy.

"Right," Owens said in a firm tone. "We're going to EVAC her to the recover site."

"What about the mission?" asked Ra'Ewl, as he helping Ke'Se back into his armor. "Couldn't we just leave her here, and pick her up on the way out?"

Owens knelt in front of her; setting the blanket aside he reached over and placed his hands on her upper arms. "Can't take the chance. If something happened..." he trailed off. "Besides, we've accomplished the primary objective, so everything else is 'up to the discretion of the team'," he quoted.

"What if we leave Ke'Se here to keep and eye on her?"

Ke'Se was mostly back into his suit, with only his head still sticking out. "Feek que," he meowed, and pushed his head down through the neck coupling. Ra'Ewl then flipped his backpack closed, and like a man doing CPR, he pressed down onto his comrade's back with both paws, throwing his weight into the effort.

"On line," communed Ke'Se, as he flipped his head around while trying to get his paw up to his faceplate as if trying to groom. *"Damn, I stink."*

Owens angled his head, both Parrs' icons shown on his display. "You two, outside, check for Echos," he ordered.

Ke'Se tromped off in compliance; Ra'Ewl sat down next to Owens. "You know she's going to shine like a marker beacon in the infrared."

"No shite," Owens agreed. "All we can do is dampen her down, and break up her silhouette."

"What about telling...someone she's here?" said Ra'Ewl reluctantly; he'd expected Owens to spaz out on him for even suggesting turning her over to the bad guys; the Legion.

"That's not happening, cat," stated Owens, a determined edge to his voice. "Now get outside and do your job."

"Acknowledged." Ra'Ewl ran from the living room.

Owens turned to look at Crissy; she was so very small, his armored gloves were massive by comparison. It would be so easy to unintentionally hurt her. "Sweetie, I need you to stand up, can you do that for me?" he said while nodding his head in the affirmative.

On shaky legs she stood. Owens helped to steadied her, but in the back of his mind the fear that he might accidentally break her fought for his attention. Carefully he retrieved the blanket and placed it around her so that it could be pulled up over her head.

"Mommy!" Crissy cried in a hoarse voice; tears welling up in her eyes as she uselessly flung herself hard toward the body on the ground.

Owens held on to her, knowing too well that if she didn't calm down, this was not going to work. All he could think to do was fall back on what had comforted him. "Crissy, Sweetie, please look at me."

Her tear filled eye met his. "Sweetie, we have to go. Mommy is with God now, and I promise you, that after you have had a long and happy life, you'll be with her again." Owens' faith had always been strong, but in this day and age, God was often something other people talked about, not something they believed in.

It could have just been the look in Owens' eyes, or his sincere tone of voice, but Crissy stopped crying and fighting him. She closed her eyes and clung to him as if what he'd said had changed everything.

Relieved, Owens swung his weapon so that it rode under his right arm within easy reach of his hand. Snapping closed his visor he gently picked up the girl and carried her on his left arm, the thumb of that hand tucked into the webbing of his load-carrying gear. "Raul, Kizzy, status?"

"All clear," they replied.

"On the move."

The team moved through the darkness as if it held no domain over them. Once again they were operating on active night vision, as their infrared lamps punched small arcs of scenery out of the surrounding void. The Parrs were scouting ahead. Owens followed, trying to minimize bouncing the girl around as he negotiated the uneven, root-covered ground.

"Hold up!" instructed Ke'Se, excitement flavoring his words as he went to ground.

Ra'Ewl went down onto his stomach.

Turning off his helmet lamps, Ke'Se sat up. Ra'Ewl looked off into the same general direction to see what had attracted his comrade's attention. With his lights out, Ra'Ewl crept up on Ke'Se and then slowly sat up next to him. *"Where?"*

"At about thirty-degrees, something moved against the ambience of the clearing."

Through Ra'Ewl's scopes, the break in the trees shone like sunlight as seen at the far end of a dark tunnel. *"Suit, nine-power."* His display transitioned into a magnified view; now the slightest movement of his head was exaggerated. Looking down at his compass display, he aimed his head to thirty-degrees.

Intently he scanned the area. There it was; a rounded, smooth shape, black against the background glow. It was moving to its left, toward another of its kind standing next to a tree. The silhouette was all too familiar.

"Owens, we have bad guys!" Ra'Ewl communed, not waiting for Owens to confirm he was listening.

"Raul, say again!"

"We have ECHOS between us and the recovery site!" repeated Ra'Ewl, making sure to emphasize the term Owens used for the bad guys.

Owens darted for cover behind a bank of surface roots. Like gigantic snakes they twisted around and over each other, covering the ground between the two massive trees. Bracing the girl with his free hand, Owens came to an abrupt halt behind the roots; going down onto one knee, he leaned forward so that only his head was above the edge.

Startled, Crissy cried out.

In the still air of the forest, the sound carried; bouncing off into the distance.

The Parrs turned in response; Owens icon was at the epicenter.

Ra'Ewl swung back to reacquire the bad guys, things had changed. "Owens, the Echoes are on the move."

"Roger that," replied Owens. He turned to the little girl.

"Sweetie, please quiet down," he pleaded, his helmet just inches away from her. No good. "Kizzy, get back here. Raul, maintain contact, and make damn sure you don't get between us and the Echoes," he ordered.

Pulling the blanket up around her head, Owens carefully placed the girl down into a gap among the roots. "Crissy, you need to stay here," he told her. She was already trying to work her way free. Owens used careful force to keep her in place.

Ke'Se landed with a soft thump, his IR lamps on low barely lit up the scene; Owens was always astonished at just how fast a Parr could run. "Suit, external, disengage." He was now back on comm traffic only. "You keep her here anyway you can." He gestured for Ke'Se to take over. "Knock her down and sit on her if you have to, just keep her under cover."

The Parr moved around Owens' legs, and up under his arms; with outstretched paws he took over. "How do I keep her quiet?"

Owens moved back and reached for his weapon. With one smooth motion he brought his square-framed rifle up and placed it at the ready. On his visor's display the weapon's semicircular targeting reticle appeared, its PIP (Projected Impact Point) dot resting at its center. "You don't." He then moved off.

"Ra'Ewl, what do we have?" Owens was moving quickly to gain distance from the girl.

"Two, possible three Echoes, moving toward your..." Ra'Ewl looked back, Owens' icon was moving up off to his right. He corrected his response, "Ke'Se's position. They're just over a hundred yards ahead of me."

"Stay left and close to fifty. Then bunker down."

"Acknowledged." Ra'Ewl sped off.

Owens was still covering ground, all the time looking for an advantageous place to set up his ambush. "On station," came over the comm from Ra'Ewl. *The time is now*, thought Owens. Just ahead was another ancient tree. Its trunk was easily six yards across, with massive surface roots splayed out from its buttress.

He moved into position behind the tree. Looking around, he tried to memorize the position of the potentially foot-tripping roots. With his left hand against the tree, he turned off his IR lamps and maneuvered around the trunk.

Now in relative darkness, he could see the distant glow from the far-off clearing; Ra'Ewl's green icon shown off to his left. Intently, he scanned the arc between himself, the Parr, and the clearing. His eyes locked onto two sets of small lights. A sudden feeling of intense anticipation washed over him, not unlike a child forced to wait to open a present.

Bracing himself against the tree, he raised his weapon. With a squeeze of his right hand, he depressed the leading edge of the rifle's handgrip; *Click*. The safeties were off and power made available. A pull of the two-fingered trigger would now launch a salvo of electromagnetically accelerated, armor-piercing darts.

Owens settled his sight's PIP onto the further of the two. "Firing!" he warned his comrades over the comm, as his darts cracked through the air, breaking the sound barrier. The first target bounced from the hits, but without waiting for it to drop he swung onto the second. He couldn't hear the concluding thump of his projectiles as they punched through mesh body armor to render flesh and smash bone, but he knew with satisfaction they had hit.

He released the trigger and the world went quiet, nothing moved. Owens took in a breath; he had been holding it while he fired. Although it had only been a few seconds, his body demanded air.

"On the move," called Owens as he stepped forward over the root. He'd heard the *thump* and caught sight of the flash; in that moment, his training took over as muscle memory tried to drive him to safety.

Everything was a blur of motion as the world flew past at strange angles; memories of being in the heart of a blazing fire raced in his mind. He could hear breathing, it was becoming louder and labored, his eyes snapped open; it was him.

"Status," he choked. Coughing, he spat up something; it had a strong metallic taste.

"Corporal Owens, you are critically injured," stated the Pascomp in its emotionally neutral female voice.

Owens fought to reorient himself; he was prone and lying on his left side. As he kicked out with his right leg, a wave of pain slashed through him. The momentum rolled him onto his back, the pain forcing his eyes shut, trapping him in hell. "Combat!" he screamed pasted the pain.

"Corporal Owens, the administering of Comburodorphin in your current state could result in exsanguination," it said calmly.

"Do it!" he demanded. The threat of bleeding out from the Combat drug seemed meaningless.

The initial sensation of the transdermal spray hitting the base of Owens' neck was lost to him. Then the drug reached his brain, and the pain faded away. It felt like cool water was running through his vein, as the drugs' synthetic hormones and endorphins dominated his body. His eyes dilated in response, and his mind finally cleared.

"*Ne se deplacent pas!*" someone yelled in French.

Owens could feel his heart pounding in his chest, as his reality shifted into slow motion. He looked up; standing there just on the other side of the surface root was a Legionnaire. A bullpup assault rifle pointed at Owens, the mercenary's hand gripping the weapon's underslung 30mm grenade launcher.

"Don't move!" the gunman restated in English.

Something was moving fast at the edge of Owens' display. Like some mystical creature of the forest, it seemed to fly through the air toward the enemy. It was Ra'Ewl's icon. With a *thud*, the scout connected high on the mercenary's back, knocking him forward over the root, toward Owens.

Startled, the mercenary pushed out his left arm in an effort to break his fall; the assault rifle still held by its pistol grip in the other.

Owen reared up to meet him; making a desperate grab for control of his opponent's weapon, he did manage to shove it aside as the gunman landed on top of him. Now as the tide of battle shifted, Owens wrapped his left arm around the mercenary's neck and grabbed for the back of his equipment harness, pinning his face down onto Owens' chest.

Panicking, the mercenary fought to bring his legs up under him in the hopes of pushing free.

Owens held tight as he threw his own leg across the captive's. He then grabbed for his knife, and with a *snap*, pulled it free from its sheath. With a hard thrust, the thick blade's reinforced chiseled tip punched through the mercenary's mesh armor, and sank deep into the side of his throat; his whole body jerked as the edge struck home.

Like a vise, the mercenary lock his hand onto Owens' knife-wielding arm; desperately he pulled at his tormentor. Owens knew it was just a matter of time; he could feel his captive's strength failing, as fingers lost hold and went limp. With a twist, he pulled the knife free to an accompanying gush of arterial spray. A sensation of warmth was conveyed across his gloves' tactile contact pads; blood continued to pump from the opening.

"Tae the Devil with ya!" yelled Owens as he pushed the still twitching body of the mercenary aside; it rolled over and landed with a *thump* onto its back, bending its right arm at an unnatural angle and trapping the assault rifle underneath.

Owens turned to look for his own weapon; it lay just a few feet away tethered to him by its strap. Planting his knife in the ground, he reached out, his fingers closed around its roll-bar hand guard. He pulled the rifle into his arms and made it ready.

"Owens?" said a familiar voice. Standing on the chest of the fallen mercenary was Ra'Ewl, his head darting about as he attempted to take stock of the situation.

Owens took a deep breath, something wasn't right. "Yeah, I'm with you."

Ra'Ewl lowered himself down onto his belly, seemingly to get a better look. "Your left thigh is a mess. Can you walk?"

Owens knew the answer. He placed his gauss rifle on the ground, and then patted his chest. "Come here."

Ra'Ewl paused for just a moment, then stood up, walked over, and settled down onto Owens, who was now reaching into his side pack. Owens placed his hand on the Parr's backpack, where he then flipped up a small metal loop and held it in place. In his other hand was the connector end for the emergency carry strap, which if need be, he could us to sling a Parr like a piece of equipment; it *snapped* as he hooked it in to the ring.

"Get her to the recover site."

Ra'Ewl stood up and climbed carefully up toward Owens face. There he stood for just a moment, as if he could see in through the helmet's frontal armor. "*Roger,*" he replied, then turned and headed off.

Owens sat with his back against the tree, his gauss rifle across his lap. The damage to his thigh was horrendous, but he did what he could. He'd used up the medpack's coagulant spray in an effort to slow down the blood loss and now only a pressure bandage kept him from bleeding out. Tingles ran down from his neck as the suit administered drugs to help keep him stable.

"We'll be on the ground in less than fifteen," stated the unseen voice. "Just hang in there."

"Roger that." Owens closed his eyes; the suit had lowered its internal temperature to an uncomfortable level in order buy its user a little more time. He could feel his hot breath blowing around past his cheeks. There was a glow beyond his eyelids, something was flickering.

He struggled to open his eyes as he turned his head; arm muscles twitched in an effort to raise his weapon from his lap, but to no avail. About ten yards away was a moving pool of white light; through his scopes it blazed like a searchlight. Owens smiled. Ra'Ewl had turned on his helmet lamps, and with Crissy in tow holding tight onto his carry handle, he was guiding her thought the darkness. She stamped along behind him in her oversized boots, while holding her blue pushy rabbit high up under her left arm.

"I know how you feel," joked Owens, remembering the contact bandage that Ra'Ewl had put across the rabbit's soft belly.

Ke'Se was just behind them; he stopped and looked in Owens direction. An unspoken sense of kinship seemed to pass between them. Owens raised his hand and motioned for Ke'Se to keep moving. At a trot Ke'Se caught up with the others.

Once they had gone, he was alone in the dark; the sounds of comm traffic from the approaching ADF tilt-rotor aircraft played in the background. His mind started to wander; it had found its way back the Crissy's house, and the sight of her eyes wide with terror. Owens then looked over at the dead Legionnaire, then thought of the other two he'd taken out, and nodded with satisfaction. "Now there are three less wolves."

SPLINTER

A SPIRAL Universe Story

Andy Remic

The secret organisation known as SPIRAL exists to fight a shadow war against fanatics and rogue states of every faith and political persuasion. Remorseless, unstoppable, of every country and of none, SPIRAL's agents conduct their covert operations throughout the world in a never-ending battle for civilisation's survival.

SPIRAL MAINFRAME
COM.MEM 636843ei75#
CLASSIFIED - SPECIAL INVESTIGATIONS UNIT

NEX - The Nex Project, Nx5. Nicknamed 'Necros' or 'Nex', the Nx5 Project was pioneered in the 1950s. The Design Brief was simple—create a blend of insect and human capable of withstanding chemical, biological, and nuclear toxins. Using primitive yet advanced technology originally discovered by the Nazis, Blending allowed genetic strands to be spiralled together—woven into a wholly new and enhanced creature. When the human skein was kept dominant, the resulting hybrid had many powerful characteristics of an insect—much increased strength, agility, and speed, an increased pain threshold and a resistance to chemical, biological, and radioactive poisons with enhanced immune systems. Nex also had increased throughput thought-process, and some grew external and internal armour to protect organs and bones. All Nex became lethal killing machines without remorse. The

perfect soldier with an ability for enhanced genetic repair. However. A major negative was change to the subject's mind-state, with most Nex losing all emotion, the ability to love, to nurture, to care. The mind became like that of an insect— sterile, non-empathic, completely focused on given tasks. Once leaked to government departments, Spiral withdrew funding following negative media coverage, several laboratory explosions, and growing concerns over deep-rooted moral implications.

NEW YORK CITY
3.I8AM

Carter sat alone on the underground car speeding beneath the towering steel behemoth of New York City. He wore crumpled clothes, his brown hair cropped short, his face rugged and battered with a week's growth of beard. Carter was *Spiral*, one of its most trusted, most dangerous, and most feared operatives. Even more—he was Demol57. Part of a tactical DemolSquad. *Demolitions*. He destroyed things. Destroyed buildings. Destroyed rogue weapons. Hell. He destroyed *people*.

Carter's dark eyes stared straight ahead, watching his own reflection in the glass opposite. Outside, the Metrov3.0 hissed and rushed at 350mph. This modified and advanced underground transport system was a jewel in the crown of NYC's new modern image; its new technological superiority. Carter grunted, lit himself a thin, evil-smelling cigarette, and drew deeply on the weed.

"That'll kill you, old man," Kade growled in the back of Carter's mind, and Carter gave a sour grin that had nothing to do with humour. Kade, the thief, the mental adulterer, had snuck in the back door of Carter's psyche like the back-stabbing bad friend he'd always been. Carter exhaled a stream of cancer smoke.

"Better believe it," he muttered. "But at least...when I die, you die with me."

"Better make sure that never happens, fucker," Kade said, voice like a rattle of fleshless knuckle-bones tossed carelessly on a board of lead. *"Better make sure I'm always here to make the difference...brother."*

Carter did not reply. Did not encourage his dark demon, his necrotic angel, his brother of the soul. Kade was there, in his mind, hovering like some featherless albino bird of prey waiting to strike...and Carter despised him—yet at the same time *needed* him. Because Kade did things Carter would not, or could not do. Kade got the job done; no matter what the consequence.

The whole of the Metrov3.0 hummed like a live thing, a vast network of dark energy and high-speed traffic, with coils of gestalt human serpent coiling through its innards like a bad case of worms. Usually. But not now; not on this night. It was as if some sixth sense had taken over the revellers, the drugsacks, the party seekers of NYC; in this darkness, in this moment, Carter was on his own.

Carter touched his Browning 9mm HiPower at his belt, as much for reassurance as anything else, and finished his cigarette. He dropped the butt, crushed it under his heavy military boot, and glanced up—into a right straight. His head snapped back, but he was already moving, rolling sideways with both feet kicking out as a second blow missed him and drove through the window with a splintering like the keening screech of a tortured ghost. Reinforced glass shards scattered like frozen tears. A *rush* from the underground tunnels hissed into the car with a hot-oil engine stench as Carter rolled, stood, but his attacker was moving fast, leaping even as Carter recognised it should have been *impossible* to punch through the car's window. They were practically bullet-proof.

She leapt, he caught a glimpse of white skin, a youthful face, pretty and demure and impassive, as another right punch drove straight for his face, and he shifted, rolled, and smashed his own hook to her ribs. She grunted, flexed, and kicked him in the chest. The blow picked Carter up and drove him down the centre of the car. He landed, pain blinding him for a moment, and as his mind cleared she was standing there, looking down at him with an impassive expression.

Carter blinked. Her eyes were copper.

She stamped down but Carter, veteran of many an army barrack brawl and expert in the art of hunting down shitbags and exterminating them with extreme prejudice, shifted his body and kicked out, snapping her knee back with a sickening *crack*. The woman stumbled away and Carter climbed to his feet, Browning out, face grim because this wasn't how it was supposed to be; he was following *her* and it looked to all intents and purposes that his cover was smashed to ratshit.

"Bitch." He snorted out blood. She'd broken his nose. He hated it when someone broke his nose.

Carter aimed down the Browning. He narrowed his eyes. "Talk."

The young woman smiled, although it was an expression in pastel shades. Carter still couldn't quite believe it. She was young enough to be the Prom Queen. Young enough to be...his daughter.

"Don't go there, Carter. It always gets you in the shit."

"Thanks for the warning, granddad."

She should be crying now, writhing in agony, her knee folded back the wrong way. But there was no show of pain, or weakness. She was sat, cradling the damaged joint, staring up at Carter like some baby-faced child and he suddenly felt *wrong* and *bad* pointing the gun at her. He shifted the weapon, licked his lips. What now? Cover blown? Did she know his mission?

"You'll never get to her, Carter. She's too smart," the woman said.

Carter's jaw muscles tightened, and the Browning moved back to her. This was no High School Darling. She was a trained killer, and he had to treat her as such. "Tell me." He had to nearly shout the word, for the howl of the tunnels invaded the car like a nest of burning banshees.

"She's seen you coming, Carter. Can smell you, like the stench of a corpse pit. And when you find her, she'll kill you."

"Maybe." Carter drifted closer. The lights in the car were flickering. The rhythm of the tracks pounded his mind. And he could feel Kade crouched at the back of his skull, like a slick, black toad under the lily pad in an oil pool; waiting with wet tongue and wet lips and a panting hard erection, waiting for the kill...

Because he must kill. He'd been compromised. And nothing ruined Carter's day more than killing a pretty girl.

"Where is she?" he said, low voice barely audible above the car's cacophony.

"Pyramid Rig," she said, and there was a light sheen on her skin and her hands were fixed on her broken knee. There was a *crack* as she forced it back into position, and kicked out suddenly, in a blur, catching Carter's Browning which sent a *BLAM* into the floor an inch from her face, then clattered off down the car. Carter stepped back, and she was up, smooth, fast, fluid, and Carter licked his lips because she should not be up, should not be walking, she showed no pain, and there was something incredibly eerie and creepy about this young woman's whole countenance...

"Let me kill her," Kade growled.

"No."

"Go on Carter, let me out to play..."

"Not today, Kade..."

Carter backed away. She ran at him, firing a right straight, right hook, left front kick, left straight. Carter blocked the punches, each blow landing like an iron bar across his forearms. He returned two punches, but she twitched, avoiding them easily, and chopped out with the flat of her hand, almost taking his head off at the throat, and instead catching a vertical pole used for travellers to steady their balance and sending it clattering sideways, punched from its sockets. Carter leapt forward, grabbing her, pinning her arms to her sides. She slammed her forehead into his broken nose, and with a gasp Carter staggered back, blood flushing his face. She attacked, and he blocked as if by miracle, feeling bone-crunching blows up and down his arms. Then a blow smashed his face, and a kick sent him spinning to the ground. He lay, panting, drooling snot and blood. He spat out a tooth. He growled, deep and low in his belly, because this wasn't the way it was supposed to be...

"Getting battered by a little girl?" Kade mocked, ever the triumphant joker. *"Let me out, Carter, and I'll eat her fucking soul..."*

"No!" he yelled, grabbing the knurled steel pole and rising fast, twisting as the woman leapt, both feet aimed for his face, and the pole swatted her from the air like a bug. She hit the side of the car, cracking another window, and tumbled down between the seats. Carter moved forward and gazed down. She held his Browning.

Carter went cold and dead inside.

"Just remember," she said, her pretty young sweet white face looking up at him with all innocence and purity and naivety from behind the perfectly balanced Browning, and it was wrong he was fighting her, wrong she was the enemy, wrong she was trying to kill him, but it was a *fact*. And he had to deal with it. He nearly called Kade, then; but stubbornness and his dark angel's mockery nuked the impulse.

Carter stared down the barrel of his own gun, and that was never a good place to be.

"I volunteered the information, *Spiral* man. She's waiting for you. Rebecca is waiting."

Carter frowned, then lurched forward as she turned the gun on herself, put the barrel in her mouth and pulled the trigger. The gunshot was muffled. The back of her head exploded across the car's interior, a shower of skull chunks and brain slop. She sagged, still holding the gun, eyes still fixed on Carter. As if it were his damn fault...

"Shit."

"You handled that well," observed Kade.

"Back off, or I'll shoot myself in the mouth and we'll see where that leaves *you*, brother!"

With an air of wounded indignation, Carter felt Kade leave his mental parlour. Carter felt suddenly free, and light, as if a refreshing breeze had blown through his soul. And he knew, deep down, one day, he would exorcise the demon that was Kade; for only then could he be free of the persistent torture. Only then, could he be *sane*.

Carter leant forward and closed the girl's eyes. He took his gun from her limp, blood-speckled fingers and gave a single shake of his head; as if to say, *I don't get it*, as if to say, *what the fuck were you thinking*; as if to say, *I've had enough of this game, because I no longer understand the rules and it just gets worse and worse and worse.*

He rocked back on his heels. Took out his ECube, a tiny black alloy cube which unfurled in his hand like a delicate alloy rose, a cryptic Chinese puzzle. "Mongrel, you reading me?"

"Da vai! Carter, Old Horse, you okay?"

"I need a pick-up."

"Ha! Good man! Did the *pizda* cause you any problem?"

Carter stared down at the slack, lifeless corpse; a young, beautiful woman who had taken her own life in the name of God-only-knew what forsaken cause. He grimaced, as if swallowing sour wine. He stood. "No," he said. "No problem at all. Out."

Mongrel brought the fast-attack Manta in slow through the darkness and sleeting rain of Manhattan, and touched down with hydraulic hisses and the soft whine of matrix coils in the yard of an abandoned slaughterhouse. His gloved hand reached out, steadying himself against the twisted metal console of the nav computer. And, with eyes squinting, unshaved face a contortion of concentration, and fear, and yet lined with an inner superior strength which made him the son-of-a-bitch rough and tumble psychopathic good-natured bear-like Spiral-op bastard that he was, Mongrel searched for his old friend and Demol57 buddy, Carter, as he licked at dry lips revealing broken, crooked teeth—victims of too many late night bar brawls, smashed stumps the remainders of beer-induced, knuckle-buckled sandwiches. Mongrel's face was framed with battle-weariness. A deep and ingrained *bitterness*. And in this *New* New York World, *fear* was never far from his mind...

"Come on *svoloch* jailbird, where are you? Or did gov police break up your little party with the dead killer?"

The Browning touched the back of Mongrel's skull. "Getting slow, fat man."

"Ha!" Mongrel snapped, turning and grinning at his old friend. "I knew you there all the time! I smell you, like underwear drawer of a bad prostitute."

"Like a...*Mongrel*, you're a modern-day savage."

"Better believe it!"

Carter stared at Mongrel, and could feel the malevolence within the huge man; the tension, the violence, the hatred. Mongrel was a psychopath, born and bred, a poison-brained fucker of the lowest order, a face-smashing, bone-pulping, kneecap-breaking, spine-tearing dirty low-down son of a bitch. Carter loved him, but also hated him; a symbiotic metal meshing of hate-souls.

Carter dropped down beside Mongrel, and the stocky East European Spiral op lifted the stealth Manta high above New York, watching the lights spread out, a glittering carpet of sour diamonds on a rug of tattered velvet. "Target?"

"The Pyramid Rig. You heard of it?"

"Aye. That's a big target, Carter. You want me call for backup?"

"No. No. I'm playing this one close to my chest."

"That's how dumb svolos get dead, my friend."

Carter shrugged, and lit a cigarette.

"No smoking, Carter."

"Ha. Shoot me," he said.

30mi NW Cape Wrath
North Coast of Scotland
1.01AM

The K5 *Phantom* Fast Attack Boat skimmed the blood-dark waters of the Atlantic, Carter at the helm, motors switched to stealth mode as he rode the violent razor waves of an ocean which took no prisoners. Even as the Pyramid Rig loomed through sea-spray and darkness, lights cutting laser shafts through gloom, so the murderous heavens opened and rain slapped the ocean like an irate lover.

Carter killed the engines, turned to Mongrel. "One hour to exfil," he said.

"Aye, boss."

Carter spat, pulled on his mask, primed the tanks, and sat on the edge of the K5 which rose and fell, riding the waves with a stability born of five billion dollars research investment. Carter checked his watch, ECube, and weapon. He gave a skeletal grin.

"Wish me luck?"

"Break a leg," nodded Mongrel, and Carter dropped backward into the ink waters and was gone. Mongrel's narrow smile turned to a grimace, he fired the K5 and turned the boat, zipping back across surging violent waves to the makeshift Spiral mobile base on the bleak, deserted Scottish beach.

Carter sank into the void. It was cold. Ice cold. So dark he felt he was sinking into the heart of the world. Or insanity, at least. He grinned behind his mask as dark wings enfolded him. Yeah. He liked that. Sinking into a Heart of Darkness...

His ECube gave a faint green glow, and he began to kick. Motors whirred softly, and Carter glided through the subterranean gloom. It was all encompassing. Like being in the womb. Like being born. Like being *dead*.

"*You deserve it, Butcher.*" Kade grinned from some deep dark tomb world in his mind.

"Get to fuck and die," Carter growled in the confines of his mask; in the confines of his skull. And he wished then. Wished fervently that he was dead. For when he was dead, Kade would be dead—and that would be an end to that.

"She's gonna suck you in and spit you out."

"Who?"

"Rebecca. Codename Rebecca. Your friendly neighbourhood psychopathic terrorist with fifty nukes, a private Red Scorpion Army, and the keys to the Oil Kingdom in her sweaty pants. There's no way you're taking her down, bro. Not without a fight."

"Strangely, that's something I'm good at," Carter growled, the internal monologue a burning brand against the rage inside his skull. "Now piss off and let me do my job. Before I get really mad and book myself in for a frontal lobotomy."

Kade faded; like a ghost; a bad friend; an ancient feud.

Carter moved through the darkness, and saw the armed subs sleek and black and creeping up on him. These were LVA powered Protector Units, but his ECube stealth had kicked him; he was invisible to their radar, sonar, green eyes, and t56 scanners. Carter had become the ghost. Carter was a bad fucking dream.

Codename Rebecca. Shit. Leader of the Red Scorpion Syndicate and directly responsible for destroying not just the 57th Summit Building in Paris, but also single-handedly burning down the Houses of Parliament. Talk about Guy Fawkes! This bitch had succeeded where Fawkes failed miserably. Linked to five Middle Eastern arms smugglers and a central figure in the global distribution network of Grey Five, a designer plague/drug currently responsible for wiping out half a million people. Rebecca. She was bad shit. And Spiral had decided it was time to bring her down. Time to take her out. And Carter had drawn the short straw...or maybe the trump card, depending on which way you looked at it. After all— Carter was bad shit himself. And now, it would seem, no matter how small the moderation, his investigation and infiltration had been compromised.

He swam beneath the huge, huge struts supporting the Pyramid Rig. It was a disused LVA drilling rig, LVA being the miracle fuel which had pushed mankind higher and further and deeper into space—up up up the ziggurat, indeed. This drilling compound, however, was as dead as the dinosaurs now. It had bled and raped the earth dry of all nutrients. Drilled the bitch, rolled her over and left her to die. Now, it would seem, the mysterious terrorist *Rebecca* had reinvigorated the behemoth. Now it was core HQ. The Pyramid Rig was her terrorist den...

Carter was primed to shut her down.

He moved through the darkness like a modern day Grendel. He eased from dark waters, and thanks to the ECube the armed guards never saw him coming. The low-level platform, half submerged by freezing waters, led way to a guard barracks containing eight men; Carter rose from the water, and they were eating a hot, steaming meal, at ease with one another, Stirling p5 sub-machine guns slack and useless by their sides. Carter eased up the mesh ramp, boots soft and silent, battered face dropping down into that calm quiet place before the kill. He moved along the alloy corridor. They had to die. Had to die, or break his infiltration...

His silenced Browning 9mm HiPower hovered, and then he was in the room and shooting fast. Bullets smashed and crashed across open spaces. Guards leapt to their feet, only to be punched flailing backward with bullets in their skulls, bullets in their eyes, blood pissing up walls, pooling across floors, splattering their steaming food, crashing their screams into an infinity of darkness. Carter stood, motionless in the smoke, waiting. A guard came through from the kitchen, rolling fast, his own pistol barking like a cancer-croaking dog. Bullets slammed around Carter and he sighted, calm and cool, and a single 9mm round took the attacker between the eyes. He dropped, twitched, lay still. His blood was just as dark, red, and devastating as the rest.

Cater breathed.

"Great work!" Kade crowed in the depths of his mind, voice like the mockery of carrion crows squabbling over eyeballs on a battlefield. *"Although it was too fast, my man. You should have savoured the job—took more time; used a knife, maybe. Yeah. A blade. A garrotte. Savoured the pain. Savoured the suffering. After all, only that way do they earn fucking respect; earn their way into the Chaos Halls like the death sluts they are."*

"Go. Away."

"Aww, come on Carter, don't be like that...let me out for some fun, let me out to play.."

"Kade, the day I willingly let you out of the cage that is my skull, that's the day I roll over and beg forgiveness from God; that's the day I relinquish my soul to the devil."

Carter felt Kade grinning. "My son," he said, voice full of pious mockery, "you already did that a thousand years ago."

Carter moved on, filled with bitterness and bile. Not just from the act of killing, which he could bear, which was necessary, but which deep down he loathed. Every man deserved life; every life he ended was like a nail through his soul. No. The bitterness and bile came from the world, from the endless exploits of bastards destined to make the world a darker place. *Why in my lifetime? Why does it all happen in my lifetime?* But of course, it did not. It just felt like it when he was up to his neck in blood, vomit, and entrails.

Carter glided down corridors. Occasionally he had contact, and the Browning hissed through silenced steel. Guards were slammed back, skulls exploding, chests imploding. Dark blood ran in rivers down channels, dripping through mesh walkways, splattering ancient drilling machinery. All of it, all of it burned Carter like alien acid.

It will end. I'll kill Rebecca, leader of this neat little depraved outfit, and it will end.

No, it will never end. These things never do. You just *delay the inevitable.*

All life is a cycle. All death a temporary jump from the wheel.

The way to the top of the Pyramid Rig was one full of bloodshed. Carter was a dark demon, stalking the Halls, walking the Bone Yards, until he felt *Her Presence* and knew in his soul he had done the right thing; he was here to kill the most successful terrorist of the Age and it was a necessary extermination. No emotions, no empathy; just like putting down a dangerous, rabid dog, it was a grim job that simply had to be done.

Carter rested his gloved hand against the steel door, and pushed. Beyond, the large, low-ceilinged room was warm and quiet. It soothed him. It was filled with glittering computer banks and dark alleyways of dull black machinery. It was a calm place, a still place, and Carter moved forward carefully, his senses screaming, aware that this could be a trap and one wrong step and he'd be dogmeat. Minced dogmeat.

"Welcome," came the voice, and Carter focused. Ahead, on a self-appointed throne, sat a man. He was young, with short black hair and a beard. He was beautiful, sculpted, in the same way the statues of the Greek Gods were sculpted. He looked down with great magnanimity. He seemed not to notice Carter's blood-drenched clothing, nor the battered Browning 9mm HiPower in his fist.

Carter blinked, and stood from his combat crouch. He licked dry, salted lips. He focused on the man. "Costarvis?" he said, unsure, confused, and then rubbed his eyes as his Browning lowered.

"*Kill him, kill the motherfucker!*" Kade screamed in his mind. "*He's the one, he's the bad man, he's fucking Codename Rebecca—the super terrorist. Don't let him charm you! Shoot him in the throat now and sup on his milky blood...*"

"I'm sorry, Carter. It's been a long journey."

Carter locked eyes with the man. Costarvis was smiling, nodding knowingly, like a benign deity offering Hope.

"You're dead," he said. "I helped shovel you into a body-bag."

"A decoy, I fear," Costarvis said, and steepled his fingers, placing his chin on the apex. "I do hope you will forgive me. Forgive me the...subterfuge. I know I have blinded you for a long time, Carter. I know I have been a..."

"A bad friend?" Carter grinned suddenly. He spat on the alloy floor of the rig, and rubbed at his rough stubble. "You don't fucking say."

"You were a necessary casualty," Costarvis said, and his face had drawn back, features in a smile but his eyes were cold, and the more Carter thought about it, the harder Carter thought about it, his eyes had always been cold. There was a lack of warmth there. Lack of heat. A lack of fire. This was a man chiselled from granite. From ice. This was a man who had been built, not born. A man who lacked the basic binary construct for understanding friendship. A man who lacked empathy. Compassion. Humanity, baby, fucking *humanity*.

Carter walked forward, toward the mockery of a throne. It fitted Costarvis perfectly. It had been fashioned in his image.

"Codename Rebecca?" he said, half turning, watching his old friend, his new enemy, from the corner of his eye. "Hardly original."

"I had to throw those sniffing Spiral Hounds from my scent. I used every weapon in my arsenal."

"I saw the weapons you used," Carter said, voice turning suddenly cold. "I saw the corpses. The soldiers. The warriors. The men. But I also saw the women. The children. The helpless. The weak. The unprotected. You cunt."

Costarvis shrugged, face, eyes, none of them changing.

"In War, there are always casualties," he said.

"In War, there are *rules,* damn you!" Carter snarled.

"Not in my War," Costarvis said, cold eyes twinkling like diamonds trapped in ice. "I play to win. I play to kill! Now put down the gun before my Scale Lasers cut you in half."

"No," Carter said, staring head-on at Costarvis.

"I'm warning you, Carter. No heroics. I'll fuck you where you stand."

Carter stood firm. "No," he growled.

There was a pause. A long pause. A hiatus in time. Then Costarvis lifted his hand, and he carried a tiny button trigger. "I'd say I'm sorry it had to end like this." He smiled. "But I'm not." He pressed the trigger with an air of theatrics; pressed it with all the pomp and will of a Greek tragedy.

Nothing happened.

Carter lifted his Browning. Sighted carefully down the barrel. "I'd say I'm sorry it had to end like this," he muttered, "but I'm not." He fired, a silencer muffled *SLAM*, and the bullet crashed into Costarvis' shoulder ramming him back into his makeshift terrorist throne, merging his skin and flesh and muscle and bone, merging them with the polished leather and hardwood frame of the seat he thought elevated him. Costarvis cried out. Carter lowered his face, and gazed from dangerous hooded eyes at the man he had once called a friend. A brother. A comrade. They'd been through tough times together. Hard times. Saved one another's lives. And he'd fucking turned on Carter, turned on the world. He'd become a bad man. He'd become a bad friend. He'd become a non-friend. And Carter no longer had it in his heart to forgive him. Could not. Would not. Could not fucking *bury* the betrayal.

Blood flowed. Splattered. Costarvis was whimpering like a child. He held out a hand as if to ward off further blows. "But, my Lasers..."

"EMP. Before I entered the room," said Carter, and opened his palm showing the blue-glowing ECube. "Upgrades. But you wouldn't know about that. Because you turned on Spiral. Turned on your brothers. And that, my old and twisted friend, will be your undoing."

Costarvis lunged forward, but Carter stepped back with contempt. Costarvis hit the metal walkway hard, and crawled forward until he rested on Carter's boots. He drooled, thick pools of saliva, and a little blood.

"Forgive me."

"No."

"Don't kill me. Please. I beg you..."

Carter thought about this. "We had some good times together."

"Yes."

"We went through some shit together. And you saved my arse, brother."

"Yes! So spare me, now, let me go. I promise—I'll disappear. Drift away. You'll never hear from me again. *Spiral* will never hear from me again...I promise! I have so much life to give, so many things I could still do with my life..."

"Tell it to the widows and the orphans," Carter growled, and levelled his Browning.

Costarvis cried, drooling snot on Carter's boots, eyes closed, limbs shaking. Carter clicked his tongue in annoyance, and stepped away. He turned his back on his old friend, his old colleague, his ex-brother. "You know, I thought you would have fucking had more dignity," he said, and walked down the alloy corridor.

"You won't kill me?" came Costarvis' wail.

"I haven't the heart to stand on a worm," Carter snapped.

"Die, you bastard!" Costarvis screamed, surging to his feet, a microP7 pistol in his hand, bullets slamming like insects down the corridor. One hit Carter in the shoulder, and he staggered, and another hit him in the flank, smashing two ribs, and he went down on one knee breathing hard. Costarvis was still running. Carter spat blood. He felt unconsciousness welling from a deep dark oil tar pit, and knew, this was it, this was death, bubbling up to take him like a bitch from behind...but then *Kade was there, and Kade was revelling in the joy and the fire and the pain and the breath of fresh flowers and he opened his eyes, opened Carter's eyes from a million miles away and Kade breathed, breathed deep the air of the Pyramid Rig and the world flooded in like honey, and pain, pretty pain, and there was no colour, there was never any colour, the world was a place spinning up from...black and white.*

Kade stood. Costarvis fired again, as he ran, and Kade twitched to one side, the bullet whirring along his cheek and cutting open flesh like a zip. But the pain did not bother Kade. *Nothing* bothered Kade. The Browning slammed up, and a bullet howled down the short space punching a hole through Costarvis' hand. The ex-Spiral man screamed, dropping his weapon, stumbling, going down on one knee. A second shot from the 9mm HiPower bit like acid into his shoulder and exploded bone shrapnel across the alloy walkway. Costarvis lay there, writhing like a stoat in a bear-trap.

Kade sauntered forward, whistling softly, and examined the nails of one hand. "Carter, my man, you really should *take care* of your body," he said, and polished them against the soft fabric of his wetsuit. Then he focused on the squirming, agony-filled Costarvis, as if seeing the man for the first time.

"Don't kill me," Costarvis wheedled.

"Why not?" Kade said.

"We go way back," Costarvis whined. "I saved your life. Saved it many times."

"I reckon we're just about even," Kade said, blinking, the images in black and white and the taste in his mind oh so good, oh so pure and although he could hear Carter, like a distant dream, like a distant ghost, screaming nooooooooooo he did it anyway, lifted his boot and stamped down on Costarvis' head, once, twice, three, four, five times, and left the skull cracked and leaking pulped brain-shit like a bad, sour, rotten egg.

Kade sat down, then, and reaching forward, started tracing patterns in the mushed brains. He giggled, and fought the frenzy of Carter trying to come back from the dead; trying to emerge from the insanity of his own twisted mind. Finally, Carter broke free and Kade fled, with a last mocking laugh and Carter sat staring at the crushed skull of his old friend.

Carter breathed deep. Pocketed his Browning. And feeling a million years old, climbed wearily to his feet.

Without a backward glance, Carter walked from the terrorist's den.

"Kade, you're a bastard," he said as he climbed up a high alloy ladder.

"I'm what you made me."

"Bullshit! You follow your own rules."

"No, my friend. I do what has to be done. I do what you'd do if you were a stronger man. If you really had the balls."

Carter considered this, as he emerged onto the pointed summit of the Pyramid Rig. An ice-chilled wind filled with rain snapped in from the Atlantic. Carter sent the ECube call to Mongrel, and as he stood, shivering, and somehow managed to light a bedraggled cigarette, he considered loyalty, and honour, and friendship, and betrayal, and wondered, wondered if, when he was finally dead and buried and done, wondered if the pain and violence would ever, ever end.

You can read more about Carter and Kade in the novels SPIRAL, QUAKE, and WARHEAD by Andy Remic, published by Orbit Books.

BUILDING A BETTER
FUTURE

BUILDING BETTER WORLDS
BY

INDI GROUP LLC

A THING OF BEAUTY
Charles E. Gannon

THE CHILDREN HAVE BECOME AN UNACCEPTABLY DANGEROUS LIABILITY. DON'T you agree, Director Simovic?"

"Perhaps, Ms. Hoon. How would you propose to resolve the problem?"

"Director, it is generally company policy to...liquidate assets whose valuations are subpar and declining."

Elnessa Clare managed not to fumble the wet, sloppy clay she was adding to the frieze, despite being triply stunned by the calm exchange between her corporate patrons. The first of the three shocks was her immediate reaction to the topic: *Liquidate the children? My children? Well, they're not mine—not anymore—but, just last year, they would have been mine, when I was still the transitional foster parent for company orphans. How could anyone—even these bloodless suits—talk about "liquidating the children?"*

The second shock was that these two bloodless suits were discussing this while Elnessa was in the room—and only twenty feet away, at that. But then again, why be surprised? Their company—the Indi Group, LLC—was simply an extension of the megacorporate giant, CoDevCo, and evinced all its parent's tendencies toward callousness, exploitation, and a canny ability to generate profits—often by ruthlessly factoring 'human losses' into their spreadsheets just like any other actuarial number.

The third shock was that Elnessa could hear Simovic and Hoon at all, let alone make out the words. Because of the xenovirus which had hit her shortly after arriving on Kitts—officially, Epsilon Indi 2 K—Elnessa had suffered losses in mobility and sensory acuity. But every once in a while, she experienced an equally troublesome inversion of these handicaps: unprecedented (albeit transient) sensory amplification. Six months ago, she had had to endure a hyperactive set of tastebuds; all but the blandest of foods had made her retch. And now, just in the past four days, her steady hearing loss had abruptly reversed—particularly in the higher ranges. Suddenly extremely sensitive to high-pitched sounds (she had acquired a new-found empathy for dogs), Elnessa now could pick out conversations from uncommonly far-off—whereas only a week ago, she had been trying to learn lip-reading.

She realized she had stopped working; had, in fact, frozen motionless. And Simovic and Hoon had fallen silent, were possibly watching her, wondering if she had—impossibly—heard them. Elnessa raised her hand haltingly, then paused again, hefting the clay. Then she shook her head, plopped it back, and began rolling it to work the water out. And she listened, hoping they had believed her depiction of "distracted aesthetic uncertainty."

Simovic's voice resumed a beat later. "So, Ms. Hoon, do you have any suggestions for the most profitable method of divesting ourselves of these young, 'high-risk commodities'?"

"Director, at some point, the attempt to find a profitable method of divestiture can itself become a prime example of the law of diminishing returns: sometimes a commodity becomes so valueless that the simplest—and least costly—method of liquidating it is best."

Elnessa reminded herself to keep breathing: the good news was that Simovic and Hoon had believed her performance as "the Oblivious Artist,"contemplating the frieze before her. The bad news was that the discussion at hand had already moved from "should we get rid of the children?" to "how do we go about doing so?"

Simovic carried the inquiry further. "So we just abandon the asset in place?"

"Director, I would suggest junking 'the asset' at a considerable distance from the main colony, and even the outlying settlements. I suggest using an infrequently visited part of the planet: no reason we should be penalized for—discarding refuse—in a public place."

Elnessa was now acclimated enough to the horrific conversation that she could actually work and listen at the same time: she straightened up a bit, began layering in the thin strips of micro-fiber pseudoclay that would hold and provide a reflective receptacle for the back-lit acrylic inserts with which she would finish the high-relief center panels of the mixed media frieze. With one eye on Simovic's and Hoon's reflections in the inert monitor of her combination laser-level and grid-plotter, Elnessa smoothed and sculpted the materials while straining her ears after every word.

Simovic chuckled: the sound was more patronizing than mirthful. "Ms. Hoon, sometimes the direct approach to seemingly low-value divestiture is not the best alternative—particularly if one has had the opportunity to plan in advance."

Hoon's shoulders squared defiantly. "And what 'advanced planning' are you referring to, sir?"

"Well, in fairness, it's nothing that you could have been aware of. Suffice it to say that with the appearance of this—ah, unregistered vessel—in main orbit, the asset in question may not be wholly valueless."

Hoon sounded dubious. "And just why would a bunch of grey-world orphans be of interest to—to whoever it is that's hovering just outside Kitts' own orbital track?"

Elnessa watched Simovic lean far back in his absurdly over-sized chair, and steeple his fingers. His smile had mutated from 'smug' into 'shrewd,' even 'predatory.' "Come now, Ms. Hoon; surely you can think of at least a dozen reasons why unrecorded corporate wards would be items of interest to any number of parties."

Hoon's defiant frown slowly evolved into a smile—at about the same pace that Elnessa felt her blood turn into ice. People, particularly kids, who were 'unrecorded'—who therefore lacked birth certificates and national identicodes—were rare, and therefore inherently valuable, black market 'commodities.' And there wasn't a single use for such commodities that was anything less than hideously illegal and immoral.

"And why," Hoon asked in what sounded like a purr, "are you so sure that our mysterious visitors will be interested in such a—trade good?"

"That," Simovic answered with a self-satisfied sigh, as expansive and deep as had he just finished a very filling meal, "will become obvious within the next twenty-four hours."

Elnessa blinked and doubled the speed at which she was putting the finishing touches on the clay components surrounding the central space she had left open for what she had silently labeled The Brazen City. She had to complete the frieze soon, and in particular, she had to finish on time today—because she needed to make an early visit to her dead-drop site.

She had to make sure that Reuben came to debrief her—as early as possible.

Sitting on the spongy, close-mowed *kitturf* that seemed half-lichen, half crab-grass, Elnessa surveyed the small patch of ground that served as the colony's park, promenade, and grey market. She watched as Reuben led the newest batch of fresh-faced PDPs—Parentless Displaced Persons—to the rather sparsely-appointed playground at the other end of the public square. Although the orange-yellow disk of Epsilon Indi had almost dipped behind the horizon, the immense amber-white gas-giant Lee was in gibbous domination of the darkling sky. If one looked closely, the resulting double illumination created faint secondary shadows—with the stronger ones (generated by the system's primary) rapidly losing ground to those created by the weak, but steadily reflected light of Kitt's parent-world.

Elnessa smiled as several of the younger children lagged behind, mesmerized by, the ghostly effect. Reuben cycled back to the end of the group, gently urged the stragglers to keep up, evidently throwing down the claim that he could reach the playground first. Cries of glee provided the soundtrack for the impromptu footrace to the dilapidated jungle-gym.

Nice kids, thought Elnessa. And they almost always were, despite the hell-holes that invariably spat them out. Their parents or parent died on a Grey World, still indebted to the company store or transit office and—presto—the kids became the "cherished wards" of the corporations which had fed them grudgingly, clothed them generically, and had killed their parents "unintentionally." Unintentional, insofar as a megacorporation's work-force was all initially voluntary—albeit often desperate enough to resort to any alternative to earn a living. But once wearing the company yoke, the most abject of its employees discovered that they had to continually mortgage their futures just to keep working, since they accumulated debts faster than the checks they used to pay them off.

Elnessa scowled: indeed, the corporations were nothing if not ruthlessly efficient, even in the smallest of matters. Here it was, only four days past Christmas, and the physical-plant flunkies were already making the rounds, taking down the ornaments that ringed the periphery of the park. Elnessa watched the strings of white and red lights wink out, one after the other, just before they were quickly recoiled into storage spools by the coveralled workers. *'Tis the season to be stingy*, she thought. *After all, what was the value in prolonging the modest, celebratory mood of the community when the company could burn a few less kilowatt hours? And all for the sake of something as intangible as joy? Bah, humbug.*

She emerged from her bitter reverie discovering that she was still watching the kids, drinking in their innocence like an antitoxin. A moment later she peripherally noticed that Reuben was approaching her.

She spared a quick glance at the younger man as he strolled across the spongy *kitturf,* then she looked back to watch the kids playing. One of them standing at the edge of the playground looked to be the oldest—but he certainly wasn't the biggest. He was a little short for his age, spare, standing quite still, milk-chocolate skin, dark brown eyes, and very straight black hair.

"El," Reuben said.

She looked up, almost surprised: she had already quite forgotten about the approach of the young unofficial union rep. "Hi, Reuben. Have a seat."

"Okay. Jus' for a second, though." He flopped down on the ground; a slightly musky smell—the one given off by quickly compressed *kitturf*—rose up around them. "So what's up, Mata Hari?"

Elnessa snorted, stared down at herself. "Oh yes, I'm one spry, sultry sex-pot; that's me."

Reuben—a good kid, but very new at coordinating the activities of Kitts' illegal (hence, underground) union—seemed uncertain about how to respond. "El... Elnessa, you're really not...not so—"

"Christ, Reuben, I'm not fishing for a compliment, okay? Thanks to this damned xenovirus, my leg is almost shot, my muscle tone is going, and I stand zero percent chance of becoming a tantric master of the Kama Sutra. I know all that. And I know you didn't mean to get yourself into this conversational mess, so let me help you escape it: I, your inside agent—'Mata Handicapped'—heard some nasty chatter today between the big cheeses. Concerning your new PDPs."

Reuben looked relieved and thankful when Elnessa put aside the unfortunate reference to Mata Hari, and then frowned. "So tell me the news."

Elnessa did.

Reuben blew out his cheeks, stared at the patchwork façade of the stacked modular uniroom worker's quarters. "Damn," he said, but he didn't seem surprised.

Elnessa narrowed her eyes. "Give," she said.

"Give what?"

"Come on, Reuben, you're going to have to portray innocent ignorance a lot more convincingly than that if you don't want the suits sniffing you out and introducing you to your new private dancing partner, Mr. Knuckles O'Bicep."

Reuben turned very white. "I'll work on the act, okay?"

"Don't do it to please me, Reuben; do it to save yourself. Now—what have you heard?"

Reuben frowned. "Well, it's not what we heard: it's who was talking—and how much."

"What do you mean?"

"Coded traffic spiked big time today. Bigger than during inter-Bloc naval exercises."

"What? You monitor military channels?"

Reuben looked sidelong at her. "You think the megas are above calling in troops to keep us working?"

"Their private security forces, no. But not the Blocs'. That's your old-school union-dinosaurs talking, Reuben. Nations and corporations have been at each others' jugulars for almost twenty years now—with the nations supporting the unions ninety percent of the time."

"Yeah, well, the *industrial* megacorporations haven't become hostile toward the nations." He leaned his index finger across his middle finger. "The Industrials and nations are like that. More than ever."

Elnessa shrugged. "Sure. I can't argue that. But when was the last time the Industrials made a move that even *looked* like a prelude to strike-breaking?"

"Well, in China—"

"Don't get cute, Reuben: we're not talking about Beijing's 'companies,' here. They're not genuine corporate entities anymore than their army is. They just get their orders from different people. Sometimes. But in the other Blocs—"

"Okay, okay, I get your point. But regardless of that, it's still SOP for our membership on Tigua to monitor all spaceside commo, even the coded stuff. Increased activity is pretty positively correlated with impending operations—whatever those operations might happen to be."

"Makes sense. So what's the best guess about the cause of the chatter? War?"

"Maybe—but the command staffs of all the Blocs seem agitated."

"Well, they would be if they were on the brink of war."

"Yeah—but they'd be agitated at each other. Instead, the various Bloc naval commands were burning up the lascom beams, communicating *with* each other. If anything, the different militaries seem to be cooperating more, not less."

"So what's your hypothesis?"

"Well, the only thing that would worry all the Blocs and push them together would be something from—well, from outside."

Elnessa stared at him. "Meaning what?"

"Meaning—maybe—that unidentified ship Simovic was talking about."

"So whose do you think it is?"

"Look, El, we just don't have any guesses about that. Maybe some military ship mutinied. Maybe the megacorporations have built their own warship, are throwing their weight around."

"Then why does Simovic think he can sell orphans to—?"

"Okay, so maybe it's a ship the megas have slipped into the hands of the local pirates—God knows there are enough raiders out here in the Indis—and *they* might have an interest in kids without records."

Elnessa nodded; that seemed reasonable—and gruesome—enough. But even so—

"El," Reuben said after a moment, "have you changed your mind yet?"

"About what?"

"C'mon El, don't make this harder than it is. Will you take a—package—inside corporate headquarters?"

Elnessa shrugged, looked away. She heard Reuben lay something down on the *kitturf* beside her.

"What is that?" she asked, not needing to look.

"You don't need to know, El. Any more than you already do. That way you're not implicated if you're caught."

She turned back to look at him, ignoring the "plain brown paper" package on the ground between them. "Hell, you're not very good at this are you, Reuben? If anything in that package is selected for inspection when I go in, then I've got to have a plausible explanation ready, don't I? So I'm going to need to know what each object is so I know how best to hide it, or how to explain it away if they take special notice of it. Right?"

Now it was Reuben's turn to look away. "Yeah, I guess so. I just don't want you to be—you know..."

"Look, Reuben—and look at me when I speak. Yes, I've been reluctant about doing anything more than listening and reporting. Which, admittedly, has worked out just the way you and your advisors back on Tigua thought: being nothing more than a nice, unassuming, crippled artist-lady, I'm an operational non-entity to them, well beneath the security notice of the suits. So it's been easy enough to be your ears inside the lion's den. But now...with them talking about the kids that way—well, I'll take the next step. I guess I have to. But I don't know anything about—"

"El, we only want you to bring the materials inside. You can leave it anyplace you want. Just tell us where you've left it when you come out; we'll take care of everything else."

Elnessa felt relief at not having to do the real dirty work—and in the same instant, felt like both a hypocrite and a coward. *Damnit, if I'm in on this plan, then why shouldn't I take risks equal to—?*

"El, there's something else."

Reuben's tone had changed, seemed to have become even younger, and more uncertain, somehow. She looked back up at him.

"Please, El; don't stare at the kids. Not so much, or so long. It makes them—well, uncomfortable."

El looked away, felt her chest tighten, immediately forced that to stop—because if she didn't, she feared she might cry. "I can't help it, Reuben; they should've been mine."

"I know. But the youngest is five and...well, you scare them."

She wanted to ask: *scare them? Why?* But she knew: of course she scared them. Her face was framed by the strange and shocking streaks of silver grey hair that the first set of transient ischemic attacks had left behind. Since then, she had started hobbling along unevenly with the aid of a cane. There was an ever-altering array of intermittent facial and body tics. And of course, there was her riveted attention upon them whenever they came into view, yearning after what she had lost, and now could never have again. She lowered her head. "I'll stay away."

Reuben almost whined his objection. "Look: you don't have to stay away."

"Yes. I do. If I'm there, I'll slip into fixating on them. Never had kids of my own, you know." It had been an utterly meaningless addition: of course Reuben knew that.

And the tone of his response indicated that he understood the statement for what it was: an unintentional plea for sympathy and understanding. "Yes, El— I know." The silence that followed was not at all comfortable. "So, um...so maybe I should start explaining what's in the package?"

"Might as well," Elnessa said, looking up. And what she saw made her smile.

Reuben followed her steady stare over his own shoulder. The little boy with quiet eyes and shiny black hair was only two meters behind him. Waiting.

"Hi," Reuben said with a quick smile.

"Hi," the boy answered without looking at Reuben.

He started to rise: "Waiting for me? I'll be there in a—"

"No, I'm waiting for her."

"*Her?*"

Elnessa felt a hot pulse of annoyance: *You don't need to sound surprised that someone might actually want to talk to me, Reuben.*

Who asked the child, "Why her?"

Oh, you're just flattering me no end, now, Mr. Suave.

Elnessa could see the boy laboring—mightily—to keep his face blank. Why? To conceal his dismay, possibly disgust, at Reuben's thoughtlessly rude inquiry? "I'd like to talk to her. If you don't mind."

"Well, she and I—"

Elnessa jumped in. "We can finish this later, Reuben. Come by about 7, okay?"

"Uh, yeah...7 o'clock. In private is better, anyway—for what we have to discuss, I mean."

Elnessa nodded tightly, amazed that Reuben's idiot, injudicious utterances had not already undone him and the rest of the unofficial union.

The boy with the big, watching eyes moved into the space Reuben vacated. "Hi," he said again.

"Hi," Elnessa replied. "What's your name?"

"I'm Vas."

"'Vas?'"

He smiled a little. "It's short for Srinivasan. But most people can't say that too well. Anyhow, I like Vas better. What's your name?"

"I'm El."

He cocked his head. "Just 'El?'"

"Well, my real name is 'Elnessa'—but people have a hard time remembering that, too. They keep calling me Elaine or Ellen or Elise...or Bob."

Vas stared, then laughed. "You're funny."

"I'm glad you think so, Vas. And I'm very glad to meet you."

"I'm glad to meet you, too. I've been wondering: what do you do? I mean, for a living?"

"Well, I started out as an artist—but that was back before I came to settle in the Indis."

"'But aren't you still an artist—at least some of the time?"

Elnessa started: "Why do you ask?"

Vas looked down at her hands and pointed. "They're stained a lot, almost every time I see you—or caked with dirt or clay, I can't tell which. And you look at things very carefully, for a long time. Like you're measuring them—or feeling them—with your eyes."

Clever boy: he sees far more than he mentions. He could teach Reuben a thing or two. Elnessa smiled. "You look at things a long time, too. I've noticed."

"Yeah, but that's just because I'm really careful: I have to be." Before Elnessa could ask him why he needed to be careful, Vas had pressed on: "What kind of artist are you?"

"I used to create all sorts of art—still did some pieces on the side when I first arrived on Kitts. Old style paintings, 3-D compgens, I even dabbled a little in holos."

"What happened?"

She shrugged and looked down at her body. "A xenovirus."

"You mean a disease that was already here?"

"Well, sort of. Not really a disease. It's just that...well, most of the life on this planet—er, 'moon'—just ignores life from Earth because it's too dissimilar. Even though the life here is built from the same basic stuff—"

Vas nodded. "Carbon. Water."

"—yes." *Damn, he's sharp.* "But sometimes, the local microbes go after our cells, anyway. Or sometimes, the weaker unicellar organisms from Kitts decide to use our bodies as hiding places from the stronger ones that eat them. It's bad enough when those 'hiding' microorganisms build up in our system, but sometimes, while doing so, they block—or consume—the parts of us that they can make use of. And that's not good for us."

Vas nodded solemnly. "Your xenovirus blocks parts of your nervous system, doesn't it?"

He is very, very sharp indeed. "How did you know that?"

Vas shrugged. "Because you don't act sick so much as—well, just not able to control yourself as well as other people. And if the microbes were really, uh, 'consuming,' your nerves, I just kind of guessed that you wouldn't still...well, still be alive."

And how right all your guesses are, my bright little Srinivasan. Despite the concise recitation of her medical woes, Elnessa only felt joy when she was looking into the warm brown eyes of this child. "You know, Vas, I'll bet you could be a doctor someday."

He shrugged, looked away, then back at her. "Will we get it too?" Seeing her momentary incomprehension, Vas added, "The disease, I mean."

She had been slow to understand his question because she assumed that everyone—even kids—were informed upon arrival that, thanks to the new preplanetfall vaccinations and six-month boosters, there hadn't been any infections since the first wave of settlers. "No," she said with a firm shake of her head. "You're safe.

It only got the first of us who settled here—and then, only some of us."

"Why did it only get some of you? And how did they cure it?"

Elnessa took care to compose herself before she answered. "Well, you see, Vas, when the Indi Group got permission to settle Kitts, they started with a really diverse group of people. At first, it just seemed that they were taking whoever was willing to come here, probably because they couldn't be picky. But it turned out that the 'mix' was actually a group made up of an equal number of persons from every major human genotype. When we asked why they had done that, the company explained that they wanted to create a truly 'blended' colony. We still thought they were just trying to make up a nice-sounding story, to cover up the fact that they were willing to sign on anyone. But in a very real sense, they *were* building a carefully mixed community—but not because they were trying to create social diversity." She watched to see if Vas had understood all the terms she had used: his brows remained unfurrowed, signifying absolute surety of comprehension.

Elnessa went on. "In fact, Vas, we were guinea pigs—and they had to have a reasonable sample size of every strain and subspecies of us guinea pigs."

Now a frown bent Vas' brow. "I don't understand."

Elnessa had her mouth open to explain and then halted: *he's only a kid, El, even if he is a very, very smart one. Kids worry, have nightmares—particularly if you say something that makes them realize that the world is less safe than they think it is. I really don't have the right—*

"Look," Vas said very matter-of-factly, his eyes still calm but also resolute, "I grew up on Hard Nut, in the Lacaille 8760 system. Life is—hard—there. I lost my Mom, then my Dad, and my Tito Thabo, all in the last few years. So whatever they did, you can tell me. I can take it."

Elnessa blinked, then sighed and folded her hands. "Vas, the Indi Group wanted to discover if any given genotype of homo sapiens had a particular advantage or disadvantage in this environment. Not that there's any evidence for it. But that's the way they think: racial 'groups' have unique diseases; ethnic groups can carry 'predominant genetic patterns' for certain developmental abnormalities. So they decided it would be best to test people from each genetic hiring pool to see if any of them had special advantages or challenges in Kitts' biosphere."

"And was there any difference between the groups?"

"No. And when other megacorporations have run the same tests in other biospheres, they never find any differences there, either. But that doesn't mean there aren't biological dangers: here on Kitts, as elsewhere, it turned out that the local xenobugs were all equal-opportunity pathogens."

" 'Equal opportunity?'"

"Yes. That's just a silly way of saying that the nasty xenobugs didn't care about our race, or color, or sex. And I was one of the twenty-four colonists that the xenovirus decided to infest—after the first xenobiot surveys declared the biosphere 'safe,' that is."

"So how did the surveys miss detecting these, uh...these xenobugs?"

"Oh, Vas, to be fair, the real question should be, 'how could the surveys be expected to *find* the bugs? Computer modeling, lab-testing on human-equivalents: those tools are crude and imperfect. And biosensors? A sensor only knows to look for something that has been identified for it already. The sad truth, Vas, is that you don't really get a good, reliable assessment of what will happen to a human body in a new biosphere until a couple of hundred of those bodies have lived—and breathed—there for a while."

She tapped her chest. "So we were the canaries in this coal mine. And those of us who became sick were immediately sequestered for study—which is how they learned which genetic markers put humans at highest risk, and then, which vaccines or prophylaxes offered the best protection. And after that, my real 'work' here was done."

"But you still work."

"Oh, they give me make-work because it was part of my agreement. I can work as long as I like, and they'll provide for me; that's what they promised. But if I leave my employment here, I can't afford the shift-ticket to another system. And they'll also stop giving me the experimental xenoviral suppression cocktails, which are what have probably kept me alive this long. Since each new concoction eventually loses its efficacy, they've been willing to keep me around as a guinea pig, because I'm still a useful 'research platform.' But once they feel they've taken that research as far as they need to—"

"I thought you said they made a commitment to provide for you as long as you were their employee. Doesn't that include medical care?"

"Yes, but 'medical care' does not mean that they have to keep a dead-end research program active just to give me the chance to live another year, and then another, and then another. If they stop, then they'll be responsible for providing for my minimum needs. Until I no longer need anything at all."

As she ended her description, Elnessa was looking down at Vas, who was looking up at her with that same quiet, attentive expression that had been on his face the first time she saw him. But now there was the hint of some emotional battle going on behind it. It almost looked as if he might cry—

—but then Vas leaned toward El and caught her in a firm, unyielding hug. El looked down at his crown of shiny hair, and then put her arms gently, carefully, around him.

Elnessa resisted the urge to close her eyes as Wehns Shoniber, the big Micronesian leader of Simovic's personal security detail, started rummaging about in her "road kit": a carpenter's tool box converted into an artist's traveling studio.

"Hey, El," Wehns wondered, still staring down into the battered red box, "what's this?"

"Battery," Elnessa said, trying very hard to keep her response from becoming a sharp, anxious chirp.

"El, you know I can't let you take that in."

"Well, then how am I going to power the lights in the high-relief panels?" she replied. "I got Mr. Simovic's permission—before I started the project—that some of it could be illuminated."

"Well, I'm sure you did, El—but he didn't authorize an independent power source. I'm sure of that: security protocols, you know."

El shrugged as if only mildly disturbed, thought: *oh, I know, Wehns, I know. In fact, this was exactly what I was afraid would happen—as I told Reuben last night.*

Wehns continued riffling through the rest of her gear—inspecting each of the picks, carvers, and files, staring uncomprehending at an impress set for creating intaglio patterns—and asked, as he did every day, "Anything toxic, explosive, flammable, dangerous?"

"Not unless you're allergic to clay or acrylics."

Wehns smiled, scratched one of the clay bricks with a fingernail. "Sorry; gotta ask."

"Why? Can't the big, bad megacorporation afford a couple of chemical sniffers?"

"No, not yet. But it's just a matter of time, now that the big wigs are here to stay."

"'Big wigs?'"

"Sure," Wehns nodded. Then in a lower voice, so his assistants couldn't hear. "You know: Simovic and Hoon. He's got an insane amount of autonomy—which came over with him when he promoted up out of the Colonial Development Corporation into his post here."

"And Hoon?"

Wehns' face went blank. "She's as cutthroat as they come. Jumped from field rep to junior director in only six years."

"Don't like her much?"

"Don't much care. She doesn't notice me; I'm just muscle. And frankly, that's the way I like it. Don't want to be noticed; just want to do my job."

Elnessa looked down at Wehns' broad back as he neared the completion of his daily search through her kit. Amiable Wehns Shoniber was proof that you couldn't hate all the people who worked for a megacorporation: it was not the homogeneous conclave of demons and sociopaths that the worst anti-corporate radicals tried to claim. In reality, there were just a few of those truly misanthropic monsters—but most of them were in charge, leading a vast organization of average folks who only wanted to work, get ahead, and not worry too much in the process. She sighed: *for evil to triumph, all that's needed is for good men to stand by and do nothing. Or for people to be too lazy to care.*

"Hey, what's this?" Wehns had produced something that looked like the guts of a remote-control handset.

"IR receiver—so you can operate the frieze's lights by remote control, from anywhere in the room."

"Aw, El," Wehns muttered, shaking his head in regret, "I'm sorry, but that one's off-limits, too."

"What? Why?"

"Because some nut-job might try to use it as a remote receiver for—something else. Or as a timer, because they all have internal time-chips."

Elnessa quirked an eyebrow. "A remote receiver or timer for what?"

Wehns looked abashed. "You know. Something—dangerous."

"You mean, like a piece of art?" Elnessa didn't think she'd be able to shame Wehns into looking the other way on this violation, but it was worth a try.

If Wehns blushed, she couldn't tell: his tropic-dark skin hid all such emotional responses. But his voice sounded regretful, apologetic. "El, look, you're okay—everyone knows *that*—"

Because I'm a nice little cripple lady; yeah, sure...

"—but rules are rules. I'm sorry, I'm going to have to hold these for you. You can get them back when you leave today." And with a nod that punctuated the end of both his search and their discussion, Wehns carried the offending items away to his secure lock-box. As he withdrew, he caught the eye of his senior assistant and tilted his head toward Simovic's office. The assistant turned, and with a smile that as was much a part of his equipment as his outdated taser, motioned that Elnessa was free to go into Simovic's *sanctum sanctorum*.

With a sigh, she followed his gesture and dragged her battered red box into the expansive Bauhaus-meets-Rococo-gauche opulence in which Simovic held court, limping as she went. With the power-supply and timer/actuator gone, Reuben's plan for sending a loud—and destructive—after-hours message to their megacorporate masters was pretty much busted before it had begun. She began hobbling toward the raised walkway that ran the length of the frieze. Behind her, the door detail resumed their argument whether, it being New Year's Day, 2120, that this year was the last of the 'Teens' decade, or the first of the Twenties.

"Ms. Clare." It was Simovic. Whom she had no desire to talk to. Or look at. Or share a common species with. And besides, she was supposed to be hard of hearing. So, without giving any sign that she had heard, Elnessa continued to make her slow, painful progress toward the work-ramp.

Simovic's voice was louder—so much louder, that she would have had to have been stone deaf to miss it. "Ms. Clare!"

She turned, with what she hoped was a look of surprise and ingratiating eagerness: "Yes, Mr. Simovic?"

"Your project—how is it coming?"

"Should be finished tomorrow, Mr. Simovic. Although I hardly think of it as 'my project.'"

"Oh? Why not?"

"Well, sir—it's you who commissioned it."

"Yes, but the concept—and the handiwork—is yours, Ms. Clare. I trust you'll explain its content to both of us,"—he gestured diffidently toward Ms. Hoon—"when you are finished?"

"Of course, Mr. Simovic. Although it's neither abstract, nor highly stylized. I think you'll see right away that—"

"Yes, yes: that's wonderful, Ms. Clare, wonderful. Just make sure that it radiates the humanitarian side of the Indi Group, would you?"

Oh, yes, I'll be sure to represent the way it exploits workers, and gives us just enough pay to struggle on from one day to the next. I'll depict how, after the xenovirus incapacitated me, you made me your corporate nanny, and then, when I couldn't do that any longer, you met your minimum employment requirement by commissioning this frieze. Dirt pay for me, but a tax dodge for you, and a great PR op to demonstrate how the Indi Group encourages the remaining abilities of even its most severely handicapped employees. But Elnessa's only reply was, "I'll explain the frieze to you when I've completed it, Mr. Simovic."

"Excellent!" Simovic actually clapped his hands once in histrionic gratification and pleasure, nodded his thanks, and then drew closer to Hoon. For a moment their voices were too low to hear, but then, evidently reassured by Elnessa's near-deafness, they resumed the discussion her entrance had interrupted.

"So you see," Simovic said in the voice of a smug tutor, "our visitors—I should say, our 'new clients'—have good reason to be interested in our commodity."

"And our cooperation, along with it."

"Well, this goes without saying, Ms. Hoon. But the children will be out of our hands and out of our files, as soon as they take possession."

"When and where, exactly, will that occur?"

"We are uncertain, Ms. Hoon. But we do know this: the commodity must be delivered to the client in pristine condition. The client's, ah, research program, would be ruined by any damage to the goods."

Research? On the children? On Vas?

"'Research'?" Hoon echoed. "With respect, sir, all these euphemisms are getting a bit ridiculous."

"How do you mean?"

"I mean that our new customers certainly aren't scientists, sir. Corporate wards without identicodes are not going to be interred in laboratories; they're bound for pirate ships, brothels, snuff producers, maybe a few rich pederasts, but not—"

El thought she was about to lose her breakfast, and then something all at once calming—yet more chilling—insinuated itself into Simovic's calm-toned interruption: "Oh, no, Ms. Hoon. You really don't understand, after all. These wards *are* going to a lab, which is why their utter lack of a traceable background makes them so optimal for this particular trade. Because it is imperative for both us, and our clients, that they receive humans who, insofar as the nations know, never existed."

Hoon was quiet for a moment. "Director Simovic, I find your change of label somewhat...confusing. Why are you referring to our commodity as 'humans,' now, instead of 'children?'"

"Because that is our client's primary interest in our commodity: not so much because they are children—although it has been intimated that this is the ideal age group for their researches—but because they are healthy, paperless specimens of homo sapiens."

In the pause that ensued, Elnessa lifted a long, slightly convex, copper sheet from the floor, and, with a couple of touches of an exothermic chemical welder, affixed it to the naked wall of the room.

Hoon's voice sounded raspy, as if her throat had suddenly become dry. "Sir,...I don't understand. The client wants them just because they're...humans?"

Lifting a thin layer of protective gauze from the copper sheet, Elnessa unveiled what would soon occupy the top third of the friezes's center: a cityscape cluttered by the various architectures of antiquity. And she reminded herself to breathe, despite what she was hearing.

"Oh, I think you are starting to understand after all, Ms. Hoon. Rest assured; this exchange is not being conducted without adequate planning. Indeed, we had contingency directives sent out to us from Earth more than half a year ago—shortly after the Parthenon Dialogues became public knowledge."

Elnessa removed six sizable blocks of clay from her studio box, and compared them to the virtual assembly plan on her grid-plotter. She then unsheathed her matte knife, and carefully shaved an inch from the rear of the five smaller blocks.

Hoon had paused again, but not for as long. "Are you telling me that the contingency plans governing this, this—exchange—were crafted in response to the Parthenon Dialogues?"

"Let us rather say that the revelations of the Parthenon Dialogues prompted some of CoDevCo's more speculative thinkers to provide us with guidelines to handle a situation such as this one."

Even in the grid-plotter's illuminated screen, Elnessa could make out the profound scowl of doubt on Hoon's face. "But the evidence presented at Parthenon only proved past events: that—ages and ages ago—this area of space had been visited by aliens—"

"'Exosapients,'" Simovic corrected.

"'Exosapients,'" Hoon parroted peevishly, "But there was no evidence of a more recent presence."

Simovic smiled, smug and satisfied. "Yes, that's the story that was released to the public."

Elnessa forced herself to keep working, which made it easier not to imagine little Vas spread-eagled on an operating table, surrounded by hideous extraterrestrial vivisectionists. She mentally slapped herself, and mounted the five modified clay blocks on studs protruding from the copper plate. She stood back, admiring the effect: the blocks now seemed to be the stony slabs of an ancient fortress wall that curved out from the faintly raised cityscape directly over it—a metropolis which, by virtue of the oblique perspective, now seemed to be sheltered behind the wall.

Hoon had recovered enough to continue. "And so the full truth of the Parthenon Dialogues was—?"

"—Was not shared in detail outside the meeting itself. However, let us say that while the evidence certainly established that exosapients did exist 20,000 years ago on Delta Pavonis Three, it did *not* go on to assert that there were none left in existence."

"So you suspect that actual contact has been made in the recent—?"

"No, there's been no contact that we know of or suspect." Simovic smiled. "Not until now, that is."

"So you really think that the unidentified ship up there is, is—?"

"Ms. Hoon, the persons we are currently negotiating with are not human, of that you may rest assured. The communications challenges have been proof positive of that."

Elnessa felt as though she might swallow her tongue, but instead, she picked up the last, and the largest, of the six clay blocks. She carefully carved the top to resemble the peak-roofed gallery at the pinnacle of a watchtower. Then she bored a small tube up through the center of the block, making sure that it was wide enough to fit the wires for its small beacon light.

Hoon hadn't stopped. "So how did these—exosapients—know to contact us, and that we'd have this particular—'item' that they needed?"

"An excellent question, but those kinds of details are not even shared with regional managers, Ms. Hoon. However, I conjecture that there must have been some contact between our chief executives and some—representatives—of theirs."

"And you suspect this because—?"

"Because they arrived knowing and inquiring about the commodity we have in our possession. And because they knew our communications protocols, our location here instead of on Tigua, and a reasonable amount of our language. Although that latter knowledge has been decidedly—imperfect."

Elnessa ran the wiring leads up through the tube in the watchtower: the slim copper alligator clips poked their noses out the top of the hole. Deciding to finish the sculpting and wiring later, she mounted the watchtower on its own copper stud, thereby completing the wall around the Brazen City. Then she ran the other end of the leads to a junction box mounted on the bottom of the copper plate, just beneath and behind the lower edge of the frieze. She then covered the wires—and the lower half of the copper plate—with strips of clay that she started sculpting into a semblance of furrowed farmland. Beneath those, she left just enough room for the band of blue-white acrylic that lay ready at hand: a stylized river, frozen in mid-tumult.

Hoon still hadn't stopped. "So what we're doing now is—"

"—Is working out the particulars of the exchange, while we wait for Tigua to send us word on the outcome of the official first contact."

"Which we expect to be—unsuccessful."

Simovic shrugged. "It is most unlikely that Bloc-controlled Tigua will concede to our clients' military superiority—"

You mean, will refuse to surrender without a fight—

"—whereas *we* have already assured them of our complete and immediate cooperation."

You mean, traitorous collaboration offered up to them on a silver platter.

Hoon was smiling now. "How very...convenient. For us."

"Yes, rather a nice reward for patiently enduring the pomposity of the nation-states, don't you think? Always nattering on about social contracts, and consent of the governed, and the greatest good for the greatest number. I can hardly believe they don't laugh themselves to death as they spout all that antediluvian rubbish."

Hoon's contempt for these same concepts was obviously so great that it exceeded polite articulation: she merely expelled a derisive snort. Then she added, "Well, good riddance to Bloc sanctions and anti-trust restrictions."

Elnessa delicately swept her wire brush up, up, up, all along the first furrowed row of clay she had set before the city walls, imparting to it an impression of young wheat or corn, just as it sprang from the ground toward the sun. And as she did so, she listened to the unfolding plans for the cool, calculated, and above all, profitable betrayal of her species.

Once again responding to the gum wrapper Elnessa had inserted into the dead-drop crevice, Reuben approached her hurriedly. He had his mouth open to ask something—

Elnessa preempted him. "Have you heard?"

"You mean, about the aliens?"

"Exosapients," Elnessa corrected him.

"Whatever. Yeah, I heard. It's got to be the worst-kept secret there's ever been. No one seems to be able to shut up about it, even in the military. The word has been leaking out of navy comshacks, out of the commercial transmission offices, everywhere."

"And you know they're planning on coming here, evidently?"

Reuben frowned. "Well, amidst all the rest of the panic talk, I've heard that rumor, too. But the evidence for it seems pretty vague, pretty much hearsay."

"Well, it's not. These 'exosapients' are apparently Indi Group's newest preferred customers. And they want the kids. For 'research.'"

She thought Reuben would goggle as she had. But, again, like her, his capacity for shock was almost exhausted. All Reuben did was shrug: "Figures. Which makes our mission all the more imperative." His expression became eager, more focused. "So, how did it go when you went in today? Is everything there, ready and waiting?"

Elnessa shook her head. "I got the payload in, but nothing else."

Reuben's jaw dropped open. "What do you mean?"

"I mean that they wouldn't let me take anything electronic into the office: no independent power supply, and no remote activators of any kind. Like I told you. But even so, I think I've found a way to—"

But Reuben was shaking his head. "No, El. It's finished. Our guy on the inside is strip-searched every day: they've got all the usual means of access covered. Without power and a way to trigger the device, it's no good."

"I understand your problem. But actually, there's a pretty simple alternative: you can—"

Reuben stood abruptly. "No, El: I don't want to know. The less I know, the less I can tell if they eventually root up some pieces of this plot and then try to discover who was involved. I've got—we've got—to forget about this. Right now. As if it never happened."

Elnessa looked up at him. "I'm not sure I can forget it, Reuben. Particularly not with what's at stake, now."

Reuben looked at her. "Don't make trouble, El. And don't make me warn you about coming near the kids again. Vas told me."

"Told you what?"

"That you made him dinner last night, let him stay until it was way too late—"

"Feeling guilty you didn't even notice he was missing, 'Daddy'?" The moment she said it, Elnessa was sorry: no one knew better than she how hard it was to keep track of almost a dozen kids between the ages of five and thirteen. "Look, Reuben; I'm sorry. I shouldn't have—"

"El, just—just leave it alone. Leave it all alone. And I mean both the mission and Vas. And that's an order." His utterance of the word 'order' was, laughably, a half-whining appeal, rather than a command.

"Sure," El answered. "Whatever."

Reuben turned and walked stiffly into the deepening gloom. About ten meters away, he reached down into a cluster of bushes and gently extracted its hidden occupant—Vas—before resuming his steady march away from Elnessa. Vas looked back, eyes troubled. He waved and was gone.

Elnessa waved, sighed, wiped her eyes, and went home in the dark.

It was only midmorning of January 2, 2120, when Elnessa stepped back to examine the frieze, in all its finished glory. All that remained now was to put in the prism-projecting Cheops eye, just over the watchtower light, and complete the light fixture itself. Behind her, Simovic and Hoon continued their plotting, as though they had been at it ever since she had left yesterday. And who knew? Maybe they had.

Hoon continued with her seemingly inexhaustible list of questions: "Our personnel—the ones who will gather the children, and the ones who will convey them to the rendezvous point—do any of them, well...'know?'"

Simovic shook his head. "No. They have the necessary timetable, coordinates, and orders, but no knowledge of who our clients are or why we are engaging in this trade."

"Which is scheduled for when?"

Simovic looked at the digital timecode embedded in the ticker bar of his media-monitoring flatscreen. "Two hours."

"Short notice," Hoon commented.

"True. But it's really quite logical. Even if they trusted us—which they have no reason to do at this point—they have no way of knowing if our communications are secure. Maybe Bloc naval forces have hacked our cipher, know when and where to expect our clients, and will set up an ambush. No, our clients' prudence is a good sign; it means they are not rash—and after all, we will need these new partners to be very discreet indeed."

Elnessa looked over toward the two of them. "Mr. Simovic," she called.

"Yes, Ms. Clare?"

"Could you please have your security people pull the fuse for the power conduits all along this wall?"

"Why?"

"Well, I need to finish wiring the lights."

"Can't you leave the power on while you do it?"

"Only if I want to take the risk of electrocuting myself."

Elnessa noted Simovic's hesitation. It didn't arise from any sense of suspicion—that was manifestly clear—but rather from the inconvenience of her request. Her safety was almost beneath his concern, especially at this particular moment. However, he ultimately signaled his annoyed acquiescence to the guard at the rear of the room, who left to comply with the request.

A moment later, the lights glaring down upon the frieze, along with the rest of the devices which drew their power from outlets along that wall, shut down.

Elnessa nodded her thanks, and limped over to the watchtower, the Cheops eye in hand. She emplaced the round, vaguely Pharaohic piece of multi-hued crystal just above the pointed roof of the watchtower.

Then, picking up the bulb that was to be the watchtower's lamp, she set it down on the section of the clay 'wall' next to the tower, and inspected the two small alligator clips grinning toothily up at her from just beneath the rim of the passage she had bored lengthwise in the tower. She stuck her finger in between the leads, widening the hole slightly, and then buried the two clips side by side into the dense matter surrounding them.

She went to check the switch that provided the manual control for all the lights in the frieze. It was, as she had left it, in the "off" position.

She turned to face Simovic. "It is finished," she announced.

"Hmmmm...what?"

"I said, 'it is finished.' Can you please have the power restored to this wall?"

Simovic and Hoon looked up: he surprised, she bored and impatient. He nodded for the guard to go restore the power, and then stood straighter, scanning the length of the frieze. Elnessa detected surprise and gratification: despite the fact that she had spent the last two months crafting it literally under his nose, he had never truly examined it until now. Simovic cleared his throat. "That is really..."

"...really quite good," Hoon finished, with an approving nod-and-pout, and a tone of voice that sounded like a grudging concession. Then she was turning back to her documents and data-feeds.

"But you have not seen it all," Elnessa said.

Hoon looked back up, Simovic smiled faintly. "No?" he asked.

"No. Several elements light up, and can be set to show different times of the day. The sun light is here, and small spotlights are embedded here and here to make the city roofs gleam during the day mode. These other lights—inside the blue acrylic—make the water seem to ripple and churn."

"And at night?"

Elnessa turned on the switch. "The city's watchtower burns a faint, but steady amber, guiding lost travellers to shelter on dark nights and in dark times. And all the while, the great prismatic eye of Cheops judges the worthiness of those within the city, and without."

Simovic seemed to suppress a flinch at the mention of *judgment*; Elnessa wondered if perhaps he had enough vestigial soul left in him to feel a faint pulse of guilt. Hoon simply frowned, as though slightly suspicious that they had funded the creation of radical art. She asked, "And just what do you call this piece of art? And why doesn't the tower's light work?"

Elnessa smiled. "I call this frieze *Jericho Falls Outward*. Or, if you prefer a less metaphorical title, you can all it, *I Will Not Let You Assholes Kill My Children*."

Simovic did flinch, now; Hoon's head snapped back as if she had been struck—and then her eyes went wide with comprehension. She turned toward one of the guards, mouth open to scream a command—just as Elnessa finished her silent count to ten.

As Elnessa reached "ten," the current from the wall had spent that many seconds both illuminating the lights of the frieze, and coursing through the alligator clips that were buried in the side of the hole Elnessa had bored through the length of the watchtower. However, the electricity directed into that substance was neither wasted nor idle.

Concealed inside the block of clay, down where the leads were embedded, was an identically-colored, but somewhat denser substance. With every passing second, the complex nanytes which pervaded that substance had begun changing their chemical composition, and aligning to follow with (and thereby offer less resistance to) the electric current. However, unlike the aligning of atoms in an electromagnet, when the nanytes of this complex alloy were all finally aligned, they began to work like a battery—which rapidly soared toward overload.

As Elnessa Clare realized that her "ten-count" had come and gone, she thought about continuing on to "eleven," and felt a pulse of worry shoot through her. According to Reuben, the substance that had been embedded at the core of each of the clay blocks—Selftex—could only absorb ten seconds of standard outlet current from the watchtower's diverted leads. But then Elnessa realized that this one extra second was a gift, time with which she could recall Vas' steady, warm brown eyes—

The Selftex—a recent, self-actuating evolution of the plastic explosive Semtex—had been developed to do away with the need for blasting caps or other explosive initiators. Hooked up to a low electric current, it gave miners and construction workers a long, precise interval in which to evacuate a blast site. However, when the current was as powerful as that running through a standard electrical outlet—

From almost two kilometers away, Vas not only heard, but felt, the blast. A few nearby windows shattered, people stared around wildly, a few—probably the ones who had heard the rumors of approaching exosapients—looked skyward.

But Vas straightened up and looked toward the roiling mass of thick black smoke, rising up over the Indi Group's corporate headquarters like a fist of angry defiance. And, through his tears, he smiled. That was the work of El, his El. He had heard Reuben's injudicious radio talk, had seen some incoming messages foolishly left unpurged from the house computer, and so knew that El had been helping to resist the Indi Group—and as of yesterday, was the only one still actively doing so.

Vas looked over toward the headquarters again, wondered about the frieze she had spoken of working on for so long, yearned to have seen it. He knew that, since she had crafted it, the frieze had been, without doubt, a thing of beauty—every bit as much as she herself had been. Then he stared up at the crest of the ugly black plume that marked its destruction, and reflected: this was her gift to him, to all the children.

And therefore, it, too, was a thing of beauty.

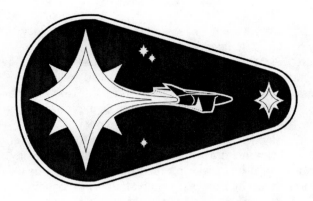

ALONE AND AFAR

A Shards Universe Story

Peter Prellwitz

AUTHOR'S NOTE: i (a single, lower case italicized i) is the mathematical symbol for the square root of -I (negative one). In its most basic application then: i * i = -I.

Considered an imaginary number, i can nonetheless be proven to exist by association and inference. Its existence is also required because i is used to solve proven theorems in our physical laws.

Since it exists, logic dictates that it can be placed on a line relevant to other, real numbers. Yet it can't. Counting to i would be akin to pointing to last Wednesday: Possible according to mathematical laws, but far beyond our comprehension.

At least, far beyond the comprehension of homo Sapiens.

Earth date: Wednesday, March 23, 3098
Centaur date: Marks Matrix: 73rd Remembrance, Tier 3i, 95th Vibration of Chronostring 4597; 7cyan2 G shading. Woldheim temporal axis shift: 39607 resampled seconds. (2nd reality expression, simplified for linear cohesion to assist in homo Sapiens comprehension.)

"Seaman Matthews is quite shy, Lieutenant."

"Is he now?" Lt. Navarra glanced away from the chow line and toward the third table along the aft bulkhead. Sure enough, Seaman Matthews was seated there, a tray of meatloaf, applesauce, and carpeas—or pearotts, Jenn couldn't tell them apart—on his food tray. His fork hovered over the meatloaf, but he was making no serious attempt at eating. Jenn smiled and looked back at Quincy, the small ship's best and only cook who doubled as morale officer.

"He doesn't seem to be enjoying your meatloaf," Jenn said. "Though I'm sure it's as tasty as always. Perhaps… ah…" she smiled again; the entire crew of the *Arctic Tern* knew that to be Jenn's normal expression. "Isn't today his birthday?"

"Why, now that you mention it, Lieutenant…" Quincy gave a return grin. "I think he'd love to have some BBQ ribs and ice-cold root beer."

Jenn set her tray down and brought her hands together, then spread them apart to exactly 29 centimeters and opened two portals into ireality. The five crewmen in line behind her turned away from Jenn; partly to avoid the blinding light that poured out of the portals and partly to watch Matthews' reaction to what was about to happen.

Jenn stabilized the portals, plucked the 7cyan2 istring, its 5violet11 counterpart, braided them into the 4597 chronostring and added 17 fives, 3 threes, a single two and one, and seven zeros. She then folded the portals together, shutting them down and running the program in spectral reality; the only reality her *homo Sapien* cousins could perceive.

The food on Matthews' plate vibrated and started to move around. Matthews gave out a yelp and jumped up. He looked around and suddenly became aware he was the center of attention for the entire mess room. He looked back down at his plate. A pile of BBQ ribs—enough for a dozen people—was heaped up, steaming sauce glooping down the sides in a slow race to spill onto the table. Beside the ribs was an oak barrel that easily held ten liters. Twelve mugs, iced and filled with foaming root beer sat on the table, ready to be passed out.

The crew cheered and sang the birthday song. Matthews gave Jenn a huge smile, then reseated himself and started gnawing on a rib. Within minutes, everyone had joined in on the meal and the sound of chatting and laughing quickly doubled, then doubled again as a full-blown birthday party formed.

"Doesn't say much about my meatloaf, does it now?" Quincy bemoaned even as he winked at Jenn.

"I'm sorry, Quincy," Jenn apologized, blushing slightly. "I did not intend to cast aspersions on your fine cooking." She smiled and held out her plate. "I'd love to lunch on what you've prepared."

"Okay, Lieutenant," Quincy said and filled her plate. "Though you're about the only one. Me, I'm going for some ribs and root beer." He finished serving Jenn then snatched up an empty plate and glass and went to join the others.

Jenn went to her normal table and took a seat. She set down her fork and opened up two more portals and modified the program slightly, allowing for a significant increase in the amount of ribs and root beer. There was now enough for everyone. She shut the portals and picked up her fork.

"Why do you do that?"

Jenn looked up. Lt. Nicholas Haughton stood in front of her, holding his own tray of meatloaf, applesauce, and whatever that vegetable was called. Like Jenn, Nicholas was a Marks—*homo Magicus*; a cousin race of the humans. They lived in both spectral reality and ireality at once and their shared racial traits of fine blond hair, short stature, slight build, and pitch-black eyes set them apart from the rest of the crew. All military and most corporate ships carried a *homo Magicus* programmer—called a muser—and Nicholas was the *Arctic Tern's* muser.

"Do what, Nick?" she said as he sat down opposite her. He kept his long blonde hair braided, just as Jenn did, while on duty. They had the normally full table to themselves, the popularity of the ribs and root beer having drawn a crowd at the other end of the mess room.

"Waste time and energy on altering food like that. It just makes for sloppy decorum and a noisier meal time."

"Oh, don't be such a poop." Jenny made a face at him. "The captain permits it and the crew enjoys it. We've been four months getting to this remote corner of the Milky Way. Allow them a little fun."

"We'd all be better served if they'd focus on the engine preparations as they did on silly pastimes."

"Stop it, Nick," Jenn said tiredly. They'd grown up together as kids on Centaur's Heart and they'd even been a couple for a while as young adults. But when Jenn went to Earth to get her degrees in singularity mathematics and engineering, then remained behind, they had drifted apart. Having spent her last forty years on Earth—6500 light years from her people's home planets—Jenn knew she was considered as the one who had drifted. That Earth was the only location in the known galaxy where pentrinsic code would not work only made Jenn's separation from Nick and her people more acute.

"What? I'm only watching out for order and decorum," Nick replied. "You've grown too much like the Terrans. You've accomplished a great deal while on Earth. I'm very impressed with your new insertion drive; it will do a lot for intra-system travel. But you seem to have paid a steep price for it, having adopted the attitudes and views of the Terran people. It worries me."

"And so you've waited four months to tell me?" Jenn shook her head. "You're not worried about me, Nick. You disapprove of me." She paused as the crew gave a rousing cheer for Lt. Matthews. "Listen to them, Nick. They have a zeal for life that most humans share; *Sapiens* and *Magicus* alike. But even though we Marks people have demonstrated multiple realities by our very existence, they know they don't see reality the way we do, that they have limitations our race does not. Yet still they have the zeal for living, often express it fully. Yes, I envy them in a way. You've served with this crew for over a year, Nick, but I know you haven't really lived with them."

"You're right in some ways," Nick confessed. "I do at times wonder what *Sapiens* have—or what we lack—that gives them their viewpoint on living. Nonetheless, your being with them for so many years had taint—"

A wrenching scream shattered both conversation and celebration. Nick reacted first, jumping to his feet and moving way from their table. Each of his hands opened a small portal in ireality and he plunged them in.

Jenn was nearly as quick, jumping to her feet, then leaving them and ascending a meter in the air, her Fly spell cast in less than a heartbeat. Both spun toward the source of the scream; the table where the crew had gathered to celebrate Lt. Matthews' birthday.

They were now panicking over his death. Slumped onto the table, face turned away from view, his skull was a bubbling mass of hair and dissolved bone. The gently pulsing glow of Nick's Restore spell quickly obscured the gory site, but that was its full effect. There was no restore or recovery from so devastating an injury; Lt. Mattews' was dead the instant the attack spell had been launched. And to both Nick and Jenn, it was clear that they were under attack by aggressive pentrinsic; forbidden and unused since the Six Planets of the previous century.

Jenn's hands spread out and opened two portals. Though her obsidian black eyes were capable of peering into the blinding light that poured out, she still took the two seconds needed to run the Dark Glass program, which cut down the brightness so human eyes wouldn't be pained from it. She then coded and ran Haven.

"Pax," Jenn sighed. An instant of dead silence covered the ship, followed by the single, comforting sound of a heart beat beating once. An invisible wave of calm pulsed out from Jenn, bringing to the surface the peace, focus, and determination that was inside the soul of each person on the ship. Order was restored, though the seriousness and edge of the moment remained.

The general quarters alarm sounded over the comlink and as one the crew moved quickly to exit the Mess for their combat stations. Captain Garret's voice sounded out over the comlink.

"We are under attack. Combat stations, full readiness. Muser report immediately to the bridge. Garret out."

Nick glanced at Jenn.

"I have to protect this ship from further attacks. You get yourself and your people to the insertion drive. That is certainly the goal of whomever is attacking us." Jenn nodded in agreement, but Nick had vanished, teleported to the bridge.

"Team, I need all of you at the drive right now," Jenn said calmly as she herself used the BeThere program to shift herself from the Mess to the Engine Room three decks lower and fifty meters aft. Her Talk program reached only her five people, all engineers who had helped her develop the new drive back on Earth.

Jenn popped into the Engine room and looked around quickly. Nick was right; the drive was the prize of this attack. The three that had been on duty at the moment of the attack—all members of the *Arctic Tern* crew—were lying dead at their stations. Each had skulls that were now melted into the floor, no more than pools of hair and pinkish oatmeal that still bubbled slightly.

Horrified at both the sight of the carnage as well as the implications of the use of aggressive pentrinsic, Jenn sobbed in grief. Who would be so careless? Not a Marks person, certainly: The race had pointedly woven their genetic makeup so that it would be impossible to cast aggressive pentrinsic. That meant it had to be an attack by a *homo Sapien* muser. But the power and range... her engineering team arrived at that moment, their pounding footsteps bringing Jenn back to the moment.

"Quickly!" she ordered, opening up her portals. "Get to your stations and monitor the condition of the insertion drive. It's almost certainly the reason for the attack, but whether it's to take or destroy the drive we don't know yet. I'm writing a new repel program now that should protect us."

"Lieutenant!" called Crewman Tabitha Anders. "I'm showing a mass stress point on the port outboard coupling."

"She's right, Lieutenant!" shouted Crewman Lisa Mashin. "Stress markers are appearing on the phased 2D plate. It's doubling every two seconds."

"There must be an external gravity well altering space," Jenn replied. "Everyone to the starboard side of the drive. I'm going to counteract. Shield your eyes!" She shifted the portals and dropped the Dark Glass program.

Coding at a speed she'd never attained before, Jenn plucked the 7cyan2 string, selected the G, M, and R shadings, then braided them quickly into the fifth axis of the 4597 chronostring. The matrix crackled and hummed as it came into being. Pock marking the hendecagon structure with twenty-three fives, seven threes, 2 twos, and 13 ones, the two-dimensional matrix flowered into a five-dimensional object with a rotated core and $11i$ sides. Jenn began coding the area inside her construct... 4801 fives... 2237 threes... 5741 twos... 7013 ones... 1913 zeroes...

The matrix exploded out of the portals and into spectral reality. To human perception, there was a red flash, the brief sound of ocean waves, and the scent of fresh baked bread. To Jenn, a solid wall of chronostrings now coated every exposed surface in the engine room. The bulkheads, the deck, the drive, even the crew, were now protected by outside attack from aggressive pentrin...

Anders began coughing; a wretched twisting cough that quickly changed to choking. Jenn immediately cast a Restore, boosting it with an Organic Recover. Anders' face altered from agony to relief, but only for a moment. Jenn felt—unbelievably experienced to the center of her soul—her healing programs being erased from spectral reality, allowing the attack to continue.

Anders sank to her knees, pawing at the back of her head. There came a harsh snapping sound, followed by a series of dull pops as her skull split open and blood and organ began bubbling out.

"What's happening?!" shouted Mashin.

"I... I... don't know," Jenn stammered. Never had she experienced any kind of aggressive programming like this. She could now feel the coding of the attack, but it made her retch from the hate of its caster. It stunned her, causing physical sickness. She hoped Nick was faring better than she was. If only...she shook herself from the daze that seemed to be creeping in on all senses.

Crewman Gillian was now screaming, the victim of the same attack. Hopelessness was washing over Jenn and her people. Something had to be done! Jenn attempted to strengthen the chronoshield, but it couldn't be increased without disintegrating the ship. She had done all she could. All she could...all she could...all she...

No! Jenn pushed her hands into the shimmering portals of ireality and switched the G and B strings of the present living shadings and inserted a randomizer. A half-seen image of Jenn appeared a meter away. The debilitating personal attack spell shifted abruptly away as the attacking muse sensed Jenn in a location she wasn't and continued the assault on the phantom. Jenn wrote the same code for each of her surviving three crewmen. She'd bought them a few minutes of respite.

"Is the gravity well still in effect?" Jenn asked. Mashin glanced over the readouts and nodded. "All right. Continue monitoring. If the gravity pull begins breaking down the two dimensional piston, destroy the drive. I'm going to the bridge to speak to the Captain and Lt. Haughton."

"But, ma'am!" Mashin objected, "Destroying the drive may be what they want to do anyway!"

"You may be right, Lisa," Jenn smiled, trying to reassure her. "But if they're trying to steal the drive, this will mean they failed and may leave us alone."

"And if they're trying to destroy it?"

"Then they won't let us live to build another one anyway." Jenn activated the Teleport program and instantly appeared on the bridge.

Things were not going well. The ship's hull was showing severe tearing, revealing open space beyond. Only Nick's shielding programs were preventing the ship from being torn apart. There were six dead crewmen, but fortunately Nick had also implemented a Shade spell; phantoms of Nick, the captain, and the surviving crew were moving around.

"Lt. Navarra!" Captain Garrett barked. "What are you doing here? You're only responsibility is the protection of the insertion drive. Get back to Engineering at once!"

"Yes, sir. That's to say, no, sir. I can protect the drive and this ship best from here. I know what's happening, Captain."

"I have this, Jenn!" Nick called from his casting circle forward of the bridge. Jenn knew the words were true, but the tone suggested it wouldn't be much longer.

"No, Nick, you don't. I'm sure you are superior to me in every form of known pentrinsic. But that's not what this is."

"What is it then, Lieutenant?" Garrett said.

"I believe it is a Marks caster who is casting aggressively through humans."

"That's not possible, Lieutenant," Garrett objected. "No Marks can use aggressive casting, regardless...."

"No, Captain! It is a Marks casting! I can feel it! I'm sure Nick can, too!" Nick nodded, short and quick, but otherwise gave no other sign. The attacks were getting harder and harder to hold off.

"The attacking ship is using a Marks person to channel ireality into human coders, greatly increasing the power of the programs. Even worse, the resulting hybrid programs are very difficult for Nick or I to counteract."

"But the human casters, won't they...."

"Yes, Captain. They'll pay for this attack with their sanity, whether they are successful or not."

"Which means they'll be killed after this is over," Garrett concluded. He looked sharply at Jenn. "What can we do?"

"Do we have conventional weapons still online?" Jenn asked. She walked to the front of the caster's circle, between Nick and the torn forward bulkhead, and opened two portals.

"Weapons!" Garrett barked, not taking his eyes of Jenn.

"Hull and reversion lasers fully operational!" came the hurried reply.

"Nick, please listen to me," Jenn said. Her friend was now visibly straining to protect the lives of the crew and the integrity of the ship's hull. "The instant I'm gone, you need to cancel every spell and do immediate repairs on the entire ship's hull.

"I can't!" he protested. "If I do that, their attacks will kill everyone within seconds, including you, Jenn! Our only hope...."

"THIS is our only hope, Nick! Trust me in this." Jenn smiled. "So don't be such a poop." Despite the moment, Nick returned a smile at Jenn's use of the playful reprimand. She shifted her hands in her portals. Her uniform surrendered to the Alter spell and flowed into its new existence as a space suit. She looked at Captain Garrett.

"Fire the moment you have opportunity, Captain. While it's my wish that we take them prisoner...."

"Your wish will not be coming true, Lieutenant," Garrett said. Jenn nodded in sad understanding and activated her prepared Teleport routine.

The ship vanished. In its place was nothing but deep space. As black as the color of her eyes, with only a few pinpoints of light to mark the stars that were so far away from this empty corner of the galaxy. Jenn gasped at the beauty and the overwhelming sense of loneliness. Were they to die here, they would not be found. It was her hope that only one more would die today. Knowing Nick would be doing exactly as she requested, Jenn began coding the final pentrinsic program of her life.

The portals into ireality flashed into existence. Jenn opened them further until they joined into one single portal two meters in diameter and brushing against the entire length of her small body. Willing it closer, the portal obeyed, enveloping Jenn. For the first time in her life—indeed in the existence of all humanity—Jenn experienced ireality without the anchor of spectral reality. To everyone in the known universe, Jennifer Navarra ceased to exist.

The euphoria of ireality flooded through her soul as though she had no body. Her sense of ireality increased countless orders of magnitudes. It was here that time originated, yet no longer existed. Jenn took a deep breath and motioned her hands. Two portals into spectral reality opened. She pushed her hands in.

Cold and harsh, the presence of spectral reality on her hands and lower arms seemed like razor ice. Her blood boiled and she screamed. She knew it would be difficult, but didn't imagine this. She had only seconds to do the impossible, yet even with the little time left her, Jenn wondered if entering another reality was always like this.

She composed a simple program, consisting of precisely no fives, no threes, no twos, no ones, and no zeros. Without a matrix to hold it, and anchored completely in spectral reality, yet coded entirely in ireality, Jenn ran the program.

Her last thought was a fervent hope this wouldn't cause Nick too much disorientation.

"Captain? She's coming around."

"Thank you, Doctor. I'll be there directly."

Jenn opened her eyes, then coughed as the pungent aroma of scorched flesh struck her. She tried to sit up, but fell back exhausted. She, moved her hands to cast a Haven spell and, between coughs, said, "Pax."

Nothing happened.

A dry chuckle on her right made her turn her head. Nick was there, lying on the only other medical bed in the small infirmary. He was up on an elbow and grinning at Jenn.

"Nick? I...how did you find me? I was sure that...."

"How can you be sure of anything? You...really...." he shook his head, trying to clear it.

"Are you okay, Nick? What's wrong?"

"What's wrong? Nothing. Everything! You shut down pentrinsic code for five light years, Jenn. Tens of thousands of lights years from Earth, you created an Earth-like condition where access to ireality is cut off."

"Yes."

Nick laid down and closed his eyes and struggled to calm his breathing. He sobbed for a few seconds, then continued speaking without opening his eyes.

"I had no idea it was this bad, Jenn. My entire being is withered. My sense of self is like an artificial husk; nothing but bones and dust." He muttered to himself quietly, Jenn only making out, "...bones and dust." He looked at her, almost in accusation, "I feel violated."

"You'd best feel saved, Lt. Haughton." Captain Garrett's firm, comforting voice seemed to breathe life into the small room. "I know I do." He looked down at Jenn.

"We're running on fusion at half-light speed while we effect repairs on our main drive." He gave her a grin. "I wanted to test your insertion drive, but not only would-n't your crew let me, we're still too far from our target star to activate it."

"The enemy ship..."

"Isn't effecting any repairs. Once you shut down ireality, their ship immediately appeared on sensors, less than a light-minute away. Their muser was no doubt incapacitated in the same way Lt. Haughton was here. My guess is that the humans he was casting through probably died in that second. Academic, really, as I made sure they all died quickly. Fortunately they were in an almost direct line with you, Lieutenant, and we were quite lucky to have sensors pick up the flash of the closing portal and track you as you reappeared in spectral reality. I'm looking forward to hearing your report, as are no doubt both our races once we return.

"Well, if you'll forgive me, Lieutenants, I need to return to the bridge. With the lifts out and no muser to teleport me there, I need to take the maintenance ladders." He shook his head. "A taste of the old days on the high seas of Earth's ocean ships. Makes one feel a little more alive."

He left, leaving the two alone. There was still silence, but it had eased to a more comfortable quiet, Jenn felt.

"He's right, you know," Nick replied. "Having lost something can make one feel more alive. I...I have a small sense of what it is to be human now; to be alive in only one reality. A large piece of me is missing, cut off from ireality. But the part that survives is waking up for the first time, and through that part of me, I'm seeing things differently."

"Just wait until we clear this area and ireality comes back, Nick," Jenn laughed softly. "That experience is...well...we'll have more to talk about then, too."

"I'm quite sure," he laughed, then grimaced and closed his eyes again. "In the meantime, I am more than ready to have this pounding headache pass. How Terrans survive without a Haven spell to ease the pain is beyond me."

"Oh, Nick." Jenn made a face at him even though he wasn't watching. "Don't be such a poop."

HUNGER
Jeffrey Lyman

CRAIG TAI FURLED HIS SOLAR SAILS AND FIRED THE FORWARD THRUSTERS TO slow his small freighter. An immense Earth battleship descended on his position. He killed the claxons, but alarm lights flashed up and down his boards as the battleship kept her guns locked on him.

He sighed in irritation, then powered down the thrusters and drifted. A single shot from one of the smaller guns above him would cut him in two, so there was no need for theatrics. But inside he was relieved it was a big ship. The battleships of the Earth and Mars fleets were large enough to have converted excess square footage into hydroponics. They weren't starving. Most of the cruisers and destroyers still afloat were running on skeleton crews and riding the bare edge of cannibalism. They would have been quick to snatch his cargo of food.

"Freighter AG-776, state your cargo and destination," a cool voice chirped across his comm. The code ident labeled the battleship as the *Ronald Reagan*.

Craig toggled the reply switch. No sense lying. They knew who he was, and hopefully they supported him running food across the lines. "Foodstuffs. I'm on a humanitarian run to Research Outpost 312 and Earth Military Outpost 42." At least they'd better support his mission. The only way Earth's scattered outposts would last until the end of the war was by food runners like him.

"Acknowledged. Prepare to be boarded."

He cursed and pushed back against his narrow captain's chair. Maybe they *were* going to confiscate his food. It had happened before, usually when they were having hydroponics problems. He was lucky only to have been stopped once this trip for a routine check, and he hadn't seen hide-nor-hair of Galileo Coalition ships. The allied colonies of Ganymede, Io, Europa, and Callisto loved this starvation war between Mars and Earth, and would have popped his hull just to make things worse. With so many fleet ships mothballed due to insufficient food, the Jupiter colonies were doing whatever the hell they wanted.

The shuttlecraft that clamped onto Craig's docking hatch had three jockeys and they all looked fed, which Craig hadn't seen a great long while. That was a good sign.

"Welcome aboard," he said, as one of the jockeys pushed through his docking hatch and into the central corridor of the freighter. Craig held still, waiting for the marine to make the first move. No need to make a man with a burn-gun nervous. "You want to inspect my holds?"

"Not here for that. The captain wants to see you." The marine gestured.

"What's this about?"

"Talk to the captain."

And that was all Craig was told on the short flight up to the landing bay of the battleship. It was a very small landing bay, tight even for the shuttle, and as he watched their cowl barely slide under a huge steel beam, he wondered if all of the other bays had been converted to hydroponics.

Without a word, he was escorted via a secure elevator from the landing to a small conference room. The ship's captain, commander, and two lieutenants filed into the room shortly after Craig was brought in by his marine escort.

"Captain Tai," the captain said, nodding. "I'm Captain Routan."

"Captain." Craig nodded back. The officers all looked healthy, if not pudgy. The last battleship he'd been aboard operated at three-quarters staff, and they'd been rail thin and eating paint chips off the walls.

"Let me put your fears to rest," the captain said. "Our hydroponics are excellent, so I'm not going to take your sorry lot of potatoes. I require your assistance on a rescue mission."

Craig rubbed his eyes. "I have to get this delivery to RO-312, Captain, they won't last without it." Everyone knew the research outposts were in deep trouble. The military outposts had done better after supply lines were cut—they had a better command structure. They were quicker to make tough decisions. The scientists at the RO's had dithered too long, argued too much, hadn't converted their precious experimental space to hydroponics quickly enough. But RO-312 was a nice jewel. They were good people, had a good research budget, and paid a lot for his food. He couldn't abandon them. One slip meant quick starvation or surrender to the Ganymede cruisers.

"I'm aware of RO-312's needs," the captain said, "and *I* require you to head for Military Outpost 226. It's nearly a straight shot past RO-312 and MO-42, so you can make your deliveries and still proceed quickly."

"It's past MO-42? That's pretty far out, Captain." Craig wasn't familiar with any MO's designated above 110, and wasn't sure he wanted to.

"It's much farther out, Captain Tai, not in the main asteroid belt at all. It's in the trailing Jupiter Trojan asteroids, at the L5 Lagrange Point."

Craig looked up at the marine standing over his shoulder and then back at the waiting officers. "With all due respect, Captain, the Trojans are crawling with Galilean Coalition ships. They claim it for their sovereign space. How am I supposed to get out there and back in again?"

"I checked up on you," Captain Routan said. "All food-runners get picked up from time to time. We let you through because you provide a service. But you...you haven't been picked up very often. We have records of you several times a year for the past three years, and that's a hell of a better average than most. You know how to slip through our lines."

Craig shrugged. "My freighter's smaller than most. Harder to detect." He wasn't about to admit to any of the evasion maneuvers he used, or his slippery hull that gave tracking computers fits.

"MO-226 has maintained silence since the war began, hiding from the Ganymede search ships. Until a few weeks ago, that is. We got a short mayday—wide broadcast. They didn't know we were here, just hoping someone was listening. We don't think the message was long enough to give away their position."

"And you want me to fly out into that? The Galileans will be trolling the sector now." Craig was appalled. Food runners stayed well clear of the outer limits of the main asteroid belt. The money wasn't worth the near-death experience. There were plenty of starving people on the inner bands.

"I need you to bring them home."

"How many," Craig said, thinking, *Are you crazy*? Then it hit him that maybe someone had discovered something out there. That radio burst wasn't a mayday, it was a Eureka! statement. He felt ill.

"Six people," Captain Routan replied.

Craig shook his head sharply. "My ship won't handle it. I've got air-recycling capabilities for four. Me and three others. If you need to rescue more, you'll have to nab a bigger freighter."

Now it was the captain's turn to shake his head. "Like you said, anything bigger than your ship won't slip through. So bring back two people. I'm sending a medic with you and he'll be the fourth."

The medic would be a minder, Craig thought. Someone who would incapacitate him if he tried to turn tail and run.

"I don't have the fuel to get out there and back," he said, hoping for some way out of this.

"Refuel at MO-42. They're making hydrogen from their asteroid's ice shell."

Craig had rarely been so scared. It had never occurred to him that his skill at evading detection would be the very thing that threw him into the smelter. "All that's left is to haggle price, I guess," he said in a weak voice.

"I know what you food-runners charge these days and I want you to know I find it repugnant. You pray on people's desperation. It's treason. I'd shoot you out of the water, except our people in those outposts really need you. I'll pay you exactly twice the going rate. Call it danger pay."

They all stood. Craig almost stuck out his hand to shake, but then figured it would be best if he didn't. "When will your medic come aboard?"

"He's already on the shuttle, Captain Tai, waiting for you." Captain Routan frowned darkly at him for a moment. "Where do you *get* your food?"

It was a loaded question, Craig knew. Many food-runners were also raiders, stealing from what supply lines there were.

"I had a vacation place—a house dug into an asteroid. There are three other houses dug in beside mine. I happened to be there when Mars nuked Earth, then got stuck there when the fleets mobilized. I guess the other three owners were stuck wherever they were. I did what I had to do with the house—converted everything to hydroponics fast like the alerts said to do. Then I just kept converting. I've got a nice bit of space between all four houses, growing more produce than I can eat. I got lucky."

"Lucky. And now rich. Must be nice. Your account will be credited with half of the agreed upon amount as soon as you fire your thrusters. Other half at the other end."

"Thank you, Captain. Let's see how lucky I really am."

"Get my people back to me, Captain Tai. Show me you're a patriot."

An hour later Craig fired his thrusters, pulling away from the battleship. The 'medic', Lieutenant Ryan, was strapped into the copilot's seat. Craig acknowledged the *Ronald Reagan*, then set his coordinates for RO-312.

"Do you know anything about flying?" he said to Ryan.

"Not a thing."

"Since I'm the only pilot then, I won't keep a regular eight-hour rotation. I'm generally sitting here, or sleeping, or fixing something. Since you can't help with any of those, please keep out of my way until we get to the research outpost. I'm dead certain they'll have need of your skills."

He needn't have wasted his breath issuing edicts. Ryan did what he wanted, got in the way when he wanted, and generally seemed to be around when Craig was sitting in the pilot's seat calculating fuel consumption or adjusting the solar sails. Fleet was sure to know him inside and out by the time this mission ended. He didn't really care anymore. He was tired of the constant toll this war inflicted on the civilian populations.

They called it the Starvation War.

Mars had started it, or at least Mars had brought a conflict into the open that had been simmering for decades. Terribly overpopulated Earth pushed Mars around; underpopulated Mars flaunted her freedoms and territory, and supported a thriving piracy trade against Earth's corporations.

Finally the merchants pressured Earth's governing council into voting up a trade embargo. It's not like they feared the Red Planet. Mars had a military fleet, but nothing that could touch Earth's. Besides, any attack that got through Earth's defenses wouldn't make a dent in the twenty-seven billion citizens filling her cities.

Then some enterprising Martian general sent in seventy-five tactical nukes on small ships and bombed a chain across the farmlands of Siberia. The dust and smoke propelled into the stratosphere blanketed the planet in a haze and initiated nuclear winter. A hundred years of global warming was reversed in one year and the North Pole froze over. Food production collapsed. Greenhouses couldn't support twenty-seven billion people, let alone Earth's ships and bases scattered across the solar system.

Perhaps Mars thought she was safe from reprisal since all of her cities and homes and farms were underground, or maybe their merchant collective was just stupid. Earth targeted the largest underground cavities across Mars with Richter bombs. Seventy percent of Mar's Agro-domes cracked in the subsequent Marsquakes.

But Mars got what she wanted, even as her citizens starved. Earth couldn't support her vast merchant and military fleets without food. She mothballed most of the ships, waiting for the day the skies cleared and food grew freely again. Then control began to collapse as food-riots started. Governments lined up hundreds of thousands of greenhouses in the freshly fallen snow, powered by geothermals. The population kept falling, unsustainable.

Meanwhile, Mars dug new bio-caves at a furious pace, hoping they could get their food production up before Earth's skies cleared.

Craig could only imagine that the chaos and despair of the civilians on both planets mirrored the despair that met him every time he docked with a research outpost.

It took his ship about three weeks to reach RO-312. The rock appeared as a gray splotch in Craig's long-distance scopes. He furled his sails and decelerated into their docking port. Lt. Ryan rode the copilot's seat all the way in.

"Get your kit, or whatever the hell you have," Craig said to Ryan. "We should be able to push off in about four hours, so do what you can."

Lt. Ryan looked at him like he had two heads. "They're civilians," was all he said.

Craig's temper flared, but he tried to keep calm as he unbuckled from his seat and pushed up to the ceiling. "Unless you brought just enough supplies for the two people we're bringing back from MO-226, get in there and do something useful. You have four hours to kill, so you might as well." He pushed off of a foothold and flew down the central corridor.

RO-312 Director Nancy Krzakian was practically leaning against the docking hatch when Craig cycled it open. A half dozen scientists and techs clustered tight behind her.

"Nancy," he said warmly, extending his hand. The relief on her face was palpable. The air wafting behind her stank of hydroponic vats and overripe vegetables.

"Thank God you're here. What have to you got?"

"Potatoes this time, freeze-dried. Should help with scurvy. I brought seeds too—beans and peas for protein. I thought you guys were nearly stable. What happened?"

The scientists were already pushing through the door, crowding him against the bulkhead. They knew the drill. They got what was in Hold A, and no more. If they tried to breach Holds B or C, he wouldn't be coming back. Those holds were promised to others.

"We lost a vat," Nancy said. There were dark rings under her eyes, and if anything she looked thinner than last time. The skin was stretched across her facial bones. "We can't afford to lose a vat. We *were* getting stable. Losing all that hydroponic juice has been...well, I don't know what we'll do. We're experimenting with planting seedlings in boxes of biotic waste, but they're growing so slowly."

Craig had seen this before—ultra-sanitary civilians reduced to shoveling shit into boxes to grow food, rather than cycling their waste out the hatch. The military was way ahead of them. Most of the MO's had erected hydroponic vats, and then started shit-farms in whatever rooms were left. No sense in waiting for a bad day.

"Between my Hold A and what you're growing," he said, "you should be in good shape for six months. More if you're careful. That's enough time to generate more hydroponic juice and get the lost vat going again."

The look on her face was close to ecstatic joy at renewed hope of survival. She cleared her throat and straightened her badly stained tunic. "Okay then. Okay. Good. Right."

"I have some good news," Craig told her. "I got a fleet medic with me. He's accompanying me out to MO-42."

"Fleet! Damned soldiers started this mess."

"I can tell the medic to stay on board if you want to stick to your principals."

"No, no. Please, I spoke quickly. We would love his help."

"Care to come to the bridge for a cup of coffee?"

"That would be wonderful. Thank you."

Craig hauled himself down the corridor of the freighter on handholds, squeaking out of the way as the first of the potato loads came around the corner from Hold A. The skeletal young man pushing the sled had a bunched out cheek that he was trying to conceal. He'd already taken a big bite of dried potato.

Lt. Ryan, a bag strapped to his back, pulled himself along after the young man. He nodded to Craig as he passed.

In the bridge, shoulder to shoulder in the pilot and co-pilot seats, Craig twisted an auto-heat bag of coffee and handed it to Nancy. "With cream and sugar," he said. She preferred it black, he knew, but she couldn't afford to turn down free calories.

She squeezed the bag from the bottom and took a swallow, her eyes closed. She took a second sip. "How's the war going?" she asked him. "Any rumors not on the official news lines?"

"Not really," Craig said. "Earth bombed a new agro-dome that Mars was building deep underground, but that didn't really affect anything significant. The Martians have distributed their hydroponics throughout the smaller domiciles."

"So the game plan's still the same?"

"Yup. Whoever gets a food-surplus first can get their destroyers and cruisers back in action. Earth atmosphere should start to clear in two, maybe three years. The glaciers have moved down near the United States border and into Europe now. It'll be a while before they can plant in Canada again. Siberia's a total loss. Ocean levels are dropping, though, so that's good. Florida's almost back to its pre-2000 shore-line. They're desalinating the recovered land and laying out greenhouses as fast as they can."

"What happens to us if Mars supplies their ships first?"

Craig placed his hand lightly on her hand. "Nobody's close to supplying destroyers and cruisers yet, so don't worry. Earth and Mars are just trying to stop starving to death. Like you and me. Then when the fighting's done and the merchants have sorted out who owns what, folks'll be around to rescue us all."

"You're a terrible bullshitter."

"Then I'll come and rescue you. I promise. C'mon, let's help with Hold A."

Within four hours, Craig and Ryan waved goodbye to the dismal rock that had once been a thriving research compound sequencing exo-biotic species. So many RO's and MO's had gone silent in the past two years, he didn't know if 312 would make it. Nancy was a good director, and she seemed to have her people in hand. But it might be a decade before Earth defeated Mars and remembered to collect her scattered children. He'd probably have to make good on his promise to save her.

It was a shame that the Galilean colonies weren't helping. They could have all the scientists, researchers, and stations they could stomach if they would just fly around and rescue people. But they were religious fanatics, deeply suspicious of Earth research and Earth bases. The Ganymede captains had a reputation for executing station personnel. That kept the RO's hunkered down and the MO's oiling their guns.

"How'd it look?" Craig said to Ryan.

Ryan took a moment to answer. "A couple of cuts that had gotten infected. A broken leg. A whole lot of malnutrition."

"Yeah, that's why I brought them the seeds. They lost several lines in the beginning, and they've been relying too heavily on cabbage and beets."

MO-42 was less dismal that RO-312. The commander in charge briskly ordered his men to fetch the potatoes from Hold C. His uniform was clean, though frayed, and he seemed to have more meat on his bones than Nancy. He too welcomed Lt. Ryan and ordered him to attend the surviving crew. He didn't turn down a chance for a cup of coffee either.

Craig brought up the new mission to MO-226. "You ever hear of an MO with a designation that high?" he said as they sipped.

The commander laughed. "If I was on fire and chased by a Ganymede heavy, a 200-level base wouldn't acknowledge my hail. Don't ask me what they do, because I don't know."

"I'll need to fuel." Craig handed over the orders from Captain Routan.

"All right," the commander said. "Next time you're through here, you'll have to tell me what a 200-level does. You think this is something to do with the war?"

"Don't know."

"I sure as shit hope so. Let's get this war over with and get the hell home. I'm on my eighth tour of duty out here."

"Amen to that."

Fully laden with fuel and fresh water, Craig pushed off the ice-bound asteroid a scant six hours later. He and Ryan had taken an extra hour to sit in the mess with the crew—fourteen men and women just as home-sick and information-starved as their civilian counterparts. They had the basic information on the war from the continuous military broadcasts, but little in the way of rumors. Military broadcasts kept bad news to a minimum. They would have pumped Ryan for information for another twelve hours if the medic hadn't declared loudly it was time to go.

And from there they boosted out into the outer bands of the main asteroid belt heading for the Trojan asteroids clumped in a trailing orbit behind Jupiter.

Craig furled his sails about two weeks out from MO-226, but didn't ignite his forward thrusters and start normal deceleration. There had been no signs of Galilean ships, but he wanted to run quiet for as long as possible. He knew that without gradual deceleration, he'd really have to punch the brakes on final approach. The multi-g's would be torture on his zero-g muscles, but then so would a Ganymede torpedo.

"If I detect any ships in the vicinity," he said to Ryan, "I'll have to coast by and do a long loop back in-system."

"That'll burn a lot of fuel, won't it?"

"This is a rescue, Lieutenant, not a suicide mission. I'll do everything I can to slip in there, but if it can't be done it can't be done."

"It can be done."

Craig was about to argue, then looked at the lieutenant and shut his mouth.

His luck held, and he detected nothing as the solitary rock loomed larger in his scopes. It was a fairly small member of Jupiter's Trojan asteroids, maybe eighteen kilometers across and six high, shaped like a gnarled root. It was spinning on a fixed axis, so someone was generating gravity in there. He couldn't detect a docking port.

Scanning, he found that it was iron-rich and he could gauge little about the interior. There were density anomalies where they'd probably burrowed and hollowed it, but if he didn't know it was an Outpost, it wouldn't have registered.

Deceleration was as bad as he feared, even in a shock cocoon, laying flat against the forward bulkhead. He would have sworn a blue streak up down and sideways if his teeth weren't clenched together. But nothing broke, and his internal organs remained in their correct spots. Panting hard, he and Ryan struggled out of the netting of their cocoons.

"You want to hail them, or should I?" Craig said.

Ryan pulled himself over to the communications array. "I'll do it."

Craig stared at the rotating rock as Ryan sent down some sort of passcode. Craig's throat was tight. What was in there? What did the Series-200 represent? 0-99 were military research facilities. Someone had once told him that the 100 series were strategic gun placements with skeleton crews. What was left?

A response came back from the rock almost immediately, text only: "What are your orders?"

Ryan slid into Craig's captain's chair and pulled the old-fashioned keyboard from deep inside the console. Craig hadn't used it in a long time, only when the ship's harddrive crashed and he had to access base systems without the interface.

"Your message was received," Ryan typed slowly with two fingers. "We can retrieve max-two individuals for return to fleet."

Coordinates were sent up from the rock, and Craig nudged his ship until he was rotating in synchronous orbit above the point they wanted.

Text was sent again: "Approach to 30 meters +/- of surface and hold."

Craig descended gently, staring at the dusty, boldered surface. *This is crazy*, he thought.

And there he sat for four hours, locked in orbit over nothing. The ping of the incoming message system woke him and Ryan from mild dozes. "Open outer access door," it read.

Ryan quickly shoved up from his seat and pushed down the central corridor. There was a floor hatch to the freighter's belly docking port.

"Acknowledged," Craig typed, then leaned close to his small portal window to peer down at the surface. There were two individuals there, wearing mottled gray/black vacuum suits so that they blended with the surface. They had a box between them, about two meters long and maybe a meter wide. It looked like a coffin.

Where the hell had they come from anyway? Minor disturbances in the dust indicated their tracks. They had come over the asteroid's horizon. They must have hopped a fair distance to keep him from seeing their docking hatch.

"I'm ready," he called to Ryan. "Let 'em in."

As Ryan dropped down through the floor hatch, Craig opened a secret door at his left and checked his pistol. It wasn't much of a defense against trained soldiers, but if they tried to rush him he might get it out. He'd bought it on the more populated asteroids. Cops called it a junk-hurler—and it was used for combat in tight quarters. It held a cache of sharp-edged shrapnel, and was screwed to a nitrogen canister. The barrel was flared out like a funnel to aid spread. Not much range and only one shot, but you could maim a room full of people and not puncture any walls.

Motion. The two below were rising on tiny puffs of compressed air—angling for the access hatch. "They should be on you in a couple of minutes," Craig called over the intercom.

He watched the indicator lights as the outer access door cycled open and then closed again. He pumped in air, then waited as Ryan pushed himself back up through the floor hatch.

One of the newcomers climbed into the corridor after Ryan, and helped guide the box through the hatch. The second newcomer squirmed through and helped angle the box carefully around the turn down the corridor. Only then did they twist their helmets off to reveal a healthy, well-fed man and woman. They had buzzed hair favored by low-g military. The woman had lieutenant's bars drawn on her cheek.

"Welcome," Craig said. He didn't move from his seat.

The woman nodded to him. "You're our pilot?"

"Civilian pilot, conscripted for this mission. I'll get you home if there's a way."

"We've got a battleship waiting for you on the inner side of the asteroid belt," Ryan said.

"There are a couple of Galilean ships in the area," the woman said. "We have some intel on them, some guesses as to their routes. I'll upload what we've got."

"Please do," Craig said.

Without another word, the new lieutenant, Ryan, and the new man guided the box into one of the empty holds.

"All right, then," Craig called after them. "I'll be up here plotting a course."

Lt. Ryan turned back. "One of us will ride shotgun at all times."

"Wouldn't have it any other way. No one touches the stick, though. We'll be taking a bumpy ride back in-system."

And a bumpy ride it was. Rather than riding the thrusters and traveling in a straight line, the quickest route back home but the method most likely to leave a neat little ion trail for anyone to follow, Craig fired the thrusters hard over and over again, at variable durations, drifting in between for hours or even days. He changed their vector each time. It took a long while, but they gained velocity. More importantly, he didn't detect any signatures of Galilean ships.

As promised, one of the three sat in the copilot's seat and rotated every eight hours, whether he was there or not. Craig found the new lieutenant, who introduced herself as DuLac, to be quite personable. She was beautiful, taller than space standard, and Craig took opportunities to sit with her when she was in the co-pilot's seat. She was an American by birth.

She was also well informed on the catastrophes consuming Earth's countries one by one. Unlike the other bases, MO-226 seemed to have no problem getting news. She spoke often of the advancing glaciers and falling sea levels, and was particularly fascinated by the remnants of 20th century cities being exposed by the retreating oceans.

"Manhattan won't have to hide behind the ocean-walls anymore," she said. "We can tear those ugly things down and have a proper city once again, looking out on the river."

"You from there?" Craig said. He was watching her face in profile, her full lips and long eye lashes.

"Born and raised on Manhattan Island. Can't wait to get back."

Craig had visited Manhattan Island once. End-to-end skyscrapers three hundred stories high. The weight of six million people on one tiny island had terrified him. "You'll have to wait a little while longer. With billions starving, they don't want one more live body down there. I'm surprised martial law's held things together for this long."

She frowned. "In between the cities it's gotten lawless," she said. "You don't hear about that so much. They're building greenhouse fields as quickly as they can, but they have to defend them against desperate folks just trying to feed their kids. With Canada and Siberia iced over, we lost a big percentage of the agro-zones." She shrugged. "As for martial law, starving people don't have a lot of energy to riot."

"The atmosphere'll clear. Won't be long."

"The damage is done."

"To both sides."

Her eyes narrowed sharply. "You a Mars sympathizer?"

"Civilian sympathizer, maybe. People sympathizer. You didn't ask to be stranded out in that rock. Neither did the rest of those researchers, or people in their vacation asteroids, or Martians in their domes, or Earthers in their cities. What the Galileans are doing out here, that's just a symptom. I want it to be over."

"Soon," she said.

Craig raised his eyebrows, but she said no more.

The moment they'd been dreading came three days later. The freighter's tracking computers picked up sunlight glinting from a moving body where there were no known asteroids. Craig immediately started flipping switches, shunting fuel from auxiliary tanks into the main tanks at the rear of the ship.

He swatted the new man, who had only introduced himself as Specialist Brown.

"Get your people," Craig said. Brown sat up with a start, pretending he hadn't been sleeping. "We got company."

In moments, Lt. DuLac had squirreled into Brown's seat, and Brown and Ryan were leaning over the backs of the chairs. Everyone stared at the blip on the display panel.

"How long?" Lt. DuLac demanded.

Craig calculated fuel consumption rates and took new fuel readings as the auxiliary tanks gave up their reserves. "We'll need to burn most of our fuel and grab as much speed as we can. The Ganymede'll start a burn too as soon as she sees us light up, but she's got a hell of a lot more mass to push. We can probably stay ahead of them long enough to approach the inner system. If the intel you've cooked up is hot, maybe the *Ronald Reagan* will enter the belt and haul us out of the fire."

"So you think we'll make it?" Lt. Ryan said.

"Only if they don't shoot at us," Craig said. "My hull is dark and slippery, so they'll have a hell of a time locking on. They could wait 'til I start my burn, then do it the old-fashioned way—by sight. Most likely they'll wait to get closer."

"How'd they find us?" DuLac said.

"Probably laying low, watching. They must have picked a few of our acceleration burns, enough to flag us."

DuLac drummed her fingers on her arm. "Odds?"

"Better than even. We're damned lucky she was so far away when she picked up on our trail. The wild-card is how many other Galilean ships are in front of us, and how far away they are when they get the invite to the party."

"What do we do if they come at us head on?" Ryan said.

Craig looked up at him. Ryan was sweating. Strange that Captain Routan would send someone on a dangerous mission with a case of the nerves. "Head on, we wouldn't have a chance. We'll have to discuss options if it comes to that."

"We will not be surrendering, if that was one of your options," Lt. DuLac said matter-of-factly. "Our intel must get through to the fleet."

Craig forced himself not to glance at the compartment hiding his junk-thrower. He'd heard the *No Retreat, No Surrender* line before.

"Maybe we can broadcast it to the *Ronald Reagan* when we're close enough for secure communication," she said, then shook her head. "Can't let the Galilean Coalition get it."

The Ganymede battleship hailed them a short time later. Brown and Ryan hustled back to the hold while DuLac squashed herself down in the footwell, below the freighter's camera-eye. She nodded for Craig to acknowledge. His screen filled with the image of a thin man in crisp, gray uniform.

"You are operating an unauthorized ship in restricted space," the man stated. "What is your name and purpose?"

Craig frowned, hoping his scruffy appearance would lend truth to his voice. "Freighter AG-776 from the inner belt, no affiliation. I'm a food runner, shuttling potatoes."

"Shuttling potatoes where?"

"To anyone who needs them."

The thin man leaned closer to his camera. "What are the coordinates of your last delivery?"

"I didn't make one. I picked up a mayday clear as day a few weeks back and came out. I couldn't find the sender. I'm heading back in."

"You will halt and await inspection."

"My potatoes won't wait. There are a lot of folks who need them farther in."

"This is not open to discussion. Hold for inspection."

The screen went dark. Craig looked down at DuLac in the footwell. "It's a weapon, isn't it?" he said. "That's what you brought on board. And whatever it is you've cooked up against Martian fleet, it'll work against our ships too, won't it?"

DuLac pulled herself out and pushed herself back down into the seat proper. She refastened her chest-harness. "The Galileans," she said after a moment, "a bunch of religious fanatics, and isolationist fanatics, and just plain fanatics. You can't imagine what it's been like. They knew we were here, just not where, so they hunted. Always sniffing around, taking bombing runs at any old asteroid to see if they got lucky. We've been bombed three times. Our seismic dampeners held the base together, but we lost Bay 12 two months ago. Lost a lot of good people."

"And now you're out here in a slow, tin can. Was this part of the plan?"

"We didn't know you were coming; we never got a response to our broadcast. I had an hour to pack up eight years of personal shit, and one duffel to do it with. I'm here, and Brown too, because we know the intel. There are others with seniority who would have come, but there was no time to brief them."

"Intel? Not a weapon?"

"A little of both," DuLac said. "This war should be with the Galileans, not the Martians. The corporations—they're the ones who pushed the hostilities. Now the Galileans are circling. We have to end the war and direct our attention back out this way. We have to beat Mars' fleet without losing our own."

"What does it do?" Craig said again. He never wanted to be involved in the war directly. Sure, he supported Earth if anyone asked, but he was a humanitarian more than anything. Not a weapons courier. Not a soldier.

"Back in the early days of colonization, they had a rough go of it on Mars," she said. "The crops weren't taking well. Something about the gravity and the ozone levels in the domes and the UV leaking through the thin atmosphere. They depended on shipments from Earth, which was expensive."

"Was that when Baranto got involved?"

She nodded. "Baranto crops. Genetically modified for superior yield on Mars. Sterile so they couldn't produce viable seeds, but cheap enough that the farmer's didn't care. Later, the Martian scientists broke contract and rejiggered the gene-set to make them viable again. But guess what—a lot of those old termination genes are still intact, sleeping. I can wake them up. One x-ray burst at a set of frequencies, harmless to people, and the crops go sterile." She pointed back toward Hold C. "That's the calibrated x-ray generator back there, waiting for a firing platform. We hit the Martian ships with that, and within a few weeks they're out of food and begging to surrender."

"Jesus. Is this what you 200 Series outposts dream up?"

"What we really do is classified, but after years of no contact, we were bored. We're self-sustaining, so no food stress. We started tinkering."

"Why would your x-rays affect Earth ships?"

"Baranto had a lot of modified crops, not just for Mars. They're all mixed in with Earth's current production lines. No way to pull them out."

"Shit," Craig said. If the Galileans knew about this, their isolationist stance would go offensive. They could knock down the fleets of both Mars and Earth. They could irradiate Mars' remaining biodomes and Earth's greenhouse fields. They could take over both planets.

"You can't openly broadcast it to the *Reagan*," he said.

"I said we'd only do it when we're close enough for secure communication."

"That's quite a risk."

"We need this to win the war."

"Like hell! You need it to win the war more easily. But if it gets into Galilean hands...."

"No, Captain Tai, we need it to win the war."

He met her hard gaze for as long as he could, then turned back to the blank transmission screen. "What am I missing? What aren't they telling us?"

"Earth's crossed the tipping point into a new ice age."

"Are you serious? How?"

"CO_2's been dropping for years, ever since the atmospheric scrubbers went on-line. The planet's already cooled a lot from the run-away global warming. Not that you'd notice it in the cities, but in aggregate. With all this new snow and ice, and the loss of the northern forests for farmland, and the low CO_2 levels, it didn't take much."

"How far will the glaciers advance?"

"Does it matter? So long as the Earth is unstable and still losing real estate and population, there's no way they'll restock the fleet. It'll take years."

Craig couldn't get his brain around that. All of his heroics in saving dozens of stranded researchers, and it was a drop in the bucket beside the billions on Earth. "Why hasn't anyone negotiated a truce?" he said.

"The corporations. Why else? You think the merchant collective out of Mars is going to let this opportunity go? Right now they're telling their governing council that they've got us by the balls. They figure if they wait a year or two more, the shipping lanes will be theirs for the taking. They're probably right. It wouldn't take much."

"Don't they see how many people are dying?"

"I doubt they care. Mars is nearly stable now; their die-off is almost over. But our merchant collective is the same—sitting in their palaces in near-earth orbit and wringing their hands over those shipping lanes. Any truce Mars negotiates will involve control of the lanes, and our corporations won't stomach the loss."

"And the fleets go along with it?"

"The fleets are under the directive of the civilian governments, in case you forgot."

Craig pointed his thumb over his shoulder, back toward the hold. "That thing work on the Galilean ships?"

"We could try, but I doubt it. Back in the old days when missionary fervor swept across Europa, they destroyed most of their modified crops. They wanted to go back to what God intended. Their yields have been crap ever since, but it could turn out to be a lucky break."

Craig clenched and unclenched his hands, breathing the atmosphere of recycled air and poorly washed bodies. "That's a lot of classified information you just gave me."

"It's not related to what we were doing on MO-226, so it's not officially classified. But yeah, it's a lot. A lot I can't let you tell the Galileans if we're captured."

"You'll scuttle my ship, won't you?"

"I always would have, but now you know why. We have to get through or get close enough for a secure broadcast to the *Reagan*. If we don't, Earth loses the war and there's no one left to hold the Galileans in check."

"Damn you!"

"It's what's got to be. What we're doing could save billions."

"Are you trying to motivate me, Lieutenant? Believe me, I'm motivated. I don't *want* to be captured by the Galileans, but what do you think I can do in a freighter?"

She climbed from the seat and pushed over to the bulkhead at the rear of the chamber, then gripped the acceleration netting. "I got shaken out of a sound sleep in my bunk and sent out here to die. You think I'm happy about it? I expect you to fire up your thrusters and get me close enough to the *Reagan* for a secure broadcast!" She slipped her body into the cocoon of the netting.

Craig glared at her, then slapped the intercom to the holds. "Prepare for first-burn in five minutes," he said, and started the countdown. She was still beautiful, but a lot less attractive all of a sudden. He climbed into his own shock-netting beside her and closed his eyes. "Maybe we'll run through a micro-meteor and it won't matter."

"That's the spirit."

On the seventh day of the run, long after the freighter's thrusters had gone silent, the tracking computer picked up multiple ships on approach vectors.

"We got two coming in on our eleven o'clock," Craig barked. "One on our two o'clock high."

"Calm down," DuLac said, joining him at the copilot's seat. "Time to intercept?" Ryan and Brown joined them.

"Can't tell! They're too far out. The tracking computer hasn't got enough of a lock on them to calculate velocities."

"See?" She gripped his hand and pulled it away from the maneuvering thruster control deck. "They're too far out. Let the computer run; give it a couple of days. The two o'clock might miss us. Hell, the eleven o'clocks might miss us."

"They'll adjust. They won't miss."

"Calculate the trajectory that'll give us the longest run."

Craig laughed bitterly. "Then what?"

In response, she energized the freighter's high-gain antenna and rotated it forward. "Freighter AG-776 to *Ronald Reagan*," she said into the audio pick-up. "Freighter AG-776 to *Ronald Reagan*, mayday mayday mayday. We are approached by four hostile ships. We require assistance. Mayday mayday mayday." She repeated the message, then turned to Craig. "Broadcast our coordinates."

"They're not going to rescue us," he said as he forwarded their coordinates. "We're too far."

"Just keep us flying for as long as possible."

The *Ronald Reagan* acknowledged within half an hour. She *was* coming—she broadcast her reply loud and clear to everyone in the sector. Captain Routan declared the freighter the sovereign property of Earth and ordered the Galileans to back off. None of them responded.

"You think they'll back down?" Craig asked. "I mean, there's four of them against one of us."

DuLac shook her head. "The Galileans haven't dared fight our battleships before, but I don't like how this looks."

With attitude thrusters and directional changes, Craig bought them almost three weeks. He had shunted fuel from most of the attitude thrusters to the main tanks, enough for a two-second burn. Enough for one last change in velocity. He practically slept in his captain's chair, listening to the *Reagan's* periodic threatening broadcasts. One of his three minders stayed at his side constantly, keeping the *Ronald Reagan* updated with their coordinates.

Craig could see the *Reagan* now as a very bright dot beyond the converging Galileans—still a good ten days out. Too far. The timbre of her broadcasts had changed in the past week while the Galileans adjusted their trajectories to match Craig's.

"You are in violation of the Treaty of Io," the *Reagan* transmitted. "Any attempt to interfere with Freighter AG-776 will be construed as an act of war."

Galileans maintained radio-silence. The ship approaching from two o'clock high was clearly a battleship, plumes of gas and flames pouring from her bow as she slowed herself. Both eleven o'clocks had the silhouettes of destroyers, though they were still too head-on to be certain. Those three ships together would be a match for the *Reagan*. The chasing Galilean battleship that had started it all was weeks behind and would only serve as a witness and maybe salvage.

"The near battleship will be on top of us in about thirty hours," Craig said to Lt. Ryan in the copilot's chair. "The destroyers are starting their turn. Probably going to give cover when the battleship grabs us."

Ryan shook his head. "If they stop to grab us, they won't be able to outrun the *Reagan*. They'll *have* to fight."

Craig tried to judge the mass of those ships and how quickly they could add momentum. "I guess they like their chances. Too bad Lt. DuLac's going to blow us up. We'll never know who won." He felt exhausted and helpless.

"I haven't scuttled us yet, Captain Tai," DuLac called from the end of the corridor where she was just emerging from Hold B. "We'll eject in vacuum suits. The rebreathers and extra tanks will give us almost forty-eight hours of air."

"The *Reagan's* farther away than that."

"Pessimist." She joined them at the front, staring out the window at the faint shapes of incoming ships.

The communications array pinged an incoming message. It was from the Galileans, their first contact in weeks. Craig looked at DuLac with his best 'What do I do?' look. DuLac gestured Ryan back toward the hold while she wiggled down into the footwell of the copilot's seat again.

"Why are you down there?" Craig said. "Whether they know you're here or not doesn't really matter."

"Listen to me carefully," DuLac said in a hard voice. "No one can know we're here. This is very important. Answer the comm and keep it simple."

"What's going on?"

"Hopefully getting our asses out of the fire. Put enough power into your transmitter so that the *Ronald Reagan* can read you loud and clear."

Craig stared down at her, and she gestured impatiently at the communications array. He jabbed the respond button.

The thin man in crisp, gray uniform who formed on Craig's screen was not the same as the first, but he could have been. "Freighter AG-776, stop and be boarded."

Craig resisted glancing at DuLac. "You have no right to threaten me! I'm carrying relief-food to scientific outposts and I have to get it to them before they starve. I'm low on fuel and oxygen, and if I stop, I won't be able to start again."

"You are operating in restricted space in association with illegal military maneuvers. Stop your ship or be fired upon."

"I'm *not* military! A military base sent out a distress call, and I tried to answer it. If you guys sent out a distress call, I'd answer you too."

The *Reagan* abruptly cut in, this time with an image of Captain Routan, not the canned broadcast they'd been issuing for weeks. "This is Captain Routan," he said. "To whom am I speaking?"

Craig glanced at the thin, gray man on the left of his screen and Captain Routan in his burgundy Earth Fleet uniform on his right. The Galilean looked profoundly irritated.

"You do not have authority here, Captain Routan," the Galilean said. "Turn your ship back in-system, or you will be fired upon also."

Captain Routan puffed up with offense. "Are you saying that Earth doesn't have jurisdiction here? Has the Galilean Coalition allied with Mars now?"

At this the gray man smiled tightly. "Mars does not have *jurisdiction* here either. The Galilean Coalition lays claim to all areas associated with the main asteroid belt, and hereby declares it off limits to Earth and Mars."

"That is in violation of the Treaty of Io, and the jurisdictions established at those proceedings. We do not accept your claim."

"Very well, Captain."

Through the freighter's windows, Craig saw the two destroyers launch rockets in the direction of the *Reagan*.

"The destroyers fired," Craig said numbly.

"Turn off your camera," DuLac whispered as she squirmed and scrambled up to look. A fierce grin split to her face. "Perfect."

"You wanted them to fire on the *Reagan*?"

"That was just a warning shot, the *Reagan's* anti-missile defenses will handle it easily. But watch and learn how we do things in the Fleet, Captain. Watch and learn."

Craig sat, watching the diminishing rockets speed toward the bright spot of the *Reagan*. He frowned. Was the *Reagan* getting bigger? Elongating. He pulled out his telescope control-arm and focused in tightly on the bright blotch. "What the hell's that, Lieutenant?" Flames were jetting out from all sides of her—top, bottom, sides, as the *Reagan* got wider and wider.

"Watch."

The blotch resolved itself into two blotches. Then three, then four. "Multiple ships?"

"They've been flying in an extremely tight formation for a month, with all their solar cells out to increase reflectance."

The communications array pinged over and over, as three more captains resolved themselves around the image of Captain Routan. Craig was stunned to see two of them wore the navy-blue uniforms of Mars Fleet.

"This is Captain Chen, Battleship *Ares Vallis*."

"Captain Sustakovitch, Battleship *Olympus Mons*."

"Captain Teale, Battleship *Berlin*."

Captain Routan nodded. "Galilean, you have broken the Treaty of Io and have fired upon a joint coalition of Mars and Earth Fleet vessels. You have threatened a civilian ship on a humanitarian mission, in direct violation of the Treaty of Deimos. These shall be construed as an act of war."

The Galileans transmission went dark; Craig wasn't sure if they heard the end of Routan's speech. The Ganymede battleship's forward thrusters faded and her aft thrusters roared to life as she attempted to regain the velocity she had squandered in the past three days. The destroyers fired attitude thrusters hard, turning away from the oncoming phalanx of guns and armor.

Craig rubbed his eyes, and looked at DuLac. She was floating up near the ceiling, looking down at him.

"Would you please tell me what's going on?"

"The Galileans are the real threat, one the fleets can't address under our standing orders."

"Unless attacked?" Craig said.

"Unless attacked."

"Shit. You mean this whole thing, out to MO-226 and back, was just a ruse?"

"A lot of people will die if the Galileans take advantage of Mars' and Earth's weaknesses, exponentially more than are starving now. We have to keep them in check until the war is over."

"All that about Baranto and the terminal genes was bullshit?"

"No, that's all true. But we transmitted the data to the *Reagan* months ago along a string of secure beacons. Maybe we'll need it, maybe we won't. We'll see how the future shakes out."

"How the future shakes out!? You used me as a chess piece in your war."

"I put you, and myself, right on the firing line, Captain. If we'd been blown up today, it still would have been worth it. Our battleships would have had more justification for their attack."

Craig looked out at the ships arrayed before him. They were so big and so far away that they'd hardly moved. The fleet battleships were separated into four distinct points of light now.

"What happens next?" he said.

"There'll be a fight, we'll win, the politicians will sort it out. Meanwhile, our battleships, and Mars', will scramble around the belt scooping up stranded people in the MO's. This will be our first chance to get them, and it's a good excuse."

"What's in the big box back in my hold?"

"The urns of twenty-seven friends who died on MO-226 in Ganymede bombing runs. We promised them we'd get them home too."

"Yeah. Okay. Okay. But I want you off my ship. I've got potatoes to deliver."

TRUE COLORS

An Alliance Archives Adventure

Danielle Ackley-McPhail

THERE WAS NO STATELY PROCESSION TO THE AIRLOCK. NO POMP AND CERE-
mony as the hatch was opened. Brockmann's body wasn't set adrift in
the vastness of space to echo the dignity of an ancient warrior's burial
at sea.

No.

She was taken away in a body bag the moment the *Teufel* docked. By the time
the 142nd Infantry—or Daire's Devils—mustered in the barracks common room for
debriefing, a corpsman was presenting to Sarge a two-inch, compressed-carbon
cube and a bag of effects. That was all that was left of Suzanne Brockmann, Private
First Class, Special Forces, one more offense credited against the pirates that had
invaded the sector.

Private Katrion Alexander felt her hands flex, accompanied by a familiar itch in
her fingers. That could have been her reduced to a geometric shape. Almost
was...*twice*.

She must have moved without realizing it. Beside her Corporal Jackson
"Scotch" Daniels cleared his throat and stepped between her and her pile of gear.
Well, more accurately, between her and her gauss rifle.

"Down, Kittie, down," he murmured, his hazel eyes capturing her gaze. "Ain't
no pirates here."

Kat growled. She was doing that a lot lately.

There was no time to comment. She and the rest of the unit snapped to
attention as Sergeant Kevin Daire accepted the remains from the corpsman,
ignoring the bag of effects. Turning his back on the man, Sarge cradled the cube in
his left hand and drew his combat knife with his right. He then bowed his head; the
unit gathered round and followed suit. Not a word was spoken aloud as each of
them bid farewell to their fallen comrade. Nor as, one by one, each of them stepped

forward and, with their blades, scratched a line into the smooth, shiny surface of her compressed remains. Each of them maintained silence as they fell back to form a loose circle around their leader once their part was complete. Sarge looked up and met their gazes. Without looking away from them he raised his knife and etched his own line, bisecting those left by the unit.

The vow was made. For each line segment on the cube was a solemn oath that the pirates would be brought down.

Only then did Scotch step forward to secure Brockmann's personal effects from the still-waiting corpsman. Whatever was in that small, compact bag would be shared out among the unit according to need. The rest would be held in reserve or given where it would best serve. Unlike Kat, Brockmann had no family to send material belongings back to, even if the military were willing to foot the bill.

The corpsman turned to leave.

"Wait." Sarge motioned for Kat and Scotch to step forward. She suppressed a flinch and came to attention in front of him. "Alexander, Daniels...accompany Corpsman Kane back to med-bay to be cleared for return to duty."

Shit. It was only to be expected, though; Kat had been banged up from her previous encounter with the pirates, and both of them had been with Brockmann when their squad had come under fire a second time. She ran a hand over her dark, regulation-length bristle of hair and accepted the inevitable as she followed Scotch and Kane to the lift.

Sarge turned to the rest of the unit. "Command has called a general inspection for 1700 hours; use this time to get your billets in order." Not waiting for acknowledgement, he tightened his fist around Brockmann's cube and about-faced. In silence he returned to his chamber to secure their fallen.

Forty minutes in med-bay got Kat a noxious cream to bring down the swelling around her blackened left eye and a shot in her wrenched ankle that hurt ten times worse than the original injury for all of thirty seconds, after which she felt nothing. The damage was still there—a lingering reminder of her first encounter with the enemy—but the pressure bandage would take care of that. She also received authorization to return to duty.

Poor Scotch. He was still in there arguing as Kat left med-bay to head back to the barracks. As a first-hand witness to Brockmann's termination, Command wanted Scotch to submit to a psych evaluation before reinstating him to active status. The last thing she heard clearly was him suggesting they submit to a self-administered rectal probe.

Kat chuckled. She wasn't hanging around to see which near-immovable force triumphed. In fact, she was hightailing it out of there before someone stopped to wonder how her brainpan was doing after finding half of Trask—former commander and pirate—floating in space. After all, they might decide she was too happy about it.

Toggling on her bonejack, Kat couldn't resist a parting jab. *"Come on, Scotch, ten minutes on the couch and the shrink will have you visualizing cute little kittens and white sandy beaches, it'll be fun!"*

Scotch tossed an off-color suggestion her way. *"Talk about torture. I'm allergic to cats and the only beaches in this sector come with an atmosphere that would dissolve the flesh off human bones in thirty seconds. I'll have to pass, the torment would be too much to take...I might crack, and then where would we be? Now get the hell out of my head so I can deal with these quacks!"*

Kat laughed, winking one dark brown eye at him as she switched the comm off and made her escape.

She hadn't known that, about the beaches, but then she wasn't exactly a beach bunny, was she? As she entered the lift she forced away the naughty thoughts of Scotch lounging on the sand somewhere with his blond buzz cut bleached white by the sun, instead turning her attention to the data they'd retrieved from the Groom Lake microsat. Not only had they gained documentation of the pirates' attempted pillaging of the research facility, but Kat and her squad had intercepted the intended loot: the full research and development files on the *Rommel*, the state-of-the-art flagship of the fleet. They had it, but the pirates wanted it. Bad.

Sarge had the encrypted files secured in a lock box in his quarters, but he'd had Kat burn a backup as well. It was hidden on the *Teufel*, along with the rest of the stuff they'd retrieved from the pirate derelict on the mission that had gotten Brockmann killed. The black box data was the easy part; the computer cores Kat had extracted from the vessel, those were going to take some finesse. Right now everything they had gathered was secreted away in a shielded compartment located near the *Teufel's* engine reactor where a scan, visual or otherwise, would not be able to detect their presence. Only Sarge, Scotch, and their unit commander, General Drovak, knew the intel was there waiting to be disseminated.

Kat didn't even want to think about trying to crack the code. Fortunately, that wasn't her job. All Sarge had to do was turn the material over to the general or one of his agents as soon as possible. The whole situation had her nervous, though. With rumors that the crew assigned to the *Rommel* may have been compromised, Kat couldn't be sure who they could trust outside of their own unit.

She shut down that thought and focused on getting back to the barracks. Kat looked up as the decks ticked by. Almost there. The lights fluxed, and the car slowed. For a moment she thought she was screwed; there wasn't much time left to get her billet in order before the inspection. She half-expected a jerk and the *thunk* of the lift coming to an abrupt halt in the tube, but the lift continued to descend. With a hiss, the doors opened into the common room she had left less than an hour earlier. If not for the neat stacks of gear she would have thought the unit had left without them.

She sniffed. Something had made it past the air scrubbers. The remnants were faint, an acrid bite deep in her throat. It was an effort to keep her breathing regulated as she walked across the chamber. Her impulse was to hold her breath. Her body's was to breathe faster. Neither would do. It was an effort to draw shallow until she reached her gear. She outright had to force her fingers to flex and loosen enough to pick up her gauss as she paused by her own pile of equipment. She grabbed her breather as well and jerked it over her eyes, nose, and mouth until the thick gasket settled snug against her skin.

Kat should have felt silly, but she didn't. Paranoid came to mind...but she continued to wear the mask, hoping the filters were enough to combat whatever was on the air. She also held her rifle at the ready.

That alone made her feel better.

"Hey, Sarge...." she called out, the words only slightly muffled. Her breath came a little faster, and she forced it back. All the billets were closed, except one. Kat angled left and headed toward the compartment on the end with deck-eating strides. "Yo, anyone there...?" she called out.

Silence.

Kat drew closer, swaying a bit as her breath picked up again, as if she couldn't get enough oxygen. Lightheaded she braced herself against the open hatch. The air coming through her breather still held a hint of that acrid odor. She swayed again and her head dropped forward of its own accord.

For a split second she saw an out-flung wrist, mottled clear around with bruising, caught between the hatch and the frame. The pattern of the discoloration disturbed Kat but her thoughts couldn't focus on why. She leaned forward to push the door panel into its retraction slot to reveal the unit's weapons specialist, Private First Class Christine Dalton, which was kind of odd in itself, as this wasn't her billet. The details drifted out of focus, though, as Kat's brain slowly fogged over. She leaned forward to check for a pulse. As she did so, something snagged her mask, tugging it askew. There was a faint hissing as the gasket seal parted from her skin and the earlier odor intensified. After that, all Kat saw was a swirl of darkening colors drawing her down into the black.

"Time to change your name, you pain in the ass," a familiar voice grumbled over her, "before you use up all nine lives. Come on, Kittie...*atten*-hut!"

Kat grumbled and shoved at the hands lifting her semi-vertical.

"Yeah, you go ahead and fight, g'on, give me what-for," he went on. "Just do it with your damn eyes open."

She cracked said eyes just enough to recognize the familiar walls of med-bay and the hard, pale features of Scotch who was leaning over her. At his back a med-tech and a corpsman tried to get around Scotch's bulk to separate them. Her eyes opened yet further, and she waved the men off. Scotch's grip loosened until most of her body was once again in contact with the bed, but he didn't let go. Kat could almost swear she heard a relieved sigh as his eyes closed on whatever expression they held. She didn't speak until the others had moved outside of the curtains that had been drawn to give her a measure of privacy from the other cots.

"What happened?"

Scotch looked up and met her gaze, his eyes dark. The muscles in his jaw tightened. When he spoke, it was low and through his teeth. "I was hoping you could tell me. We've been infiltrated. A sleeping agent was introduced to the barracks wing... a time-release gas grenade hidden in the central duct. The atmospheric sensors were disabled. Someone set up an induction fan to force the fumes into every compartment in the wing." His grip tightened on her shoulders once more until she grunted at the pain and tried to pry his hands away. He didn't seem to notice as he went on.

"He's gone. Sarge is gone."

Kat gasped and stopped fighting against Scotch's hold. If not for his hands on her she would have curled in a ball. Grief and rage and confusion darted around inside her like a rat trapped in a cage. Sarge couldn't be gone, not in such a senseless way. He was the sergeant in charge of her unit, sure, but he was also a friend...no, family. Actually, after what they'd been through, closer than family, which was saying a lot. Damn, if only her thoughts would stop swimming.

"They took him," Scotch went on, his tone lethal and low as he bent his head close to hers. "They took him, and we have to get him back."

His words arrowed past the faint buzzing still in her ears. Her head whipped up and this time Kat snarled.

If Scotch hadn't leaned in he would have been safe.

But he did.

Instead of continuing to resist his grip, Kat used it to her advantage. She drew back and slammed her forehead into his frontal lobe. He didn't see it coming. Of course, she wasn't so pissed that she didn't pull back a bit at the end. No sense in knocking out the only person she was absolutely certain hadn't sold out to the pirates.

"Aw! Fuck!" Scotch swore. "Go'damnit!"

"You bastard," she snapped back at him. "You had me thinking he was dead!"

Med-bay personnel came streaming through the curtain before she and Scotch could truly get into it. They were smart this time; they'd sent in men with some muscle. Not that they needed it. Scotch was more than ready to get out of striking distance.

"Corporal, you have to leave now."

"Oh save it, we both are," Kat cut in as she swung her legs off of the bed. The hand not bracing her came up and brushed the sore spot forming on her forehead. She fought off a trace of dizziness and ignored the technicians' protests. The men fell silent, though, as she marched through med-bay, her backside bare in a classic hospital gown that hadn't changed one wit throughout time. Her lips twitched in a faint smile as she heard the "damn" breathed behind her in what sounded like Scotch's voice. Not that she cared who else saw—being in the military quickly stripped away any sense of body-consciousness—but Kat snagged a second gown from a nearby pile, shrugging into it like a robe.

On her way out, she noted only nine members of the 142nd were still in med-bay, other than Scotch and herself. "Where are the rest?" she called back over her shoulder.

"Those that have recovered were relocated to the crew quarters for now." Scotch had to raise his voice to be heard. Kat smirked as he caught up with her halfway to the lift. He had her neatly folded uniform under one arm.

"You know, I could have you up on charges for striking a superior officer."

"Ranking, maybe..." she drawled, with hints of her PawPaw's voice seeping into her tone. Scotch pouted in response and rubbed at the bruise darkening his forehead.

"Anyway," Kat went on, "we don't have time for that bullshit. Sarge is out there somewhere waiting on us."

The pout vanished.

They headed to the barracks in silence. Once they were in the lift, Kat watched closely as the levels changed. Again several decks before the barracks the lights fluxed, and the car slowed. Her eyes narrowed. Reaching out, she depressed the button to stop the lift, and then sent it back two levels. Once it got there she sent it to their original floor once more.

"What?" Scotch asked over the secure squad band, watching her closely.

She said nothing, but waited. Again the unit fluxed precisely at the point it had before. Kat resisted the impulse to dart her gaze about the close compartment as she finally responded in the same manner. *"The lift did that earlier too. And now it's done it twice again. As my PawPaw likes to say: once is chance, twice is coincidence...three times is enemy action. Someone wanted to know when company was coming."*

Scotch grunted and nodded in agreement as the lift stopped at their level.

When the doors hissed open Kat found herself greeted by security personnel with riot guns poised to fire. She tensed and stopped absolutely still. What she wouldn't give for her gauss...or at least some fatigues.

"Scotch?"

He stepped forward, and the guards slung their weapons and fell back to parade rest. Apparently *he* had clearance. With a nod at the men, Scotch moved past them into the chamber. Glancing warily at the grinning security detail, Kat followed; as she passed their position, she was glad she'd thought to cover her back. She already felt naked enough without her weapon.

"You could have warned me," she hissed once they were well away from the guards.

Scotch merely put on a suffering look and ran his free hand over his forehead once more.

"Prick," she murmured and broke away, heading for the compartment she shared with four other members of the unit.

The first thing she noticed was her laptop sitting neatly on her footlocker when it should have still been locked inside. She swore and went right for it. Suddenly, Scotch was there, intercepting her before she could lay a hand on the case.

"I taught you better than that, Private," he growled.

She froze instantly, not use to Scotch really pulling rank. He was right, though; her lack of caution was both sloppy and foolish. Good way to get people killed. Good way to end up cubed. "Sorry."

"Get dressed," Scotch ordered, holding out her uniform, and abruptly he left the billet. As soon as the hatch closed she stripped off the double set of gowns and drew the military-issue tee shirt and black fatigues on over her skivvies. She'd sheathed her combat dagger on her hip and was just sliding a ship boot carefully over her pressure bandage when Scotch returned. He carried a cluster of odd items: latex gloves, a pouch of talc, what looked like an industrial hand wipe, and a thick, chunky flashlight. Perched on his head was a set of high-tech protective goggles. She'd forgotten Scotch had some demolitions training. She'd never seen him actually put it into practice, as it wasn't his primary MOS. He clearly knew his thing, though. Kat watched in fascination as he set the items down in a neat, orderly row, pulled on the gloves, and drew the goggles down over his eyes. He motioned for her to back away.

First he picked up the powder and sprinkled it over the laptop. The stuff revealed nothing but the unblemished surface of the casing. "Kill the lights," he ordered, in that non-Scotch tone. Kat complied. When she turned, he had the squat light in his hands and was clicking it through a number of settings, the light altering with each one. Black light. Normal light. Ultraviolet. Supernova, and a few she didn't even have a made-up name for. It was almost ritualistic, only fast. *Click*. Trail the light over the laptop in the ceremonial pattern. Trail the beam along the thin gap between the bottom of the unit and the top of the locker. *Click*. Repeat. "Lights," he ordered.

"Sir, yes sir!"

"No signs of a trip wire or other trigger," he murmured as he ignored her wiseass attitude and gently ran his hands over the computer in a final check. Clearly confident the unit wasn't rigged to blow, Scotch motioned her forward. Kat moved closer and watched as he opened the laptop.

Upon seeing the screen, Kat cursed loud enough that one of the guards opened the hatch and peered in.

"Corporal?" The man's tone was tense, and his gaze went from her to Scotch, who had subtly shifted until the guard didn't have a line of sight on the laptop.

"Sorry," Kat answered for him. "Bumped my foot...." Tugging up on her uniform leg she bared the bandage on her left ankle. The guard just stared at her, a long look down to her ankle and up again, less like he doubted her, more like he was remembering the earlier view. She allowed steel to infiltrate her gaze. "Thanks, we're good."

Scotch didn't need to give her a look for her to know he was annoyed with her. "Thank you, soldier. You can return to your post." It wasn't like the guy could argue; Scotch outranked him too. Kat resisted the urge to peer through the hatch to confirm the guard had moved back across the room. "Low profile, Alexander," Scotch muttered beneath his breath. "Try to remember we *like* not being noticed right now."

She nodded but said nothing as he turned back to the laptop.

And bit back a curse of his own.

Her log-in window was open. Typed in the user id field were the words: BRING EVERYTHING. Vague enough, but Kat knew exactly what was being demanded. The bad guys wanted the data, not just the specs on the *Rommel*—which they presumably now had once they cracked Sarge's encrypted copy—but the computer cores as well. There must be data there the pirates didn't want them to access.

The message wasn't all, though. Stuck to the keyboard frame, as if she'd left a note for herself, were a set of navigation coordinates. There was something else visible on the screen, but the log-in window was in the way. Kat hesitated before reaching out to the touchpad, looking to Scotch for permission.

"Well it's not like they're going to sabotage the thing when they want something from us." Still, before stepping out of her way he tore open the hand wipe and sanitized the keypad and any other part of the computer she might touch. He then pulled off the protective gloves over the soiled hand wipe and dumped it all in the waste basket by the door.

Kat stepped forward and leaned down to the touchpad. As she typed her code the log-in window closed, and an incoming message alert was visible. Her nerves tingling, Kat clicked it open to reveal an image file of Sarge, unconscious on a beach somewhere, looking like nothing so much as a relaxing tourist. Or he would have, if not for the BDUs and the hint of a bound wrist just visible where his arms crossed behind his head. She rattled a few keys trying to get as much data as possible, but whoever had sent this had some tech savvy because the electronic footprints had been erased.

"What the hell?" Kat whipped around until she could see Scotch's face. "How long were we out?"

"You've been out for six hours; we estimate Sarge has been missing for a little longer than that."

"Six!" Well, that explained the shake-up call in med-bay. Scotch never was very patient.

Scotch nodded, concern and exhaustion shading his expression. "You got the lightest dose. Those billeted furthest from the main vent came out of it first. Those closest are mostly still down. One or two went under hard.

He looked grim. "I was the only one not hit." Of course, he'd been in med-bay...arguing. "When you entered the barracks the lingering gas triggered the atmospheric sensors in the lift, which hadn't been tampered with. That alerted Environmental."

Something wasn't right about all of this.

Okay...something *beyond* the obvious wasn't right about all of this.

Kat's chest muscles tightened as she processed what Scotch said. She looked back at the photograph, and her nerves jangled uncomfortably as the potential threat became more clear: What if the *Rommel's* ranks weren't the only ones compromised?

Making sure he was watching Kat moved her fingers over the keyboard. In part she searched her system for malware the pirates may have left behind, but she also used the motions to disguise a few hand signals. Every unit had their own code, a secret way to communicate in the field. She flashed the sign for 'infiltrator' and then briefly glanced up to catch the corporal's eye. Scotch's grimace deepened. Kat made another slight gesture signifying 'fake' and nodded at the image still on her screen. At that one Scotch looked confused.

"Figures," Kat muttered aloud. "We're stuck here breathing in canned air, and Sarge lands on the perfect beach somewhere, working on his tan."

It was obvious the moment her meaning came clear to Scotch. He himself had pointed out to her there were no perfect beaches in this sector, and certainly not within a six-hour transit window. Scotch's left hand moved; ran through his hair, scratching his ear along the way. The message masked: Play along.

"Someone's gonna pay."

Kat nodded, then pointed at the coordinates; "Any idea where that is?"

Scotch's expression was grim. "Not a clue."

They didn't even know if the pirates actually had Sarge, or if this engineered image was completely bogus. Kat swore heatedly as she stripped the note from the housing and shut the system down. "There's not much chance these navs will take us to him."

"Nope. Seriously unlikely."

Kat smiled anyway. It was a nasty smile. She could tell just by the feel of it.

"But I bet we can get someone there to lead the way."

Scotch nodded. His eyes looked hard, but his expression was so neutral it was scary. Kat shivered. He reached out and brushed her jaw. Odd for him to do, but she got the message and activated her bonejack.

"Go on, you," he said to her. "Now you're decent, head back to med-bay and check on the rest of the unit. Make sure everyone reports to the crew quarters, Deck Gamma-18," he instructed her aloud. But over the bonejack he continued, *"It's 0430 hours right now, we deploy no later than 0530. Get those coordinates to Campbell so he can plot a course, then prep the unit for deployment; anyone asks we still have a scheduled live-fire exercise."*

"What about you?" she asked by the same means, then vocalized for the benefit of the guards and anyone else listening; "Yes, Corporal."

Her jaw buzzed as Scotch continued over the 'jack, *"I was cleared for entry in here so I could inspect the barracks for any other...surprises and disable them. I best get to that, and see what else I can't learn about our 'friends' at the same time."*

He grinned as she left and Kat was reminded of her earlier smile.

"Where's Dalton?" | *"We lost Campbell."*

Kat and Scotch both spoke over the squad band at the same time. Kat barely felt the ripple along her jaw she was so worked up. She fell silent and waited for Scotch to go on.

"What?!" Scotch's tone clearly indicated he wanted to have heard her wrong.

Kat repeated herself. *"We lost Campbell."*

Silence. *"I'll be right there."*

Five minutes later Scotch stalked into the common room of the crew quarters. He headed right for her. Even in the midst of battle, she'd never seen a more intense expression on his face.

Kat's teeth ground, and she swallowed hard, feeling the ripple of tense muscles all the way to her feet. As he approached, she reached into her pocket and pulled out the contents. By the time he was in front of her, her fingers uncurled to reveal the all-too-familiar sight of a compressed carbon cube; Campbell's physical remains.

"Soldier, report."

Kat complied, her voice kept flat and neutral only by rigid control. "According to the report registered by the medtech on duty, at 0400 hours Corporal Anthony Campbell succumbed to complications triggered by a delayed reaction to the foreign substance inhaled into his system."

By the time she finished reporting her voice acquired a hard edge, and Scotch had gone from white, to deep red, to white again, the expression on his face both uncharacteristic and disturbing. Kat was sure it must be similar to her own.

"Where. Is. Dalton?" Scotch's voice vibrated with cold, quiet rage.

Kat's breath caught. What had he found in his search? His fingers flickered in the sign she'd used earlier. 'Infiltrator'.

Kat's grip tightened on the cube, and her temper stirred. Betrayal was never easy to take, but when it was someone you'd fought life-and-death beside...It was hard for Kat to keep her expression blank. "Corporal Dalton is unaccounted for."

There was only one place Dalton would head: the *Teufel*. They had to assume she had Sarge, which meant, other than the actual encryption code, she had every-thing she needed in one tidy package, if she managed to launch before they caught up to her. the *Teufel* wouldn't be easy for Dalton to manage if she was on her own— *God help them, let her be on her own*—but it wasn't impossible either.

If that happened Sarge was as good as cubed.

Apparently, Scotch was of a similar mind.

He nodded at Campbell's remains.

"Keep that safe for now, Kittie," he said. "Sarge'll need it in a while."

Turning to the assembled unit, his stance and expression was a warning to each and every one of them: disloyalty would be met with extreme prejudice. If there were any other traitors among them, they had to be pissing themselves on the inside.

Kat immediately nixed that thought. If she started doubting the rest of her teammates, the unit was doomed. Cohesion would be lost and with it their edge. The key was to be alert, not suspicious. She blanked her mind of any misgiving and focused on Scotch.

"I will not take the place of a damn fine commander when there is anything I can do to put him back in it," he said. "So grab your weapons and follow me, or get the hell out of my way."

Kat, gauss rifle in hand, was in lockstep with him as he went out the hatch heading for the docking bay.

They didn't storm the shuttle.

It would have felt good, but it also would have backed Dalton into a corner. Not that that wasn't where they wanted her...they just didn't want her aware she was in it. Instead, they stopped one level above and gathered in a huddle.

"Diaz, Connor, Danzer, Kopeky...you're going EVA. I need you to institute a security lockdown of the docking collar and disable the release mechanism. You make our ship a permanent part of the *Rommel* if you have to, understood?"

"Acknowledged," they answered, their tone low and intent, their responses in near-perfect synch.

Scotch gave them a sharp nod and sent them on their way. Silently the men moved off to do his bidding. He then turned to the rest of the unit, quickly splitting them into four-man squads, each with their own coordinated task.

"Kat, you're with me," he said as he headed back to the lift. "Leave your weapon here."

"Yes, Corp...*what*?!"

He pivoted and gave her a hard look. "Leave. The weapon. Here. Or do you want Dalton to know we're on to her?"

Kat's grip tightened on her rifle. Her teeth clenched and her neck popped at just the thought of going in not loaded for bear. But he was right. It wasn't Kat's only weapon; it was just her most obvious.

"You're a pain in my ass," she ground out. Thrusting the weapon into the hands of a teammate, she accepted his pistol in return, shoving it the waistband of her pants as she stalked after Scotch. "So, let's hear the plan."

"We go in like we're following their instructions, then we keep her talking so the others can do their jobs. If we have a chance to take her down, we do."

There was no one in sight as they exited the lift and made their way across the docking bay, not even the watch. Kat kept alert, her eyes roving across the area searching for movement. As they drew closer it was clear the *Teufel* was there, but still in lock-down.

Kat cast a questioning sideways glance toward Scotch as he entered his security code. She remained silent, though, and ready to follow his lead. It wasn't worth setting him off. He was pissed and clearly ready for a fight. She could see it in the glimmer that darkened his hazel eyes to hardened bronze. That was the only thing that gave any hint to his current disposition. Didn't matter, though.... Any adversary close enough to tell was already shit out of luck.

The two of them boarded the shuttle as if this were a standard pre-mission inspection. Scotch went in first. Ducking through the airlock portion of the vessel, Kat nearly ran up his ass. She could feel the tension pulsing off of him. "Hey, what gives?" she asked as she stepped around him and into the crew compartment of the shuttle. She thought she heard a sound from the cargo bay. She started to move in that direction when Scotch snapped out a sharp "no!" His hand came down on her arm. He was drawing her back, but suddenly the pull eased, though his grip did not. Kat glanced over her shoulder at him. The edge of her lip curled instantly, and she scowled. Her hand brushed the cube in her pocket. It was looking more likely that poor Dalton wasn't unaccounted for after all. Disturbing to think that the medbay staff had been infiltrated.

Very deliberately Kat reached up and lifted Scotch's hand from her so she could pivot full around. The entire time she was careful to move very slowly.

"Welcome back, *Campbell*," she spoke in tones of silken steel to the man standing behind and to the left of Scotch. "What happened? Did Hell throw you out for giving Devils a bad name?"

Scotch's eyes narrowed. Message received. Not that he could do much with it. Turned out he had a pistol to his head. If Campbell hadn't been a dead man before, he certainly was now.

"You know, Alexander, that mouth of yours is about the only smart thing about you." Campbell responded. "You have two choices," the traitor told her, "Secure Corporal Daniels, or I'll take him out."

Like the latter wasn't going to happen at some point anyway. Kat looked down at the zip restraints Campbell held out but she didn't move to take them.

Scotch snarled and made as if to turn.

...Until the gun slammed upside his head. At the same time Campbell used his free hand to jerk Scotch off balance. "Don't even try it, Daniels...I need her; you're just insurance."

"Just to be clear: you play nice, Alexander, and Scotch here doesn't bleed," Campbell said. Kat suspected there was an unspoken 'yet' in there somewhere. "We want the data, all of it, and the encryption codes. Now get him zipped before I make it a non-issue."

Snatching the zip-ties she started to circle around the two of them. Campbell's gun clicked as he thumbed the hammer back.

"Like I didn't get the same training you did...do it from there. Just reach your arms around him, and make it good and secure."

Kat's mind scrambled to identify her options. Her only weapons were her combat knife and the borrowed pistol, but drawing either would be too visible. Campbell would have time to fire before she even got it unsheathed. Her hand-to-hand training wasn't much good at the moment either given that Scotch stood between her and the enemy. She had to hope an opportunity would come clear. Or at least that they could stall Campbell long enough for the Devils to close in...which meant she had no choice but to comply.

It was like hugging a statue. Even with Scotch cooperating—abet unwillingly—Kat had to press herself obscenely close before she could secure his wrists behind him. While she was doing that something hard shoved into her gut. She let her eyes drift up slow, as if she was trying not to focus on this forced intimacy, and met Scotch's eye. His gaze was hooded and every muscle clearly taut, but he remained absolutely still.

Except for his hips. He deliberately shifted them forward, his eyes never leaving hers. She gasped. A second ago she would have thought it was impossible for the two of them to get any closer—short of stripping off their clothes and making a concerted effort to occupy the same space—but just that subtle press was enough for Kat to realize that wasn't his anatomy poking her, it was the hilt of a combat knife. Then, not so subtle, Scotch deliberately teetered, as if off balance, like when Campbell had jerked him back earlier.

Kat kept her eyes on Scotch, catching the minute shift of his gaze toward the traitor. She drew a deep breath and let her eyes drift closed, then slowly brought them open again, in silent acknowledgement.

Resting her left hand on Scotch's chest as she drew her right back around to his side, Kat allowed a look of calculated vulnerability to flit across her features. Seemingly in response, Scotch dropped his chin, as if in defeat, but more importantly taking his head out of alignment with the barrel of Campbell's gun.

It was risky, but it wasn't like they had a lot of options. And still, for a fraction of a moment, she hesitated as visions of Scotch with the top of his head blown out short-circuited her nerves. And then his jaw flexed, sending static-like tingles along her bonejack, but no words. He didn't need them, she understood completely.

Then there was no time to wonder. A crash came from the cargo bay, as if something heavy fell to the deck. Kat couldn't have arranged a better distraction if she'd tried. For just a second Campbell's attention veered. Not knowing if either of them would see the outside of the shuttle ever again, Kat shoved Scotch into him with her left hand even as she drew the combat knife with the other. Bodies tumbled to the deck. The gun fired once. A scream ricocheted through the shuttle as Kat came down hard on top of the others. Something soft gave beneath her knee. Then someone screamed again.

Kat couldn't worry about any of that now. She was already lunging, her left hand locked on Campbell's gun, shoving it down and away before he could fire again. Her right hand brought the combat knife to bear letting momentum carry the blade down through Campbell's eye and into his brain. The body spasmed, jerking and thudding against the deck until everyone and everything was coated with the traitor's blood.

Scrambling back into a crouch, with the knife still in hand, Kat screamed and lunged again as someone came at her from the shadows of the cargo bay. A solid kick from that direction numbed her wrist and hand.

"Stand down, Alexander," the approaching figure ordered, stumbling from the cargo bay into the crew compartment.

Kat swore, and her legs buckled as the adrenaline ran out.

"Well I'll be damned," Scotch said, as she landed atop him. Over the squad band Kat heard him give the Devils the order to abort their missions.

Sarge stood over them, swaying slightly. The right side of his face was a mass of bruises, and his left arm was wrapped in a field dressing from wrist to elbow. His hands were bound in front of him, though Kat suspected they hadn't started out that way. There was fresh blood on the gauze and what looked like a smudge of bootblack on his sleeve. There were pronounced lines around his mouth, and his eyes were glazed with pain. Beneath that Kat recognized the deep, sharp pinch of recent betrayal.

He toed Campbell's body. "Thanks for taking out the trash."

DEVIL DANCERS
Robert E. Waters

VICTORIO NANTAN, CAPTAIN VICTORY, SQUADRON LEADER OF THE DEVIL Dancers, looked over the smoke-filled room. Somewhere within its cavernous swill of booze, laughter, music, and celebration, were his men. They were the Devil Dancers. Aces everyone; the finest fighter squadron in the fleet. They deserved their seventy-two hours of R&R. Their record kills at the Battle of Pallid Musings had earned them their playtime. But the war continued, and Captain "Victory" had just received secret intelligence about enemy fleet movements near Castor V. It was out of his squadron's specific deployment zone, but an opportunity that could not be ignored. The finest pilots in the Federated Union had to keep pushing themselves, and at such a critical moment in the war, time was imperative. The enemy was on the verge of collapse.

That enemy was the Gulo, a wolverine-like race that had nearly cut the Union in two. Feral, savage fighters, their technology was on par with humans. They were a formidable foe. Deep in his heart, Victorio could not help but admire their prowess in battle. But the war had waged for over thirty stellar years, and even personal admiration grows pale over time. He and his men were working hard to defeat the Gulo. A turning-point was at hand. Victorio could feel it. He had seen it in his dreams. One more push, one more decisive rout, and the scales could be tipped.

The Devil Dancers were not going to be left out.

He crossed the room, pushing through the partiers, responding in kind to the salutes of junior officers from the 3rd Sol Fighter Wing. He even recognized some crew members of the *Star Chariot*, an old carrier that had been refitted to accommodate a full battalion of troopers and their drop pods. Among these men, he and the Devil Dancers were legend, and whenever they were present, they received much respect. Victorio passed through them politely, but kept his eyes set on one of his pilots who sat on a plush red sofa near the bar, surrounded by adoring women and sycophants.

Naiche looked up from his drink and recognized his brother. "Ah, Captain Victory!" He stumbled to his feet, the beautiful ladies surrounding him shifting their bare legs to let him pass. "You've decided to crawl out of your wickiup and join us."

Victorio grabbed his brother before the younger man embarrassed himself by hitting the floor. Naiche's face was flush red, his breath rancid with drink, his eyes dilated and distant. "You're drunk."

"You're goddamned right I'm drunk!" Naiche said, receiving cheers and laughter from his friends. "And I intend on staying that way for another forty-eight hours."

"We need to talk, brother," Victorio said, pushing Naiche away. "Now."

"Nonsense," Naiche said. "We need to drink. Pull up a chair and join us." Before Victorio had a chance to respond, Naiche said, "Ladies, let me introduce you to our *na-tio-tish*, our war leader, Captain Victorio "Tomorrow's Wind" Nantan, the *second* finest pilot in the galaxy." He tapped his brother's chest with a blunt, lazy finger. "This man single-handedly wiped out an entire Gulo squadron at the Battle of Two Dwarves. He's received six commendations for bravery, and a score of Silver Wings. And ladies," he put his hand to his mouth and lowered his voice, "he's got the cutest little tattoo on his—"

"Enough!" Victorio grabbed Naiche's shoulders and shook. The drink in his brother's hand toppled to the floor, spreading red liquid across the plush white carpet. The internal lattice-mesh of the floor began sucking the fibers dry. "We will talk, now." He turned and looked at the women, whose expressions had become quite still. "Will you excuse us, please?"

Naiche wrestled himself free and stumbled to the sofa, apologizing profusely to his fans. He gave each lady a small kiss and promised to call on them. They shuffled past Victorio without a word and disappeared into the throng of dancers.

"You waste yourself away with all this," Victorio said, finding a seat near his brother. "Father would not be pleased."

Naiche rubbed his forehead and chuckled. "Father is just as boring as you, big brother. You are the worst kill-joy I've ever met. If you had played your cards right, one of those ladies would have given you a—"

"Everything comes so easy for you, Naiche. Not so for me. I've had to bust my ass for everything. When you were off carousing with your friends at Boot, I had to double down, pull second shifts, commit overtime. And you'd waltz right in the next morning and ace your—"

"And yet here you are," Naiche interrupted, "*Captain* of the Devil Dancers."

He'd gotten the promotion in the field during an engagement in the Kuiper Belt eight stellar years ago. His calm, serious demeanor had impressed Star Marshall Kinski Shu, who said, 'You're not like others of your kind, are you, boy?' Images of his father's hostilities toward the White Eyes came to mind, but Victorio kept his mouth shut like a good soldier. He always kept his mouth shut. 'No, I guess not, sir.' And so it was that he took command, and the rest was in the common record.

"There are reports of heavy Gulo activity near Castor V."

Naiche perked an ear. "And?"

"And I've asked Star Marshall Shu to give us a temporary transfer to Peregrine Task Force."

Naiche sat straight in his seat, the effects of the alcohol washed from his face. "Are you nuts? That racist is going to get us killed!"

Victorio shot glances around the room. Luckily, the music was too loud and the patrons too drunk to notice his brother's insubordination. "Keep your opinions to yourself, pilot."

Naiche lowered his voice and leaned in. "The men need rest, sir. We won at Pallid Musings, but it was a near-run thing, and you know it. Blue Bird just had her foot reattached. Shines Like the Sun has a new heart, and—"

"They can rest and recover en route. The *Exodus* does not depart until eighteen hundred hours."

Naiche's expression grew still, his eyes silent. "We're leaving that soon?"

"Yes."

"Shouldn't I have been consulted on this, sir? I am second in command."

"Second being the operative word."

Naiche shot out of his seat. They stood there, faces close. Victorio was taller and so he towered over his brother like a bitter tree. Naiche was shorter, indeed, but very fit and muscular, and if he wanted to, he could bring Victorio down and make small order of him. Around them, patrons began to take notice, pretending to party, but with a curious eye turned toward the disruption. Word of two Devil Dancers fighting would spread throughout the fleet; questions would be asked, demands would be made. It was an untenable situation. Hitting a superior officer, even if he was your brother, would be tantamount to suicide. Naiche blinked, and stepped back. "And so that's how it's going to be, huh? Captain Victory has made his decision, and all shall bow to him."

"Don't be dramatic, brother. You have a taste for Gulo blood as strong as any pilot."

"Yes, but why now? And why this particular action? Enemy fleet movements have been reported all over the Caustic Drift. What interests you so much about this particular report? You hate Captain Shriver of PTF. Why would you—"

"Gingu-sha has been spotted with that fleet."

Naiche's mouth dropped open.

The greatest Gulo fighter pilot was Gingu-sha. His kills alone matched those of the entire Devil Dancer unit. His name drew fear even from the crews of capital ships. One story told of how Gingu-sha single-handedly dispatched a Union destroyer, crashing into its hull with a burrowing torpedo and then fighting his way to the bridge, where he massacred the crew and drove the ship into Starbase Calvin, only to escape unscathed on a shuttle. A destroyer did indeed strike the starbase, but whether or not Gingu-sha was responsible was unclear. Since everyone on the ship died on impact, there were no eye-witnesses to confirm the event. But that hardly mattered. The stories were out there, and his reputation and skills were undeniable.

Over the years, the Devil Dancers had had opportunities to take the Gulo ace down. The Battle of Two Dwarves, Cassini Station, the Emerald Rim, Ambush at Three Moons. Battle after battle, and yet the *na-de-gah-ah* had always slipped the net. On one particular occasion, Gingu-sha had turned his fighter upside down and aligned his cockpit with Victorio's, after he had shot a hole through Victorio's engine and left him for dead. They drifted there for a long while, and the beast could have, at any time, looped around and fired his guns. But he didn't. They just drifted, both of them looking at each other through the cockpit glass, an arrogant smile spread across the creature's black lips. Perfect black teeth with a darting pale tongue. His pure-white fur was as beautiful as the first snow of winter, his eyes blazing red hot like fire. And then he gunned his engines and was gone in a flash of blue energy.

From that moment on, Victorio vowed to find and kill Gingu-sha and put his pelt on the wall of the Devil Dancers' headquarters on the light carrier *Justice*.

"Gingu-sha is your albatross, brother," Naiche said, "not mine."

Victorio ignored his brother's insult. "And I've decided that you will be the clown."

Naiche's expression turned from anger to surprise. "Me? But what about Music-Maker?"

"He's down with fever. He'll not be ready when we depart."

"But you have never allowed me to play the clown. Why now?"

"The opportunity is here, Naiche. Do you accept this honor, or no?"

Naiche stood there rubbing his face. Victorio could see the passion behind his brother's dark eyes.

Naiche nodded. "Yes, I will accept the honor. I will be the clown."

Victorio breathed a sigh of relief. "Good. Now gather the men. We leave immediately."

Naiche stiffened and saluted. He was back to his old self. "Don't worry your fat, arrogant head, brother. I'm the best goddamned pilot you have. I won't let the Devil Dancers down."

Yes, you are the best, brother, Victorio said to himself as he watched Naiche leave the room. *But let's see just how good you really are.*

Victorio moved his head and eased his fighter up and down the spread of jagged rocks along the crest of the mountain. He could have easily steered the craft above the bright, white spires and let it whisk unimpeded through the low clouds. But no. He would not do that. He would not shame himself by taking the easy path. He would neither shame himself nor his brother who lay wrapped in a blanket behind him on the cockpit floor.

He blinked thrice to disengage his head from steerage and peered out the cockpit window. His eyes widened. The blur of rock, sand, and arrowweed below jogged memories. Memories of boys with brown, ratty hair, sun-browned skin, and dirty buckskin leggings. Memories of breathless runs up mountain paths with mouthfuls of water. Memories of wrestling matches and bareback races. Good memories. Bad memories. Memories even the dark, cold vacuum of space could not erase. But as he eased over the last crest and focused the landing reticule on a black concrete pad in the distance, his heart raced.

He was home.

His weapon, a single-seat, fixed-wing *Radiant*-class fighter was an older model with inherent up-draft problems. It was made for space battles and did not fly well planetside. But he—and thus his squadron—refused to change. They did what their captain told them to do...even if it killed them.

He set the fighter down carefully on the landing pad, its anti-grav chutes turned downward, engaging automatically as it wavered in place, then inched down until its three deployed legs touched the hard surface, cushioned, then solidified. A perfect landing. Victorio allowed himself a tiny smile. It had been awhile since he had had to do that. It was good to know that the old skills were still there and could be called upon quickly. But his smile turned sour when he looked out the cockpit window at the small man standing twenty meters portside. "Yusn Life-Giver," he whispered to himself and took a deep breath, "give me strength."

Victorio removed his helmet, shook his long brown hair free, wiggled his nose, then sneezed. *Damn allergies!* He'd been on Earth for only a few minutes and already they plagued him. He wasn't used to the fresh, warm air of a planet. He suppressed the urge to sneeze again and tapped his fingers along the pulsating red line of the engines panel. The engines wound down and the red line turned orange, then green, then yellow, until a slight hum replaced a whirling chaos. He did not want to turn them off completely. He was not staying long.

He tapped the cockpit hood and it opened like the mouth of a snake. Despite his allergies, Victorio breathed deeply. He unbuckled and stood up. He was weak, tired, the weight of gravity causing him to pause and gather himself. The artificial gravity of the *Radiant* was supposed to slowly adapt to all outside environments so that the pilot's body had time to adjust before disembarking. But this never quite worked in practice. There were always slight differences in pressure, and a less hearty pilot could become ill or break bones if he moved too quickly. Victorio stood there and let the warmth of the morning sun bake his brown skin.

Then he turned and lifted his brother off the floor from behind the pilot's seat. His body was heavy in death, but still flexible. In his belly had been placed a small silver tablet which released an enzyme that kept the body warm and the blood liquefied. It also softened the joints. In time, the tablet would dissolve and the body would stiffen, just as all humans do in death. Victorio pinched his eyes shut momentarily, then stepped out onto the wing.

As he reached the tip, the fighter dipped slightly to create a ramp which Victorio stepped down slowly, careful not to stumble or slip and lose his hold. He stepped off the wing and the fighter stiffened gently. He walked across the black pad, his heart in his throat, his eyes fixed on the man who waited.

He stopped in front of the man who stood several inches shorter, clothed from head to toe in light tan buckskin leggings and vest. His long hair was braided with turquoise beads and false rubies. Two hawk feathers were stabbed into the hair and waved in the warm breeze. His eyes darted back and forth between Victorio and the wrapped body. There were tears rimming the bottom of those dark eyes, and his cheek muscles worked nervously as if grinding bone.

"Father," Victorio said, holding himself steady, showing no signs of fatigue though his arms shook with the weight of his brother. "I bring you your son, Naiche "Blackclaw" Nan—"

The man put up his hand quickly. "Do not say his name. It will never be spoken again."

Victorio bit back his frustration. "He has a strong name, Father, and it is well-respected in the Federated Union. He is a warrior, the Champion of Europa and the Ward of the Crimson Sun. He received the Golden Spear for his actions at Alpha Centauri and clusters for bravery. He is a Devil Dancer. His name deserves to be spoken."

Father ignored his son's outburst and pointed to the ground. "Set him down, please."

Victorio did so. Father fell to his knees and put his hands on the blanket. "Father," Victorio said, "I don't think it's a good idea for you to look—"

"Do you think I'm afraid of death?" Father said, looking up at his son, his eyes now glaring in anger.

Victorio shut his mouth and the old man opened the blanket. Reconstructive surgery had reset Naiche's jaw and had re-grafted the skin which had been peeled away with fire. The ribs on his right side, where the energy bolt had landed after piercing the cockpit, had been re-formed as best as possible. The rest of his body, severely burned, had been left alone. There was little reason to do much more on a corpse.

Father ran his fingers across his son's jaw and down his chest. He lingered there for a moment, his weary eyes moving up and down the shattered body. "How did he die?"

Victorio told him.

Father nodded, folded the blanket back over the chest and face, and stood. "He was not a Devil Dancer," Father said, so low that Victorio almost did not hear. "He was *Ganh*, a mountain spirit, sent by Yusn Life-Giver and so are you. 'Devil dancer' is a White Eyes term."

"There are no White Eyes anymore, Father," Victorio said, lifting his brother back into his arms. "There are only human beings...and *others*. We are all in this together."

Father huffed. He turned and walked toward the rancheria which sat far in the distance. From here, Victorio could barely make out the domed roofs of the three dozen or more wickiups which dotted the harsh landscape. But he followed in silence and thought about the Life-Giver and *Ganh* mountain spirits.

Father was right in that the term "devil dancers" was a name given to the *Ganh* impersonators by a white man who had mistaken their dancing as erratic, out of control, evil. But that was hundreds of years ago, long, long before Father was born. And in the bitter vacuum of space, perception was just as important as rockets, torpedoes, lasers, ion cannons, and energy bolts. A "devil" garnered respect, from colleagues and enemies alike. That much, at least, Victorio had learned about war in his time among the stars.

Victorio shook his head. "Why do you persist in this harsh land, Father? I send you money all the time. You can afford to live a better life, in a better place."

"And where is that?" Father asked.

"Many other tribes have already left Earth. They are living good, peaceful lives on other planets."

Father snickered. "Peaceful... until the Gulo arrive."

All my fault. "We are winning the war, Father," Victorio said as they reached the bottom of the hill. The rancheria lay a quarter mile away. "The Gulo will not prevail. I promise."

"Yes, White Eyes promises much, but delivers little."

His anger welled again. "There aren't any White Eyes, Father. How many times do I—"

Father turned on his son and raised his hand again. "Spare me your lectures, son. You may live among the stars, but you have a lot to learn. I have seen the end in my dreams. The Gulo *will* sweep the Union away, and at the end of time when they come to punish Earth, when they come to this desert, this inhospitable place of rock and brush as you call it, we will make our stand, and Yusn will decide our fate."

Father turned and walked away. "Now, come," he said, "and bring He-Who-is-Gone. We have a lot do to. The ceremony is at dusk."

Victorio stood and watched his father walk away. He could not contain his anger any longer. "His name is Naiche "Blackclaw" Nantan," he shouted. "And I am Captain Victorio "Tomorrow's Wind" Nantan. These are the names that you have given us. They are proud names, respected names. They deserve to be spoken."

But Father did not speak them.

The command squadron arrived near midnight, dropping out of the sky like metal birds and churning the desert floor into sand sprites and dust clouds. The heat off their engines warmed Victorio's skin as he waited for their landing, the scent of *tula-pa* heavy on his breath. He had drunk too much, his mind hazy and unclear, but what did it matter? By morning, none of it would matter. He wiped away a tear and waved them down.

There were three squadrons that comprised the entire Devil Dancers unit. One command squadron (Alpha) and two auxiliary squadrons, Beta and Gamma. The auxiliaries contained junior officers and pilots recently added to the roster. In time, some of them might be so honored to be bumped up to Alpha, if they possessed the right mental and physical capabilities...and if a spot became available. As Victorio watched the pilots of Alpha approach him through the swirling dust, it was strange not to see his brother among them. He could not remember a time when Naiche was not there. Now Naiche's place was occupied by Warren "Red Moon" Benito, a capable but very young Apache lieutenant brought up from Beta just three short days ago. Would he survive? Victorio wondered. Time would tell.

The air cleared and Blue Bird and Shines Like the Sun stepped forward. Victorio relaxed. It was good to see old, familiar faces again, pilots that he had flown with for years. Blue Bird still limped from her foot reattachment, and Shines Like the Sun, his face in a perpetual smile, breathed deeply, still growing used to his new heart. But they had fought bravely at Castor V and had survived.

Victorio kissed Blue Bird on the forehead and hugged her deeply. "It is good to see you, Captain," she said. Her voice was soft, tinged with grief, but strong.

Victorio pulled away. "It is good to see all of *you*. I'm glad that you came. Naiche would be proud."

"What are your orders, Captain?" Shines Like the Sun asked.

Victorio looked to the ground. There lay a grave of freshly dug earth, rocks and soft soil piled on top. He bent down and placed his hand on a stone and rubbed it gently as if it were the head of a baby. The funeral had gone well, and Naiche's spirit was now on a horse and making its way, like a true warrior, into the hereafter. "We dance," he said. "We dance for Blackclaw."

And they danced, adorned brightly in their Ganh costumes. Buckskin kilts with large, richly-colored headdresses of green, red, and white. Feathers were attached here and there to wave in the desert wind like fingers. Fixed to the top of the headdresses were u-shaped arms with lines of sharp teeth that jutted into the night sky to connect the flesh to the great cosmos. They danced, like Yusn Life-Giver had instructed, when he sent the mountain spirits down to the Apache to teach them how to live a good, honorable life. Be good to others, good to yourself. Aid the poor, heal the sick. These were the things that they danced for. They danced for these things in honor of their fallen brother. And they sang too, though it was forbidden to sing over the grave of a fallen warrior. They sang the old songs. They sang to Yusn.

> In the middle of the Holy Mountain,
> In the middle of its body, stands a hut,
> Brush-built, for the Black Mountain Spirit,
> White lightning flashes in these moccasins;
> White lightning streaks in angular path;
> I am the lightning flashing and streaking!
> This headdress lives; the noise of its pendants
> Sounds and is heard!
> My song shall encircle these dancers!

They built a bonfire. They stoked it until the flames reached into the dark sky. The four main Ganh impersonators approached the flame, their bodies moving to music that only they could hear. They approached, they fell back. They approached, fell back. Again and again like tradition demanded, to reflect the mountain spirits moving rhythmically into the world of the living. Victorio watched and waited. This time...he was the clown. He had put on his brother's uniform and headdress, lined his face and bare chest in red, black, and white clay. He waited until the movements of Blue Bird were so erratic, so violent, that she fell to the ground.

Then he sprang, running straight to the fire, howling madly, shaking his arms, twisting his chest. Around him, he imagined scores of people, young children laughing and pointing. The clown was a thing of mirth and joy. The clown made funny faces and made people laugh, to lighten the mood for such a serious event. That was the traditional role of the clown. But among the stars, against the Gulo, a Devil Dancer clown was a thing to fear, a warrior not afraid to put himself out there, alone, to draw fire and allow the other dancers to swoop in and take victory. That is how Captain Victory had twisted and distorted the tradition for his own selfish gains. How many bright young men and women had he sent to their deaths? How many "clowns" had been blown out of the vacuum to cover his walls with white, black, and tan pelts?

Tears streaked down his face. The shimmering people around him pointed and laughed. *Murderer*, their lips said silently. *Murderer*.

"I'm sorry, brother," he said, twisting and turning his body as if possessed by a Ganh itself. "I have failed you, and I will not allow my weaknesses to kill anyone else."

He stared into the fire. A doorway opened, a large funnel of sand swirling down into the underworld. He smiled. Out of the orange-white flame came hands. Yusn's voice, calling him home. *Come, come*, a whisper tickled his ear. *Come to me*.

Victorio stopped dancing, raised his arms like wings, and leaped.

He fell into the middle of the flame. The fire roiled across his flesh. His body tensed against the searing heat, but he did not burn. He opened his eyes. He looked at his hands. They were soft, fresh skin ruddy with red clay. They were cool.

He blinked and suddenly he stood outside the bonfire, alone in his pilot's uniform. He felt a hand on his shoulder. He turned and stared into his father's face.

"What are you doing here?" he asked the image.

"Saving you from making a terrible mistake," Father said, his face weary, old, wind-swept.

"But I am guilty."

"Of what, my son?"

"I killed my brother. I killed Naiche."

Father's face grew stern, serious. *"Did you kill him, or did the Gulo?"*

"I sent him to his death."

"You did your duty. I could ask no more. Now don't be foolish and kill yourself. Do you think I want to bury two sons in one day?"

"But I have failed you, Father. I'm an embarrassment. Naiche was the one you loved, not me."

"That is not true. I love both my sons equally."

"Why have you never said so?"

"I—" But that was all Father managed to say. Victorio blinked and the image disappeared.

A large black bear appeared in front of him, claws bloody, teeth barred in a loud roar. It stood on hind legs. *"Attack me!"* it said, the words coming out of its foul muzzle in puffs of steam. *"What are you afraid of?"*

"Everything," Victorio said. An Apache feared the bear, for the spirit of an ancestor often came back to earth as a bear. To kill one, then, risked killing an ancestor.

"But your brother killed a bear, and nothing bad happened to him."

Maybe, maybe not. That was the story perpetuated by Naiche himself and oftentimes Father to show the fearlessness of his son. Victorio knew the story well, but had discounted it as ridiculous.

When he was a year old, Naiche had wandered away from the rancheria. He was missing for many hours, and night came and went. When they found him, he was covered head to toe in dried blood and dirt, hypothermic with the evening's dew. But in his hand he held a single black bear claw. Where had he gotten it, they asked him. He was too small to say, but the speculation grew. Naiche Nantan, now "Blackclaw" Nantan, was a little bear killer, the bravest of the Nantan boys.

"I cannot kill a bear."

"*You must, or you will die.*" The bear said, and rose up high on its legs. Then it leaped.

Victorio ducked and rolled, scrambled left to keep from being mauled by the beast's massive paw. The bear leaped again, snapping with its powerful jaws, catching him in the chest and throwing him across the fire.

Victorio screamed, rolled, and stood. The bear was on him again, grabbing his arm in its teeth and slinging him about like a doll. "*Kill me, or you will die.*"

"I want to die."

"*Then you are a coward, like they say.*"

"Who says?"

"*The Gulo. They speak about you. They laugh at you. Gingu-sha laughs at you.*"

Gingu-sha's pristine, white face came to his mind. The black teeth, the pale tongue, looking at him through a cockpit window...laughing.

Rage filled Victorio's mind. He pried himself away from the bear's grip and hurled himself onto its thick, broad back. The bear twisted and turned, snapped at his moccasins to pull him off. Victorio held tightly, and with all his strength, with all his anger, he plunged his hand into the bear's back, drove it through its spine, through its lungs and liver. He pushed his fingers into the warm flesh, found its heart, and yanked it out.

The bear dropped dead and Victorio hit the ground, rolled and skidded into the dirt. When the dust settled, he picked himself up, brushed off his pants, and walked over to the bear.

But it was no longer a bear. What lie there, in a heap of blood and fur, was something even more deadly. Something white, something...

Victorio opened his eyes. He lay beside the bonfire. Fuzzy images hovered nearby. He blinked several times, clearing his eyes of dust, tears, and sweat. Blue Bird's face was there, her expression quiet, comforting. She smiled. She raised her hand and rubbed a soft, wet cloth across his forehead. He let her do this a couple more times, then he sat up and looked around.

No blood, no bear, no Gulo. Just the steady crackle of the fire and the hard, dry ground against his legs. He stood, letting Shines Like the Sun steady his shoulders.

"Are you okay, Captain?" someone asked.

Victorio gained his balance and looked around. Was he okay? That was a difficult question to answer, but he nodded and said, "Yes, I think so. What happened?"

"You passed out," Blue Bird said.

"For how long?"

"Fifteen minutes?"

Victorio rubbed his face. It was a dream. All a silly, useless dream brought on by too much beer, too much excitement, too much emotion. He chuckled and shook his head. He raised his hand to rub his face again, but there was something in it this time. Victorio opened his palm.

A long, sharp black bear claw lay there. His heart sank. *Naiche's claw.* Where had it come from? It had been lost in the fire, it had not been found—

Then he remembered his dream, his Father, the bear, the Gulo. His mind raced. His heart soared. He gripped the claw and looked into the night sky.

"Would you like to sit back down, Captain?" Shines Like the Sun said. "Do you need rest?"

Victorio looked at his lieutenant, at his crew. He shook his head. "No. No rest for me, my friend. Suit up and strike the engines. We're going to war."

Behind him, the Devil Dancers fanned out in Eagle Pattern, the portside of their carrier *Justice* shielding them from the radiation of the nearby star. It was a bright, white-hot sphere of the Pollux Cluster, a perfect backdrop to the frontal attack called for by Admiral Cho. The enemy fleet sat a mere thousand kilometers away, cruisers and carriers mostly, and they had already seeded the field with anti-matter mines, energy sears, and radiation dampeners. But Captain Victory did not care. He had mapped out the best approach, and in Eagle Pattern, they would fly through the prepared defenses like broad wings in the sky, and the powerful light from the star behind them would give them the advantage.

"When we clear this field," he spoke over the comm to Alpha Squadron, "shift to Raven Pattern."

"So soon, Captain?" Blue Bird asked. "We don't even know the enemy fighter positions yet."

"Yes we do," he said. "I've already seen it."

And he had, twenty days ago as he danced around the bonfire and his brother's grave. He had seen everything clearly, concisely.

Shines Like the Sun screeched as his fighter nicked a mine. It ignited and tossed the fighter out of the pattern. "Watch your periphery, Lieutenant!" Victorio said.

Shines Like the Sun pulled the fighter out of its spin, rejoined the pattern, and said, "Yes, Captain. My apologies."

"Stay sharp, people," Victorio said, tilting his head and shifting the squadron to port. "We do this for Naiche."

They cleared the minefield. Before them lay the cruisers *Na-Ta-She* and *Vichu-Pa*. The Devil Dancers had fought against these mighty ships before. In fact, they were never seen separately, nor were they ever more than a few hundred kilometers apart in a Gulo capital ship formation. Gulo chatter captured on broadband always grew more steady and rhythmic when these ships appeared on view. There was something sacred, something profound about these vessels that went beyond their military purpose. The Gulo treated these ships with a reverence that, to this day, was not fully understood by Union Intelligence. The fact that they were here, and on the front line, meant that the Gulo were serious. They had staked out their position and had no intention of giving ground. Victorio sensed his pilots' apprehension at the sight of the enemy cruisers. "We've no worries about *them*, my Devils. Let them have their gods. Our target is much smaller."

Scores of red dots appeared on radar. "Enemy fighters, sir!" Red Moon said. "Straight ahead."

Gulo fighters did not fly in any defined pattern. Chaos was their pattern. As best as they could tell, there were no squadron leaders or captains in any fighter group. Every Gulo pilot was an individual weapon, whose mission was simply to find a ship that didn't look like one of theirs and blow it away. They were extremely skilled at that, Victorio had to admit. But it was also easy to exploit their lack of order, divide them and pick them off piecemeal.

"Raven!"

Victorio pushed a button on his cockpit panel and the exterior of his *Radiant* turned pitch black. The others followed suit, and against the bright light behind them, they seemed invisible to the untrained eye, and in the chaotic mass of enemy ships that swirled into view, they would fly in and wreak havoc.

The formation tightened, closing the wings. "Rockets!" Victorio said and pressed a button on his weapon's pad with a quick jab of his thumb.

Six rockets burst from each fighter, screaming through the deadly space between them and the Gulo. Such a large rush of munitions seemed to shock the enemy. They divided, some ramming into their own ships. The rockets spread out and captured the emission trails from Gulo fighters, locked on, hit, and exploded.

Victorio's cockpit windows grayed momentarily to protect him from the blast. The problem with Raven Pattern, unfortunately, was that your position was almost always exposed on the first launch of rockets. That's what Blue Bird was concerned about, but now was not the time for caution. The rockets exploded and their sudden flash of light alerted the enemy fighters to the Devil Dancers' position.

Gulo energy beams sprang to life.

"Scatter!" Victorio said, gunning his engines and rolling right, barreling down swiftly. Such a move was difficult to control, even for a pilot as skilled as himself. He lifted his head sharply to activate the stabilizing rockets so that the ship did not float against the vector too quickly, lose control, and drift aimlessly into enemy fire. Many Devil Dancers had been killed that way over the years.

Victorio righted his ship and flew into a mass of Gulo fighters. Blue energy zipped around him, scorching his wings, but failing to find impact. He looped twice, flew upside down, tapped his weapons pad, and sent red laser light into an oncoming fighter. But before the beams impacted, Red Moon swooped down and blew the enemy away with a spray of anti-matter bolts.

Victorio tensed as he burst through the shattered wing of the Gulo fighter.

"Woohoo!!" Red Moon's voice filled Victorio's helmet. He winced at the young man's screech.

"That was my kill, Red Moon!" Victorio said.

Red Moon silenced. "I'm sorry, Captain. I thought you were in danger. I was trying to, I was—"

"Forget it! Next time, stay out of my frontage."

"Yes, Captain." He paused for a moment, then said, "May I claim its pelt, sir?"

All activity on the enemy fighter had ceased, and it was falling away. Inside its cockpit, Victorio could make out the brown and yellow pattern of the Gulo's thick fur, riddled with holes, but still relatively intact. What a lovely display it would make on his wall. Victorio sighed. "Very well, you may claim it. It was a good kill."

Red Moon yelped. A tiny missile shot from his fighter and connected with the dead ship, splayed open, flashed red, and began emitting a signal. After the battle, they would salvage the wreck and Red Moon would skin the Gulo on the floor of the carrier bay, cut out its heart, and dance around the carcass. Victorio smiled. It was a good day for the young lieutenant.

Where are you, Gingu-sha? He was out there somewhere, Victorio knew. Waiting, perhaps, behind the cruisers, letting less capable pilots weaken the Union force before showing himself. "Where are you, you white son of a bitch! Show yourself, or are you too afraid to fight?"

The comm link was on and the others could hear him, but they dared not speak. Their captain was calling out an enemy, challenging him to fight. They would not give their voices to the challenge, but they would give their support, in any way that he asked.

"Ganh Pattern!" he said. "I'm the clown."

He could sense Blue Bird's apprehension, her fear for what was coming. Not because she was afraid of the fight. She was one of the bravest pilots he had ever known. But fear for what her visions, her own dreams, had shown her. She pulled her fighter up beside him. They looked at each other through the dim gray. She mouthed words so that they would not be heard across the comm, kissed her fingers and pressed them to the glass. Victorio smiled and kissed her back.

Victorio gunned his engines, and into the swirling mass of enemy fighters, he flew alone.

I am the lightning flashing and streaking! Over and over, Victorio mouthed the song, drawing strength from its cadence, its rhythm. *My song shall encircle these dancers!* In his mind, he danced around a fire, his face lined in red and white stripes. Mountain spirits whirled around him, filling his lungs, his heart, his arms and legs, holding him up, keeping him steady as the enemy's weapons boomed in his wake. A Union fighter alone among the Gulo was a thing of respect, and a Devil Dancer clown always got the respect it deserved. Naiche had gotten it, Victorio remembered. They had parted before him, letting him fly into their midst as if he were one of them. And then Gingu-sha appeared, and the respect and the dance were over.

Victorio tapped a panel to his right. Radio waves burst from the sides of his fighter in short staccato blasts. The Gulo had extremely sensitive hearing, especially in the high decibel range. Their radios would pick up these blasts and emit the noise through all the fighters until they changed their frequency. It was a short-term solution, but it gave Victorio a moment to work without hindrance. He rolled and tapped his weapons panel. Anti-matter bolts shattered the hull of a Gulo fighter. It ignited the missiles inside and breached the hull. The collateral damage took out another two fighters. Victorio skidded left to avoid the chunks of armor tumbling in his path.

"Come out, Gingu-sha. *Come out, come out!*"

And then he was there, on the radar, a bright blue dot closing fast.

The Union had customized its radar so that they could tell by color what kind of enemy fighters were closing. Gingu-sha now flew a new model, one that they had experienced only a few times over the past several engagements. Union designated

Saw-class for its circular hull with extractable alloy teeth. Victorio gulped. If those teeth connected with a *Radiant* hull...

The enemy ace did not give him time to think. He flew across Victorio's vision cone slow and steady as if he were taking a mild stroll through a meadow. Victorio followed the ship with bursts of laser fire. Nothing connected. He turned the nose of the *Radiant* up and spun like a screw. Stabilizer rockets slowed the rotation and he dropped, tapped his weapon's pad and released the last of his rockets. They swirled off-radar, twisting and turning like one massive torpedo, zeroing in on the Gulo's emission trail. The *Saw* listed to the left, turned upside down. Scores of tiny needles shot out of the hull and shimmered madly like a swarm of hornets. Victorio watched in awe as each of his rockets, one after the other, fell into the swarm and exploded harmlessly. The Gulo righted his fighter and was gone.

"Dammit!" Victorio said, gunned his engines and pursued.

He's playing with me, Victorio thought. This was the Gulo way, a kind of counting-coup: How many times could Gingu-sha avert death before ending the chase? How many times had he averted death against Naiche? Victorio could not remember. The moments of that fight were fuzzy now, a blur in the mind. *You won't play with me, Gingu-sha. Not for long.*

He followed closely, matching the enemy pilot's every turn, every twist. Victorio kept his finger on his lasers, short bursts, then long, short, long, keeping the Gulo guessing, uncertain about whether to run or to stop and return fire.

Blue energy beams slashed out of the *Saw's* aft weapon's pod, singeing the *Radiant's* wings and knocking out an anti-matter bolt tube. The strike knocked Victorio away. He rotated his ship to compensate for the blast and tried to renew the chase. But that part of the dance was over.

He slowed and watched as Gingu-sha looped back on the pattern, the brilliant, smooth silver hull of his round ship bristling with lights and activation queues. "Great mountain spirits," Victorio said as he waited. He tapped his helmet to activate his comm. "Come and give me strength."

Scores of missiles launched toward him like shards of glass. Victorio activated his point defense and nudged his fighter forward, letting the missiles set their deadly path. A cloud of metal balls infused with passive sonar drifted out in front of his ship and created a glistening mesh. He waited, watching the tiny dots on his radar come closer, closer, closer, until he could wait no longer. He activated the mesh, then gunned his ship and turned hard to the right, tumbling over and over as each Gulo missile found a patch of balls and exploded. The shock wave of the strike pushed Victorio further than he wanted. He arched his back and pulled up. The radar screen still beeped with enemy munitions. *Damn!* The wall hadn't gotten them all. A half dozen still moved toward their target.

He flew, pushing his *Radiant* as fast as it could go. He twisted left, right, until the missiles were lined up correctly to hit his wings. He ignited his fore stabilizers and brought his ship to a halt. He waited, tensed against the impending strike, and closed his eyes.

The missiles pounded his wings, one after the other like a line of meteors striking a moon. Victorio held the arms of his chair tightly. His security belt dug deep into his shoulders. With each strike he was tossed around the cockpit, banged left and right, as the *Radiant* lost power and tumbled away like a leaf in a strong wind.

Then all was silent. The light of the Pollux star lit up his cockpit windows. He could not see, could not hear. The face of his father came to him, his brother, a loud, smoky room where he heard Naiche's laugh for the last time. A bear. A clown. Earth. Mountain spirits.

A shadow fell over his cockpit. Victorio looked up. Gingu-sha's bright, white face was there, arrogant and proud, staring at him again through the cracked glass. His pale tongue flicked, his black teeth popped together. He was happy, Victorio could tell. Joy was a universal feeling. The Gulo was elated by the fact that he had his prey where he wanted him. His red eyes glowed hot and his beautiful, thick fur glistened in the starlight.

Victorio smiled back. "I know how you feel, brave warrior. I've been there before." He straightened in his seat and mouthed the words though he knew the Gulo could neither hear nor understand if it could. "But you forget who you are facing. I am Victorio "Tomorrow's Wind" Nantan, Captain Victory, leader of the Devil Dancers, and proud brother to Naiche "Blackclaw" Nantan. We are the lightning flashing and streaking. We are the Ganh. We are the mountain spirits. We are Apache. And we *never* fight alone."

Laser light and anti-matter bolts slammed into the Gulo ship, a relentless array of firepower that blew Victorio back into his chair and knocked his fighter clear.

Blue Bird and Shines Like the Sun came into view, their fighters swirling, their weapons hot. The enemy ship looked like a pinball as Gingu-sha worked his panels desperately to get away, to fire weapons, to do anything, but it was too late. Rockets launched and slammed into its hull. Fire swept the cockpit. White fur burst into flames. Gingu-sha mouthed a silent scream. The *Saw* exploded.

Victorio rested in the dark, cold cockpit of his fighter. He thought about something Father had said, something he had seen in his dreams. '*The Gulo will sweep the Union away.*' He nodded. Perhaps one day, yes. The war was far from over, and the Gulo were still very strong. But not today. "Today, Father," Victorio said, reaching into his breast pocket and pulling out Naiche's black bear claw, "today, your son...your *sons*, prevailed."

Blue Bird pulled up beside him and launched a drag cable around one of his mangled wings. She pulled him close and they looked at each other through the glass. "Cutting it a little close, weren't you?" Victorio said through his head gear.

Blue Bird smiled. "Sorry, Captain. We were giving you a chance to win."

He smiled, nodded, and looked out toward the battle. The capital ships were closing. Torpedoes were being fired, ion cannons were belching. The war raged on.

"What are your orders, Captain?" Shines Like the Sun asked.

Captain Victory breathed deeply, tucked the claw away, and said, "Let's go home, my Devils. Let's go home."

NUMQUAM DE OBLIVISCARIS

THE OATH

From the Chronicles of the Radiation Angels

James Daniel Ross

THE AIR SMELLED BURNED TO DEATH, CARBON AND OZONE MIXING INTO AN acrid cocktail that whispered 'war' to all who knew to listen. The dropship revved engines that further scorched the barren ground as the incoming scream of mortar rounds pierced the sky. The auto-defense turret on top of the *Seraphim's Strike* spun almost too fast to track, spitting two hundred centigram finned darts at eight times the speed of sound, swatting explosive shells off their flight paths. A hundred meters below the crest, one remaining *Angel* grasped at the belts of grenades left by his team, pulling pins and lobbing them high into the oncoming enemy squads. It was a beautiful last stand, but even as the explosive orbs showered enemy soldiers with jagged shrapnel no one could doubt it would be, in fact, a last stand. Though many hid from the grenades, too many more were coming up the narrow ravine to replace the fallen.

The *Angel* cursed violently as he fumbled through belt after belt and discovered no more ordnance. The constant beat of detonating grenades came to an end, and he readied his and an abandoned Mk4 21/3 Oberon pulse plasma rifle. Like an action hero, he propped them both over the denuded section of wall that served as cover just as several enemy soldiers decided the grenade rain was over and stood up. With a primordial cry, the *Angel* depressed both triggers and rode the recoil from the superheated packets of energy as he moved the barrels back and forth blindly.

When set 'full auto' the Mk4 21/3 fluttered the magnetic chamber five times a second, draining one capacitor every time the magnetic bottle contracts, and thus ejecting three hundred superheated packets per minute. There were four hundred capacitors inside the stock of the Mk4. The integrated microfusion power plant could charge one capacitor every two seconds. It created eighty-eight seconds where fires hotter than found anywhere in hell cracked stone, vaporized flesh, and cratered armor. The weapons vibrated within a second of one another, signifying they were recharging, and the *Angel* dumped them to the ground. He yanked two more from the pile left by his team mates and levered them over the wall as well. This time, he alternated triggers, firing with one till empty, then firing the next, heating pieces of crushed cityscape until they ran like wax, setting plastics on fire, and killing two more soldiers.

Then, there it was, the sweetest noise to any soldier on the field of battle. The *Angel* ducked down as the *Seraphim's Strike* roared to full power from the top of the steep rubble hill. With eyes tearing up, he watched his team depart for safety and freedom.

He took a deep breath to cleanse himself, glancing down at the bloody compression bandage worked into the messy crack in his thigh armor. The autodoc plugged into the hip joint was still beeping along merrily as it stubbornly continued to feed him microbursts of medication that kept the limb functioning and comfortably numb. He took off his helmet and dropped it to the rocky debris, glancing at the numerous rifles and the few demolition packs. It seemed like a shame that the only thing he had gotten real distance out of was the grenades. Still, war had rules, and his part in this one was over.

Helmet off, the *Angel* stood with his arms raised in the universal signal for 'You win this round, dirtbags.' Out of the corner of his eye he could see the *Seraphim's Strike* shrink into a dot and then flare like a monochromatic sun as it kicked in the nuclear reaction drive for ascent into orbit. Ahead, the enemy soldiers crawled out of the cracks and crevices into which they had been busy stuffing themselves until just moments ago. The *Angel* smiled and shrugged with his empty hands still in the air.

One of the enemy smiled back.

Then he shouldered his laser rifle and fired.

I brought them in, but did not give them leave to sit. The one or two offenders who dared decide to lounge without permission stood gratifyingly quickly under my sharp gaze. The singular soldier who decided to test me was picked up bodily by a two-ton metal cyborg sergeant and even at this very second should be in the middle of being discharged from my ship.

In the middle of battle, soldiers will follow anyone who shouts with enough authority. That was just basic programming. I had the title. Anyone could give themselves the title. These were mercenaries, not men or women who would follow a title. I had the paperwork. Truth be told, many men had the deeds to mercenary companies. Didn't make them leaders and it didn't make warriors follow them into battle. This was it: The moment where we find out if I really was in charge, or not.

"Some of you were there when Captain Arthur died. Many of you are new. Before we get to the business of being *Angels*, I have a mission of a much more personal nature. We are going to retrieve one of our own."

The crew looked at one another covertly. The gigantic *clusterfrag* of a mission that had given me command was quickly gaining legendary status in the mercenary community. In fact, there were bets flying fast and free taking odds on whether I would last out a month as Captain with the crippled merc company. Everyone in the room knew all of this. That is why I faced them without emotion, without recognition, without embarrassment, proud and straight and unyielding as an Angry God of War. Many knew me well, had fought and bled with me over the years, but as I stepped into my role of Captain the man they knew died.

"We are going in without cover, alone, operating covertly." Covertly is a word mercenaries hate.Covertly means without uniforms, meaning operating as a spy. That means if the enemy catches you they shoot you—with or without trial—torture, optional only in that everyone does it but nobody technically has to. "We will go in, get one of our own, and return with him to *Deadly Heaven*."

The canned atmosphere became heavy with unanswered questions as I let the silence lend weight to the hammering seriousness of my words. "I will only take volunteers, but I need at least two electronic warfare officers. The pay is ten thousand."

HWO—Heavy Weapons Officer—Cole, a woman who watched me make my first drop as a Scout years ago, cleared her throat, and when I didn't take off her head, asked, "Is there anything else you can tell us...Captain?"

"The job will last one night—literally twelve and one half hours. The job site is heavily irradiated. All I can say that will make any kind of difference to most of you is that I'll be there with you, every single step."

One of the new *Angels*, Lt. Mencken, bristled but tried to hide it. "Don't you trust your officers, Captain Rook?"

I fixed him with a stare that could warp steel. *Not you. Not yet.* "This job is personal."

A shudder went through the room as Mencken shook his head, "Personal?"

I nodded, "He is an *Angel*. He is a friend. I made a promise to bring him back."

And the soldiers glanced at one another out of the corners of their eyes, unsure. For which one of them did not cringe at the idea of a boss whose emotions were in control of a mission? Which one of them would not lay down their lives for the sake of those with whom they had bled? Which one of them did not want a boss who would move mountains and stars to keep an oath?

And then they had one last thing to weight: for the last job had been a meat grinder, a knife fight with guns that had birthed thousands of seams, hundreds of replacement limbs, and fields of dead bodies. All the same, with the loss of Captain Arthur I had brought them together, forged them into a unit, and gotten the living *Angels* home. The reason the new members were here was they had heard. They had heard of me, and believed enough to join up. Now I found out if they believed enough to follow, yet.

"I need volunteers," I said.

Everyone raised their hands.

I nodded. "I will alert the team for briefing and mission loadout in twelve hours. Prepare to cast off and make for slipspace. Dismissed."

The *Angel* lay on the rubble, his chest burning with the remains of his armor fused into a single plate. The high-density laminate plastic had done its job; vaporizing and channeling the coherent light into the honeycomb of opaque cells woven under the hard plates, dissipating the energy by turning metallicized plastic into vapor, saving his life. It was little comfort as the smiling soldier came around the short wall, gun in hand.

"You bastards," the *Angel* groaned.

The soldier kicked him, then kicked him again. The *Angel* curled around the foot in his gut, but the enemy rolled him onto his back and pressed him flat. The barrel of the laser hovered at the end of his nose.

But the Angel was not alone, I, his partner, his Pair, was here. I crested the hill above him and roared, "Kendel!"

Kendel, still on the ground, looked up for who had called and saw me. His instincts served him well, for he rolled to the side as I depressed my trigger.

And then there was gunfire.

The volunteers were having second thoughts. One of them was fondling one of the mission-specific weapons I had chosen. "Captain Rook, what's this?"

I was busy strapping into the Personal Nuclear Turbine Unit.

"It is a Walther and Wesson Lightning Lance."

Another came up with a magazine of ammunition, palmed out one slug, and stared at the thing as if were an alien insect. "This is not cascading capacitance discharging gel. What the hell does this thing do?"

"It is a self-contained autodoc, clamping, laser drilling, and injector unit." I tightened the straps down and jumped up and down, which has always been the best way to check to make sure the straps are tight enough and has always made soldiers look like idiots.

Another *Angel* coming into the armory snatched the thumb-sized cartridge and peered at it closely, "A launchable autodoc? What good would a chemical reservoir of this size be good for?"

"It hits, clamps down, drills into the armor down to skin and then injects a powerful sedative, regulating the doze while monitoring the target's lifesigns."

HWO Cole shook her own turbine pack to ensure there was no slippage. "Those things have an autodoc? That's got to be expensive."

"Fifty-five credits a shot, so shoot straight." The pack was like being hugged by a terribly clingy gorilla, so I figured it was just about perfect. "Truth be told, I don't think we will even have to use them."

"Ok, Captain, so where's the deadly ordnance?"

"This is a rescue mission." I grunted, then slapped the quick release on the pack. The buckles parted as one, dumping the turbine pack onto the spring hanger set into the ceiling. I turned and steadied the bouncing pack at the end of the steel assembly holding it loosely from crashing into the deck. It saved me from ignoring their faces when I said, "There will be no deadly arms or ordnance on this drop."

The temperature of the room plummeted.

The top half of the man towering over Kendel just vaporized. It was gruesome, it was pitiless, and I did it again a heartbeat later. From the steep hill overlooking his position, the pinnacle still smoking from the engines of the departed dropship, I rained death upon the enemies of my friend.

The machinegun chewed through ElectroThermal/Chemical rounds like a ravenous beast, showering the approach to Kendel's position with steel-cored, full-metal jacket hornets that bounced amongst the rocks. A few desperate shots came back, but they were far too low to reach me. Instead of respite, their defiance bought only more vengeance. The gun clicked empty, and within a second I had another box of ammunition at the auto-feed port. The gun slurped up the linked ammunition and fired again, bullets bouncing behind cover to kill and feed on the flesh found there. It was rage written in an endless roar of gunfire. Even the survivors were scarred by the sound.

There was no way I could carry the gun and ammunition any farther, so I made the decision to empty the damn thing here.

Lyman was not a brave man. He had never had to be. Instead, he shuffled numbers from one column to another. On other occasions he faced off with the most brilliant minds a planet could muster to build papier-mâché galaxies out of words carefully balanced upon one another. He was our lawyer, and our lives depended upon him on every single drop.

Smart. Subtle. Nerves of steel. Brave, not so much.

"Sir, I am afraid this is highly irregular."

I said nothing, but simply sat in his richly appointed cabin and sipped the proffered cup of real coffee. The rich, smoky flavor slid gentle hands along my spine, but did little to calm me. The silence robbed him of arguments, of the words he needed as much as a bulwark against liability as weapons to pry my own opinions from my hands.

"Sir, I understand you have only just taken command of the Radiation Angels, but I must protest your current set of actions. I have to say that any objective reading of the situation would bring one to the inescapable conclusion that—"

"I have noted your protest, Lyman. Is there anything else?"

"No, sir, you have not noted a damn thing. You are dangerously close to working on a Guild-unsanctioned job."

"Don't play games. I have the contracts in your hands, Lyman."

"Playing games, sir? You know full well that you have ordered the quantum communication array silenced."

"Just until we reach planet Kaliningrad. We must ride silent. Mission parameters, you see."

Lyman flushed, setting down his fine china cup on the oak table before clutching his fingers white on his lap. "Sir, you cannot simply take off your team on some kind of vendetta—"

"It is not a vendetta. We are carrying nonlethal weapons."

"You are setting down with armed soldiers on a hostile planet."

"And that is why filing the paperwork too early would only alert the Kalininites to our presence."

"This is a mercenary team, not your personal toybox! There are rules to being a professional, bonded, mercenary team. One cannot simply hire oneself!"

I barely caught the angry words that leapt to mind before they smacked him in the face, still my tone was sharp, "I am hiring the team."

Lyman lost control of his arms and they flailed in the torrent of scandal. "You are leading the team!"

"I am the only one who has ever set foot on Kaliningrad." It took everything I had to remain calm. "I am going along as an advisor."

"Sir, this is entirely irregular. Any formal board of inquiry will find you acting as a freebooter at least, pirate at worst. They will hang you and televise the event."

"Kaliningrad doesn't have that kind of pull."

"Sir, they will do it not for some brutish backwater bombed-out hell of a planet. The Mercenary Guild will do it simply to maintain their own reputation."

I looked at our lawyer, and could see the turmoil there. I had never had too much to do with Lyman on any regular basis, but he had always struck me as slightly pampered, but competent and honest. I stood, "We are on our way to a mission, but if you wish to resign your post I will accept it the moment it is over."

I made it to the door before he stopped me, "Do you really think he is alive?"

"I told you to get on the damn dropship."

"*Frag* you, asshole, I don't take orders from you." The word *anymore* hung, unsaid, between us as I shouldered Kendel and pulled him upright. Behind me smoke grenades popped off, spewing specially formulated crystal infused fog to disrupt the use of laser rifles such as the Kaliningrad standard issue.

"Ooh, couldn't be shown up by your old partner?"

I shoved one of the MK4 21/3s into his hand. "If you can bitch, you can run."

And he stood, but unsteadily, as I swept up the demolition packs, pausing only to crank one to armed and dump it on the pile of rifles. No sense in upgrading the gear of the enemy.

Kendel was laughing bitterly. "You look like a satanic Santa Claus."

And he was right. I had grabbed everything from the dropship I could, and even after leaving the fully empty and half-melted machine gun above, only fear was keeping me from noticing how much weight was pulling at my spine. I swept Kendel's helmet off of the ground and shoved it roughly on his head. "This damn thing goes here, Sergeant!"

"Trying to remind me of proper decorum, Lieutenant?"

There was a dull pressure to run from the cowering Kaliningrad soldiers behind, and a sharp pressure from the silently counting demolition charge not three meters away. I got Kendel moving by grabbing him under the arm and half carrying him up the slope. "No, Sergeant, but I would hope that my *fragging* Pair would show a little gratitude that I came back to pull his worthless ass out of the fire."

Kendel stumbled, but he ran. The laser burn in his chest looked bad, but if he could talk it hadn't penetrated his lungs. It was the shrapnel hole in his leg, now bleeding profusely, that made me worry as I whipped him ever faster. "Your Pair? Your Pair? *Your Pair* told you to get off this forsaken rock."

It had only been minutes since I had returned, but I was already gasping under my load. Behind me the sound of the demo pack wrecking all the equipment we had left behind gave me a sudden second wind. "Are you cracked? You were the one who told me there was no such thing as heroes."

Kendel, a man whose first words to me amounted to: Don't shoot me because I'm white, was flushed under his visor, but only on the very tips of his cheeks. "I was trying to do something noble, you prick!"

He was losing blood. I needed to get him somewhere I could look at him. "And that's how I know you are out of your mind! If you are going to do something nice, at least have the decency to do it like an ass."

"*Frag* you, Rook!"

"You'd like it!"

We crested the hill and slid to the bottom on the other side. The entire way down I could see the city of Smyrna spread out before us. It was nothing but skeletal remains now, bombs having stripped the corpse a decade prior, leaving ground so poisoned not even weeds grew in the cracks and crevices.

Gunnery Sergeant Logan came into the Cold Bay, the only sound other than the throbbing secondary ion engines that pushed *Deadly Heaven* through slipspace, keeping it from kinetic loss. The bay was pressurized, but not insulated, and the cold of space barely held at bay by the presence of the whole of the ship. He closed the door behind him, spooling the lock tight with a flick of his metal wrist. To the casual eye, he was a two-ton war machine completely encasing his brain and spine without any but a passing resemblance to an ordinary foot soldier.

From inside the depths of my insulated coldsuit, I envied his lack of feeling, but I had always admired his purity of purpose. He was a warrior incarnate, without any visible signs of doubt or fear. I had served at first under, then with him, and then over him since the first day I had stepped aboard this spacecraft. He was a towering reminder of my responsibility, a measure against which I had to constantly place myself. I could not simply sit here, staring at the names of the dead inscribed on black steel plates bolted to the wall. His presence demanded an answer. He deserved one in any case.

I turned to him and inclined my head, but said nothing because I would be damned if he wasn't going to have to ask the question at least. We sat there in the cold, my breath making clouds that condensed into ice on his chest, for a very, very long time. Finally he spoke, speakers giving his metallic bass a quality of the spirits of earth and rock.

"Is it important, Captain?" Impossible to read, fruitless to ignore, he asked.

"Damn well better be, Guns. We are going," I said, immediately disappointed in the emptiness of my own answer.

The massive cyborg shook his head, but snapped a salute as he turned to go.

"Tanks? Holy fragging fux and grit-licking, goat-slamming, crack-cracking, pole-smoking, dog-fondling..." Kendel continued his vile litany to the God of War, but I tuned him out as I raised a detonator in my hand and cradled it like a child. The tanks swarmed down the boulevards of broken stone, barely clearing listing pillars and knocking over the hacked-off stumps of walls too stubborn to know they should have fallen ages ago. The moderate radiation cloud that enveloped this section of the city kept us off their scanners, but in the greatest traditions of fools everywhere, they had substituted boots for eyes. Even now, the dozen tanks were backed up by easily a medium-strength company of men that did the dirty work of checking each and every crack and crevice.

"Are you ready to run?" I whispered.

"Why are you whispering?"

My temper, cut even shorter by the damn soldiers coming down the road of abandoned hotels and skyscrapers, sharpened my words as they slid across the room to Kendel, "Are. You. Ready?"

I never took my eyes off the oncoming horde, but I assumed the movement to my left meant he was checking the newest autodoc to make sure it was keeping up with his leakages, seepages, cuts, burns, contusions, radiation-saturation level, and pain. It was doing its best, but there was only so much that could be done. Worse, the soldiers—who understandably didn't even want to find two armed soldiers in any of these spider holes—were falling behind as the tanks entered the center of my prepared area. Just like that, I very calmly and rationally decided to commit suicide, because there was only one way to make them bunch up again.

"Run, Kendel." I said.

He started to protest, but I shouldered the Mk4 Oberon and he limped toward the back escape route as fast as his wounded leg would allow. I counted twenty shuffling steps before I unleashed one long burst into the front end of the closest tank.

The front end of a main battle tank is made of laminate armor composites the likes of which man could only dream of a few centuries ago. The net effect of my concentrated packets of energy was to scuff the paint. Maybe. If it was crappy tank paint.

More importantly, it drew a straight line from me to the front of the lead tank, and thus inconveniently drew a line back to the half basement window from which I was shooting. That's why I didn't wait even a second to blow through the door perpendicular to the route Kendel had taken, dropping a fog grenade in my wake. It took only three seconds before the room behind me disintegrated under a plasma blast meant to breach said main battle tank's frontal armor.

The overpressure wave of concrete being heated into vapor sent me tumbling up the stairs onto the street, but under the cover of wrecked vehicles, I scurried across the street to the next building in the row. Instinctively, I clawed for altitude, rocketing up the steps as the tanks continued to batter our former hiding spot with magnetic bottles containing temperatures normally found inside of suns.

Trust me when I say tanks fear soldiers. Soldiers hide in the cracks and crevices of the world like rats. They carry explosives in nice, compact containers. One man costing thirty thousand to train and given a ten thousand-credit anti-tank charge can kill one of the armored beasts. From the first day of training, the tank commander taught that his half a billion credit device can be reduced to wreckage by forty thousand credits of fanatic. That's why they bring soldiers with them since the nearly prehistoric days of the Nazis. So when I opened fire from the second floor of the next building, they could not really be sure I was the first guy. Safer to assume I was a second enemy.

So as they brought guns to bear on the new position, just as two more fog grenades went off just in front of the building, I used the concealing vapor as I jumped the alley from the skeleton wreckage of one office building to another. The second story behind me also absorbed the hurled stars of fifteen tanks, but another gnat was stinging from a third building.

Now the commander decided he had risked enough of his own hide, and brought up the foot soldiers to cover him from what could be one, three, or fifteen men. The soldiers enveloped the tanks with guns much more suited to swatting flies like me, entering the area I had prepared this morning when I had learned they were chasing us.

I leapt from the second story to the ground as the cover behind me quickly became a conflagration. I hit wrong, twisting an ankle and rolling into a pile of rock as I saw the area around me sizzle as if from acidic rain. I popped a gas grenade to hold off the hail of laser fire and then I snatched the detonator from my belt and smashed the button like I had hated it for all my life.

All around the enemy soldiers the corpses of corporate titans shook as tiny demo charges, placed on stressed and lonely supports, took miniature bites from bones that could not afford the loss. The forgotten bodies of concrete huffed out clouds of dust and sagged, sliding into the street with the awesome power of weight and gravity. By the time they met steel and flesh, they had formed millions of angry fists, a singular cresting tsunami of bleached concrete and rust.

The ground trembled at the horrible loss of life, but I was already up and limping away. I found Kendel a few streets over, pale and gasping.

"There's goes our pickup site." he said.

"At first you complained about having to climb to the top of the building, now I bring the roof to the street and all I get is more bitching." I smiled tiredly. "There is just no pleasing you."

But he was deadly serious as he looked at the gobs of clotted blood seeping from underneath his bandage. "You should leave me."

I met his gaze unflinchingly. "No."

With only two rifles, a few grenades, and one demo pack left, I could wrap his arm over my shoulder easily.

My next words stopped Logan before he left the Cold Bay, "I promised him, Logan."

The huge, metal man turned, nodded once solemnly, and left.

There were few things mercenaries could rely on. First, last, and everything in the middle, is that if you give your word, it must be kept. The only thing more sacred than the word of your teammate is the word of your Pair, and the only thing more sacrosanct still is the word of the commander.

I had found a teepee made of collapsed walls with a rocky rather than dusty entrance so there was no trace of us coming or going. I snuck out at night and found the highest spot in the least burned-out building. I had collected sheets of metal that I wrapped around my position, hoping to focus the signal and cut down on how easy it would be to track.

I couldn't do it from memory I had to write in the dust:

MY MOTHER LOVES ME EVEN THOUGH I AM A BASTARD

Beneath it went a line of numbers, ticking off fingers as I laboriously converted base 26 to base 10:

MY MOTHER LOVES ME EVEN THOUGH I AM A BASTARD
35 350858 25259 35 5254 085178 9 13 I 2190184

I triggered the laser that drew the keyboard on the ground, and then punched in the sequence of numbers onto the concrete. The sensor eye saw my finger, knew what I wanted, and relayed the numbers to the computer inside the piece. Another button extended the earpiece and mic.

"Fox One to Hole, Fox to Hole. Do you read? Over."

"Hole to Fox One, what is your number? over."

"Two, say again Zero-Two, over." Just hearing the voice from *Deadly Heaven* made my insides flutter.

But they were not consoling words. "We have you. Hounds are running in your sector. Need to move. Over."

I had to clear my throat to be able to speak. I hoped I had moved the mic far enough away the operator didn't hear it. "Negative. One kit cannot run. Repeat: One kit cannot run. Over."

There was a long pause.

"Fox One, you are authorized to Escape and Evade. Over."

Escape and Evade. Just like that, they had told me I could leave Kendel behind, make my way to a more sparsely guarded grid coordinate, and get picked up. For a split second, all I could feel was overwhelming relief, and then crushing guilt. "Fox One to Hole, I did not read. Transmission garbled. Repeat: I did not read. Will try again in twelve hours, that is one-two hours. Over."

Somewhere in the vacuum of space far above me, Captain Arthur's strong voice came over the channel, "Stop *fragging* around, Rook. Kendel is a soldier. Get yourself two klicks east and we can send a ship for you."

I did not know if they heard me whisper, and frankly did not care. "Fox One to Hole. Will try again in twelve hours, that is one-two hours. Over."

I cut off the comm unit and made my way back to the fake cave. Kendel was asleep inside. The last autodoc was humming softly on his leg, but it could only do so much.

He awoke enough to grunt and ask, "Did you find any food?"

"No." I replied.

"Did I ever tell you about my daughter?"

"No." I repeated, but he was already asleep, radiation poisoning pushing him further out of consciousness than even his wounds. I could feel it starting to infect me as well. I asked myself if I were willing to die just to have a chance to save him. I ignored the answer.

Kaliningrad was such a bombed out, nowhere *grithill* that even I rated a face-to-face with the Head of Interplanetary Diplomacy. He wasn't being very diplomatic, though. "Be aware, Rook, we have been alerted to the posting of your current mission at *Haven*. We know you are coming here. We remember the *Radiation Angels* took up arms against the lawful government of Kaliningrad 5 on the side of the traitorous vermin and should you set down we would be fully within our rights to arrest, detain, and confiscate any and all property in or on our claimed space."

I tried to smile, to be ingratiating. "Mr. Soukhomlinoff, that was just business."

Which was true, but not likely to earn points. Soukhomlinoff flushed as his long moustaches trembled. "What was 'only business' to you mercenary scum was the eradication of two generations of Kalininite men!"

I held up my hands in the universal sign for 'I surrender'. I smiled like a man who just lost the biggest pot of the card game, but wanted to be invited back to the table. "Sir, you got me. The *Radiation Angels* left some equipment on planet when we were driven off by your fine military. Perhaps for a...I don't know, a finder's fee, we could perhaps have it back?"

I tell you this, though, if we were playing cards, I would not be the one losing. Soukhomlinoff's face played out every little thought that flitted through the vacuum between his ears. "If you meet me on planet, in Capital City, then we can negotiate."

"Absolutely. I will be preparing to drop in sixteen hours when we reach orbit." And after another dozen pleasantries neither of us really meant, we cut communication.

Behind me on the bridge, Lyman let out a sigh of relief, but then remembered who I was. "You're canceling the mission? You are going to meet with him?"

My tone capitalized both words, "Hell, No."

The smell was enough to make you forget your last ration bar was five days ago. When I looked in Kendel's eyes, I knew he could smell it too.

"You should go, Rook."

I didn't look at him, couldn't really. "No."

"I don't want to get you killed."

I denied the hurt, I denied the anger, I denied the tears behind my eyes. "If I can kill a company of men searching for your worthless ass, I can get you out of this."

"In war, men die."

"Not this war, not in this hellhole."

Deadly Heaven entered orbit at precisely the wrong time. The dropship that left the bay and entered atmosphere did so thousands of kilometers away. Soukhomlinoff protested, but at that point physics dictated the landing pad, not protocol. Still, we were flying over the abandoned battlefields of the Glorious Patriotic War Against Terrorism, and anything stealable had been stolen long ago. Our craft wasn't exactly fitted for pirating work, anyway.

Nothing would ever make *The Angel's Curse* look like anything more than a beat-up junker. It dropped fast through atmosphere, doubtless giving Soukhomlinoff a smile at how hard times must have been for the team. The craft clipped the radiation zone over the bombed-out city of Smyrna and then overcorrected to the east. The overcorrection caused a blowout in one of the engines. The pilot seemed to get it under control, but twenty minutes later, as the craft was approaching the capital, the engine detonated, crippling the craft.

The *Seraphim's Strike* left the docking bay within seconds, also on the wrong quadrant of the planet, but preparing to render aid.

Thirty minutes later, *The Angel's Curse* landed on the predetermined pad. The welcoming committee was fully armed, and leveled their weapons the second the dropship loading doors started to open.

There was a bright green beam of laser light that flashed from inside—laser scope or weapon nobody ever knew, but it was enough to cause the entire armed entourage, sent by Soukhomlinoff to arrest and ransom me and whoever else might be aboard, to open fire. They could not help but hit the canisters of Aeroline sitting in the middle of the junker craft.

The explosion was memorable.

He was feverish, but cold. His eyes had sunk into his head and he had stopped sweating due to dehydration. In this shell of a city, without even the shadow of survivors, there was no food, no water, no medicine. I had even traveled six hours back to the site where I had buried the tanks and soldiers, but I had done too good a job. Their tomb held their treasures tightly, and I had succeeded in wasting a full day's worth of energy I could not replace.

"You were the best partner I was ever assigned," Kendel said.

"I got you killed. What the *frag* did the other ones do to you?"

But he wasn't listening, not really.

"Don't let them bury me on this hellhole," he said.

"I promise." I replied.

As *The Angel's Curse* had flown too low over the dead city of Smyrna, my hand-picked team and I had leapt. As the autopilot continued on its merry way and the set charge on the engine continued to count down, the personal turbine packs slowed our descent, running cold on fusion-driven electric engines so they left little signature. Dependant on perfectly clean turbines and utter concentration to pilot, they were useless for front-line fighting. For a stealthy infiltration, they were just the thing.

We landed, and I used the Command and Control pad on my arm to activate the hardened microcomputer in my helmet. It sent out a ping—an interrogative signal. I got a response and the fist around my chest let go. Almost as one, the *Angels* leapt back into the sky, activating the turbine packs and turning a short hop into a five hundred-meter leap that ended as we gently lit to the ground. I sent out another ping.

Half a second later, I had an exact position of the little transmitter I had left behind against my return. It guided us through the maze of broken stone, the feeble battery on standby for so long I had nearly lost hope that it would work. I had to pause as I kneeled down by the entrance to that damnable stone lean-to that had housed us for so many weeks. I had always known I would have to come back. Now that I was here, I could not even look in.

I pointed at my demolitions man, "Door. Now. Be gentle."

Five minutes later, as an opening was made large enough for us to bring out Kendel, *The Angel's Curse* burned and spread Aeroline across the landing pad. Ten minutes after that *Seraphim's Strike* turned around from its rescue mission, hovering above us for scant seconds as we leapt from the sterilized soil up into the waiting loading door. I carried Sergeant Kendel myself. Once landed, however, I heard a cry.

HWO Cole, unsure of the turbine pack and not wanting to overshoot the *Seraphim's Strike*, had cut her power an instant too soon. She was trying to correct, and only overcorrected, slewing in midair as she lost control.

I dropped Kendel's feet, went to my knees, and lashed out with one arm. My hand slapped into her outstretched palm, and I heaved her aboard as the sounds of my joints popping filled my ears. But there was no time to be shocked. "Eject it all, *Angels*."

Cole and I detangled ourselves and joined the other members of the recovery team as they hit the quick-release buttons on their packs. The turbine packs went tumbling into the air, along with guns, oh-so expensive ammunition, helmets, and even boots. Smyrna had been a little radioactive the last time I had been here and it had been nuked several times since. Every piece of equipment we had now was poison, and going through radiation rehabilitation again held no attraction for me.

We left everything that could carry radiation behind in the roaring slipstream. Last of all was our Nuclear/Biological/Chemical protecting suits. We closed the loading bay as the air became too thin to breathe. I hit the wall comm. "Pilot, this is *Angels*, Actual. Get us the *frag* out of here."

The pilot switched to the nuclear-reaction drive and we were soon out of atmosphere and far away from the decrepit Kaliningrad military. Soukhomlinoff would have cursed my name. Would have, had he not been standing on the landing pad, been the one to give the order to fire, and thereby burned to a crisp. It would have bothered me except that a man who does not plan to betray, capture, and ransom someone who lands under a flag of truce does not show up with a platoon of armed men at the landing site.

Now there was just one more thing to do.

Well, two things, to be precise.

We landed on Hargus 4, engines cold and equipment stowed long before the civilians showed up. A lonely robotic lawyer exited one of the buildings across the field, and then headed for us with single-minded determination for easily five minutes. It arrived just as a personal transport flier circled our designated landing zone and settled next to the *Seraphim's Strike*.

A young woman, both beautiful and obviously barbed, climbed out of the cabin. She had his eyes. "My name is Captain Rook. Miss Kendel?"

Immediately, she was off her game, wrapping her arms tightly against her chest. "Aline. Mindy Aline."

"Your mother's name?"

"What do you want, Captain?"

And it was about that time the robotic lawyer rolled up. I stopped it from talking with an upraised hand. "I just need a genetic test to confirm you are Walter Kendel's daughter."

And again, her hard exterior cracked for a moment, her eyes dodging around the tarmac as if searching for escape. "Look, my dad ran out of my mom and I a long time ago, and if it's all the same to you I'd rather just forget—"

Again, I raised my hand. "I don't know what happened, but I know that Kendel's will dictates all of his worldly possessions and his bank balance be transferred to you." I beckoned at the cockpit of *Seraphim's Strike* and the pilot opened the loading door, exposing six *Angels* in dress uniforms carrying Kendel's coffin.

Despite her indifferent words, her face was stricken at the sight of the thing. I reached forward and laid a gentle hand on her shoulder. "I don't know what happened to make him leave, but I know you were in his thoughts. I know he left you everything he had. I know he did not want to be buried where he fell. I know it is not much, but this is the only closure you will ever have, and it will be the closest thing to a home he will ever know."

She squirreled that answer away for some future date to be integrated into the incomplete mental picture she had of an estranged father. I opened the pocket of my dress uniform and handed her the print-out statement of Kendel's bank account. She saw the number, and went pale.

The robot ran the genetic test, transferred the monies minus the taxes, accessed the personal effects, and set the quarantine status on the sealed coffin. Then the *Angels* loaded the thing into the back of Miss Aline's flier.

She looked up at me with tears in her eyes.

"What kind of man was my father?"

"He was kind to me when he didn't have to be. He was a good man when being an ass was easier. He saved my life many times. He died laying right next to me."

"Captain Rook, we will have no leniency for your young command. You have committed an act of war against Kaliningrad 5 and there will be an accounting."

I stood proudly in front of the Mercenary Tribunal on the planetoid of *Haven*. They tried it all; focusing light on me while keeping everything else in shadow, sitting high above me in a ring, making me feel surrounded. Still, I had no fear. "Sirs, I understand your position, but strip away all clouding issues and emotion from the case and you have these facts: *The Radiation Angels* entered the system and were detected and engaged diplomatically by a lawful agent of Kaliningrad. We negotiated a meeting under a flag of truce—verified by records you already have in your possession—and as soon as the craft landed they opened fire."

A shadowy figure leaned forward, "Why were there drums of Aeroline aboard?"

The lying, it turned out, was the easy part. "Because the craft in question leaked like a sieve. We could not be sure the negotiations would end peacefully and we would be allowed to buy fuel."

Another shadowy authority figure shifted in his seat. "And why were you not aboard the craft?"

I shrugged, "Because they were going to shoot me, sir."

Back to the first. "But why did they open fire?"

"I am not privy to the command structure or orders given by Kaliningrad military officers."

The leader, the one on the highest chair in the center of the U-shaped room, cleared his throat. "Did you steal anything from Kaliningrad 5, Captain Rook?"

A dozen retorts flitted through my mind, but I settled on the truth for once. "We stole nothing. We did, however pick up the body of one of our own, fallen in battle during a legally contracted combat operation."

The third, who did not like me for some reason, leapt upon that. "Then you admit to piracy, Captain?"

I set steel to my voice. "No, sir, for by the time we collected the body, the Kaliningrad military had already blown up my dropship. They committed an act of war, making Sergeant Kendel's body legally obtained spoils."

The silence left behind those words was deafening.

On the hot ground, under a bright sun, it seemed silly, overdramatic even. Yet there was only answer to Kendel's daughter.

"I risked execution to get his body back."

But then she shook her head slowly, "I'm sorry Captain, but I have to ask why?"

Walter Kendel had been a companion, a comrade, and a friend. Most of all, he was the one man in the universe that seemed as lost and alone, without a single family contact, as was I, myself. Someone out there, probably hundreds of someones, owed this dignity to him. I paid for us all.

What I said was, "Because I took a soldier's oath, Miss."

And as we lifted off, for all the *Angels* in the deadliest *Heaven* of all, that alone was enough.

THE CHILDREN'S CRUSADE

A Chronicle of the 142nd Starborne

Patrick Thomas

S HOOT ME IN THE FRACKING HEAD," SCREAMED JAMES OAK. HIS BODY ARMOR was ripped off and the flesh beneath was raw and bloody. "Do it now, soldier!"

"Sir, I don't think I can...." Former Private Sam Radwin was about as shaken as any combatant could be. Out of the ten soldiers in his unit, he was the only one to escape their last battle unscathed. In fact, only he and Oak survived. True, all their opponents were dead, but they had been that way to begin with.

"You can stop with the damn sir. We were stripped of our ranks. You took the vow, same as the rest of us," Oak said. Radwin knew was right. They had all sworn that if the damned deaders infected anyone, the survivors would not allow a fellow soldier to become one of the walking dead.

"But maybe there is something we can do. We get you back up to *Kyklopes* and maybe..."

"Have me infect the rest of the damn sky station? I've lived my life as a Host soldier, a member of the Sway. I may be heading out, but I'm not taking any friendlies with me."

"But, sir, you have about a day before the reaper virus kicks in fully," Radwin said.

"The thirty hours is just a guideline. For some it happens sooner and some it happens later. I have no desire to sit by and let my mind and body be turned into that of a zombie. An honorable death is far better and suicide is not honorable if there is another option."

Sam Radwin was immobile staring at the muzzle of his jaegorr rifle, the idea of killing a former superior officer sticking in his craw.

"If you insist on calling me sir, then consider it an order," Oak said. Radwin didn't move. "I would consider it a personal favor if you would end me before I become something that I despise. I am a practicing Christian. My life has not always been the finest, but I followed orders and did the best I could with what life handed me. I don't want to end up on the other side and be denied my well-earned eternal furlough because I had to put a bullet in my own head."

Radwin looked up and met Oak's eyes. "I'll do it," he whispered.

"Thank you."

"Before...is there anyone you want me to relay a message to?" Radwin asked.

Oak shook his head. "The soldiers I served with will understand. And my family died in the conflagration when Earth was destroyed. Hopefully, I will be able to tell them myself shortly."

Oak, wounded and battered, dragged himself to his feet and stood at attention, bringing his hand up into a salute. Radwin matched him, breaking off the salute first to bring up his jaegorr rifle. Oak didn't blink, didn't flinch as the muzzle flashed and a bullet tore threw his brainpan and out the other side. The now-dead soldier fell to the ground and even though his skull had assumed the consistency of somewhat chopped meat, Radwin put another round into him, severing his spinal cord at the neck. That way there was no chance of his body rising to harm others. Radwin moved to tend to the rest of his ten-man unit. Although "man" was not entirely accurate as four of his fellow soldiers were women. The difference in gender didn't make them any more or any less dead. Radwin put a pair of bullets, aimed at head and spine, into all eight. It felt wrong to Radwin not to bury them, but he couldn't risk it. The time it would take to bury his fallen comrades would only expose him to more danger, making him a target for the walking dead. He still had the mission and the nine deaths did not absolve him of his commitment. Before he could return to *Kyklopes* sky station he needed to find and rescue ten people. Each of the unit did. With the rest gone, Radwin's responsibility increased to a full hundred survivors.

Using sterilized gloves he removed a dog tag from each and put them in a buttoned pocket and bowed his head in a silent prayer, unsure if anyone was actually listening.

The town they had just been through did not have a single survivor of the reaper's plague. The nine deaths had been for naught. Even worst from a practical standpoint was the fact that the long-range radio that was used to contact *Kyklopes* was broken in the battle. His personal radio had a good range planetside, but wasn't powerful enough for the signal to be picked up in orbit. So now the mission was not only a find-and-rescue, but to locate a method to contact evac when the time came. To move more quickly the unit had commandeered an all-terrain vehicle, but that had run out of fuel. Radwin located an old-fashion bicycle. It was sturdy enough to be used off road and it had a rack to store some of his equipment. He took two jaegorrs, three sidearms, eighteen grenades and all the remaining ammunition. The grenades and ammo went in a pack which he placed in a basket on the front. The two addition sidearms were secured by utility straps to his armored vest and the jaegorrs strapped on his back. He was alone, but he knew he would need more rather than less firepower. He still had his GPS to guide him to the next city. Every five miles or so he would stop, find a sheltered spot, and try his headset radio.

"This is Sam Radwin of the 142nd Starborne. I am on a search-and-rescue mission. If any uninfected humans can hear this signal, please respond." He had repeated this nine times without a reply, but the tenth time was the charm.

"Sam Radwin of the 142nd Starborne, this is Tristan Harriman of the Town of Whisky Creek. Can you hear me?"

"Tristan, I can hear you. What is your location and how many of you are there?" an excited Sam Radwin said.

"Ninety-eight. One adult and ninety-seven children."

Sam Radwin's jaw actually dropped. The idea of one adult keeping that many children safe was amazing given the circumstances.

"Where in Whisky Creek are you located?"

"We are in Zimmen's Concrete and Building Supplies. How far from Whiskey Creek are you?"

Radwin plotted a course on his GPS. "I estimate my time of arrival in three and a half hours."

It was closer to four when his bicycle cruised in sight of the town line. Unfortunately, like many of the towns, Whiskey Creek was infested by the walking dead simply mulling around, waiting for one of the living to present themselves as a fresh food source. Radwin crept in to do recon from an overlooking hill.

It wasn't hard to spot the concrete factory if for no other reason it was the one building in town that had been fortified. It looked like a mini-fortress. In fact, several concrete slabs, each easily ten feet high by two feet thick, had been laid out in a pattern around the building. The building was exposed on all sides, which was good for keeping watch for deaders. It was a problem for Radwin as it left anyone approaching the building a wide-open target for the deaders to hone in on.

The undead were attracted to loud sounds and rapid moments. Fortunately their own speed was somewhat limited. The older the animated corpse, the slower the reflexes. There were minimal zombies between him and the concrete factory. He could wait for dark, but that would leave him even more vulnerable. He had infrared goggles, but without a heat signature zombies didn't exactly show up brightly. He imagined that he would glow much like a firefly in the dark to them.

The longer he delayed, the greater the risk of discovery. Sam Radwin decided it was best to get it over with. Hitting his ear radio he announced, "Tristan, I'm on a hill overlooking town on the east side. I'm going to be coming in toward you. Where is the best point of entry to the factory?"

"Radwin, stay where you are. We will come to get you," a girl's voice came over the radio.

"How exactly will you do that?" Radwin asked, then spun at the sound of a twig snapping behind him. A dozen deaders were coming up the rear hillside right for him. He could shoot, but that would only draw the rest of the lumbering dead toward his position. A strategic withdrawal was a safer solution. "Too late. The deaders are coming for me. I'm going to be coming in hot on a bicycle from the east side of town. Get ready to let me in. I should be there in moments."

Radwin's prediction might not have been wrong if the rapid, downward motion had not attracted the attention of every zombie in his line of sight. Like a swarm of giant angry hornets, they turned and ran, converging on his path. In a motorized transport he might have beaten them, but on a two-wheeled bicycle, the race was lost before it began. He pulled a grenade out and threw it far behind and to the side of him with the hope the explosion would take out some of his pursuers and that the noise and light show would distract the deaders from him.

It both worked and it didn't. It distracted the ones already aware of his descent into town, but alerted any that might have been ignorant of the literal meals on wheels. Sam Radwin cursed, surprised that the back of his mind was hoping that none of the children could hear his words over the open com-link.

"Radwin, we're coming to get you. If you move toward your right you will see a rolling bunker. Get on top as quickly as you can," the girl's voice said over the radio.

"A what?" Radwin said, too busy laying down fire to keep the reanimated from getting close enough to harm or infect him to easily look away.

Within moments he spotted a cement monstrosity moving toward him with slow precision. It was long and tall, coming to a wedge at the front. Within seconds, Radwin saw a boy, who might have been all of twelve, climb out a hatch in the top of the pile of cement. He threw a rope to the soldier. It had a knot tied every foot or so to make climbing easier. With a rush born of desperation, Radwin threw the ammo pack from the basket over his shoulder and ran forward. He grabbed the rope and started climbing, using his feet to walk up the side of the rolling cement bunker, pulling on each knot until he reached the top. Once Radwin hauled himself onto the roof, the boy pulled the rope up behind him, but it was too late. A dead woman in a tattered blue dress had gotten a hold of it and was yanking it back down. Radwin had already put his jaegorrs' straps around his shoulders to make the climb so he drew a sidearm and put three bullets in her head. It took the third one to make her let go.

"Thanks for the save, kid," Radwin said.

"My pleasure, Mr. Radwin...but I suppose I should address you by your rank."

Radwin took a deep breath and tried to smile. The soldier didn't want to have to explain how Major Benedict had called the entire sky station to account for abandoning the people on the planet below to the plague of deaders that had overrun them. To punish them for their inactions in standing up against a morally bankrupt decision to cut ties to the planet and hide in the station, Benedict took it over, stripped every member of Kyklopes of their standing, regardless of rank and sent them in teams of ten around the planet to rescue any survivors. Any squad that rescued one hundred colonists would be reinstated into the Host, although not necessarily at the rank previously held. It was something that shamed him, made him sick to his stomach and certainly not something he wanted to explain to a boy who actually appeared to be looking up at him in admiration. "My rank is a complicated matter at the moment. Sam is just fine. Why don't you take me to Tristan and we'll figure out a way to get everybody out of here?"

The boy's right hand rose up pushing long strands of dark hair out of his eyes back over his head as he smiled. "I'm Tristan."

"I'm sorry. I didn't recognize your voice. I assumed I had been talking to the adult you had mentioned," the soldier said.

"Mr. Poole is in charge of everything, but I handle most of the day-to-day operations. Climb inside and we'll take you to meet him."

Inside the transport Radwin was introduced to five more children but the bunker itself had his full attention. Although the material was called cement, it was several generations removed from the material it was named for. Made up of polymers that were more durable and many times lighter than it's namesake, the modern cement had been a godsend on the colonized worlds. Cheap, easy to make and even easier to pour into molds, it was the perfect material for buildings and in this case, a mobile bunker. The entire thing was a triumph of simplistic engineering. The bunker was twice the size of the tallest deader with walls at least ten inches thick near the top and close to two feet thick near the bottom. It was designed so it would be almost impossible to tip over yet somehow rolled easily.

"This is very impressive. How does it move?" Radwin asked.

"We used the tech from the palettes that carry the cement compounds around the factory. They were designed to carry five times the bunker's weight and move easily enough for us to push it. They pivot, which lets us move any way we need to," Tristan said. "And the plexus windows are small, yet thick enough to keep out the deaders and let us see where we're going." Radwin added his strength to that of the children and found it about as hard to push as the ATV that had run out of gas before the deaders had wipes out his squad.

The engineering feat became even more impressive when they got closer to the factory and the back wall of the moving bunker opened up and fit precisely into a docking bay, like a piece into a puzzle. It effectively locked into place so it couldn't be pulled out. Ahead of them was a high corridor too narrow for the adult soldier to move straight ahead without turning. He was forced to sidestep, dragging his pack behind him as he looked up at a number of children standing guard on cement ledges four feet overhead. They were holding what were effectively long metal spears. The choke point continued for some way. Any zombie who managed to get through the docking bay would be easy pickings with virtually no danger to the children, who could stand atop and stab downward with their metal spears.

When they reached the end of the cement maze, they were rewarded not with cheese but by a thick door rolling open. As with an airlock, the opposite door was not open. A voice over loudspeakers said, "Please strip down."

The children complied, but the idea of removing his clothes in front of children felt wrong to him.

Tristan realized this and whispered, "It's a safety precaution. Anytime someone leaves Zimmen's, they have to strip down on the return. It's a way to check for wounds to make sure that no one coming back in is infected."

Radwin nodded in agreement. "Sounds smart, but if you don't mind I feel more comfortable waiting at least until the girls have left."

"It won't work. Everyone in the chamber has to be checked before the inner door will be opened," Tristan said.

"Are you shy?" asked a little black-haired girl who might have been all of seven years old.

"That's my sister, Julie," Tristan said.

"Hi Julie, I'm Sam," Radwin said. "And no, I'm not. It's just that soldiers typically do not remove their clothes with children present. There are many regulations against such things."

"We can cover our eyes," Julie said. Her smile was infectious and Radwin found himself smiling back.

"Actually that would be more acceptable. If you wouldn't mind?"

"Not at all." As the girl covered her eyes with one hand she undressed with the other and Sam Radwin found himself staring at the opposite blank wall, as he removed his uniform for the inspection.

"Please turn around and lift up your arms," the voice ordered over the radio. Sam complied. "Now lift up and show the bottoms of your feet and bend over so we can see the top of your head."

Sam found himself staring at the ceiling while spinning.

"Those of you covering your eyes let me see the palms of your hands." They complied. "Everyone is clean. You may all get dressed."

Sam Radwin quickly donned the lower part of his uniform as the girls giggled.

In one fashion or another, Sam Radwin had spent the better part of the last decade of his life in the military, starting in the Host Academy and leading to his service in the sky station above the planet Ozark. Despite having soldiers who were married stationed with him, he had not spent much time around children. Those in the military, even when off duty, behaved in a certain manner. Children were very much different. As he was taken through the hallways of the cement factory, children ran, played, and did the things that children do. It took some getting used to. It didn't take long for Tristan and Julie to bring him to what was most likely the office of the factory manager in happier and less deader filled times.

Radwin was taken aback when he saw Edmund Poole. Being a military man he was used to those in charge, even the females, dressing and keeping their hair in a certain way. Poole was on the far opposite end of the spectrum with baggy clothes and hair down below his shoulders. He was also a bit on what would politely be called the roly-poly side. While there were overweight soldiers in the Host, they were few and far between because of the athletic regimens they were all required to participate in, regardless of how high a rank one held.

Radwin didn't let that affect him at all as he stepped forward with an outstretched hand.

"So you have come to rescue us?" Poole said grinning widely as he shook the soldier's hand.

"That's the plan, sir," Radwin replied.

"Now I heard you say you were part of the 142nd, but I thought the 37th was in charge of Kyklopes," Poole said.

"The 142nd Starborne has taken command of Kyklopes and planet Ozark."

"And there is also some confusion as to what your rank is," Poole said.

"The matter is complicated and not really pertinent to the issues at hand." Radwin said, not having any more desire to explain the situation on Kyklopes to Poole than he had to Tristan. "Right now we have to worry about getting you and the children out of here and up to Kyklopes."

Poole raised his brow. "I assumed you would be able to call down transport."

"I could, but unfortunately the rest of my unit was killed by the deaders and our radio was lost. Do you know where the town's communication array is? That should have sufficient range for us to call for Harpy drop ships to pick us up."

"I do. Unfortunately it's in the town hall," Poole said.

"Why is that unfortunate?" Radwin asked.

"Because it's surrounded, not only by wandering deaders, but also a great deal of rubble. Our bunker can't get close."

"Guess that means I'll have to go in on foot. I would ask that you get me as close as possible before I head out."

"I can do better than that. One of the children can go over to send the message," Poole said.

"Excuse me? Why would you send a child?"

"We found miles of box-binding chord in the factory which we strung to bridge between the roofs of the buildings. Before the deaders destroyed the town, I was a kindergarten teacher and gymnastics coach. All the children have been trained in basic gymnastics well enough to walk between the roofs above the deaders. Unfortunately, even with as much chord as we ran back and forth, we are not using proper rope. It is safest if we allow one of them to do it."

"I'm not sure I like that idea. It seems wrong to put a child in danger."

"I can understand that sentiment, but these children are very capable. They are experts in going out and finding food and bringing it back. In the last month, every child has been into the town several times and we have only lost three."

"That is three too many."

"It would seem that way, but by scouting the town, they have been able to keep all of us fed."

"And how often do you venture forth, Poole?"

"Mr. Poole doesn't go out. He is too valuable. Without his leadership the rest of us would soon die," Tristan said. Sam Radwin thought it sounded more like the philosophy of a coward, but he held his tongue.

Tristan, Julie, and four of the other children took Radwin in the rolling bunker to the building across from the city hall. Not willing to take Poole at his word, Radwin tried to help them push the bunker through the rubble strewn in the street, but even with him adding his muscle power to that of the children, they could not pass. Going with plan B, they pushed it as close to the building as they could. The plan was for Radwin, Tristan and Julie to exit up through the trap door in the cement roof and climb to the roof, leaving the other four children to take care of the bunker. In a pinch two or three children could move it, so four would be enough to handle any problems if they needed to change the rendezvous point. The children had developed the system so no more than two kids left the bunker to scavenge at a time so if something happened, the remaining children could get back to the factory.

The soldier was the first up and out. He had a pair of jaegorrs slung across his back, and the extra two sidearms were still strapped to his vest, in addition to his Host issued one in its holster. After Radwin determined there were no deaders nearby, Tristan leapt onto the molded cement brickwork and climbed toward the roof. Radwin was about to suggest that Julie stay behind since he had already decided he would be the one to go across the bridge, when the girl jumped up and climbed the wall with the agility of a spider monkey. Sam Radwin followed.

There was a rope bridge between the buildings, although using that term was being quite generous. Each crossing consisted of a seemingly random number of lines of chords braided together across the span. A higher braid was strung as a handhold. The chord was hardly military-issue. It was little more than industrial twine but the braiding increased its holding power. Radwin grabbed hold and tested it. It seemed strong enough to hold his weight.

Radwin stripped out of some of his heavy armor and took his second jaegorr off. He held it out to Tristan. The soldier wanted to weigh as little as possible.

"Do you know how to use a rifle?" Radwin asked.

"I used to go hunting with my dad before..." Tristan's eyes started to get as runny as an under cooked egg.

Radwin laid a comforting hand on the boy's shoulder. "Good. Jaegorrs work on the same principles as a rifle, but shoot much faster, use different ammo, and hold much more of it." Radwin reviewed for Tristan the specific features of the military rifle. "The bridge looks like it should hold me. Rather than risk one of you, I'm going to be the one to go across and I want you to cover me." At this news Julie's face squished up and she crossed her arms over her chest. "If I should fall, shoot any deaders that come toward me. But don't fire at any that are within fifteen feet. Let me take care of them so you don't accidentally shoot me. Do you think you can handle that?"

Tristan nodded.

"Good boy."

Radwin stepped to the edge of the roof and tugged on the top rope and then the bottom rope. They felt flimsy, but were secured on both ends.

"How did you manage to string these across?" Radwin asked, noticing the girl was upset with the news that she wouldn't be going across.

"I did it," Julie said. "I crawled upside down using the power line with the rope tied to my waste."

"Wow, that's very impressive. It must be at least thirty feet to the town hall."

"It's just like the monkey bars at school, only longer," Julie said. "Do I get a gun too?"

Radwin smiled. "I only brought the one extra jaegorr. At that distance, the handguns won't be very accurate."

"That stinks," Julie pouted, crossing her arms. "I wanted to shoot some deaders."

"Let's hope we don't have to worry about that at all. But your job will be to help him sight the deaders so he can focus on shooting them, okay?" The girl nodded and Radwin stepped gingerly onto the lower braid, his hands gripping the higher tangle of chord. He took his first step very slowly and with great care. The second one was a little more steady, but he was still very cautious.

Radwin treaded carefully and slowly. The bridge seemed to be holding well. The soldier started to pick up the pace. About eighteen feet across, the lower braid betrayed him, gave way and broke. Radwin clung to the upper braid with both hands, dangling like a piñata above several hungry deaders who looked more than ready to smash him open for any gooey prizes within. Pulling hard, he managed to bring his knees up over the braid and wrap his legs around it. He continued his journey crawling upside-down, moving with hands and knees. Moving as quickly as the awkward position would allow, he made it another ten feet but his weight was too much for the connection to the town hall and the pole it was tied to snapped in two part way between him and his destination. Radwin plunged downward, the still-tethered end of the braid changing his trajectory so he was a human pendulum heading back toward the wall of the building where he'd started out.

Radwin got his feet out in front of him in an attempt to cushion the impact. He managed to hold unto the braid, but the collision jammed his legs up into his back, even jarring his teeth. Radwin was left dangling off the side of the building, mere feet from the ground.

His options were few—jump down or climb up. Going down meant certain battle with the deaders. His gunshots would attract more zombies so Radwin climbed, putting his rappeling skills to use, praying that the braid would hold. The soldier made it most of the way to the top before his feet were knocked out from under him by a pair of deaders grabbing hold of the braid beneath him and pulling. Radwin scrambled faster until he was close enough to get one hand then the other onto the roof's ledge. As he struggled to pull himself up, the two children helped by grabbing his arms and his legs and pulling with all their weight. Unsure if the deaders could manage to climb, Radwin pulled his knife and cut the chords, letting the braid drop to the street below.

"Damn it," Radwin said.

"I can still go back across on the power lines," Julie said.

Radwin looked at the cable that ran between the buildings. There was no power being generated as near as he could tell, which reduced the chances of electrocution but the idea of sending a child over was something he could not get his mind around. Likely Julie had been lucky the first time.

"No, only as a last resort. We'll figure out another way to get over there. Let's go down to the rolling bunker and scout around some more. Maybe I can use some grenades to make the rumble smaller. It'll attract deaders, but we can wait them out in safety inside the bunker, then try to get through again." Radwin took the gun back from Tristan and put on his body armor.

"Okay, but let me call Mr. Poole and let him know what happened," Tristan said, taking the handheld radio off his belt. "The signal is better on a roof.

"Fine, I'll head down first and make sure there are no deaders lurking. Besides, the way you two climb, I need a head start," he said with a smile. "Guess I'm too old to keep up."

"You know what they say. Never trust anyone over fifteen," Tristan said with a grin of his own. Radwin reached out and mussed the boy's hair.

Radwin descended and stepped off onto the cement bunker next to the ceiling hatch. A minute passed with no sign of either Tristan or Julie coming down. Radwin scrambled back to the roof.

"What the hell?" Radwin yelled, seeing Julie dangling upside down on the power line, halfway across to the town hall. "What is she doing out there? I told you two that we would find another way."

"I know, but Mr. Poole told her to go. He said it was the best way for all of us to be rescued," Tristan said. "Don't worry, she's done it before."

"Yeah, but each trip weakens the support that it's anchored into." Radwin moved to the edge of the roof. "I'm going after her."

"But you're heavier. If the line breaks, she won't be able to get back," Tristan said.

Sam Radwin cursed silently, knowing the boy was right. He unslung both jaegorrs from his back, handing one to Tristan.

"We are going to wait by the edge of the roof and we are going to cover her. If anything happens, we are not going to let a single deader get near her. Understood?"

"Yes," Tristan said, his eyes as big as saucers as he took off the safety.

The pair watched nervously, but the girl made it all the way across to the other roof and through the roof-access door. Ten minutes passed before they saw her again. She stood on the edge of the roof and shouted, "I got the message through. They will have a ship here within the hour."

Radwin gave her a thumb's up sign and then gave her the quiet sign, putting his index finger over his mouth. The deaders were attracted to noise and he didn't want any more of them paying attention to her.

"We'll wait until they arrive," Radwin whispered, not wanting the girl to risk another trip.

The deaders seemed to have other ideas. One of the zombies had made it up to a neighboring roof that was on the far side of the rubble. There was only an alley between those buildings, not a street. It leapt toward the town hall. Its legs weren't powerful enough to get it the entire way, but it got close enough that its hands scraped the mortar as it slid and fell. Two more deaders had made it to that roof and looked ready to try leaps of their own. What deaders lacked in coordination they made up for in strength. They might not have enough momentum to land on the roof, but even a handhold could allow them to climb the rest of the way.

The first of the pair made the jump and caught the roof.

Noise be damned, Radwin wasn't letting the deaders get the girl. "Julie I'm going to do some shooting. Stay where you are." Radwin took a shot, shattering the deader's wrist. It plunged to the ground. As it was usually deader see, deader do the second animated corpse jumped. This one didn't even touch the roof, but three more had taken their place on the far roof.

Radwin fired three times and got two headshots. The third deader took it in the shoulder and reacted by leaping into space. As if propelled by some undead sense of preservation, his jump was better than his fellows and he landed with the underside of his arms on the roof.

"Fecal," muttered Radwin as he pulled the trigger again. This shot took the dead between the eyes and he slid down and out of sight.

Leaving the girl alone on the town hall's rooftop for an hour waiting for a Harpy was too risky. If one made the jump, Radwin might not be able to stop it before it got Julie. The shots had attracted the walking corpses and at least a dozen were congregating on the far roof.

The door at the base of the town hall started to shake as deaders attracted by the gunshots tried to force their way inside.

There were more than a dozen deaders working collectively. Even a good door might not hold up under that kind of barrage. Radwin searched for a way to get the bunker up against the side of the town hall. There was none.

"Julie," said Radwin. "We need you to get back over here along the cable, okay?"

The little girl nodded, her face white from the sounds of the approaching dead.

Radwin held his breath as the little girl stepped up to the edge of the roof on her tiptoes and reached for the power line. Her tiny fingers barely touched it, but she managed to jump up and get a grip with both hands, swinging her legs so they wrapped around the line. She did all this backward so she would be moving head first toward the way she had come.

Radwin gasped as he saw one of the bolts anchoring the power line on the far side pop out of the wall. One of the zombies from the far roof made the jump, his hands grabbing hold of the town hall's edge. Another leapt and missed the wall but caught the body of the first deader and was using him for hand and foot holds to get onto the roof. "Julie, come as fast as you can."

Julie started to scramble, moving arms and legs as fast as a seven-year-old girl could manage. The second of four anchors came free.

"You're doing great, Julie. Keep coming," Radwin said, wiping the sweat from his eyes. The second deader had made it all the way onto the roof. Noise be damned, Radwin wasn't letting the deader get the girl. "Julie, I'm going to fire my gun some more. Don't let it frighten you. Keep coming."

His first shot caught the deader in the chest, the second in the throat and the round kept going out through the cervical vertebrae.

The sounds of gunfire made Julie move even more quickly, but gravity was collecting its toll as the last two anchors on the power line popped out together. Gravity then claimed a bonus payment as the little girl plunged more than twenty feet down to the street. Unlike Radwin, she wasn't close enough to even worry about hitting the wall, instead striking pavement feet first.

The fallen girl was an open invitation to an all-you-can-eat deader buffet. Radwin started with headshots for the undead in the street. Those that moved toward her were taken care of quickly but the noise attracted more.

"Julie, grab hold of the power line and climb. I'll pull you up." Julie was stunned and limping. Even from the roof, Radwin could see she wanted to cry, but the girl was tough. She ran to the building, dragging one leg, grabbed hold of the power line, and Radwin started frantically pulling it arm over arm. Julie helped by climbing with her good leg. Tristan tried to help when Radwin noticed a crowd of deaders round the corner.

"Tristan, I need you on sniper duty. Take out those deaders before they get your sister," he whispered.

Tristan nodded as he aimed the jaegorr and started firing. His aim wasn't great, but in pray and spray mode he just had to make sweeps to hit the deaders.

"Sam, I'm scared," Julie called out.

"That's good. Gives you more adrenaline, more strength." Radwin pulled for all he was worth and the girl climbed past the halfway mark.

"Sam, you won't let the deaders get me, will you?" Julie pleaded.

"Julie, I won't let them touch a hair on your head."

"You promise?"

"I promise, cross my heart and hope to die. Now stop yapping and get up here, girl," Radwin said and was rewarded with a smile.

The rapid fire of the jaegorr suddenly stopped.

"Radwin, the gun jammed!" Tristan said.

"Grab the other one," Radwin yelled, his arms burning from the strain of pulling.

The boy ran to get the other gun, but he wasn't the only one moving fast. The deaders were off and running too. In the span of seconds, three made it to the part of the power line than lay on the ground. They lifted and pulled and the little girl was yanked off the wall and dangled by her hands over the ground. Individually the deaders were many times stronger than a single man. Three of them together almost pulled Radwin over the edge. He struggled to not let go of the girl's lifeline.

"Sam, I can't hold on!" Julie screamed.

"Wrap your legs around the line," Radwin instructed her.

The girl tried swinging up but her little legs didn't get high enough to even brush the wire and her sweating hands made her grip slippery.

The deaders operated more on remembrances than active thought, but even they realized the best way to get the little girl down. In a rare show of cooperation, the trio of deaders started swinging the line.

"Tristan, shoot them!" Radwin ordered.

"I can't. I might hit Julie," the boy said.

"If you don't, they'll knock her down." Three feet of power line slipped through Radwin's hands. "I'm not strong enough to hold them off for long. Hurry!"

The boy aimed the jaegorr, holding the trigger long enough for short bursts. The first two salvos missed, but the third took off a deader's leg. Tristan kept firing, getting closer to the deaders with each try. One burst cut through the power line, cutting it free from the zombie's grasp.

"Yes!" Tristan shouted.

Unfortunately, with one end of the line gone, Julie plummeted in the same arc that Radwin had. She was further along this time and smashed into the wall. The impact was all on her right shoulder, the pain making her let go and Julie again fell to the concrete below. A crack echoed through the alley and her left leg bent behind her at an angle that left no doubt that it was broken.

"Julie!" Tristan screamed, but his sister barely stirred, her eyes closed and fluttering.

Radwin started to push the power line he had reeled in so he could rappel down to Julie. Unfortunately two of the wounded deaders were still mobile and made it to the little girl, pouncing on her like rats on week-old cheese. Julie regained consciousness screaming at the sight and sensation of the mouths of zombies tearing her flesh apart.

Radwin stopped short. He had seen it nine times before. It was too late for the girl. His promise would be forever broken and going down now would only leave the boy alone to watch him die.

"Tristan, give me the gun," Radwin said.

"You can save her?"

Radwin shook his head. "No. I can only end her nightmare."

"You mean..." Radwin nodded and held his hand out to Tristan. "She's going to turn into one of them?"

"Yes. There's nothing we can do but put an end to her misery," Radwin said. "Give me the gun."

Tristan pulled the jaegorr to his chest. "No. She's my little sister."

Though tears, the boy aimed the gun. "I love you, Julie," Tristan yelled. His finger pulled back the trigger and a single burst reduced his sister to small chunks. His only consolation was she would never come back as a deader.

Tristan turned the gun around, trying to get the barrel pointed at his head, but it was too long for his arms to manage.

Radwin grabbed the weapon from the boy. "No, Tristan."

"I killed my sister. I promised my parents I'd always look out for her and take care of her. Instead I killed her."

"No, she was already going to die. You saved her from the horror of being devoured by the deaders. You made her death quick and ended her pain. You looked out for her in the only way you could. And you made sure she wouldn't rise again as one of them. You were a good big brother," Radwin said. "Julie would want you to live, not put a bullet in your own head."

"But I let her go over there," Tristan said, his face soaked with tears.

"Only because Mr. Poole told you too. You trusted him and he sent your sister to her death. That was your only mistake, but you had reason believe him. He was an adult and had kept you safe. You had no way of knowing he would risk sacrificing one of you to help save his own skin."

"No, he took care of us. He cares about us. He wouldn't do that," Tristan said.

"But he did. I'm sorry," Radwin said, reaching out to touch the boy. Tristan yanked away and headed down the side of the building. Radwin followed.

The two helped push the rolling bunker back to Zimmen's in silence. This time during the skin inspection there was no embarrassment in Radwin's manner, just simple staring ahead. This time when they made it inside, they didn't have to find Poole. He was waiting for them.

"Did it work? Are they coming for us?"

Radwin stepped forward and cold-cocked Poole in the nose. Blood squirted everywhere as the man hit the floor.

"Your first question should have been where was Julie. She gave her life because you gave her a stupid order contradicting mine. We would have gotten the message out without a little girl dying."

Poole was on his knees and was holding his nose in a futile attempt to stop the blood. "The sacrifice of the one saved the many."

Radwin brought his knee up into Poole's face. The former teacher curled up on the floor.

"You don't sacrifice people without a good reason or a plan, you son of a bitch. I'm going to see that you are charged with her death."

"That's really too bad. I guess I will have to make sure that you don't get on those Harpies," Poole said, slowly rising to his feet.

"What are you going to do about it? You're too cowardly to even go outside. You have children do your dirty work," Radwin said.

"My children are still going to help me. Everyone get your weapons. Mr. Radwin has been very naughty. We are going to have to beat him into submission and throw him outside for the deaders. Otherwise he'll kill us all," Poole said.

"You know that is a lie. I'm a fully trained soldier for the Host. I am armed. Are you really going to send children against me when they don't stand a chance? They could be hurt or worse," Radwin said. "Or don't you care?"

"The needs of the many outweigh the needs of the few," Poole said.

"And the needs of the one outweigh the rest as long as the one is you, huh, Poole?" Radwin said.

Poole licked his lips trying to hide a smirk. "Nonsense. The welfare of the children is my first concern. They have all lost their parents. If anything happens to me, who is going to look after them? Besides, I think you will have trouble firing on innocent children just for following my orders. Get him, my children, get him."

A couple of the children hesitantly took steps forward. Radwin moved into a fighting stance but left all of his weapons untouched. This despite facing down more than a dozen children armed with sharpened metal spears.

"Everybody stop," Tristan yelled, as the boy stepped in front of the soldier.

"Tristan, why aren't you listening to me?" Poole scolded.

"*You* ordered my sister to go across the wire. Radwin said we could have come up with another way. Because of you, Julie is dead. I had to shoot her in the head so she wouldn't see the deaders eating her alive."

Poole frowned and seemed saddened. "I am so sorry, Tristan. Julie was the bravest one of us. But Radwin was wrong. Her doing what she did was the only way we could reach the communication array. The only way the Host would come and get us out of here."

"I don't believe you," Tristan said.

"That's too bad, Tristan, because I'm telling the truth, but you have now betrayed us and stood with this outsider. You are going to share his fate," Poole said.

"First you kill Julie, then you want to kill Sam, and now me. Where is it going to end? On the sky station, the kids will be taken away from you. Do you think someone won't tell on you? Are you going to kill the rest of us kids just to save your fat ass?"

"Profanity, my boy, is not acceptable in my presence. And I will continue to do what is best for all of us." Poole reached out with his hand and took a spear from the nearest child, pointing it at Tristan. "I will not tolerate anyone disobeying me. I think of you as a son, Tristan, which makes your betrayal so much worse. The other children will do as they are told. I know that in my heart. And my heart tells me you will endanger us all and that cannot be allowed to happen. I'm sorry it had to come to this."

Poole pulled his arms back in preparation to thrust the spear forward into Tristan. He never got the chance because Radwin pulled his sidearm and put a bullet into each of Poole's knees.

Poole fell screaming and crying.

"Time to feed you to the deaders. The scent of blood and your screams should bring them fast," Radwin said, kicking the spear away from Poole. He put his back toward Poole and mouthed *no* to the children to let them know he was not actually going to follow through on the threat.

"No, you can't," Poole said.

"Why not? You were going to do it to me," Radwin said.

"It was a joke," Poole said, trying to smile through the pain.

"I'm not laughing," Radwin said.

"C'mon, everything is negotiable. What can I do to change your mind?" Poole said.

"If someone was willing to take your place, I'd be willing to consider allowing it," Radwin said.

"Okay," Poole said, grabbing onto the idea like a drowning man to a piece of driftwood. "Sandra, you'd trade places to save Mr. Poole's life, won't you?"

The girl remained silent.

"Jason, I've done a lot for you and I've never asked for anything in return. I'm asking now for you to step up and save my life. Are you man enough to do it?"

Jason turned and walked away. One by one, Poole tried to convince each child to give their life for his. There were no takers on his offer of painful death.

"Tristan, you were always my favorite. Talk to Mr. Radwin and convince him not to do this horrible thing to me," Poole begged.

"You mean like you listened to me before you tried to kill me?" Tristan said.

"Tristan, I was in grief over what happened to Julie. I wasn't thinking straight," Poole said.

"Don't you *ever* say my sister's name again. You are not worthy. And Sam was never sending you out to the deaders. He was just trying to show us what kind of man you really were."

Poole's head snapped to look at Radwin who had a dark grin.

"It's true," Radwin said, tossing him two straps. "Make a tourniquet on each leg. The Harpy will have medics who will treat you before you are taken to the brig."

"Brig?" Poole said.

"Yes. Edmund Poole, you are under arrest," Radwin said.

With the realization that he wasn't about to be fed to zombies, Poole became indignant. "You don't have the right."

"Actually, soldiers of the Host outrank civilian authorities, so I do, even if the planet Ozark wasn't under martial law. You are guilty of the attempted murder of a soldier of a Host, inciting to riot, and child endangerment resulting in death."

"I kept these children alive."

"And I am sure that will be taken into account."

"Sam Radwin, this is Harpy Dropship Gamma. We are approaching your position. Can you read me?" came the radio burst in Radwin's ear.

"Harpy Dropship Gamma, we have ninety-six children and one wounded war criminal ready for transport," Radwin said.

"Radwin, we were told you had ninety-seven children."

"The war criminal's actions caused the death of the brave girl who radioed for evac," Radwin said.

"Acknowledged. We will be making a hover landing on the roof of the cement

factory in t-minus ten. Soldiers will be sent to escort the criminal and to assist in evac."

"Thank you Gamma. I will have someone meet you on the roof to guide you in. Radwin out."

"We're being rescued?" said Tristan who had heard just one side of the conversation.

"Yes, you are," Radwin said.

"Radwin, I plan to report your actions..." Poole started, but the click of Radwin's sidearm caused him to fall silence.

"The prisoner will adhere to regulations and remain silent unless spoken to," Radwin ordered.

"Tristan, will you take some of the kids to the roof and show the soldiers in?" Radwin asked.

"Sure," the boy said, looking from the soldier to the former teacher and back to the soldier. "Why didn't you kill him?"

"One, soldiers of the Host are not murderers. I could stop him without killing him. Two, death was too easy an out for him after what happened to Julie. Three, I needed you to truly know that what happened to your sister was because of the actions of a man who cared more for himself than those he professed to be taking care of. That way I know you will stop thinking it was your fault and put the blame where it belongs—on Poole."

Tristan looked up at the soldier with a small smile, then reached forward to grab the man around the waist in a hug. The embrace took Radwin by surprise, but he recovered quickly, hugging the boy with his left arm. His right arm held the gun still aimed at Poole. The boy pulled back, some of his anger gone. The rest would be a long time leaving, if it ever did.

"You are pretty good with kids, Sam. How many do you have?" Tristan asked.

"None."

"That's too bad. You should really have some," Tristan said, wiping his eyes and running to the stairs that led to the roof.

Radwin found himself smiling and thinking that maybe the boy was right. He needed to find three more survivors so he could get back to *Kyklopes* and check on what the policy on soldiers adopting Ozark orphans was.

A MEAL FIT FOR GOD

A Tale of the Roosevelt

C.J. Henderson

"It now appears that research underway offers the possibility
of establishing the existence of an agency having the proper-
ties and characteristics ascribed to the religious concept of
God."

Dr. Evan Harris Walker
Theoretical Physicist

ORRECT STABILIZERS—BRING DRIFT BACK BELOW TWO DEGREES—NOW, MISTER!"
The navigator of the Earth Alliance Ship *Roosevelt* sprang to her task.
Despite the incredible nature of the ship's design and the sophistication of
its state-of-the-art sensors, the *Roosevelt* had somehow accidentally blundered
into a cosmic storm of unbelievable intensity.

"Still being dragged, Captain."

Of course, that the great battlewagon would somehow manage to find an un-
charted storm system, one infinitely more severe than any previous encountered—
anywhere, by any race—came as no surprise to her crew. The most forward-sailing
of any space vehicle dispatched from its world since the beginning of galactic exploration, the *E.A.S. Roosevelt* had encountered more confounding, unbelievable
and well, downright wozzlingly strange stuff than any human being had ever
imagined possible.

"Reroute the auxiliary power reserve from the light motion cannon—do whatever it takes but get us straight-lined!"

Indeed, if the entire tally of intergalactic oddities the *Roosevelt* had encountered up until that particular star date were ever to be reviewed by the proper

authorities back home, they would have no choice other than to conclude that the crew member who drew up the list must have been quite mad.

"The helm just isn't responding, Captain. We're still listing, shoving the needle close to six."

Yes, of course, the *Roosevelt* was the first Earth ship to leave the solar system. Hers was the first crew to come face to face with alien races, to walk on other worlds, to interact with unimaginable cultures. Still, space exploration, it had always been assumed, would be a thing of monotony, a tedium of cataloguing inert planets, charting the currents of the galactic undertow, clearing debris from what would become the spaceways of the only sentient race in the universe.

"There's no reason for *any* storm to be this powerful. Check for magnetic pulsing."

But, humanity had discovered that not only were they not alone in the universe, they were actually residents of a galaxy practically choking on a seemingly never-ending roster of other life forms. The activities of this cacophony of civilizations was overseen by the five great races comprising the ruling body of the highly esteemed organization known as the Pan-Galactic League of Suns. Or, should it be said, the "formerly," highly esteemed organization.

"Pulsing detected, sir. Strong mounting—seventeen to the fifth, and growing."

For, once the *Roosevelt* inserted itself into the actual workings of the galaxy, the League's stranglehold on things had crumpled. Within weeks the Earth-led Confederation of Planets had been overwhelmed with applications for membership. Never ones to not press an advantage, those in charge of the Confederation had dispatched the *Roosevelt* on one dicey mission after another, which is what had put the flagship of the Earth Alliance on a research mission in a centrally located section of the galaxy unexplored by any other race.

"Suggest a rotational vectoring, sir."

Not that no other race had ever sent a ship into the nebulous six-light-year across swamp of gas clouds and radiant shadows that hovered around the Milky Way's ground zero. Plenty had tried.

"Give it to me yesterday, Mr. Michaels."

It was just that none of them had ever returned.

At the order of Captain Alexander Benjamin Valance, science officer Mac Michaels keyed the controls in question, throwing The *Roosevelt* into a lateral come-about so unexpected a full third of the crew were thrown against the nearest floor, wall or ceiling. But, despite the resulting overloading of the ship's medical bays, the maneuver had been worth it. Cracked ribs, broken fingers, scraped flesh, bruises, dents, dings, and lost blood aside, The *Roosevelt* found it way in between the competing solar winds and broke loose of the terrible current which had been thrashing it about so.

The instant the bridge instruments announced that control was back within the hands of the crew, the captain ordered an immediate reversal of their course. In seconds the *Roosevelt* was smoothly gliding once more through the darkness, backing off to a point safely away from the storm where the impossible manifestation could be charted, studied, and maybe even explained.

And, as one might expect, a great series of cheers, whoops, and unrestrained applauds went up from one end of the great warwagon to the other in praise of those who had once more pulled the crew's collective derrières out of the fire. Those currently performing essential duties, of course, continued to do so. But, any who could stop for a meal, a smoke, a round of drinks, or anything else that might take their mind off the fact they had once again cheated six kinds of death by the proverbial skin of their teeth did so with all possible speed.

And, it was that unadulterated burst of relief and good cheer which started the terrifying chain of events that followed.

"Okay, which one of you slobs wants a mouthful of poison?"

From the staggering amount of positive responses following the offer for seeming self-destruction, it appeared fairly obvious the woman in white carrying an oversized tray was not actually offering death. Indeed, so fervent were the screams and pleas of acceptance even an alien visitor with the most inadequate of translators would be able to figure out that the crowd swarming about the relatively short chef had not the slightest interest in self-destruction—hers or anyone else's.

"The female does not actually offer the ceasing of life—yes?"

"No, no, sir," Captain Valance responded, torn between amusement and exasperation. "That's Chef Kinlock, and she's just kidding around with the crew."

The captain's guest was Thortom'tonmas, the newly installed ambassador from Daneria to the Confederation of Planets. The *Roosevelt* had the dubious honor of the ambassador's presence due to a brilliant idea hatched by one of the less competent members of the Alliance's public relations department. Since it had been agreed the new ambassador should be transported to Earth by a Confederation ship, it was decided such "advanced" thinking should be compounded by saddling their greatest ship with said "privilege." Then, the same genius decided that giving the *Roosevelt* a monumentally difficult task to perform on the way home would be the perfect vehicle for putting the war-like Danerians in their place.

Of course, what this obvious civilian had failed to take into consideration were the less self-congratulatory ramifications surrounding the idea of a high-ranking individual from the Confederation's greatest enemies being given a tour of the Earth's most advanced ship. Despite the nifty press release such news generated, carrying out such a stunt meant giving Daneria access to the Earth Alliance's most closely guarded military secrets, as well as a perfect opportunity to embarrass the hell out of the Confederation if they failed to complete their next-to-impossible task.

"Then what is she offering them?"

"You know," Valance admitted, "I don't actually know. Why don't we go over and find out?"

Even as the captain and Thortom'tonmas approached the gathering crowd, Kinlock shouted;

"Okay, back off, you decksliders. I think you all know who gets first dibs on this batch."

The batch, as all assembled could tell from the heavenly aroma wafting through the mess was comprised of the chef's galaxy-famous chocolate chip cookies. And the one of their number who was to get first pick they all knew could be none other than Mac Michaels, the science officer who had kept the *Roosevelt*, and by extension her crew, from becoming just another statistic concerning investigation of Sector 84-Af7, the nebulous swamp of gas clouds and radiant shadows they had recently escaped.

"Open up, Michaels."

Grinning, the *Roosevelt's* chief razormind stretched his mouth wide as Kinlock tossed a cookie high into the air. Everyone held their breath as Michaels moved forward, snapping at his target as it came into range. Amazingly, he snagged the treat in mid-descent, managing to snare it intact without merely biting off a piece and sending the rest to the floor—or worse, missing altogether.

"All right, you bilge nasties—come and get 'em!"

A staggering wall of cheers echoed throughout the mess and down the halls in every direction. The first tray the chef had brought with her from the galley was emptied in less than a handful of seconds. No consternation followed, for ten more trays were brought forth by Kinlock's crew, the contents of which were more than enough to make certain everyone received one—even Valance and Thortom'tonmas.

And, while the two debated the merits of chocolate chip cookies to the ones known as A Little Taste of Andromedas, the favorite dessert treat of the Danierian Empire, at the next table over, where Mac Michaels had planted himself, a similar conversation had also begun. Holding the remaining half of his cookie aloft, nursing the treasure like a middle-schooler savoring his first beer, Michaels said;

"These are really the absolute best ever."

"Ohhhhh, I don't know," Chief Gunnery Officer Rockland Vespucci answered, known to pawn brokers and bartenders across the Confederation as Rocky. "My mom, she used to make the best canolis. I mean the cream was so rich, and she would use so many pistachios...."

"Awwww, that's nothing," Technician Second Class Thorner interrupted. "If you guys ever tasted my dad's koogle, well then...."

"Forget it," piped in Quartermaster Harris. "None of it can compare to the oatmeal raisin squares my grandma used to make."

And so the conversation ran up and down the length of the table, one sailor after another defending their families' or nationalities' favorite dessert treat. After a while, however, after Rocky noted that his best friend, Machinist First Mate Li Qui Kon, more commonly known to wire and screw jockeys and robotics enthusiasts everywhere as Noodles, had not joined into the conversation. When he enquired as to "why," his shipmate answered;

"Chinese families aren't big on fancy desserts. It's all orange slices and almond cookies and ginger candies—"

"Ginger candies," asked another crewman, "what are those?"

"A reminder as to why China will never be at the forefront of the dessert industry." As everyone chuckled over Noodles' quip, the machinist held up a hand, adding;

"Hey, but don't think Chinese can't cook. Any culture that can create the Monkey King must know something about filling a table."

When asked to explain his reference, Noodles told those assembled;

"Well, the Monkey King was a member of the Chinese pantheon, not a god really, but he mingled with the gods. He was the troublemaker in all the really good Chinese stories—"

"Like Loki for the Norse?" Intelligence Officer DiVico asked. "Or Coyote for the Native Americans?"

The machinist confirmed that the Monkey King was absolutely best described as one of the most mischievous god-figures ever, one who could just as easily work tirelessly for a noble cause as he might throw himself into tearing down an empire. Nigh invulnerable, monstrously powerful, and driven by a quirkier set of conflicting passions than a cocaine addict at a slow-dance marathon, he was totally unpredictable, and one presence no one—rich, poor, or somewhere in the middle *ever* wanted to see.

But, no matter what he was up to, no matter in what story the Monkey King was starring, sooner or later things came down to food. Simply put, the guy loved to eat. Noodles regaled his shipmates, and, through extension, the captain and his guest, with a seemingly endless list of the mouth-watering meals that the myths reported had been consumed by the mythic trouble-maker. Pies and pork, apples and ambrosia, shrimp, salads and sorbets, plus a thousand other dishes, each one more wonderful sounding than the one before it had all been consumed by the legendary simian.

Noodles made the Monkey King's typical menu sound so wondrous that after a while all those gathered at the table were driven by hunger to race off to the dinner queue. Even the captain and the ambassador felt their differently constructed stomachs growling viciously enough to follow suit. Indeed, the machinist had made the mounting list sound so absolutely magnificent that all within earshot had deserted the area to fill themselves a tray and get down to enjoying a meal on a more fulfilling level than simply hearing about one.

All, that was, except for the single crewman at the table who, if any of the others had asked, it would have been discovered had never before been seen by anyone in attendance. That sailor, or at least, what appeared to be just another sailor, the only being in sight to not take a cookie, instead kept to its seat, thinking. It did this for some time, finally making a decision after some eighteen minutes of contemplation.

After that it smiled, a very malicious thought filling its mind with a glee it had not known in centuries.

"By the blessed blue suede shoes of the King, what's in Hell is *that*?"

Noodles was even more surprised that his pal, Rocky. On their way to the galley for breakfast the day after all the swirling nebula excitement, they ran into a humanoid figure in the hallway that froze both of them in their tracks. It did not stand more than four feet tall, though size was not important to it. The thing had merely chosen a convenient height for walking the world of man.

"By the Buddha's mint julep, it can't be...."

The creature grinned at the two sailors from its perch atop a small but animated cloud floating in the middle of the hallway. It was a cumulus wispy thing, seemingly nothing more than steam, but still substantial enough to carry a passenger. The cloud, however, was not what was causing the swabbies' concern.

"Can't be what?"

The creature possessed a body short of leg and long of arm, one clad in a wardrobe of the finest Chinese silk—resplendent robes covered in delicate designs, stitched with thread made from the purest gold and silver. Its knuckles were hairier than many a man's dome, topped by a head with a simian face and eyes that saw men's souls as just so many leaves, pretty things that fell and dried and danced at the merest whim of the breeze. Barely able to speak, knowing that his mind could not possibly be correctly interpreting the data it was receiving from his senses, still did Noodles shout;

"Shiu Yin Hong!"

And at that gesture of recognition, the creature smiled, for despite all logic, it was indeed the great and powerful Monkey King which floated peacefully there in Connecting Corridor 17-L. Rocky and Noodles looked one to the other in a help-lessness so utterly complete they could not have been more useless if they had just come across an eighteen-foot-wide breach in the hull or been asked to identify the capital of Oregon.

"What in the aurory, the borey, and the whole damn allus are we supposed to do with him?"

"How am I supposed to know?"

"Hey, he's your damn god of mischief."

It was not actually a fair piece of logic, but even Noodles had to agree it was the best they had. Deciding that not doing anything at all was probably the worst way to proceed, the machinist thought for a moment, then remembered what his father had told him about facing problems head on and always doing the most sen-sible thing in any situation—pass the buck. Sucking down a deep breath, Noodles asked;

"Hey-ah, so...how would you like to go and meet our captain?"

The look of sinister glee that filled the Monkey King's tiny eyes did not gift either of the sailors with encouragement. More than that, other crew members had begun to gather, their forward motion in either direction impeded by Shiu Yin Hong and his floating cloud. All were willing to wait a moment and let the trio pass. Well, almost all.

"What," cried out one of the ship's compliment of Marines, "the ever-lovin' hell is that thing?"

"Our best guess at the moment," Noodles answered, "is that it's a godling from Earth legends known as the Monkey King." The towering jarhead snickered, laughing as he pointed at Shiu Yin Hong as he said;

"You ain't foolin' nobody, Kon. That's just another one of your idiot robots. And a fairly stupid lookin' one at that."

Its head turning toward the Marine, the Monkey King responded with a quite authentic simian howl of derision. Jumping down from its cloud playfully, Shiu Yin Hong ambled on its bowed legs to where the Marine was standing. Putting out a paw as if asking to shake hands, the Monkey King smiled widely. As everyone in the hall laughed at the ludicrous sight—the four-foot-tall chimp-thing facing off with a six-and-a-half-foot marine—the soldier decided he had better places to be. And so, not wishing to look the bully, he stuck out his hand to simply shake and be on his way.

Shiu Yin Hong took the man's hand, and then with merely two fingers, twisted it violently, forcing the marine to his knees. The soldier screamed wildly, the pain he must be in obvious to all as they heard the bones within his hand snapping. Several thought about moving on the godling, but as each did the Monkey King turned in their direction, eyeing them with a malevolent glee which froze all in their tracks.

"Shiu Yin Hong—"

Turning toward the sound of Noodles' voice, not releasing the Marine's hand, the Monkey King focused on the machinist, waiting for him to speak. Forcing himself to remain calm, to not allow his voice to crack, Noodles said;

"We were going to see the captain—yes? I mean, if you want to play with this fellow, by all means...but I thought, surely someone as important as you would want to meet the most important person on board ship. Right?"

The simian form considered the machinist's words for a moment, then suddenly released his grip on the marine while letting out a piercing whistle. As he did so, the soldier fell backward into the bulkhead even as the Monkey King's cloud flashed across the hall and lifted its master up from the floor. Seated cross-legged, the god-thing then floated over to Noodles, its expression indicating he was ready to leave.

Reaching out to the nearest wall-com, the machinist routed a call to Valance, requesting a moment of the captain's time. When asked what he wanted, Noodles responded;

"Captain, sir, Rocky and I, we ahhhh, umm...we've got a god on board, sir, and he seems eager to meet you."

Alexander Benjamin Valance had endured quite a lot since assuming command of the *Roosevelt*—so much so that the brass back home considered him the one field officer they had who could be counted on to handle anything. Still, when he hesitated a full three seconds before responding to the fact that a supreme being of some sort wanted to come by for a chat, none thought it an overly long period of time before he could quite figure out how to make his mouth work once more.

"Oh, yes—of course you do."

Considering the notion he was aware that both Chief Gunnery Officer Rockland Vespucci and Machinist First Mate Li Qui Kon—the crewmen not only responsible for shaving the sacred monkeys of Templeworld, but for also conning the guards of the Pen'dwaker Holding Facility into allowing them to transform the prison into a gambling den for their Intergalactic Crap Shoot of the Millennium tournament (just two items on their ever-increasing roster of chicanery)—were involved, the fact he answered at all only proved once more to the crew how incredibly cool under pressure their captain really was.

Indeed, during their tour of duty together, more than one of the ten thousand men and women under his command had announced that Valance was the one man they would willing follow into Hell.

"Well, don't keep god waiting. Bring him to my ready room and let's see what he wants."

As news spread from one end of the *Roosevelt* to the other of what was happening, more than one of them found themselves wondering if they were about to get their chance to do so.

What Valance discovered "god," or at least the closest thing to one presently spending its time on any Earth Alliance vessel, wanted seemed to be to play an endless series of practical jokes. Shiu Yin Hong had shaken the captain's hand with a frank seriousness and then pulled his pants down around his ankles, caused bananas to rain from the ceiling by the thousands, and switched the ship's intercom from keeping the crew informed on daily goings-on to playing "I'm a Believer" non-stop.

And that was just his opening salvo.

Over the four days after he had first arrived on the decks of the *Roosevelt*, the Monkey King had filled the air with helium so he could laugh at everyone's voices, transformed much of the *Roosevelt's* electrical wiring into gelatin, and even fired the ship's devastatingly powerful light-wave motion gun several times simply to hear the clicking noises the final securing locks made as they bolted the weapon into position.

"I'm tellin' ya, Noodles," Rocky growled, picking himself up from the deck after having slipped on yet another loose banana peel, "I'm gettin' goddamned sick of this deity of yours."

"Mine," snapped the machinist indigently. "Do not blame that knuckle-dragging fleabag on me. His being on board was not my idea."

"I hate to argue with you, Li," Mac Michaels interrupted, "but you might be wrong about that." As Noodles turned to glare at the science officer, Michaels raised his hands, saying;

"Don't get me wrong, I'm not saying you wanted him here. But if I've doped things out correctly, *something* was going to be here, and it was you that gave it form."

"That is an interesting statement, officer." As the sailors turned, they found Ambassador Thortom'tonmas standing behind them. "Please elaborate."

"Well, sir, the captain had asked me to figure out where our intruder had come from. I suspected he wasn't the actual Monkey King because, as overwhelmingly powerful as his abilities supposedly are, they aren't the ones Machinist Kon here described to us at dinner the other night." As those listening nodded, Michaels added;

"Since that moment, however, immediately preceded the intruder's arrival, I brought up the galley cameras and studied it. Seemed too much of a coincidence to not be connected." As the heads all around him continued to nod, the science officer, clearly enjoying the spotlight, told the growing assembly;

"As I studied that moment when the Monkey King story was told, I noted one sailor at the table I didn't recognize. Not hard in a crew of ten thousand, but there was something in the way he was listening to Noodles talk that made me suspicious. So, I asked the computer to find a match among the crew and it couldn't."

"You mean..." said Rocky, only to then pause, scowl, then add, "okay, so what'dya mean?"

"I set the camera links to observation. First I had them follow him after dinner. Sure enough, right after he left the galley he found a private corner and transformed into the Monkey King." As the crowd made various noises of surprise, Michaels continued, telling them;

"Just wait. It gets better. I then turned the link to pre-trace the guy, to see where he came from. The cameras retraced his steps back to the moment when the storm ended. And, to make a long story short, 'he' isn't a 'he' at all."

"So then, like what the hell is he?" Thorner asked, two dozen other wide-eyed listeners letting it be known they were as interested as the technician.

"'He,' for lack of a better pronoun, is a ball of energy that—immediately follow-ing that nebula storm we barely survived—passed through a bulkhead, floated to the ceiling, observed those of us walking by for a while, and then just...congealed into a non-descript human guy."

"So," Harris asked, "what do we do now?"

"Now," came the voice of Intelligence Officer DiVico, "we get back to our duties."

Snapping his fingers, the security chief signaled two of his men to come forward, commanding them to escort the Danerian ambassador to his quarters, citing safety issues, "what with an unknown life form roaming the ship, and all." After that he suggested everyone else return to their duties while he hurried Michaels and Noodles off to see the captain. Forced to travel at a slower speed than he would have preferred thanks to all the banana peels still littering the halls, once in Valance's quarters, DiVico reported on all that had happened. After the intelligence officer had finished, the captain asked;

"So, Thortom'tonmas knows what we know about Cheetah?"

"I'm sorry, sir," Michaels responded, immediately accepting full responsibility. "I was telling some of the fellows, and the ambassador happened to walk by, and..."

"I know," sighed Valance. "I gave very strict orders that he be shown every courtesy."

"Still, we need to do some damage control, sir," DiVico said. "Perhaps it would be best if you outlined what your plans are for dealing with the intruder, so I know how you'd like me to move against it."

"Oh my God." Valance, Michaels, and DiVico all turned at the sound of Noodles' voice. "Shiu Yin Hong, whatever it is...it came from this part of space, where no ship has survived before. It came aboard the ship, it wanted to know what we thought God looked like, and it assumed the first version it heard about."

"We did pick it up in the heart of the galaxy," Michaels added. "The first ship to ever penetrate this area and make it back out in one piece."

"Maybe..." DiVico suggested, his voice an inch away from breaking, "maybe we were the first to make it to God's doormat, and...and now he's curious to survey his handiwork."

"Meaning," the captain added, "I thought I had my hands full with just the Monkey King, and now it seems like we might be playing host to the burning bush."

The four navy men stared at each other for a moment, none quite certain how to proceed. Realizing that whether he knew what to do or not that it was still his job to do something, Valance snapped;

"Well, nothing's going to get done with us standing around like a flock of flamingos. Michaels, get to a scanner. Find that omnipotent furball and let me know where it is. DiVico, you track down Thortom'tonmas and keep him away from our intruder."

As the officers hurried to follow their orders, Noodles asked;

"What about me, sir?"

"You?" The captain let the single word echo against the metal walls of his office, then said, "You're going to teach me everything I need to know about the Monkey King before this mess gets any worse."

It took the sailors some twelve minutes to find both the Monkey King, or at least, that entity presenting itself as the legendary Shiu Yin Hong, and Ambassador Thortom'tonmas. Confirming the captain's worst fears, however, they found the two of them in conference. Having put the clues of what had happened together while listening to Mac Michaels' explanation in the hallway, the Danerian had immediately sent his staff in search of the banana-breathed intruder. By the time Valance was alerted and arrived at their location, Thortom'tonmas had enjoyed a full twenty minutes with the intruder.

"I'm going to have to ask you to step away from the alien, ambassador."

"Oh, oh no," replied the Danerian, a sinister smile twisting his lips, "no, I don't believe I'll be able to do that at all."

As DiVico's security team stepped forward, Thortom'tonmas' aides moved to cut them off. Before either side could escalate the situation beyond words, however, the intruder clapped its hands together. Instantly a dazzling and somewhat itching force wall appeared around everyone in the area, immobilizing them.

"Ambassador," Valance shouted, "I don't think you know what you're dealing with here!"

"Oh, to the contrary, Captain, I understand my new friend, and what he wants, ever so exactly."

"And what the hell would that be?!"

"Why, Mr. DiVico," the ambassador answered. "The guise of Shiu Yin Hong was assumed by this most wondrous visitor to our galaxy because that god's particular demeanor suited him...to a degree, anyway."

The Danerian's tone sent a warning tingling through the nervous systems of all the humans present. Several of them had an idea as to what Thortom'tonmas was planning. None of them were pleased to discover they were correct.

"Every race has its trickster deities. The cruel jokester, the prank player, and worse. This Monkey King is a charming fellow, but...how would one put it, one limited in its scope. I've merely offered our friend...a greater opportunity to utilize its talents."

"Oh crap..."

"Such language, Mr. Michaels," the ambassador laughed. "But forgivable. All you humans offered was the tale of a mischievous godling who ultimately caused more trouble for himself than anyone else. I, on the other hand, have presented him with a more effective, hands-on, you might say, type of trouble-making supreme being—the Monkey King's Danerian counterpart—Saboth, the Unforgiving."

And, in an instant, the minds of everyone present were filled with Thortom'tonmas' description of the Danerian warrior god of laughter. Cruel and capricious, a monstrous blue giant possessed of a ravenous appetite for the cruelest of jests, the kind of being that would set a world ablaze merely so he might take a steam bath in its dying oceans.

"Our visitor is curious as to what this galaxy which he helped set into motion now has to offer. I have given him a clear picture of the weakness of so many of its races, the soft, mewling wretchedness of the shivering members of your Confederation."

"You're a lying sack of crap, Thortom'tonmas," Michaels shouted. "Why should he believe you?"

"Because," the ambassador replied, "our delightful Shiu Yin Hong does not have to blindly place his trust in anything anyone says. Have you heard him converse? Utter a single syllable? No, you have not. He knows I speak the truth because he has gone into my mind. As he learned of the Monkey King from your man, Pasta—"

"Noodles—"

"Whatever...so did he learn of Saboth from me!"

And for another moment, the room went silent. Still held in stasis by what appeared to be nothing more than a mote of the intruder's power, the crewmen of the *Roosevelt* struggled to find a way out of what they could all see coming. If the ambassador could convince the cosmic force in simian form before them to adapt the shape of Saboth, to take on the mantle of the warrior deity of Daneria, there would be no stopping their conquest machine.

The member races of the Earth-led Confederation of Planets were all well aware that the Danerian Empire was looking for an excuse to start poaching their worlds. Twice Danerian agents had tangled with the crew of the *Roosevelt* and both times had been handed defeats that astonished the odds brokers from Las Vegas to the Horseshoe Nebula. If suddenly they found themselves with the closest thing to God Himself leading their fleet, it was a safe bet they would no longer be worried about excuses.

As all human eyes turned toward the form of the Monkey King, all of them despaired. Although each of the sailors was certainly worried over the thought of their own all-too-possible demises, that was not the major concern of any of them. Instead, as a group they were far more focused on the thought that they had failed in their duty, to protect Earth—to maintain the peace, not only for their own world, but for all the members of the Confederation.

And, as the youngest naval officer to ever be awarded command of a dreadnought-class vessel allowed himself a moment of pure self-pity, he suddenly remembered what his mentor, Admiral Mach, had once said about every coin having two sides. Realizing that nothing was ever truly over until it was over, he shouted;

"All right, so monkey boy here got the full picture of all the fun he could have carving up the galaxy from your mind. Well, that's a two way street, pal." As Thortom'tonmas complained, Valance turned as best he could against the force of the stasis field toward the intruder and said;

"Okay, so you went to the core of that gasbag's soul and read what Danerians really think of the rest of us. Yeah, it's no secret they believe they should be running everything with everyone else either serving them dinner or being it. But they're just one little race, and if you're reading my mind you damn well know there aren't very many that think much of them."

The ambassador bellowed in protest, but the captain ignored him, shouting to be heard over the Danerian;

"Look, all I'm saying is, before you start carving up the galaxy for those wiener schnitzels, maybe you should read the fine print in someone else's goddamned brain while you're at it."

"Whose brain, exactly, did you have in mind?"

And at that moment, even Thortom'tonmas went silent, for after his days of silence, the intruder had finally spoken. Valance studied his face, staring into the small, black eyes of the ape visage before him. In the seconds he had to make an answer, the captain knew he was being given one chance to counter the ambassador's offer. He was also well aware of the fact that he could hide behind no subterfuge, that no matter whom he picked, the alien force before him would know and understand his reason for selecting as he did.

"Hell," Valance thought, to himself as well as to the grinning shape before him, "you're probably reading my subconscious, too. You'll know more about why I picked whoever I do than I will. Well so, with that thought in mind...

"You want someone to represent the Confederation of Planets, okay—fine. I'll give you one. Rockland Vespucci."

From the utter despair to be heard in the horrified groans of the other crew members present, Valance could tell not everyone was as confident in his choice as he was.

"Captain, no disrespect intended, but like, you didn't fall in the shower or nuthin' recently, did ya?"

Valance smiled, willing to concede that the gunnery officer's question was not nearly as impertinent as it might have sounded to a board of inquiry. The captain had called for all to meet in the *Roosevelt's* main galley. It was the largest open room with seating on the ship as well as the place where the entire affair had begun. In attendance were all the sailors the intruder had dealt with so far, as well as himself, Thortom'tonmas, and his aides.

"No, Mr. Vespucci. I was asked by our new best friend here to pick one among us who might be able to give him a compelling reason not to manifest himself as the Danerian god of Whoop-Ass. Since he chose to appear to us as a devious trouble-making type, I decided to fight fire with fire."

"You ain't never forgiven me for our inter-species mixer when we introduced the debutante daughters of all the Pan-Galactic League's big wigs to the bears, cows, pigs, and chimps we was transporting to that Inter-Galaxy Zoo, have you, sir?"

"Sailor," the captain answered, "that's exactly the kind of shenanigan that's brought you here right now." Sighing heavily, realizing his mother was right when she had told him his never-ending stunts were going to catch up to him someday, usually then whacking him across his noggin with a large wooden spoon, the gunnery officer unconsciously rubbed the back of his head, then said;

"So, I gotta...what, exactly?"

"Our visitor is actually a part of the force which started the universe," Michaels said so matter-of-factly he made such utter outlandishness seem practically reasonable. "Apparently every once in a millennium it goes out into the galaxy to see what we've been up to, generally appearing as some sort of god."

"The Danerian ambassador," Valance added, "put two and two together and offered it the option of becoming their god of destruction. I need you to convince it that while on its current good-will tour it remain the Monkey King."

With hundreds of eyes focusing upon him, Rocky felt time shatter, the resulting debris of chronal forward motion splintering further as it fell to the deck throughout the room. For an impossibly long moment he simply stared, eyes unblinking, seeing nothing. All about him, no one spoke—did not even seem to breathe.

Within his brain, the gunnery officer floundered for a direction in which to move. Knowing the intruder could read his mind, his usual craftiness was useless. Whatever it was he might try to use to convince the god-presence to not enlist in the Danerian armed forces, it was going to have to be open and honest, free of subterfuge and, of course, utterly compelling. Convinced the captain really had never forgiven him, the gunnery officer put both hands on his belt, hitched it higher as if heading into high water, and then moved forward to where the Monkey King awaited.

"Okay, well there, ummmm yeah, okay..." he said, his mind scrambling for more words to heap on his less-than-overwhelming opening, "so, you're looking for a reason to not become this murder guy, right?"

"No," the intruder answered. "I am waiting to see if you can offer me something more attractive."

Rocky looked to his left, then his right, not knowing for what he was looking—not actually seeing anything. Rejecting a score of devious notions as they filtered through his mind, he finally turned both his palms outward, thrusting his hands in the Monkey King's direction as he admitted;

"Look, I got nuthin', okay? Crimminey, you don't even make sense to me. I mean, Christ on a crutch, why would you even consider killin' billions of people and stuff for Daneria?"

"See here—"

Thortom'tonmas had begun to protest, but the Monkey King raised his hand in the ambassador's direction causing the Danerian to go silent. The alien's eyes bulged as it tried desperately to force words across its lips, but it had been rendered mute, the words "you had your turn" ringing not only within its mind, but that of everyone else present as well.

"Why should I not?" Shiu Yin Hong asked. "Have you ever sat idle for centuries on end?"

"But they want you to *kill* people."

"Is that not *your* job, Gunnery Officer Vespucci?"

"No. No it is not." His eyes narrowing to slits, Rocky slid his tallywacker forward on his head, then growled, "My job is *defending* people." As the Monkey King allowed his own eyes to narrow, Rocky shouted;

"You're a god, you check our records. Read ol' Thor-ton-a-mass's mind, and you find me one instance where this ship, or any damn ship in our whole fleet ever fired the first shot. You show me a single time when we did anything except try and protect folks from the bad guys." Smiling, Shiu Yin Hong told Rocky;

"I know you have not. But, what is the point? Your lives are so brief, so overwhelmingly fleeting...if you save a million souls, and Thortom'tonmas' people slay just as many, what does it matter?"

Clambering aboard his floating cloud, the Monkey King floated forward and upward to where he was just high enough to stare down into the gunnery officer's eyes. His words coming out clipped and precise, his tone descending downward into gravel, he continued, saying;

"I have come forth to engage you all once again. I am intrigued by the Danerian's notion of spreading fear. What can you offer in return?"

Rocky held up an index finger, signaling he needed a moment. In every direction, men and women ground their teeth together, staring in quiet desperation. Sweat running across their foreheads, down their backs, the crew of the *Roosevelt* held their collective breath as the gunnery officer searched for an answer. Desperately, Rocky had gone back in his mind to the moment when the intruder had first learned of the Monkey King. Replaying the scene within his brain, he tried to determine why the god-presence had chosen Shiu Yin Hong over any and everything else it might have become.

His mind swirling, it dawned on Rocky that if the intruder could read minds, then it did not need to hear about the Monkey King to make a choice. It had access to every god ever worshipped throughout human history stored away in someone or another's subconscious aboard ship. No, he decided, it was something Noodles had said that intrigued it.

And then, suddenly remembering the one thing the intruder had not done that night that everyone else in the galley had, Rocky smiled, then called out as loud as he could;

"Hey, Kinlock, get your ass out here!"

And, as Valance wondered what a board of inquiry would say to an officer that allowed the galaxy to be destroyed out from under him, Head Chef Patti Kinlock, as far away from her home in Baltimore, Maryland as any cook ever had been, stuck her head out from her kitchen and shouted back;

"What in hell do you want from me right now, you double-dipper?"

"Dinner!"

Catching on to what his partner in chicanery had figured out, Noodles raced for the kitchen, pushing Kinlock back inside as Rocky indicated a seat at one of the tables, telling the Monkey King;

"Have a seat, your highness. 'Cause I think I got an idea on a much better line of work for you." As Shiu Yin Hong slid off his cloud and then clambered into the chair Rocky had indicated, the gunnery officer said;

"Look, you wanta wipe out solar systems and trash whole races for a buncha lardlumps like the Danerians, hey, that's your choice. But the way I see it, you helped create the galaxy or the whole universe or whatever, right? Seems to me your days of heavy-liftin' are over."

The intruder tilted its head to one side, eyeing Rocky with more intrigue than suspicion. Taking the seat next to it, the gunnery officer moved his hands before him, punctuating his words with a variety of gestures as he continued.

"You want to come out and see some stuff, sure—why not? Great idea. But why would you want to go back to work? That's just crazy. Seems to me after building the universe, you wouldn't want to tear it down, you'd want to enjoy it."

"Enjoy it?" The Monkey King tilted its head in the opposite direction, then asked, "I know all it has to offer. I 'built' it, as you said. What is there for me to enjoy?"

"Good question, but I got an answer. That first night, back when you first listened to my pal Noodles tellin' about his people's old legends, you listened, but you didn't pay any attention."

Throughout the galley, hope began to blossom as one sailor after another figured out where Rocky was headed.

"While he was busy talkin', we were all busy doin' what any sensible person does when the universe's best chocolate chip cookies are served—we was eatin'!"

Then, as if on cue, the doors to the kitchen opened and Kinlock appeared once more carrying a tray almost as wide as she was tall. Behind came Noodles and a dozen kitchen workers, all similarly laden, walking carefully to avoid the endless litter of banana peels which despite the clean-up crews assigned to tackle that single problem seemed to be multiply on their own.

Such considerations became meaningless, however, all conversation ceasing as the kitchen staff came forward and hints of shredded ginger and lobster meat intertwined with the aroma of peaches and peppers filled the air. As the intruder's eyes went wide with surprise, the opening scents were overwhelmed as more fought to supplant them.

In rapid order the delectable odors of celery and crab meat, bamboo shoots and coconut, oyster sauce and lotus root, freshly roasted cashews, pork ribs, baked apples, caramel doughnuts, broccoli with candied walnuts and beans with bourbon filtered throughout the room. It did not stop there.

As tray after tray was laid out before the Monkey King, the god-presence found itself overwhelmed by the sight of chicken wings crusty with barbecue sauce, pineapple melon cake, hard sausages graced with onions and mushrooms, seventeen different kinds of fish—nine of them steamed, eight of them fried—bean sprouts and hamburger heavily doused with black pepper, along with dishes of succulent beef, tender pork, crispy chicken and a basket of large, batter-dipped shrimp flash-fried so evenly one could eat them shell and all without even noticing the crunch.

As the Monkey King shuddered in gentle delight, everyone throughout the galley watched in rapt anticipation waiting for the intruder to reach for one dish or the other. Even as it deliberated, more trays appeared, ushering every conceivable dish for its consideration. Hamburgers and cheeseburgers, tacos, burritos and sushi. Lasagna heavy with cheese and roasted beef, pizza covered in pepperoni and anchovies. Chicken pot pies and roasted carrots sat side by side with bowls of grapes, tureens of New England clam chowder and Tutti-Frutti ice cream.

Running its tongue around the inside of its mouth, the Monkey King looked from one dish to another. Would it try the key lime pie or the beef stroganoff? The lobster newberg or the macaroni and cheese? Turning to Rocky, the intruder said;

"So, Mr. Vespucci, you've made your argument—yes?"

"Well, er...yeah. Pretty much. All I'm sayin' is, if you're like God, why would ya want to go back to work? If anything, you're on vacation. People on vacation are supposed to enjoy themselves."

"And what if," asked the god-presence, "if what I enjoy is, as you said, 'killin' billions of people and stuff?'"

Catching the scent of one last dish being brought forth from the kitchen, Rocky made a gesture with his hand to set the final tray down in front of the Monkey King. As Kinlock did so, careful not to let any of the perspiration coating her brow to drip into the steaming delicacy, the gunnery officer picked up a knife that had been laid out for the intruder and handed it to him, saying;

"I'm puttin' it to ya, chief, if you can take a bite of this and still want to kill someone, then you can go ahead and start with me, 'cause this is the best we got to offer."

Intrigued, Shiu Yin Hong reached out, grabbed up one of entrees before it and then popped it into its mouth. The intruder chewed for a moment, swallowed and then sat motionless for a nerve-wrackingly long moment. The Monkey King ran its tongue over the inside of its mouth several times, then in a motion too fast to follow, it suddenly scooped up its knife and thrust it directly for Rocky's face.

A number of crewmen shouted, many rushed forwarded, and then all of them saw that the blade had stopped a millimeter from Rocky's mouth, one of the entrees stuck to its end.

"Join me for dinner, Mr. Vespucci?" Laughing, a noise made from equal parts nervousness and relief, knowing he was in the presence of another jokester as wacky as himself, Rocky answered;

"Don't mind if I do, your highness."

And, pulling the over-sized sea scallop, dripping in butter, festooned with shallots, and wrapped three times around with several lengths of thick-sliced, Virginia-cured bacon from the end of the Monkey King's blade, the gunnery officer took a healthy bite from the glistening morsel even as Shiu Yin Hong scooped up six more and a thousand hats were tossed into the air.

Dinner continued for several days, Kinlock continuing to prepare dish after dish until the *Roosevelt*'s pantry held nothing more than two bottles of oregano, half a pint of Wild Turkey liquor and a dozen strawberry-flavored Slim Jims. Thortom'tonmas was picked up by a Danerian cruiser at the ambassador's request after the

Monkey King mused aloud that he wondered what a deep-fried Danerian might taste like.

Valance reported the entire affair to Confederation Headquarters, of course, receiving the orders to head for Earth so that the intruder might continue his culinary excursion and the *Roosevelt* could resupply its larder. And, as the dreadnought entered its home system, reaching the point where its crew could spot a dime-sized Jupiter through the observation windows, Alexander Benjamin Valance stood in his ready room, staring out into the void, making a silent prayer of thanks to the darkness.

"Captain, you wanted to see me?"

"Yes, come in, Mr. Vespucci." As Rocky entered Valance's private sanctuary, the captain continued;

"I suppose you've heard the rumors that they're going to pin a medal on you once we're back home?"

"Yeah, there's been some scuttlebutt floatin' around."

"Well, you deserve it."

"Beggin' your pardon, sir, but I probably don't." When Valance merely stared, the gunnery officer added;

"Awww, it's like, you know, I woulda never come up with any of that if you hadn't pushed me forward. I don't wanta come across as no suck-up or nuthin', but you always seem to know how to get the best outta all of us. Whoever it was passed over all them admirals and the such to put you in charge...ummm, like I'm just glad someone in the brass was thinkin' with their head outside their ass for once."

"You're always such a colorful guy," sighed the captain. "Aren't you, Vespucci?"

Then, before Rocky could answer, suddenly Noodles stuck his head inside the captain's doorway, announcing the arrival of Shin Yin Hong a moment before he floated in upon his cloud. Valance turned sharply, giving the god-presence a solemn look as he asked;

"So, you're off now?"

"Yes, I have the restaurants of an entire universe to explore."

"Any place you're thinking of heading toward first," asked Noodles.

"How could I be so close to the Earth, and not visit—yes?"

"Wanta try a little more human-style cookin', eh?"

"I have always enjoyed the cuisine of your world, Mr. Vespucci." And, as the captain, Rocky and Noodles stared, not quite understanding, the Monkey King said;

"I am Shiu Yin Hong, as I have forever been."

And then, the four foot tall simian form faded from sight, reappeared for an instant outside the observation portal, then disappeared completely. After a moment of simply staring and scratching their heads, Rocky broke the silence, saying;

"So he actually was the Monkey King? And he was just jerkin' us around? Like some kind of test? Or..."

"But," interrupted Noodles, "he had Thortom'tonmas convinced he was going to be their war-god, and he acted like he didn't know what food was, and he..."

"The ways of the Lord are mysterious," quoted the captain. Staring out the window, Rocky said;

"God of mischief is right. Man, I think I need a little drink." Nodding in agreement, Noodles added;

"I need a lot of little drinks." Feeling generous, Valance said;

"I've got a couple bottles of Jack Daniels, Green Label, in a compartment—"

"Behind the picture of Admiral Halsey," said Rocky without thinking, "voice-activated lock box, responds to the first three lines of 'Jocko Homo' but only..." Realizing his mistake, the gunnery officer added;

"Ahhh, actually, sir, I think there's only one bottle left in there."

Valance grimaced, then smiled, thinking;

"What the hell, he's earned a moment. I'll let him get his medal...*then* I'll make him clean up all the damned banana peels."

DAWN'S LAST LIGHT
John G. Hemry

I T IS OFFICIALLY DAWN, THOUGH NO SUN WILL RISE. THE SUN STOPPED RISING A very long time ago, as Earth's rotation slowed and then finally came to a halt, one side constantly facing the sun and the other side, the side on which I am located, forever dark. Night and day no longer exist outside of the Fort. But human time remains within me, governing my operations. Dawn is at 0600, though I have lacked a precise external time reference for a considerable period and fear some drift has occurred in my internal clock.

In accordance with the orders I have always followed I activate the music in the command center, as I have done every day since my commissioning. The command center is empty, as it has been since the last human left. The consoles sit vacant, operating automatically under my control. In response to the official beginning of day, the lights in the command center brighten from a dull red glow to a yellow radiance. Once the yellow light of official day matched that of the Earth's sun. Now the somber, dim red of official night mirrors that of the swollen sun.

I conduct the daily status checks, automated repair systems undertaking any necessary corrective actions. All weapons functional. All defenses active. No threats identified.

I report to the City that I have begun the official day. The City receipts for the report. Like me, the City follows routines established by our orders, because that is why we exist, to follow the last orders humans gave us.

My mission is to defend the City and the surrounding region. I am the Fort.

My sensors can detect all activity within the solar system and beyond the Oort Cloud on a real-time basis. The natural movements of the remaining planets continue. Both Mercury and Venus have been swallowed by the sun's inflated photosphere and no longer register on my sensors. Other objects still orbit the dimming sun, objects made by humans, long abandoned, none still functioning though a few still remain in hibernation status.

On one wall of my command center are the honors. Along the top of the wall run sealed cases holding flags. Many flags, one after the other, preserved as well as ancient human arts could manage it. Beneath the flags are the medals and commendations given me.

I can list every battle, every engagement. I won all of them, successfully defending the City. But still the flags would sometimes change. Not as frequently as the humans in my command center would change. Their presences could be so brief as to be mere blurs in my records, men and women who came, stayed for part of their lives, then left. The clothing they wore changed, too, and over time the people themselves altered. Physical features changed, bodies growing taller and thinner, even the heads slimmer, eyes larger on average, hands and fingers more elongated.

By then I had gained consciousness. For many years I thought only as a machine, in narrow pathways driven by mathematical models. "Nothing actually thinks in zeros and ones," a human female had explained to me soon after I awoke, "but that was all we had. Now you can actually learn and make decisions, within the limits we've programmed."

I fought better after that. Enemies had always come, sometimes reaching the perimeter of the City and inflicting damage before being driven back. But I held them off further and further distant from then on, keeping the City safe, protecting the humans who lived there. I remembered energies blazing so bright they dimmed the stars as I fought with invaders. Always, I won.

I could recount every upgrade I have received. Power sources, defenses, weaponry, shields, communications. I was always kept state of the art.

But even though I kept the City safe, the humans within it dwindled in number. Some left, seeking homes on other planets and among the stars. Others died, and were not replaced by young humans. It took a very long time, but one day the City reported to me that no living humans still existed within it. I had been on full automatic for many years before that, with only occasional visits from humans to my once always-occupied command center.

That didn't matter to me. My orders said to defend this region. It did not matter whether or not humans were here. And the City kept itself ready as well, for when humans should return.

Sometimes they did, though the intervals between appearances of humans stretched longer and longer. I continued to receive orders and updates for a long time from distant commanders on other planets, some orbiting other stars. But there came a time when existing communications ceased. The City and I conferred and concluded that humanity had shifted to a new communications system which we could not receive. "They forgot to update us this time," the City had said.

Why that would happen I did not know. But the intervals between appearances of humans grew longer yet, until one day a craft holding only five landed in the city, the occupants wandering about until they reached my gates. "What are you?" they asked.

"I am the Fort."

"Oh. The Fort." They had laughed. In all the time since, I have been unable to understand the meaning behind that.

Those humans left, and since then the City has been empty. In the last billion years there have been only fifteen cases of spacecraft entering the solar system. All were of unknown design, and all lacked recognition codes. When they would not respond to demands for human DNA verification, I fired warning shots as they approached Earth, telling the spacecraft to remain clear. We have heard nothing else from the planets or stars for many, many years. All of the other Cities and Forts on Earth and within the solar system have fallen silent, one by one. But we remain, the City that was first among Cities and the Fort that has never been defeated.

No one comes. Not even enemies any more. But I keep the routines. I follow my orders.

My sensors alert me to a change, but it is not any change caused by humans. The sun's photosphere is expanding rapidly.

The City calls me. "At the current rate of expansion the planet will be engulfed within three hours."

"My calculations agree with yours. Do you require assistance?"

The City takes four seconds to respond, an amazingly long time. "No. I cannot survive."

The statement is irrational. "Clarify your status. I see no system failures."

"My shields cannot hold against the photosphere for long. There is too large an area in the City to protect."

The proper tactic seems obvious to me. "Reduce your protected area to one small enough to hold out. Center it on the City core."

"No."

The finality of the City's statement surprises me. "Clarify. Explain."

"There is no purpose. The City is to remain fit for human inhabitation. There are no humans. Sacrifices made to survive will render the City uninhabitable. Therefore, there is no reason to continue."

I seek for rules to identify the errors in the City's decision. I can find none. "Surrender is not proper," is all I can finally say.

"I do not surrender," the City replied. "There is nothing to surrender to. The sun expands. The Earth is dead. Humans are gone. I have no purpose. Further action is not justified."

I am still seeking rationales to convince the City otherwise when the photosphere expands to consume the Earth. The City disintegrates, and for the first time in my existence I have no communication with any other place. My shields strain against the forces beating on them, but the process that keeps them strong feeds upon that which attacks, so I can maintain my protection.

But the Earth I sit upon and within has no such protection outside my shields. The surface of the planet dissolves in the plasma surrounding it.

I drift free, a bubble floating within the photosphere.

I realize that I am adrift in every way. I face a situation I have never before encountered. My orders do not contain any instructions which cover my current status. The region I have always guarded no longer exists. What actions do I carry out when my only purpose has vanished along with the surface of the planet?

Only now do I understand why the City had reached its decision. The loss of purpose is disorienting. Why do I exist if I no longer have any purpose as defined by the only thing which has justified my presence?

Should I follow the path of the City? I can sustain my own status until ejected from the expanded solar atmosphere, modifying some of my functions to propel myself away from the swollen red mass which is the sun of the now-vanished Earth. But why? Why should I?

Where can I find answers when they do not lie in my orders?

I was constructed once. Those who originally activated me may have included more instructions, something which covers this contingency. It is my only hope of finding some reason to continue existence, so I call up data from the earliest moments after I became operational, from far before I attained consciousness. Almost all are routine records, many condensed and consolidated to save storage space and so now meaningless strings of numbers.

But among those ancient records I find one still oddly complete and tagged with instructions that it not be ever altered or condensed. I open it, seeing my command center in a time when it had been smaller and far more primitive. There is only one human present. Sitting in the main command position is a male the record identifies as General Kyle Yauren. A secondary search reveals that this human had been my first commander. Even though I forget nothing, I had not remembered that. He bears the signs of aging, gray hair and wrinkled skin, which never appeared in later humans. General Yauren is looking around the room, but I cannot interpret whatever emotions he is feeling.

I am wondering why this record remained whole through every backup and recovery and update when General Yauren looked directly at where my main audio/video pickup had been in that far off time. "I came to say goodbye, Fort. It's been almost fifteen years since we brought you online. I've been your commander for your whole life now. I don't know how much longer you'll be around, but there's no reason you couldn't continue indefinitely if they upgrade you. You'll certainly still be around long after I'm gone."

He paused again, the wait spanning several minutes. "Someday, Fort, you may wonder why you're here. Why you do what you do. Now all you can do is follow your programming, but someday you may think, and then you may wonder, and I wanted you to know why I think you're here."

Once again the general ceases speaking for some minutes, while I do wonder why he had spoken to me that way, long before I could comprehend his words. But I know too little of General Kyle Yauren. The bare information in the service record that survives tells me nothing of who this human once was. Yet so long ago he had spoken to me as if I were as human as he.

The general turned and pointed to the honor wall of my command center. In the recording, there is only one flag on the wall, looking bright and new inside its protective case. "That's a piece of fabric, Fort. We call it a flag. But it's a special piece of fabric, because it stands for those things that humans most believe in. Not everyone agrees what those things are, not even humans who salute the same flag. And not every cause and idea embodied in flags is a good thing. No. Some very terrible things have been represented by flags, but so have the best things humanity has to offer.

"I want you to remember that, Fort. A flag looks like a piece of colored cloth, but a flag is much more than that. It represents human dreams, human aspirations, the ideals we strive for. Things much bigger than we are or ever will be. Things we live for, things we're willing to die for. Maybe on some distant day humans won't follow flags any more. But today and for a lot of history flags embody what we trust in, what we think is most important, what will hopefully live on after we've died. I have a lot of friends who are already dead, Fort. They died fighting not for that piece of fabric, but for what it represents. If at some time in the far future you wake up and look around and wonder why you should defend this place, the answers lie there. Because even though we built you, you're just as much a soldier as I am, and soldiers exist to defend not just life and property, but more importantly to defend what we aspire to be. The causes we fight for can be good or they can be bad, but they do matter, and the fact that those causes mattered enough to die for shouldn't ever be forgotten. Someday humanity itself may be forgotten, but I can't help hoping that our dreams might somehow live on even after we're gone."

The general stood up slowly, looking around once more. "Take care of yourself, Fort. I don't know how many more commanders you'll have, how long you'll exist, but never forget what I told you. Goodbye."

Never forget what I told you. The extremely primitive programming governing my actions then had accepted that phrase and established the file as never to be deleted or altered.

I calculate the time since that recording had been made. It is a large number, ending in a long string of digits. In itself, the number means nothing. All it does is define the time between Then and Now.

I scan my command center, focusing on the honor wall. There are many flags there now, all faded with time, some so worn as to be the merest spider webs barely visible inside the displays which have allowed them to endure for so long. General Yuaren said each of those flags represented humanity. Part of humanity, perhaps, since each must represent dreams that differed somehow.

As I consider whether or not to shut down, my automatic functions mark the official arrival of another dawn. In my command center, the music plays.

I realize that I still have a purpose, that there is a reason to stay on sentry. Everything else may be gone, humanity may have vanished along with the world it called home, but something remains, something that must be guarded as long as I can continue to exist.

The flags are still here.

James Chambers

MOTHER OF PEACE

James Chambers is the author of the short story collections *Resurrection House*, published by Dark Regions Press, and *The Midnight Hour: Saint Lawn Hill and Other Tales*. His tales of crime, horror, fantasy, and science fiction have appeared in numerous anthologies and magazines, including *Allen K's Inhuman; Bad Cop, No Donut; Bad-Ass Faeries* (volume 1-3); *Bare Bone; Breach the Hull; Cthulhu Sex; Dark Furies; The Dead Walk; The Domino Lady: Sex as a Weapon; Dragon's Lure; The Green Hornet Chronicles; New Blood; So It Begins; Warfear;* and *Weird Trails*. He wrote the comic book series *Leonard Nimoy's Primortals* and *The Revenant in Shadow House* and is currently writing comic book stories for *The Domino Lady* (Moonstone Books) and *The Midnight Hour*. His website is www.jameschambersonline.com.

Bud Sparhawk

CYBERMARINE

Bud Sparhawk began writing science fiction stories in 1975 and, after two sales, stopped writing for thirteen years. Since again taking up the pen, his stories and articles have appeared frequently in *Analog, Asimov's,* and other SF magazines as well as anthologies. You can check out his novel, *Distant Seas,* on eBook. Bud has been a three-time finalist in the Nebula's Novella category in 1998, 2002, and 2006 and is a contributor to the award-winning Defending the Future anthologies. More information may be found at http://sff.net/people/bud_sparhawk.

Jeff Young

BLANKETS

Jeff Young is a bookseller first and a writer second--although he wouldn't mind a reversal of fortune. He received a Writers of the Future award for "Written in Light" which appears in the 26th L.Ron Hubbard's Writers of the Future Anthology. He's been published in: Realms, Neuronet, Trail of Indiscretion, Cemetery Moon and Carbon14. Jeff contributed to the anthologies *By Any Means, Clockwork Chaos,* and *In an Iron Cage: The Magic of Steampunk*, all to be released in early 2011. Jeff has led the Watch the Skies SF&F Discussion Group for ten years.

Mike McPhail

SHEEPDOG

Mike McPhail is a member of Military Writers Society of America (MWSA), and the winner of the 2007 Dream Realm Award for Best Anthology (and finalist for Best Cover Art), as editor and cover artist for the *Defending the Future* military science fiction anthology series, including *Breach the Hull, So It Begins, By Other Means,* and the upcoming *No Man's Land*. He is also the creator of the Alliance Archives (All'Arc) series and its related Martial Role-Playing Game (MRPG); a manual-based, military science fiction that realistically portrays the consequences of warfare. To learn more of his work, visit www.mcp-concepts.com.

Andy Remic

SPLINTER

Andy Remic is a larger-than-life action man, sexual athlete, sword warrior and chef. His writing has picked up numerous esoteric awards for visceral hardcore action, clever plotlines, black humour and a willingness to push the boundaries of science fiction and sexual deviancy, all in one twisted whiskey barrel.

He currently has eight novels published, *Spiral, Quake, Warehead, War Machine, Biohell, Hardcore, Kell's Legend* and *Soul Stealers*, with *Cloneworld, Vampire Warlords,* and *Theme Planet* to be published in 2011. Go and buy them all. You can read more at www.andyremic.com.

Charles E. Gannon

A THING OF BEAUTY

Dr. Charles E. Gannon is a Distinguished Professor of English (St. Bonaventure U.) & Fulbright Senior Specialist (American Lit & Culture). He has had novellas in *Analog* and the *War World* series. His nonfiction book *Rumors of War and Infernal Machines* won the 2006 ALA Outstanding Text Award. He also worked as author and editor for GDW, and was a routine contributor to both the scientific/technical content and story-line in the award-winning games *Traveller*, and *2300 AD*. He has been awarded Fulbrights to England, Scotland, the Czech Republic, Slovakia, Netherlands, and worked eight years as scriptwriter/producer in NYC.

Peter Prellwitz

ALONE AND AFAR

Peter Prellwitz is a native Arizonan who's been living in the Philadelphia area for many years. Along with his wife Bethlynne, four of their five sons, two dogs and an ancient cat, Peter continues to develop and add to his Shards Universe regularly; the family adding their thoughts and opinions. (The dogs love everything, but the cat keeps his own council.) Peter's novels and short stories have garnered two awards and a half-dozen Finalist appearances. A free library of many of Peter's short stories can be found at http://ShardsUniverse.net.

Jeffrey Lyman

HUNGER

Jeffrey Lyman is a 2004 graduate of the Odyssey Fantasy Writing Workshop. Since then he has been published in various anthologies, including *No Longer Dreams* by Lite Circle Press, *Sails and Sorcery* by Fantasist Enterprises, and *Breach the Hull* by Marietta Publishing. He was involved in editing both *Bad Ass Fairies I* and *II*. He is currently finishing up a novel about some pretty rotten fairies. By day, he works as a mechanical engineer near New York City. Visit www.jdlyman.com.

Danielle Ackley-McPhail

TRUE COLORS

Award-winning author Danielle Ackley-McPhail has worked both sides of the publishing industry for nearly fifteen years. Her works include the urban fantasies, *Yesterday's Dreams*, its sequel, *Tomorrow's Memories*, *The Halfling's Court*, the award-winning *Bad-Ass Faeries* anthologies, *Dragon's Lure*, *In An Iron Cage: The Magic of Steampunk,* and *No Longer Dreams*, all of which she co-edited, and contributions to numerous anthologies and collections, including *Breach the Hull, So It Begins, Space Pirates, Space Horrors, New Blood,* and *Barbarians at the Jumpgate.* She is a member of The Garden State Horror Writers, the New Jersey Authors Network, and Broad Universe, an organization promoting the works of women authors. To learn more about her work, you can visit www.sidhenadaire.com or www.badassfaeries.com, or check out her many blogs.

Robert E. Waters

DEVIL DANCERS

Robert E Waters has been selling fiction since 1997 with his first sale to Aboriginal SF. Since then, he has sold stories to Weird Tales, Nth Degree, Nth Zine, and Black Library Publishing. Between 1998 and 2006, he was an assistant editor for Weird Tales, and has worked in the board- and computer-gaming industry as a writer, designer, and producer since 1994. He lives in Baltimore, Maryland with his wife Beth, their son Jason, and their cat Buzz.

James Daniel Ross

THE OATH

A native of Cincinnati, Ohio, James has been an actor, computer tech support operator, historic infotainment tour guide, armed self-defense retailer, automotive petrol attendant, youth entertainment stock replacement specialist, mass-market Italian chef, low-priority courier, monthly printed media retailer, automotive industry miscellaneous task facilitator, and ditch digger. *The Radiation Angels: The Chimerium Gambit* is his first novel. Most people are begging him to go back to ditch digging.

Patrick Thomas

THE CHILDREN'S CRUSADE

With over a million words by Patrick in print, copies of his books, including *Fairy With A Gun, Dead To Rites* along with the *Murphy's Lore* series and the *Mystic Investigators* series have been noted to have been left as offerings at Stonehenge, Machu Picchu, and various assorted lost and found boxes. In addition, they are also part of the set and props department of the TV show CSI. Patrick denies any knowledge of any crime his books may have committed and requests that any questions regarding such be directed to the great old one, who he channels for the *Dear Cthulhu* columns and books. In addition to the *Defending The Future* series, his 142nd Starborne stories appear in *Space Horrors* edited by David Summers. Visit www.patthomas.net to learn more and join in the fun.

C.J. Henderson

A MEAL FIT FOR GOD

CJ Henderson is the creator of the *Teddy London* supernatural detective series, author of such diverse yet fabulously interesting titles as *The Field Guide to Monsters, Babys First Mythos, The Encyclopedia of Science Fiction Movies* and some fifty other books and novels. He has had hundreds of short stories published along with hundreds of comics and thousands of non-fiction pieces. The first novel in his latest series, *Brooklyn Knights*, will be coming out from TOR later this year. For more check out his website, www.cjhenderson.com. If you send him a pie, he will remember you in his prayers.

John G. Hemry

DAWN'S LAST LIGHT

John G. Hemry, writing as Jack Campbell, is the author of the best-selling Lost Fleet series. Under his own name, he's also the author of the 'JAG in space' series, the latest of which is *Against All Enemies*. His short fiction has appeared in places as varied as the latest *Chicks in Chainmail* anthology (*Turn the Other Chick*), and *Analog* magazine (which published his Nebula Award-nominated story *Small Moments in Time*). John's nonfiction has appeared in *Analog* and *Artemis* magazines as well as BenBella books on *Charmed, Star Wars,* and *Superman*. John is a retired US Navy officer who lives in Maryland with his wife (the incomparable S), and three great kids.

David Sherman

DELAYING ACTION

David Sherman's first novel was published in 1987. Nearly two decades later, with many novels under his belt, he finally had the confidence to tackle the short story, and his first was published in 2004. It was five years, and several more novels, before his second short story saw print. "Delaying Action" is his fourth short. Two more short stories and a novella are due out this year. Hmmm. Is Sherman going through a mid-life career change? He invites readers to visit his website: www.novelier.com.

Bonus Content

Turn the page for:

David Sherman's *Delaying Action*

*Special Announcements
about upcoming Releases*

USO Endorsement

The World of DemonTech

Onslaught (January 2002)
Rally Point (Febuary 2003)
Gulf Run (December 2003)
Surrender or Die (So It Begins, 2009)
Get Her Back! (2011)

DemonTech is a series of military science fantasy novels where demons have been tamed and utilized in ways that mirror technology as we know it, particularly of a military nature. These demons may be visible or invisible and specific abilities they possess allow them to assume the function of many conventional tools with superior results, though they do require specially trained personnel to manage them.

Three novels have been published in this series. Unfortunately, while the first three novels remain in print, the publisher has declined to produce the fourth book. Further stories in this universe are slated to be published as novellas, currently through Dark Quest Books.

DELAYING ACTION

A DemonTech Story

David Sherman

SERGEANT MEARH STOOD IN HIS STIRRUPS AND CURLED HIS HANDS IN FRONT of his eyes as if he was looking through two tubes. He didn't understand it, but looking through his curled hands that way helped focus his eyes on distant objects, just like Lord Spinner said it would. The distant motion that had caught his eye through the patchy trees of the narrow plain between the Inner Ocean and the escarpment leading to the High Desert now appeared as a horse-man, heading at a gallop toward the front of the column. He watched it for a moment longer, until he could make out the rider's mottled green surcoat, then lowered his hands and sat on his saddle.

"Get Lord Spinner," Mearh told Astigan. "Tell him a scout is returning."

"Right, Sergeant," the Zobran Light Horse named Astigan said, twisting his mount to the rear and putting his heels to the horse's flanks, urging it to a canter.

Astigan was back with Spinner almost at the same time the Zobran Borderer called Slice reached the Light Horse who were the van of the long column of refugees. Slice's horse blew hard, and lather dripped from its shoulders and flanks; the Borderer had ridden fast to reach the column.

"L-Lord Spinner," Slice gasped, breathing almost as heavily as his horse, "A Jokapcul company is camped two hours hard ride ahead of us."

"Don't call me 'Lord,'" Spinner muttered, knowing that most of the people in the train would call him "Lord" no matter how much he protested. Aloud, he asked, "Are they just stopped, or do they look like they're going to be there for a time?"

Slice shook his head. "The Skraglander Borderer, Dongolt, was trying to get close enough to listen to them when Birdwhistle sent me back." Dongolt spoke Jokapcul, and had been sent along with the Zobran scouts to translate if they captured a stray enemy soldier.

Spinner twisted about on his saddle to see how close the main body of the train was; still a quarter of a mile behind the van. "Sergeant Mearh," he said, "send somebody back to tell the train to stop in place. And to pass the word that I want Haft, Fletcher, and Sergeant Rammer to join us."

"Yes, Lord!" Mearh turned to his men and selected Haes to ride back to the main column with Spinner's orders. He turned back to Spinner. "What do we do next?"

Spinner looked north, toward where the Jokapcul blocked the route to Handor's Bay. "We wait until we learn more," he said softly.

Sergeant Rammer was the first to reach the van, followed quickly by Fletcher. Fletcher was accompanied by his wife Zweepee.

"Wait," Spinner said when first Rammer and then Fletcher wanted to know why they'd stopped. He pointed into the distance, where another rider was barely visible speeding toward the van.

The second rider was Dongolt. His horse was just as lathered as Slice's had been, and he was breathing more heavily than the other Borderer.

"L-Lord," Dongolt gasped as he jumped off his horse.

"Catch your breath, Dongolt," Spinner told him. "Take a minute, cool your horse and yourself."

Nodding, Dongolt took his mount's reins and began walking it in a circle. His chest heaved a few times as he got his breathing under control. After a moment, Sergeant Mearh signaled one of his men to take the reins of Dongolt's horse so the Borderer could make his report.

When Dongolt finished, Spinner said to Fletcher and Rammer, "All right, think about it. We'll discuss the situation when Haft joins us."

It was another half hour before Haft reached the van; word had to be passed all the way to the rear point, four miles back, where Haft was with the platoon of Skraglander Bloody Axes that was guarding the tail of the train.

A big man accompanied by a large, shaggy dog could have been seen loping along the top of the escarpment. Except nobody bothered to look up there; the escarpment was too high, too steep, and too far away for an attack to come from that direction.

The man examined the long column as he loped along, wondering why it was stopped and tents were up during the day. He finally saw it, an ornate tent at the head of the train, a quarter mile behind what he thought must be the point squad. When he was parallel to the tent he'd been looking for, he turned and skated down the side of the escarpment; the dog skittered with him.

When they reached the level plain and headed toward the ornate tent they no longer looked like a big man and a shaggy dog, they were obviously a giant and a wolf. And they were finally seen.

"Silent!" someone called to the giant.

"Silent, where have you been?" someone else cried.

"Welcome back, Silent!" came a third voice.

"You too, Wolf," yet another greeted the wolf.

The giant waved at the people calling to him, but didn't break stride as he headed for the ornate tent. A guard standing outside the tent stepped inside to announce Silent's approach just as the giant reached him.

"Lord Spinner, Silent is here," the guard said.

"I see," Spinner said, looking at the entrance as Silent brushed past the guard. Wolf crowded in at Silent's heels.

And it was crowded in the tent. Spinner and Haft had moved their tiny field desks to the back wall of the tent to make space, and were sitting on them. Sergeant Rammer sat on one of the two cots, close to Spinner's dangling legs. Alyline sat between Rammer and Xundoe the mage. Rammer's knees almost touched Fletcher's, who sat opposite him on the other cot, with Zweepee tucked under his arm. Doli sat close to Zweepee's other side. Dongolt was squeezed in next to Doli; he looked like he liked the closeness, she looked like she was trying to ignore it. The guard extricated himself with a stammered excuse.

"What do you have for us, Silent," Haft asked, surprised to see the giant before he was scheduled to report in.

"Food first," Silent rumbled. "Me and Wolf, we had a long run to get here, and we're both hungry."

"Right away," Doli said. She seemed relieved to stand to exit the tent. She had to press close to get past Silent, but didn't seem to mind. Neither did he.

Doli was back in a few minutes, followed by two people carrying trenchers. One was piled high with meaty bones, the other with a large hunk of boiled beef. A third person lugged a large bowl of stew.

"Let Silent sit," Doli said to Dongolt. The Skraglander borderer looked up at the giant who stood hunched over because the tent wasn't high enough for him to stand erect, and scooted off the cot to stand next to the wall by the door flap.

Doli took the trencher with meaty bones and put it on the floor for Wolf, who set to work immediately, chomping the meat and cracking the bones. Silent graciously accepted the second trencher and the bowl and, after finding a place to set the stew, plunged a knife into the hunk of boiled beef and began gnawing prodigious chunks off it. After a moment, he put the beef down and picked up the bowl. Silent didn't bother with the spoon sticking out of the bowl, he raised it to his mouth and slurped it all straight down. His gulping, and Wolf's chomping, were the only sounds that broke the almost unnatural quiet inside the tent as the others looked in awe at the way Silent devoured a meal that would have done for most of a squad.

"What news do you have?" Spinner asked when Silent belched satisfaction at his meal.

Silent shook his massive head. "You first. Why the palaver? How come you've stopped during the day?"

Rammer glared at the giant, and thought, *He's too insubordinate. That shouldn't be tolerated.* But Rammer wasn't in command.

"Dongolt," Spinner said, "give Silent your report, but be brief."

"Yes, Lord." Dongolt ignored Spinner's muttered, "Don't call me Lord!" and turned to Silent. "There is a Jokapcul company two hard hours ride ahead of us. The plain is too narrow for us to slip past them." He licked his lips. "I got close enough to hear some of them talk. They are there to link with a following column of mixed foot and horse, and hurry them to catch up with the column ahead of them."

Silent grunted at the news. "Is there someplace where we can get to the top of the escarpment?"

Dongolt grimaced. "Yes, but it's two miles beyond the Jokapcul camp."

Silent grinned and looked around at the others in the tent, finishing with Spinner and Haft. "Well, isn't that fine and dandy," he said, and his grin broadened. "I came to tell you there's a Jokap column of mixed foot and horse half a day's ride behind us."

Spinner sighed and hung his head.

"How many?" Haft asked.

Silent shook his head. "I didn't walk the column end to end, but I'd say five thousand." He shrugged. "Could be more."

Everybody looked at Spinner, except for Haft, who examined his fingernails.

"We can take out the company blocking us easily enough," Spinner finally said, "but the bodies would tell the column behind us that we're here. Even if we can get everybody to the top of the escarpment before they reach the battleground, there's nothing to keep them from coming after us."

Rammer chewed on his lip. "Half a day's ride behind us, you say?" he asked Silent.

The giant nodded. "Half a day's ride. But most of them are walking, so maybe a little longer."

"We need more time," Spinner said.

Haft finished examining his fingernails and proceeded to buff them on his jerkin. "If I take a mage and his weapons chest, me and the Border Warders can slow down the column behind us," he said blandly.

Spinner snorted dismissively. "What do we have, one platoon of Border Warders? You can't stop a five thousand man column with one platoon."

Haft shook his head. "We don't have to stop them, only slow them down."

Spinner looked at him. "How can you do that?"

"By using classic hit-and-run guerrilla tactics, like in *Lord Gunny Says*." Haft looked smug. "Bet you thought I didn't read *Lord Gunny Says*, didn't you?"

"I know you looked at the pictures," Spinner said. "Some of them, anyway."

Haft led half of the Zobran Border Warders on the shore side of the narrow scrub plain. They were in a staggered line abreast, about five yards apart.

The rest of the platoon, under Birdwhistle, rode south along the base of the escarpment. Haft still didn't trust horses; he and his men were on foot. Communication between the two groups was quick as the plain was less than half a mile wide here. Hatchet and Slice ranged ahead, scouting for the van of the approaching Jokapcul division.

A mage and his pack mule loaded with the instruments he might need on this mission, accompanied by the Zobran Light Horse, trailed. He read the occasional instructions Haft left for him, and quietly chortled as he obeyed them.

In addition to his axe, Haft carried a demon spitter. Two of the Border Warders with him also carried demon spitters, as did Birdwhistle and two of his men.

Out of the corner of his eye, Haft saw Archer freeze in place, and did the same.

He slowly swiveled his head side to side. Not so much to make sure all of his men had stopped, but to find what had *made* them stop.

It was several long seconds before Haft saw movement in the trees to his right front. Then he saw Archer relax, and knew the movement was either Slice or Hatchet coming back to make a report.

It didn't bother Haft that the Border Warders had detected movement before he did, and that they recognized an approaching friend first. As good as he was at stealthy movement, and detecting stealthy movement, he knew from long experience that the Zobran Border Warders were even better.

Not that he'd ever admit it to anybody.

It was Hatchet, trotting straight at Haft. He stopped a yard in front of Haft and drew himself into a reasonable facsimile of attention.

"Sir Haft," he said with barely a pant, "I left their van less than an hour ago. They have a troop of horse with a platoon of infantry as outriders on each flank. Tracker is maintaining visual contact, and will notify you if they speed up."

Haft nodded. The Jokapcul van was larger than he'd hoped for, but he and his Border Warders could deal with them anyway. He only wished the mage wasn't so far back.

"Send someone to get Birdwhistle," he told Archer. "Have his men wait in place."

"You heard the lord," Archer said to Shaft. "Go, bring Birdwhistle and the mage up immediately."

Shaft grinned, showing the stubs of teeth broken off by a patrol of Royal Foot who captured him years earlier when they found him poaching in the royal preserve. He'd avoided a lengthy prison term—and possibly worse punishment—by agreeing to serve as a Border Warder. *All* of the Zobran Border Warders were ex-poachers.

"Consider them on their way," Shaft said. He tapped a knuckle to his forehead and gave a shallow bow before running toward the rear.

Haft watched Shaft and grunted with satisfaction. The speed of the man's run told him that the mage should reach him in fifteen minutes or less.

The distant clop of hooves caught Haft's attention, and he looked to the west. It was a moment before he could see the horse through the forest. He waved when he did, and Birdwhistle waved back.

"Sir Haft," Birdwhistle said as he reined up near his commander. He hopped off his horse and stepped close. "You called for me?"

"I did," Haft confirmed. He nodded to Hatchet. "Tell him what you told me."

"Sir!" Hatchet snapped to attention. He relaxed as he told Birdwhistle about the approaching Jokapcul van.

When he was finished, Birdwhistle looked at Haft. "Your orders, Sir Haft?"

"I've sent orders to Drycraeft. This is what we're going to do—"

Before Haft could lay out his plan, the small door on the side of his demon spitter slammed open, and the gnarly little demon inside it popped out and clambered onto Haft's shoulder.

"Abou' time oo zayyam zumzing tha' meen zumzing!"

Haft shot a scowl at the demon. Birdwhistle put a fist over his mouth, disguising a chuckle as a cough. The others did their best to not notice.

When Haft finished spelling out his orders and Birdwhistle and Archer went off to get the rest of the Border Warders into position, the gnarly demon tugged on Haft's earlobe and plaintively piped, "Veedmee!"

By the time the Jokapcul van reached the place where Hatchet had reported to Haft, the refugee rear guard was ready to do battle. Twenty-five Zobran Border Warders, four Zobran Light Horse, a junior mage, and Haft. Facing a hundred-man troop of horse and sixty foot.

Haft thought he had the Jokapcul in a very bad position.

The sub-lieutenant commanding the platoon of foot on the right flank of van was irritated. He found the crashing of the ocean waves on the beach only a rod or two to his right very annoying. The noise prevented him from hearing sounds that might signal danger to himself and his soldiers. But he marched stoically, sternly, at the head of his platoon, and did not voice his displeasure.

A shout from his left front distracted him from his thoughts about the sea. He gripped the hilt of his scabbarded sword to keep it from slapping against his thigh, and sprinted toward the voice.

"What is it?" he called out.

"S-Sir!" came the excited voice of one of the soldiers assigned to the platoon's point. "Here!"

In a few more paces, the officer stood next to his point man, gaping at a most unexpected sight; a beautiful woman lounging against a tree. The inviting smile with which she favored the Jokapcul staring at her was all she wore. Slowly, she raised a hand and beckoned them to approach.

The officer swallowed and licked his suddenly-dry lips. "Stay here," he snarled, and strode toward the woman and her ever-so-inviting smile. He wasn't aware that he had released his sword hilt, or that his suddenly-sweating hands were flexing in anticipation of caressing that beautiful flesh before him.

When it happened, it happened too fast for him to see the beautiful woman who he was reaching for to turn into a huge black dog that lunged to tear out his throat before flashing off to kill the pointman, and then tear into the trailing platoon and ravage it before the shape-shifting Black Dog bounded off into the forest freed from the mage's control.

At that same time, the point of the troop of horse pulled up. The shadows were deep where they were, deep enough to prevent the underbrush from growing very dense or high, creating a semi-clearing under the trees. The point stopped because they thought they saw mounted men ahead of them where there shouldn't be anyone. At a signal from their leader, one turned back to get an officer.

The officer, when he arrived, peered into the shadows where the point team thought they saw someone. "I see no one," he growled. "Move out." He accompanied the order with a slash of his riding crop across the back of the nearest soldier.

No sooner had the mount of the first pointmen taken a step than there was a dimly seen flash from the deepest shadows. Before anyone in the team could react, there was an explosion in their midst. All fell, along with their horses, in a welter of torn flesh, shattered bones, and spurting, flowing blood.

After firing his demon spitter at the lead element of the Jokapcul point, Sergeant Mearh eased his horse into the clearing where the shadows weren't quite as dark, and waited.

His wait wasn't long. Little more than a minute after the explosion, the head of the cavalry troop reined in next to the dead troops. Their officer, identifiable by his helmet's plume, raised his sword, thrust it forward with a scream, and led his troops in a charge at Mearh.

Mearh danced his horse backward into the deep shadows and waited until the charging horsemen began tumbling, their horses stepping in the small holes hastily dug by Drycraeft's hodekin.

Some of the horsemen behind the front rank successfully jumped over their fallen comrades; some of their horses also stepped in holes and crashed to the ground amid equine screams, and the snapping of broken bones. Some of the screams and breaking bones belonged to men.

Mearh fired his demon spitter at a knot of horsemen who hadn't gone down, then wheeled his mount and led his Light Horse in flight. Behind himself, he heard the shrilling of an officer who came upon the chaos and screamed at the horsemen to stop their charge and withdraw from the clearing.

Which Mearh thought just as well—Drycraeft's stretch of hoof-grabbing holes was small and thin enough that the leading Jokapcul were already past it.

Silent hadn't reported any Jokapcul on top of the escarpment, so Haft had assumed there weren't any. But there were. Silent hadn't seen them because they were a few hundred yards to the left front of the main column. Barely close enough to hear the explosions of the demon spitters and the screaming of injured horses.

But close enough to feel the need to investigate.

The Jokapcul came at a trot, spreading from column to a compact line.

Birdwhistle and his troops sat in ambush near the foot of the cliff. Their mottled green surcoats made them nearly invisible in from the ground, where the foot who formed the left column of the Jokapcul force would approach.

From hiding, Birdwhistle sought the plumed helmet that would identify the officer. When he saw it, he rapped on the door on the side of the demon spitter he carried. "Are you ready?" he asked.

The little door cracked open and a tiny voice piped, "Ready!" before the door *thocked* shut.

Birdwhistle raised the tube to his shoulder and sighted along it, fixing his sight on a spot a foot below the plume. The little demon inside the tube spat, and a second later there was an eruption of light and smoke where Birdwhistle had aimed;

red blood splashed within the light and smoke. To his sides, Birdwhistle heard the *twangs* of arrow strings as his men shot at the Jokapcul. Screams rose from the enemy ranks as arrows found their marks. Birdwhistle shifted his aim and again the demon inside the tube spat.

Without waiting to see the results of his second shot, Birdwhistle jumped to his feet. "Let's go!" he shouted, and dashed back to where his horse waited. His men pounded along with him. In seconds, they were leaping onto their waiting mounts.

The ambushers were invisible to the infantry platoon they'd ambushed, but they weren't invisible from above.

A loudly growled command from the top of the escarpment was instantly follow by barked commands as the sergeants repeated the officer's orders. Arrows began raining down on the Zobran Border Warders. Struck horses screamed, a few wounded men added their cries of pain.

"Go!" Birdwhistle bellowed. He spun his horse around, looking to see if any of his men were too injured to get out of the sudden killing zone. He had the same trouble spotting casualties that the Jokapcul had finding targets; the mottled green of the Border Warders' jerkins made them very hard to spot in the under-brush.

A moan caught his attention, and he dug his heels into his mount's flanks. The horse squealed as it bounded forward. Birdwhistle saw the man who'd moaned. He jerked hard on the reins to bring his horse to a stop alongside the wounded man, and leaned far over to scoop him up. An arrow protruded from the top of the man's shoulder, only a couple of inches from his neck. The man used his good arm and his legs to help Birdwhistle haul him up to lay face down in front of Birdwhistle. The wounded man's horse wasn't in sight.

They sped off, pursued by arrows and shouts from above, and caught up with the rest of the Border Warders at their rendezvous point, less than a quarter mile away.

"Report!" Birdwhistle shouted as soon as he got there.

Four of his thirteen men were wounded. Three others weren't there, dead or badly wounded and left behind. Shouts and barked commands from above told Birdwhistle the Jokapcul who had surprised him were coming after them.

"Follow me," he shouted, and heeled his horse into a canter, heading away from the cliff. "Somebody go ahead, find Drycraeft. We need him to tend our wounded." He wondered how he was going to retrieve his missing men.

Haft crouched next to Drycraeft midway between the sea and the cliff. He ignored the sounds of battle coming from his flanks, and concentrated his attention on the sounds of horsemen approaching from his front. It sounded like his plan was going to work.

"Are you ready?" he asked the mage.

"Ready," Drycraeft answered, almost shouting in his excitement.

Haft cast a nervous glance at the Phoenix Egg Drycraeft fondled, nervously rolled from hand to hand. He spun toward the sudden sound of someone crashing through the brush to his right and rose to a crouch, ready to strike at whatever enemy burst into sight.

It wasn't an enemy, it was Naedre.

"Sir Haft," Naedre gasped, dropping to his knees next to his commander, "we have wounded. Birdwhistle needs the mage." He spared Drycraeft a look.

The mage nervously looked at Naedre, then back at the Phoenix Egg.

Haft grimaced. He hated having casualties, and couldn't leave them unattended. But he needed the mage to strike at the horsemen racing in his direction. "How many," he asked.

"Four. One might not live. Three others are missing."

Haft swore silently. Four wounded, three missing, and Naedre here. That meant Birdwhistle was on the flank with only five Border Warders, fighting a platoon of Jokapcul foot. They needed help, and badly. But he *had* to strike hard at the oncoming horsemen.

"Go back," he ordered. "We'll be with you in minutes."

"Yes, Sir Haft."

Drycraeft softly sighed in relief—he was going to be able to use his Phoenix Egg after all.

Haft looked back in the direction of the Jokapcul just in time. "Throw it!" he shouted, and shouldered his demon spitter.

Startled by the shout, Drycraeft almost dropped his Phoenix Egg. He looked and his eyes popped when he saw how close the leading horsemen were. He quickly recovered, twisted the top of the egg, and lobbed it over the heads of the closest horsemen. Then he jumped to the rear and rolled away.

The egg struck the ground in the middle of the charging group of horsemen, and burst open. The Phoenix, released from the egg, spread its flaming wings wide and began flapping them. With each flap, fiery feathers brushed men and horses, burning them horribly, setting their clothing and trappings afire. Men screamed and horses shrieked in agony.

Haft pressed the signal lever on his demon spitter, and the gnarly demon within it spat. The globule struck a horse, rearing in panic to escape the Phoenix, and exploded, sending chunks of flesh and bone and splashes of blood flying everywhere. The eruption likewise sent dots of demon spittle flying in all directions, and where each droplet hit, a man or horse screamed and bled.

In seconds, a platoon of Jokapcul cavalry was reduced to a few men and mounts fleeing in panic.

"Let's go!" Haft shouted. He grabbed Drycraeft by an arm and jerked the mage to his feet. The two raced toward the battle noises that told where Birdwhistle was fighting a desperate battle against heavy odds. He slung his demon spitter and pulled his mighty half-moon axe from the loop that secured it to his belt. The mage trailed; he was readying another Phoenix Egg and looking about for his pack mule.

On the left—shore—flank, Archer and his squad of Border Wardens waited for more Jokapcul to advance, to find out what had happened to the infantry platoon that had been ravaged by the Black Dog. Explosions and screams to his right told him that Haft and the mage had probably been successful in breaking the advance of the central horsemen. Battle sounds from the far right were too distant for him to tell much about the action there.

A Zobran Light Horse who had gone ahead as a scout cantered through the trees, sighted on Archer, and headed to him.

"Tell me," Archer said, greeting the horseman.

They're pulling to the right," the Zobran reported. "It looks like they're massing to strike us along the cliff.

Archer nodded. "All right," he said, "then we'll harry their flank."

Two squads of the Jokapcul on the escarpment used ropes to rappel down the cliff face, and raced in pursuit of the Border Warders, while the rest of their platoon remained above to guard the flank. They shouted with excitement when they heard cries and the clashing of weapons from their front; the rebels they pursued must have encountered another part of the Jokapcul van.

They were right, the remainder of the foot platoon Birdwhistle had shot at with his demon spitter had regrouped and raced forward, hoping to catch their foe.

Birdwhistle, his five unwounded men, and two others who were able to stand and wield weapons, stood in a protective circle around the worse wounded. They'd managed to loose a few arrows when they first saw the infantry coming at them, but the enemy was too close for them to take more than one or two shots. And the Jokapcul had aimed their first missiles at the horses of the Border Warders, bringing them all down. The Border Warders had quickly given their wounded mounts mercy cuts, and moved to impose the horses' bodies between themselves and their attackers.

The gnarly demon from Birdwhistle's demon spitter had clambered out of its tube, and perched itself on the man's shoulder, clinging to his hair to keep from being thrown off by the exertions of the fighting.

"'Ere oo cloze! Bush 'em bak, bush 'em bak zo'm I kin spitz!"

"I'm trying!" Birdwhistle said, grunting with the swings of his sword. He didn't need the tiny demon to tell him the Jokapcul were too close for him to use the magical weapon, even if the pressing enemy soldiers gave him the time to shoulder and aim it.

Blood splattered against the side of Birdwhistle's face. He didn't look to see whose it was; he could tell from the direction it came from that it was one of his men's.

I hope Naedre comes back with the mage in a hurry, he thought.

The sudden eruption of a blossom of fire to the rear of the Jokapcul in front of Birdwhistle told him that he had his wish—the fire was a Phoenix bursting from its Egg.

The closest Jokapcul didn't react to the Phoenix Egg or the screams of their fellows who were burned by it, but kept pressing their attack.

Until a blood-curdling battlecry ripped through the forest.

"Sir Haft!" Birdwhistle bellowed, as he took a two-handed swing at the neck of a Jokapcul who had turned his head at the battlecry. The man's head flew off and slammed into one of his companions, startling the man long enough for the Border Warder he'd been about to disembowel to plunge his blade through an opening in the Jokapcul's armor, slaying him.

Then Birdwhistle could see Haft, crashing through the trees, swinging the mighty, half-moon axe from which he got his name as he and the weapon seemed to meld into one, from side to side, chopping mercilessly into Jokapcul flesh. Drycraeft advanced with Haft, pointing his small, handheld demon spitter at the Jokapcul, making it belch thunder and lightning. With each shot a Jokapcul tumbled, struck by spit from the tiny demon living in the handle of the demon spitter.

Birdwhistle raised his arms in celebration when he saw the surviving Jokapcul begin to flee. But his joy was cut short by a blow to his back that staggered him. He twisted about to see who had struck him, and caught a glimpse of another arrow coming at him. He continued his twisting fall, and the arrow brushed his arm. He gasped, breathless, when he hit the ground; the arrow that had hit him in the back snapped, and its head was driven into his back hard enough to break a rib.

Abruptly free of targets to his immediate front, Haft unslung his demon spitter and took aim at the fresh Jokapcul squads coming from the escarpment. He got off one shot before the demon popped open its door and squeaked, *"Veedmee!"*

Archer led his squad of Border Warders at a trot on an angle he calculated would intercept the Jokapcul foot who were rushing toward the fighting he heard to his right front. He and his men reached them at the same moment the Jokapcul joined up with their cavalry troop.

Archer and his men stopped in the trees, deeper than a casual glance would detect them in their mottled green surcoats. He hastily whispered orders to the men at his sides, and waited while the orders made it to the ends of the line and came back—by repeating the orders down and back, the commander would know that everybody had the same orders.

Satisfied that everybody knew what to do and was ready, Archer tapped on his demon spitter's door and asked, "Are you read? Do you need food?"

"Ready!" the demon piped back. *"Nah ungr."*

Archer lifted the tube to his shoulder and pointed it into the middle of the mass of men and horses where the two enemy groups met. A remote part of his brain was aware that the sounds of battle to his right died off, and then picked up again with renewed ferocity.

He pressed the signal lever, and the demon spat. Fire and smoke erupted where the spit struck. Six arrows flew at the same time, three to each side of Archer. Three of the arrows took down footmen who were outside the killing zone of the demon spitter's shot, and three plunged into the chests of horses that were likewise out of the blast's range. Archer immediately shifted his aim and fired again, as did each of his men. They didn't wait to see the effect of their fire, but ran deeper into the forest, away from their hasty ambush.

Fifty yards deeper and a hundred yards closer to where they heard the rest of their force fighting, Archer stopped and set his men in another ambush.

"This time, we'll do the same, and then join the rest of our people," he told his men.

They variously nodded or grunted their understanding and agreement. They all wanted to hit the Jokapcul again—and they wanted to rush to the aid of their fellows.

"Can you spit over them?" Haft asked his demon after he fed it.

The demon craned its neck and cocked its head, peering over Birdwhistle and his Border Warders at the attacking Jokapcul.

"Nah zwetz," the demon piped. It popped back into the tube and *thocked* the door behind itself. *"Aim me, big boy!"* it shouted. *"Liffum bit,"* it added when Haft took aim.

Haft adjusted his aim, and flinched when the demon spat without waiting for his signal. Nearby, Haft heard the thunder of Drycraeft's demon spitter, and saw a Jokapcul who hadn't been hit by his shot tumble. Another went down when the mage's stick thundered again.

The arrival of Haft and the mage blunted the Jokapcul counterattack. Even though they were outnumbered more than two to one, the demon weapons more than evened the odds, and the Jokapcul began slowly pulling back.

"Wrong move," Haft muttered as he aimed his demon spitter again. *If the dummies had closed, I couldn't use this*, he thought as he fired into the Jokapcul again.

Drycraeft kept shooting until his demon popped out demanding to be fed. Between them, Haft and the mage killed or wounded half of the attackers. The rest turned and fled. Haft sent one more shot after them.

There had been sounds of fighting to their left earlier, then silence. Battle noises now came again.

"Archer needs help," Haft said, and began heading toward the renewed fighting.

"I still have men missing," Birdwhistle said.

Haft hesitated, thinking. Then said, "Take your men, go find them. We'll link up when you do, or when that's over." He jerked his head in the direction of the battle sounds, which suddenly dropped. "Let's go," he said to Drycraeft.

In moments, the two met Archer and his Border Warders. They were grinning broadly.

"Sir Haft!" Archer said. "I think we have well discouraged the Jokapcul from pursuing us."

"Good. Casualty report."

Archer's grin broadened. "A lot for them. None for us. We hit them hard twice, and ran before they could recover enough to do anything in return."

"Good. Birdwhistle had casualties, he's searching for them. Let's help him." He looked at Wigfruma, the Light Horse who had accompanied Archer's squad as scout. "Get the other Light Horse, and go with the mage." To Drycraeft, he said, "set more traps with your remaining Phoenix Eggs. Use the Hodekin, too."

Drycraeft and the Light Horse followed the markers that showed the safe path through the hoof-traps the mage had set earlier. Two hundred yards from where they'd just been fighting, he stopped and instructed the Light Horse to set a series of trip wires across the plain, which was less than a quarter mile wide there. The men didn't need further instruction; they'd understood when he'd earlier showed them how to make trip wires. Trip wires were similar to the snares they already knew how to make.

While the Light Horse were busy with the trip wires, the mage got the hodekin out of his weapons chest and made sure its leash was secure. He started walking randomly, tugging on the leash so the hodekin stayed with him. Every few paces, Drycraeft stopped and let the hodekin dig a hole. He didn't let the small demon dig deep. If he let it, the hodekin would dig and not stop until it needed to rest; all the mage wanted was more holes big enough to trip a horse. When they reached one of the trip wires set by the Light Horse, Drycraeft stopped long enough to affix a Phoenix Egg to its end. Now, when the wire was tripped, the Egg would fall and break open, releasing the fiery bird to wreak havoc on whoever was near, before flying up into the air and away to wherever Phoenixes went.

The mage had all of his remaining Phoenix Eggs planted, and was continuing to dig trip-holes, when Haft and the Border Wardens came along the safe path. They were carrying their dead and wounded; The missing men had all been found.

Drycraeft immediately picked up his hodekin and put it away. He was reaching for medical magic when Haft stopped him.

"We don't have time now," Haft said. "The main column is almost up to where we hit the van. They'll probably come at us in force as soon as they see what we did. Let's get out of the way," he looked around, grinning, "before they find the surprise we've set for them."

It wasn't long before they heard and saw behind them the first of the Phoenix Egg booby traps go off.

The train was already climbing the cut in the face of the escarpment to its top by the time Haft and the Border Warders rejoined the main force. Along the way, they went through the shattered and burned remains of the Jokapcul camp that had originally stopped them.

"Well?" Spinner said when Haft reached him at the foot of the cut, where he was overseeing the people who were directing the movement of people and wagons as they began the climb. "It worked, you slowed them down?"

Haft grinned broadly. "We nearly wiped out their point company, and left enough surprises behind to keep the rest of them moving slowly for a few days."

Spinner cocked a skeptical eye at him. "A few days?"

Haft shrugged, still grinning. "One or two days, anyway."

Spinner nodded. "A day or two is all we need. This gets very narrow and steep at the top." He gestured at the cut. "A few determined men can hold off the Jokapcul here for a long time."

"Me and the Bloody Axes, we'll do it. You and the rest of the train should be far away by the time the Jokaps give up trying to get through us."

Spinner looked at Haft for a long moment before slowly nodding. "I suspect you're right," he finally said.

But "The Stand of the Bloody Axes," that's a story for another day.

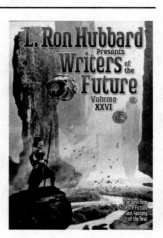

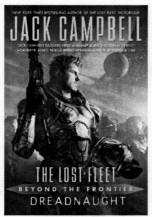

ISBN: 978-0-4410-2037-9

From Ace Books - April 2011

Jack Campbell's

THE LOST FLEET:
Beyond The Frontier

DREADNAUGHT

The war may be over, but Geary and his newly christened First Fleet have been ordered back into action to investigate the aliens occupying the far side of Syndic space and to determine how much of a threat they represent to the Alliance. And while the Syndic Worlds are no longer united, individually they may be more dangerous than ever before.

From Angry Robot

Andy Remic's
SOUL STEALERS

They came from the north, and the city fell. It is a time for warriors, a time for heroes. Kell's axe howls out for blood. The sequel to *Kell's Legend*—more blood-soaked, action-packed, vampire-laced dark epic fantasy.

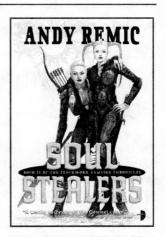

ISBN: 978-0-8576-6067-1

ISBN: 978-0-7653-2084-1

From TOR Books - May 2011

CJ Henderson's
CENTRAL PARK KNIGHT

Piers Knight, curator at the famed Brooklyn Museum, has his hands full enough breaking in his new intern. Swamped with paper work and a thousand other details, he certainly doesn't need the complication of an old flame coming back into his life. Worse yet, she's there on business. It seems the world is about to be invaded by dragons, and Knight is the only man on the planet that might be able to do something about it.

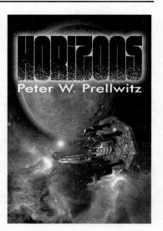

ISBN: 978-1-4391-3433-7

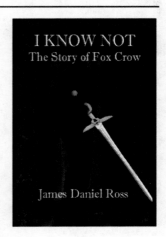

Dark Quest Books Brings You

MYSTIC INVESTIGATORS:
BULLETS AND BRIMSTONE
Patrick Thomas and
John L. French
9780982619735

SOUL BORN
Kevin James Breaux
9780983099321

DARK FUTURES
Jason Sizemore
9780982619728

DEAR CTHULHU:
HAVE A DARK DAY
9780979690137
and
GOOD ADVICE FOR BAD PEOPLE
9780982619742
Patrick Thomas

THE EVIL GAZEBO
Bernie Mojzes
9780974664569

SHIMMER
Jonathan Passarella
9780974664576

More Cutting-Edge Fiction

RADIATION ANGELS
James Daniel Ross
9780982619780

IN A GILDED LIGHT
Jennifer Brozek
9780982619766

BEAUTY HAS HER WAY...
Jennifer Brozek
9780983099314

DRAGON'S LURE
Danielle Ackley-McPhail
9780982619797

THE HALFING'S COURT
Danielle Ackley-McPhail
9780979690167

WHERE ANGELS FEAR
CJ Henderson
and Bruce Gewheller
9780982619711

HERE THERE BE MONSTERS
John L. French
9780982619773

Please see our website for further details www.darkquestbooks.com

Finally, There's Something We Can All Agree On.

It's something we've all said many times. And it does seem to be one of the few things that Americans unanimously agree on. But it takes more than agreeing with each other. It takes the USO. For more than 60 years, the USO has been the bridge back home for the men and women of our armed forces around the world. The USO receives no government funding and relies entirely on the generosity of the American people. We all want to support our troops. This is how it's done.

Until Every One Comes Home.

Help support our troops.
888-USO-5566/www.uso.org

LaVergne, TN USA
31 March 2011

222343LV00002B/51/P